7|0⁸

Praise for Award-Winr Deborah Smith

"What is it about Southern writers that make their words on paper become audible voices in readers' heads? Pat Conroy does it, with long, languorous sentences and poetically phrased prose. Roy Blount uses folksy characters and good-old-boy humor. And countless others have earned a voice over 200 years or so. Add to that list Deborah Smith."
—*The Colorado Springs Gazette*

"Smith is an exceptional storyteller . . . Exciting and heartwarming."
—*Booklist*

"A storyteller of distinction."
—*BookPage*

"Deborah Smith is one writer who definitely has become a standard of excellence in the arena of contemporary women's fiction."
—*Harriet Klausner, Amazon.com's top reviewer*

"Readers of the novels of Anne Rivers Siddons will welcome into their hearts Deborah Smith."
—*Midwest Book Review*

"[Deborah Smith] . . . just keeps getting better."
—*Publishers Weekly*

"For sheer storytelling virtuosity, Ms. Smith has few equals."
—*Richmond Times-Dispatch*

"A stellar romance,"
—*PEOPLE Magazine, When Venus Fell*

A Place To Call Home

"A gracefully written and absorbing tale . . . seductive . . .a page-turner."
—*Publishers Weekly*

"Laughter, wonderment, unrequited love! Meddling old biddies, warring families, lovers reunited. What more could you want?"
—*Rita Mae Brown*

"A rich evocation of family and place."
—*Library Journal*

"A must-read . . . sweet, salty, passionate and wise."
—*Woman's Own*

"These characters leap off the pages. A moving story that holds you to the end and has all the warmth and tenderness of LaVyrle Spencer at her best."
—*Iris Johansen*

"This incredibly magical book will bring a tear to your eye and a smile to your heart. Storytelling at its VERY best!"
—*Romantic Times*

"Clear the decks when you read this book because you're not going to be able to put it aside until you've finished the last delicious page."
—*Janet Evanovich*

"An engrossing read. The reader's sense is that these two could only belong to one another, and no one else. I also loved the rich detail of family life, especially the uniquely Southern aspects."
—*Eileen Goudge*

"Rarely will a book touch your heart like A Place To Call Home. So sit back, put your feet up and enjoy."
—*The Atlanta Journal-Constitution*

"Stylishly written, filled with Southern ease and humor."
—*The Tampa Tribune*

"A beautiful, believable love story."
—*Chicago Tribune*

"This is Southern storytelling at its best."
—*Cox News Service*

"Enchanting new novel . . . a beautiful love story of reunion."
—*The News & Observer, Raleigh, NC*

On Bear Mountain

"Beautifully written . . . A shimmering web of sorrows and joys."
—*Booklist*

"A poignant love story . . . Highly recommended."
—*Library Journal*

"One of those rare novels that stay in your heart long after the final page is turned."

—*New York Times bestselling author, Kristin Hannah*

"As addicting as chocolate."

—*Baton Rouge Advocate*

"Haunting . . . a rock-solid romantic mystery . . . reaffirms that goodness in human nature will prevail."
—Associated Press

"A rich and passionate novel."
—Pat Cunningham Devoto

"A splendid story of love and honor . . . written with easy charm and sassy wit . . . a romance to treasure."
—Booklist (starred review)

Sweet Hush

"One terrific, roller coaster of a read."
—Bestselling author, Mary Jo Putney

"A bodacious tale of Southern family heroism."
—BookPage

"The story is fresh and passionate . . . A tale about a strong-willed woman out to protect her heritage, her legacy, and, most important, her son."
—The Columbus Dispatch

Stone Flower Garden

"Readers will be wringing out their hankies."
—Publishers Weekly

"Gripping and atmospheric."
—San Jose Mercury News

Charming Grace

"Romance is about the future, and everyone gets a new one in this big-hearted Southern tale."
—The Washington Post

BelleBooks, Inc.

ISBN 0-9768760-5-1

The Crossroads Café

Published by:
BelleBooks, Inc. • P.O. Box 67 • Smyrna, GA 30081
We at BelleBooks enjoy hearing from readers. You can contact us at the address above or at BelleBooks@BelleBooks.com

Visit our website — www.BelleBooks.com

First Edition September 2006

10 9 8 7 6 5 4 3 2 1

Cover design: John Cole and Martha Crockett
Cover photo: Andrew Gunners

The Crossroads Café

Deborah Smith

Smyrna, Georgia

FIe
SMITH

PART ONE

Beauty in the flesh will continue to rule the world.
—*Florenz Ziegfeld*

The 'feminine' woman is forever static and childlike. She is like the ballerina in an old-fashioned music box, her unchanging features tiny and girlish, her voice tinkly, her body stuck on a pin, rotating in a spiral that will never grow.
—*Susan Faludi*

You know, when I first went into the movies Lionel Barrymore played my grandfather. Later he played my father and finally he played my husband. If he had lived I'm sure I would have played his mother. That's the way it is in Hollywood. The men get younger and the women get older.
—*Lillian Gish*

Prologue

Cathy
Crossroads, North Carolina

January

Before the accident, I never had to seduce a man in the dark. I dazzled millions in the brutal glare of kliegs on the red carpets of Hollywood, the flash of cameras at the Oscars, the sunlight on the beaches of Cannes. Beautiful women don't fear the glint of lust and judgment in men's eyes or the bitter gleam of envy in women's. Beautiful women welcome even the brightest light. Once upon a time, I had been the most beautiful woman in the world.

Now I needed the night, the darkness, the shadows.

"Put the gun down," I ordered, as I let my bra and sweatshirt fall to the ground. Behind me, a full, white moon hung in a sky of stars above the winter mountains, silhouetting Thomas and me. My breath shivered in the cold air. Beneath my bare feet, the pasture grass was brown and frosted, glistening in the moonlight. There were no other lights in our world, not the pinpoint of a lamp in some distant window, not the wink of a jet high overhead. There might be no other souls in these ancient North Carolina ridges that night. Only Thomas, and me, and the darkness inside us both.

"I'm warning you for the last time, Cathy," he said, his voice thick but firm. He wasn't a man who slurred his words, no matter how drunk he was. "Leave."

I unzipped my jeans. My hands trembled. I couldn't stop staring at the World War II pistol he held so casually, his right arm bent, the gun pointed skyward. Thomas had been a preservation architect; he respected fine craftsmanship, even when choosing a gun with which to kill himself.

Slowly I pushed my jeans down, along with my panties. The scarred skin along my right thigh prickled at the scrape of denim. I angled my right side away from the moon, trying to illuminate only the left half of my body, my face. Half of me was still perfect. But the other half . . .

I stepped out of my crumpled clothes and stood there naked, the moonlight safely behind me. The night breeze was a tongue of embarrassment, licking my scarred flesh. My hand twitched with the urge to cover my face. How badly I wanted to hide the awful parts. Thomas watched me without moving, without speaking, without breathing.

He doesn't want me. I said quietly, "Thomas, I know I'm no prize, but would you really rather kill yourself than touch me?"

Not a word, still, not a flicker of reaction. I could barely see his expression in the shadows, and wasn't sure I wanted to. Shame washed over me like a cold tide. Me, who had once preened for the world without a shred of self-doubt. I turned my back to him, trying not to shiver with defeat. "Just put the gun down. Then I'll get dressed, and we'll forget this ever happened."

I heard quick steps behind me, and before I could turn, his arms went around me from behind. His hands slid over my bare skin. I twisted my head to the pretty side but he bent his lips to the other and roughly kissed the ruined flesh. I cried with relief, and so did he. No matter what might happen to us later, I saved his life that night. And, for that one night, at least, he saved mine. Hope is in the mirror we keep inside us, love sees only what it wants to see, and beauty is in the lie of the beholder.

Sometimes, that lie is all you need to survive.

Chapter 1

Thomas
Ten Months Earlier

The Day of the Accident

It was never a good thing when I woke up at sunset on a Saturday in the back of my pickup truck in the café's graveled parking lot. I had a fierce hangover, and I'd spent all day snoring in a sleeping bag in the truck's rusty bed. Not long after settling in the Crossroads I'd proudly rescued the truck—a sixty-year-old Chevrolet—from a mountain junkyard. I was an architect, not a mechanic, but since my specialty had always been preservation I couldn't resist the challenge.

Admittedly, my rusty but classic Chevy deserved better than to spend its weekend nights under the café's giant oak trees. The trees housed a large clan of bad-ass squirrels who crapped on the truck and on me. They were now cheerfully showering the truck, and me, with rotten acorn shells as they did their spring housecleaning.

When shell fragments bounced off my forehead I opened my bleary eyes. I nearly gagged when I recognized the musky, ballsy, bad-feta-cheese scent that filled my nose. Squinting, I stared up into the face of a small, white goat. He stood beside my head, placidly chewing. Bits of black plastic fell from his lips. Like a dog enjoying a bone, he was demolishing my new cell phone.

"There goes another one," I grunted. I brushed acorns and cell phone pieces out of my beard. "Tell the concierge I have some complaints about the wake-up calls in this hotel. If the maid service doesn't improve I'll have to remove myself to the comfort of my cabin when I drink. Can't a man sleep all day in his truck without being disturbed?"

Crack. Banger, the goat, looked at me innocently as the last section of my phone disintegrated between his teeth. Fragments of the casing dribbled from his hairy white lips. I sighed. "I didn't want that phone, anyway."

If my brother would just stop sending me replacements, Banger might switch to something more nutritious, like hubcaps. John, up in Chicago, was determined to keep me from becoming a full-fledged Luddite. As long as I owned a cell phone, he thought there was a chance I might not end up writing crazed manifestos by lantern light in my cabin. Or shooting myself.

I was confident I wouldn't do the former.

Stretching carefully, I gave every body part plenty of warning that we were about to move as a team. Sour stomach, greasy eyes, aching head, stiff back. The rest of me was only thirty-eight, but after a few hours in the truck, my back always qualified for the senior-citizen discount.

A rumble filled my ears. I looked up, squinting, as a big, late-model SUV rolled past, heading for the café's last available parking space. Well-dressed children gaped and pointed at me from behind the SUV's windows. *Mom, what's that scary-looking man doing in that scary-looking truck with that goat?* A woman pivoted in the passenger seat and stared at me, then mouthed something to the kids. *Don't stare. It's not polite to stare at wildly bearded mountain men who sleep with livestock. We don't want to provoke him.*

Whatever she really said, it made her brood sit back quickly and look away from me. I lifted a jaunty hand and waved. Beauty, after all, is in the eye of the beholder.

My personal cache of beauty could all be found here, at The Crossroads, a small cove high in the remote mountains of western North Carolina, where an old paved road known as the Asheville Trace and an even older, unpaved road called Ruby Creek Trail intersected in front of a cluster of buildings—a former farmhouse, an old log cabin, a string of whitewashed sheds, and a pair of gas pumps under a tin awning. Grocery, gas station, post office, thrift store, diner, and more. All of it known by one name that summed up the spirit, the sustenance, and the turning points of the lives that met there.

The Crossroads Café.

I was not necessarily an upstanding citizen of the Crossroads, but I had earned the respect of the people who mattered there. Or, at least, their tolerance.

I suddenly realized my long, brown beard was wet. And also my head, and my ponytail, and my face, and, when I lifted my beard, the front of my vintage New York Giants jersey. Soaked. Someone had doused the legacy of Hall-of-Famer Lawrence Taylor. Sacrilege.

That's when I noticed the note tied to Banger's collar. Written in black marker on a piece of torn cardboard with a Dixie Crystals logo still visible on one edge, it said:

> *Thomas Mitternich,*
> *You get your behind into my kitchen by 6:30. Cathryn is*
> *on TV then. Your sore eyes need the sight. Don't make me*
> *come back with more water.*
> *Love, Delta*

Cathryn Deen. I'd never met her, but of course, I knew who she was. *Everyone* knew who she was. A bonafide, glamorous *movie star*. Not much of an actress, but what difference did that make these days? She was drop-dead gorgeous and adorably perky, her movies made fortunes, photos of her appeared every week on the covers of major magazines, she'd recently married some swaggering mogul, and now she was launching her own cosmetics line. Pygmies in the Amazon and Mongolian yak herders living in straw huts on the Russian tundra knew who she was. Even in the Crossroads, one of the most secluded mountain communities on the Eastern seaboard, people could tell you Cathryn Deen's favorite color (emerald green, like her eyes,) her favorite hobby (shopping in Paris,) and what kind of flowers (white roses flecked with 24-carat gold,) had decked the gazebo at her very expensive, very private Hawaiian wedding.

What people in the Crossroads *couldn't* tell you was why she never visited the farm she'd inherited from her grandmother, north of the Cove, or why she never replied to the cheerful, friendly birthday and Christmas cards sent to her by her devoted, distant cousin, Delta, owner of the café and unofficial mayor of the Crossroads. To me and everyone else who lived in the secluded mountain valley, Delta was a queen. To Cathryn Deen, Delta was obviously nobody.

I didn't appreciate her attitude.

Wincing, I eased out of the truck and stood up. After a polite glance in all directions, I stepped between the truck and the oak, pulled up my water-dampened jersey, unzipped my jeans, and urinated on the oak's protruding roots. "Take that," I said to the squirrels and Cathyrn Deen.

Banger dropped my ruined phone and hopped down from the truck. He affectionately stomped one hard, cloven hoof on the toe of my running shoe and butted my left knee, hooking one horn through a hole in the denim and into the tender center of my kneecap. I saw stars for a minute.

When my head cleared, I scrubbed a hand over his floppy ears. "If there is a God," I told the goat, "He appointed you to be my conscience."

Carrying a fresh Giants jersey and clean briefs—when you regularly wake up in public, it's a good idea to keep a change of clothes in your truck—I limped from under the tree. The fine, crusher-run gravel of the parking lot was a delicate material, as granite goes, yet it still managed to make ear-splitting sounds.

I tried to tiptoe, but it didn't help.

A cathedral of sky and mountain opened over my head. I took a couple of reviving breaths. Evening light cloaked the Cove in soft blue shadows; the Ten Sisters Mountains, circling the Cove like the thick rim of a bread bowl, glowed gold and mint-green above filaments of silver mist. I made my way to an old church pew that served as a garden bench beside the paved road. Sinking gratefully onto the weathered chestnut wood, I exhaled. The Trace meandered past, its aged gray surface cracked and pockmarked, its fraying edges gently disappearing into low green clumps of thrift sprinkled with tiny lavender flowers.

The Asheville Trace hinted that modern horsepower could get you to Crossroads and back to civilization without packing a lunch. Coming from its namesake, Asheville, of course, the Trace wandered out of the Ten Sisters along their foothills, curled through the grassy Cove, then yawned past the café before its intersection with Ruby Creek Trail. Finally the Trace headed west to the county seat. During rush hour, we locals might see, oh, a car every ten minutes.

Which suited me just fine.

I leaned back on the old pew and inhaled the air and the view. Almost every spring evening the Ten Sisters filled with white fog, disappearing like islands in a soft, white sea. There was a reason pioneers named the Appalachians of western North Carolina the *Smokies*.

The air and the view could almost clear up a hangover. Almost.

"Thomas! Are you still out here goofing off?" Delta's squeaky drawl stabbed my eardrums. Wincing, I pivoted toward it. She leaned over the rail of the café's front veranda, a motherly, plump, angel of food under the whitewashed halo of a farmhouse-cum-restaurant porch, surrounded by a cluster of half-barrel flower pots and rump-sprung rocking chairs.

Like everything else at the Crossroads, Delta Whittlespoon seemed to have grown out of a perfect combination of need and want and comfort. Her chef's apron hung askew over a sweaty, pink t-shirt emblazoned *Southern Gals Say: The Lard Cooks In Mysterious Ways*. An oven mitt protruded from the back pocket of her flour-dusted jeans. As I watched, a squirrel careened down the porch rails, landed right by her thick-soled hiking sandals, and grabbed a peanut that had fallen from one of the porch bird feeders. A purple finch zipped past her head to perch on the scuppernong vine twining up a post.

The woman drew wildlife and lost souls. She was a dark-haired, freckled, middle-aged, chubby, loving, tough, famous-cooking, business-managing matriarch of all she surveyed, including me. She was determined to keep me alive.

"Are you coming inside, or do I have to take a hickory switch to your Yankee behind?" Delta called.

"I'm meditating," I called. "Banger and I are working on the meaning of existence. So far, we think it involves butting things with your head."

"Spare me your ill-tempered notions. Come on, you're gonna miss Cathryn on TV! She's having a press conference for her makeup company! They're gonna interview her, live!"

Delta clearly believed a glimpse of her movie-star kin was always good for my jaded soul. And I always politely avoided telling her the only thing I wanted from Cathryn Deen was a hard-on and the deed to her grandmother's abandoned farm.

"If I come in, will you give me a hot biscuit?"

"Git! In! Here!" She jabbed a finger at the double front doors, where a small sign said, *The Crossroads Café. Good Food and Then Some.* "I haven't got time to sweet-talk you anymore! See all those SUV's and minivans in the parking lot? I got a restaurant full of family reunioners from Asheville in here. I'm volunteering you to work as a busboy!" I gave her a thumbs-up. She went back inside.

"Don't wait up for me, honey," I told Banger, who was eating a cigar butt I'd dropped.

I walked slowly toward the café, already tired of being awake and sober. All right, I'd go inside and watch Cathryn Deen be beautiful.

I could use the fantasy.

Cathy
Beverly Hills, California

The Face of Flawless, said the posters scattered around the Four Seasons' penthouse suite, beneath a smoky, film-noir close-up of my face. I loved that picture of me. Classic. Yet innocent. Yet come-hitherish. A dark-haired Grace Kelly for the 21ˢᵗ Century. The princess next door who wears thong panties. *Timeless beauty. Ageless perfection. From actress Cathryn Deen. Because every woman can be flawless.*

Yes. Like me. *Perfect.*

The hype sometimes made me blush a little. Or pretend to, at least. A Southern beauty queen is trained from birth to be charmingly self-deprecating so people will give her the benefit of the doubt and not throttle her when she sucks up all the attention in a room. Fake humility? You bet. It came in handy during interviews and when signing autographs. We super-glam movie stars are just like everyone else, you know. We don't think of ourselves as special or better than other people.

Right.

Oh, okay, I admit it: I was conceited, pampered, annoyingly coy, and way too fond of myself to be likable. But let's be real here: I *was* the most beautiful woman in the world. *People* magazine said so. And *Vanity Fair*. And even *Rolling Stone* and *Esquire*, those cynical, sex-obsessed boys.

I had been praised and petted since the time I was old enough to gurgle adorably as my father wheeled me around Atlanta's finest ballrooms and boardrooms in an emerald-green stroller custom-designed to match my eyes. Everyone loved me. The box-office reports proved it. I'd be paid twenty-five million dollars for my next film, a remake of *Giant*, co-starring me in the Elizabeth Taylor role, Heath Ledger in the James Dean part, and Hugh Jackman in the role Rock Hudson played.

I'm the new Liz Taylor, I thought, gazing at myself happily in a huge, lighted mirror while my personal stylists worked on me as if I were a life-sized Barbie doll. *Take that, Julia and Angelina and Jennifer and Reese. Top my paycheck, if you can.*

"We make fifteen-year-old girls look twenty-five and thirty-five-year-old women look twenty-five," Judi, my hair girl, was saying to the others as she fluffed a long strand of my mocha-black mane. "So our pornographic culture will want to fuck us."

"Our pornographic culture?" I said, smiling as I watched them primp me. "It's just human nature for girls to flirt and boys to appreciate it."

Randy, my makeup boy, chuckled wryly. "Not *my* nature, sweetie. But if a *boy* wants to flirt with me, that's different." His soft sable brush flicked across my forehead. His dark-skinned hand moved like an artist's. A poof of Flawless Ivory Cream Foundation Powder floated before us. Randy waved his brush at Judi. "Personally, I've got nothing against looking pornographic. Or younger."

Judi grunted at him. "You're a guy. It's not the same for you. Men are still considered desirable even after they turn into fat, wrinkled prunes with penises. When you're a crusty old queen you'll still get a lot of action."

"I do hope so!"

"The porno culture?" said Luce, my wardrobe girl. "Let me tell you about the time I managed wardrobe for a triple-X producer. It was all leather corsets and high heels. And that was just for the livestock in the cast." She hooted as she tugged a silky silver dress over my plunging silver bra. I slid my arms into lacy shoulder straps and Luce smoothed the bodice over my boobs, bending down to peer at them. *Checking for nipplage*, as we called it. "Perky nipple on the left, Boss."

I nodded. Even my boobs were proud of themselves. "Get the Band-Aids. We don't want the press to stare at my headlights when they're supposed to be listening to my brilliant and witty thoughts about my new cosmetics empire."

Randy clucked his tongue. "Boss, you could put on a burka and spray yourself with camel musk and men would still stare at your tits."

"Camel musk? Maybe I should add that to my perfume line. Judi, I'm only thirty-two. What is that in camel years? How long before camels won't whistle at me on the street? Does the porno culture include camels?"

"Oh, Boss, you know what I'm saying," Judi went on. "Women are sex objects. After decades of feminism, that's *still* all we are. If we're not young and hot, we have no value."

"I plan to be sexy even when I'm a hundred," Luce growled. "As long as there's KY and vodka, I can get laid."

I laughed. Sex appeal was just another of life's lucky gifts, and I'd been gifted more than almost everyone else on the planet. I couldn't imagine being anything but beautiful. Conceited? *Me?* No way.

My *people*—I thought of my employees the way old Southerners talk of servants, as if I owned them—my *people* always liked me. Daddy and all my Southern aunts—those golf-playing, country-clubbing doyennes of the Atlanta social scene—had trained me to be a kind and generous New South plantation mistress. I turned to peer at Judi from under a lock of my hair, which she held out like a glossy chocolate rope as she teased the underside. "Judi, is this discussion going to segue into your 'witches versus engineers theory?'"

"Isn't that a new reality show on Fox?" Randy asked. Luce chortled.

Judi scowled. "Laugh if you want to. But there are jerks out there who say women are witches—I mean wiccans, not bitches—and men are engineers. That women represent emotion and sex—the dark arts—versus men representing logic and intellect—the progressive sciences. That women have no purpose other than breeding. And thus, that it's women's job to stay desirable until they hit menopause. After that, women are supposed to just fade away."

I wagged a finger at her. "Not me. I refuse to fade. And I refuse to get old. I'm stopping my biological clock right now." I snapped my fingers. "There. Done. I'm not aging anymore. Not ever going to get wrinkly, saggy, liver-spotted, or sun-damaged. I'll never have neck jowls. I won't even get pimples from PMS."

Everyone smiled. They gathered around me, their faces around mine in the mirror, as if I were the center of a flower. Judi sighed. "Boss," she said, "You will *never* be ugly. I can't even picture it. You'll never be a mere mortal like the rest of us."

A wistful knot formed around my heart, a fluid squeeze of loneliness. Being special also meant being isolated. I never quite fit in. Men gawked at me nervously, and women were jealous of me. I had no close female friends, and no close male friends who weren't gay. I was always 'the face,' first, not a person. Someday, despite all my bluster, my face would fade. And then I'd be no one. *Don't think about it.*

I trained my attention on an elegant hotel platter of raw fruit and fat-free yogurt among the makeup kits, curling irons and other clutter. My no-frills diet reflected colorfully in the mirror. I was always hungry and always starving myself. I stared grimly at the food's reflection. *I hate eating like a rabbit trapped in a health spa.* Suddenly the reflection vanished. Instead I saw my grandmother holding out a blue-willow china plate filled with her biscuits. Covered in gravy. *Cream* gravy. With flecks of pure pork sausage in it. Heaven.

I don't mean I *thought* about my Granny Nettie and her biscuits. I mean I *saw* her, in the mirror. A vision. The irony of a life spent looking in mirrors that sometimes looked *back*. Like now. People who believe in psychic powers call it *scrying*. Granny Nettie claimed she could do it by gazing into any shiny surface. Mirrors, ponds, windows. She told me I could do it, too, when I was a child. I went home from that visit and reported that I'd seen my dead mother's face in a bedroom window of Granny's house. That the mother who'd died when I was a baby smiled as if welcoming me home. *This was my room*, she whispered in my thoughts. *It can be your room now.* Daddy told me only crazy people saw things in mirrors, and he never let me visit Granny Nettie again. I missed her and her odd little farm desperately.

I'd only seen a few images in mirrors since then – once, when a former boyfriend was killed in a speedboat accident, and a couple that portended the deaths of my aunts, Daddy's sisters. My last vision, a couple of years earlier, had been terrifying. While checking my hair in a makeup booth backstage at the Oscars, I'd seen Daddy's face.

It replaced mine for just a second. Peaceful, handsome, classic, sternly loving, silver-haired. The father who had been my biggest fan and toughest critic. The traditional Southern *daddy* I adored. I was so startled by his image in the mirror I flubbed one of my lines a few minutes later, as I read the Best Actress nominees on camera. Millions of people watching, worldwide, and I said *Merle Step* instead of *Meryl Streep*. "Do I *look* like a male country-western singer?" Meryl teased later.

When I walked off stage one of my assistants ran up to me. "There's an emergency call from Atlanta. It's about your dad."

He had died of a heart attack during his Oscar-night party at the club. Barnard Deen threw parties just to watch me give awards to other people. He was so demanding, yet so proud of me. He never believed in Granny Nettie's visions, so I never told him I'd continued to see visions of my own. Now, gazing at my grandmother, who gazed back, I made myself breathe calmly while a shiver ran up my spine. *Go away. Nothing good happens when I see things in mirrors.*

She remained there stubbornly, as vivid as life. Her green eyes were almost frightening in their passions. Her gray-black hair flowed from beneath a tractor cap that seemed as exotic to me as the turban of a sultaness. She had died when I was twelve, not long after my last visit. Her mountain farm in North Carolina had been a world as different from my Atlanta life as any foreign country. My mother didn't live long enough to raise me, and Granny Nettie didn't live to see me grown. The two most important women in my life had died without telling me how to deal with reflections.

I blinked, feeling dizzy. The vision vanished. "Boss, are you all right?" Judi asked. "Do you want something to eat? You're staring at the kiwi and broccoli as if they might bite back."

I took a deep breath, laughed, and fluttered a hand to my heart. "Why, I don't *dare* eat before a press conference. If I gain so much as *one* ounce, the porno culture will revoke my membership card."

More laughter. I took another breath. *I'm just hungry, that's all. Just imagining what I'd really like to eat. Sometimes, a biscuit is just a biscuit.*

A pair of double doors burst open. Six-foot-three-inches of elegant California business mogul strode in, dressed in gray Armani.

My husband, Gerald Barnes Merritt (never just "Gerald Merritt," that was too plain) was thirteen years older than me, rugged, brilliant, rich, and yes, wildly sexy in his own right. He had Donald Trump's flair for showmanship. We'd been married for less than a year, during which time Gerald bragged often to the media about his two beautiful ex-wives, his three beautiful grown daughters, and his successful ventures in real estate, computer technology, marketing, and now, me. Now, thanks to him, I would head my own cosmetics empire. Flawless, by Cathryn Deen. Actually, Gerald ran everything. He was the CEO. But hey, I was the *face.*

"Ready to announce your new business venture to the press, my gorgeous girl?" Gerald boomed, scattering my entourage like a rottweiler in a rabbit pen.

I preened in the mirror and avoided looking toward the mystical food platter again. "Oh, I don't know. Can you see anything about me that could be any more perfect?"

He slid his arms around me from behind, angling his head to look at me in the mirror, but careful not to muss mounds of hair and the unblemished masterpiece of my Flawless face. I felt the ridge of his penis lightly teasing me.

"You couldn't be more beautiful. I am married," he said softly, "to the girl every man wants."

Another strange little shiver went through me. *Beauty is fleeting, but biscuits are forever.* I smiled and shook off the silly thought.

I was the most beautiful woman in the world. Surely, I always would be.

Thomas

On a small portable television hanging from the café's beadboard ceiling among the pots and pans, the world's most beautiful movie star, Cathryn Deen, charmed me in ways so ephemeral, so classic that—like the faceless reporters asking her polite questions—I hardly realized she held me in the palm of her hand. Whether I liked her or not.

Dressed in a streamlined silver sheath, Cathryn sat on a chair in front of a poster of herself under the word, *Flawless.* Her voice was a husky come-on flavored with the honey of a wealthy Southern upbringing and just enough of a droll lilt to hint at self-awareness and maybe even true smarts. She tilted her face just so, and smiled just so, and a long strand of her dark hair fell *just so* along the perfect angle of her cheek. The expression in her deep-green eyes said she had never had a doubtful moment in her life, and, given a chance to kiss you with her luscious mouth, she'd make you forget any doubts you'd ever had, too.

Hypnotized, I stood in the café's cheerful fire-trap of a kitchen while a herd of Delta's immediate family, wearing the café's signature uniform of jeans and *The Lard Cooks In Mysterious Ways* t-shirts, hustled around me.

"The Lord is my shepherd," growled Delta's sister-in-law, Cleo McKellan, slapping a *Jesus Loves You* sticker on the sleeve of my jersey as she passed by with platters of collard greens, squash casserole and pear-mayo-cheese salad perched on one arm, "but if He doesn't lead you outta this high-traffic lane I'm goin' to smite you." Her husband, Bubba, hooted as he chopped onions into a pan of meatloaf. I shifted to an untraveled spot. She blew me a chaste kiss and disappeared through swinging doors to the dining rooms.

"Now, Thomas, *that's* a beautiful young woman," Delta said proudly, gazing up at Cathryn on the television. "She's my cousin's husband's cousin's daughter." Delta repeated this information and the background story at every opportunity. I nodded vaguely.

There are reasons why some people catch our attention, why their charisma makes us think that knowing them, or even simply looking at them, will elevate us to a higher plane of existence. There are reasons why women send marriage proposals to famous killers in prison and men spend a month's salary on a dugout-level seat at a stadium. We want to share the aura of fame, any kind of fame, to catch the tip end of that rainbow, as if it makes us special, too.

The allure isn't the fame itself; it's the promise that we aren't just anonymous specks of life on a small rock in an obscure universe. Anyone famous—for any reason, even a bad one—has been fingered by a mysterious fate that seems to have ignored *us*. Someone so naturally awe-inspiring must be blessed. God has smiled on this person, and if we earn so much as a glance from that sacred source, then God meant to bless us, too. The 'lightning in the bottle' we talk about? That chemistry? Secretly we believe it's not just random chance, not just good luck. It's destiny.

Cathryn Deen had it. *It*. The surreal quality that separates the ordinary from the extraordinary. I'd seen some of her movies; my wife had been a fan of hers. The films ranged from pure fluff to serious melodrama, but one factor always made them shine. *Her*. She wasn't a great actress, but she really did have what publicists and gossip hacks call *a megawatt smile*. Her luminous green eyes, filled with humor, intelligence and a tinge of self-aware vulnerability, made the whole package infinitely sexual. *I can hurt you, but you can hurt me, too,* she told us.

"Look at those eyes," Delta was saying even now, standing beside me with a pan of biscuits in her chubby hands. "You know, Thomas, all the great actors and actresses have that look. Kind of a little sad, like they know this won't last forever and the joke's on them. You know what I think? As wonderful as it would be to be so beautiful or so handsome, they wake up every day knowing they're one day closer to getting saggy and ordinary, like the rest of us. It's kind of a curse, being special just for how you look." She sighed, brightened and held up the biscuits like an offering. "'Beauty is fleeting but biscuits are forever.' That's what Cathryn's grandma, Mary Eve Nettie, used to tell me. She was a wild woman. Kept her maiden name, slept around without hiding it, voted liberal. People named the ridge after her. Wild Woman Ridge."

I nodded again, gazing up at the television in a rare moment of peaceful arousal. Cathryn Deen was sex and mystery and sweetness and fantasy and . . . magic. She was classic architecture in a world obsessed with tearing down icons. Put a fence around her; protect her from grim reality.

Delta elbowed me. "She favors me around the eyes, don't you think?"

I came out of my trance. "Definitely. But I bet *she's* too nice to dump water on innocent men who sleep under her oak tree."

Delta frapped me with a dish cloth. I took the frapping like a man, picked up a bus pan and headed for the dining room. Even a volunteer bus boy with a hangover has his dignity.

Cathy

Laughing, I led my entourage through one of the *Four Seasons'* highly discreet exits, designed especially for VIP's. The hotel is one of the most famous celebrity hideaways in the world. Frank Sinatra sang by the piano in the main bar on his eightieth birthday. Renée Zellweger was mistaken for a cocktail waitress there, and good-naturedly took bar orders from a table full of businessmen. The front-desk staff speak a mysterious dialect of English, one with vaguely euro-Asian accents, as if imported from some elegant little country especially to serve celebrities. On any given day you can glimpse a number of famous bodies being massaged in private cabanas around the pool. The lobby bars are a swoon-fest of Hollywood sightings, and also are rumored to be where the most expensive hookers hang out.

A pair of valets ran to get my car, nearly tripping over their feet when they saw me. Ah, the power of a clingy, white angora sweater, black leggings, and knee-high *Louis Vuitton* boots with stiletto heels. I looked like a wholesome dominatrix.

"You wowed everyone at your press conference today, Ms. Deen," one of the valets gushed. "You looked great."

"Why, bless your heart."

"Quit drooling and get Ms. Deen's car," a bodyguard ordered. The valet bolted.

I was trailed by two private security men, five publicists, two assistants, and one assistant to an assistant of Gerald's. Everyone but me had a phone attached to his or her ear, and they were all talking, but not to me or each other. I laughed as I signed autographs for the bellmen. My entourage chattered on without me, as perky as parakeets on cocaine.

"Yes, the press conference was huge. Fabulous. Cathryn's doing lunch with Vogue next week. Cover photos are under negotiation. Pencil us in for Tuesday, in New York."

"Marty? Book Cathryn with Larry King for the twelfth."

"No, Cathryn can't do Oprah on that schedule. She'll be in England to film a couple of last-minute scenes for The Pirate Bride. Sophia Coppola insists."

"Hello, I'm calling for Cathryn Deen. Ms. Deen wants you to find her a great, authentic voice coach to work with her on Giant. Yes, I know she can naturally do a Southern accent, but Ms. Deen says a Texas drawl is very different from an Atlanta accent. She wants a coach from Dallas. No, not the old TV show. The city. Ms. Deen requires a city-Southern-Texas-rich accent for the film. She's meeting with her producers and director this weekend . . ."

"Women like you ruin other women's lives, bitch!"

The voice rang out as I was about to step into the open door of my Trans Am. The car was a mint condition 1977 T-top, black and gold. I halted with one high-heel on the door rim. Several scruffy young women darted from behind the hotel's glorious palms, waving homemade signs.

REAL WOMEN DON'T HAVE TO BE FLAWLESS CATHRYN DEEN HATES REAL WOMEN

"You're telling women to hate themselves for having ordinary faces and bodies," one of the protestors yelled. "But *you're* the freak, not us!"

My publicists formed a circle around me, like pioneers trying to ward off a band of angry Sioux. The protestors bobbed and weaved as the guards chased them. I was open-mouthed with amazement. "Why didn't anyone tell me these girls were out here?" I demanded. "I could have invited them to the press conference. Listened to their concerns. Offered them a makeover—"

"Never negotiate with terrorists," one of the publicists said. Seriously.

"Terrorists? Oh, come on. They're just sorority girls with bad hair. They're probably sophomores at Berkeley. Maybe I'm their class protest project. " I called to the guards. "Bring them over here and let me talk to them!"

My publicists did a group pirouette to stare at me in horror. "Those girls could be carrying mace or pepper spray," one said.

"Or a hidden bomb," a second added.

I laughed. "Or iPods filled with horrifying Ashlee Simpson songs, or hair brushes with really sharp bristles, or . . ."

"Please, Cathryn. The hotel's still full of photographers. If the press catches wind of this, these protestors will make the news and that's *all* people will remember about the launch of Flawless Cosmetics."

That got me. *Gerald's put so much work and money into this venture. I can't ruin this day for him.* I blew out a breath. "All right, y'all win." They hustled me into the Trans Am. One of the publicists, a young man, put a hand to his heart as he shut my door. "Ms. Deen, I'm so sorry about this. If I ran the world, all the ugly chicks with big mouths would be sent to an island somewhere."

I stared at him. I'd never thought of myself as the poster girl for men who thought women should keep quiet and look pretty. As I drove out of the Four Seasons' elegant, palm-endowed shadow, the girls glared at me from behind the phalanx of security people. They raised their hands and flipped me the bird.

I didn't know how to deal with people who weren't in awe of me.

So in return I gave them a polite but completely inadequate beauty-queen wave.

Thomas

Just after dark, East Coast time.

Smoke break. Again I lounged on the weathered church pew at the edge of the café's parking lot. "If Cathryn Deen ever comes here and gives us any attitude," I told Banger, "I'll hold her down while you eat her cell phone."

He twitched his white tail in anticipation.

I lit a crumpled cigar butt I found in my jeans' front pocket. Hand-rolled local tobacco—a North Carolina heritage—was a smooth smoke but hard on an empty stomach. I sniffed burning hair. A fleck of tobacco smoldered in my beard. A few quick slaps, and the beard was saved. I wouldn't have to drop out of the ZZ Top lookalike contest.

More deep breaths. I inhaled the good smell of wood in nearby chimneys, the clean, springtime fragrance of earth, and the wafting aromas of dinner from Delta's kitchen. The mountains curled a breeze through Delta's cooking and carried it all over the Cove. Even out at my cabin I sometimes swore I smelled her famous biscuits.

"Hey, Mitternich," Jeb Whittlespoon yelled from the café's side door. "Poker at nine. Right after the dining room closes."

I gave him a thumbs-up.

Poker at nine, drunk by midnight, sleeping with goats by dawn.

A typical Saturday night.

Around eight, I was bussing tables covered in red-checkered oil-cloth under old tin ceiling lamps that cast warm pools of light. The café was Mayberry, a Norman Rockwell painting, and a rerun of *The Waltons* all rolled into one. Ordinarily the atmosphere soothed me, but that night I felt edgy—not just the usual blue-black mood that came on as the sun set, but something worse.

The café was full of happy, wholesome families. They came to the Cove and nearby Turtleville for the views, the campgrounds, the trout streams and the hiking. Many drove up from Asheville but others came from as far away as Georgia and Tennessee. All of them shared one common goal during their visits: To dine at the famous Crossroads Café on huge plates of the best Southern home cooking anywhere, adorned with Delta's mouthwatering biscuits.

Cleo, along with Delta's daughter-in-law, Becka, hustled between the tables. Becka elbowed me. "Move your cute butt, Thomas." Becka flirted with me harmlessly, tolerated me endlessly, and bossed me around. Cleo prayed for me. Both she and Becka warned their husbands to keep guns away from me when I was drunk.

I turned around with a pan full of dishes and found a little boy staring up at me. Gaping, mesmerized. He looked like Ethan. Even more than most. Every boy under five reminded me of my son. Every breath I took reminded me. Clouds reminded me. Toys in an ad reminded me. Spatters of fake blood on an episode of *CSI* reminded me. I wondered if I still had half a bottle of vodka under the truck's front seat.

"Mister, are you a hillbilly?" the boy asked. His voice trembled. He was *afraid* of me.

The father rushed over. "He didn't mean any harm."

I could only nod. Words stuck in my throat. A glance confirmed that *everyone* in the diner was staring at me. Six-four and bearded, wrinkled Giants jersey, faded jeans, old running shoes, blood-shot eyes. Topped with a ponytail and a long, wavy brown beard. Go figure.

Delta stepped between me and the worried customers, grinning. "Aw, this is no hillbilly," she announced. "This is just Thomas, a crazy architect from New York City." To me she whispered, "You know we all love you around here, but you've got a strange look in your eyes tonight. You're scaring kids and giving hillbillies a bad name. Take a break."

I nodded again, my throat aching. I carried the bus pan to the kitchen, then walked outside. I went to my truck, climbed in, and fished around under the seat until I found my vodka. The bottle was half-full, hurray. "Never look at a vodka bottle as 'half-empty,'" I said out the window to Banger. "Be an optimist."

The bottle's screw-top made a neat arc to the truck's rusty floorboard as I flicked it with my fingers. I had my rituals. Open a bottle, pull down the visor, then look at the pictures I'd laminated and taped there. Sherryl and Ethan on his first birthday, in Central Park, laughing for me among

19

some flowers. And the other picture, the one from the archives of the *New York Times*, a picture like dozens of pictures that had been studied, analyzed, and archived.

A picture from the morning of September 11, 2001, when my wife jumped from the North Tower of the World Trade Center with our son in her arms. I touched both pictures with a fingertip, then took my first drink of the night.

Cathy

"Caaaathryn!" A car full of teenage boys passed me in an open Jeep, waving and honking their horn.

I waved back vaguely, still distracted from the incident at the hotel, I zoomed along California's famous Ventura Highway in heavy traffic, headed northwest out of L.A. Other drivers waved and honked at me—mostly men and boys, putting their hands to their hearts. Tractor-trailer drivers blew their deep air horns as I zoomed past. I continued waving, sometimes smiling and blowing kisses too. I was gorgeous, I was rich, everyone wanted to be me. I was immortal.

The producers of *Giant*, a husband-wife team, owned a fabulous Arabian horse ranch outside Camarillo, near the coast. I planned to spend the weekend as their houseguest, discussing the script and meeting with the director. Gerald had kissed me goodbye at the hotel on his way to board our Lear jet. He was headed to London to meet with some of our Flawless investors.

My right foot cramped as I pressed the Trans Am's accelerator. High-heeled, skintight ostrich leather boots are not meant for driving a muscle car. I had a garage filled with Mercedes and Jaguars, but I loved my classic, redneck wheels. Clearly, I'd inherited some fast-car genes from my Grandpa Nettie. He died young—murdered in a fight at a mountain roadhouse, but Granny said he'd been a bootlegger and stockcar racer in his youth. Another notorious Nettie legacy my father hadn't liked. Now, as a kind of karmic compensation, I owned the Nettie farm. My business people managed it, per instructions left by Daddy's will. I kept meaning to check on the old place, but I was always too busy. Apparently, if I wouldn't go to Granny's farm, Granny and her farm would come to me. In mirrors. I shivered. *Don't think about that vision.*

I glanced at the Trans Am's speedometer. Only eighty mph. By

California highway standards, I was just coasting. "Hey, Granny Nettie, watch this," I said aloud. I wiggled my foot, pressed harder, and smiled as the needle crept toward ninety-five. The wind curled in through the car's open T-top, whipping my hair. It was a perfect spring day, the temperature in the seventies, the smog just a pretty, lavender-blue mist on the horizon. I crested a hill and grinned at a vista laced with the lime-green outlines of large vegetable fields. Open horizons. I could fly.

Lights flashed in my rear-view mirror. I scowled when I saw a familiar blue mini-van behind me. A hand came out of the van's passenger window, waved gleefully at me, disappeared, then returned clutching a large video camera. A shaggy, gray-blond guy poked his head out and fitted the videocam's viewfinder to one eye.

"Damn."

I knew him. A jerk, even by the aggressive standards of showbiz paparazzi. We had a long acquaintance, most of it annoying to me and profitable to him. He'd videotaped me as I walked through airports all over the world, trailed me on the outskirts of movie sets, hopped out of the bushes around nightclubs and restaurants, and once snapped photos of me sunning topless in Spain, which the world could still view for five dollars per download on the Internet.

And now he intended to tape me driving on the Ventura Highway? It must be a slow week in the celebrity scandals business. Were *Inside Edition* and *Entertainment Tonight* that desperate for footage?

I wasn't in the mood. *Bitch. Bad role model for girls.* Those words kept echoing through my mind.

And *biscuits.* Granny Nettie's gravy-covered biscuits. Suddenly I could almost taste them again, just as I had in the hotel suite, almost hear her ghost whispering in my ear. *Take comfort, now. Rejoice. You'll want to die but you'll be glad you lived.*

Strange thoughts. A chill on my skin. I shook it off, glared at the photographer in the rearview mirror, and stomped the Trans Am's accelerator.

For months afterwards, I would try to remember every detail of that moment. To remember every nuance, everything I felt and did, everything I *should* have done differently. I would be haunted by everything I did wrong in that split-second of eternity, when my life changed forever.

The toe of my boot slipped sideways off the pedal. The boot's long, narrow heel went *under* the pedal and jammed there. My foot was trapped for maybe two seconds, three at the most. Just enough time for the Trans

Am to slow down, just enough time to encourage the clueless driver in the lane to my left. He whipped his small, aged hatchback in front of me. I stared in horror at the car's taillights, which I was about to rear-end.

I jerked my foot free and stomped the brake. The Trans Am hunched down like a horse trying to slide to a stop from a full gallop. The tires screamed. I was still closing in on the hatchback with no hope of not hitting it. I swung into the emergency lane. The Trans Am began sliding sideways, and I couldn't straighten it.

The rear right bumper clipped a guard rail. The car spun full-circle. I couldn't hold onto the steering wheel. The front bumper slammed into the guard rail, plowed it down, and the Trans Am went airborne, riding the guard rail at high-speed, its underbelly ripping open. The roar and shriek of metal filled my ears. So did my screams.

The Trans Am shot off the road near a strawberry field. I didn't see the field's hogwire fence before I plowed through it. I didn't see the shallow irrigation ditch, either. The Trans Am hit it at an angle, tilted, and rolled completely over.

My head slammed into the steering wheel. Thank God for the wheel's padded leather cover. And thank God I was wearing a seatbelt. The car flopped to a halt in the ditch, upright but tilted, with the passenger-side wheels resting on the slope.

Quiet. Everything suddenly went so quiet, and so *still*. My head throbbed, but otherwise, I was unhurt. Dazed, I managed a few deep, shaky breaths. I heard people yelling, but for some reason, none of them came over to help me. I fumbled for the door handle. It wouldn't work. I shoved. There was no give. The door was jammed. My head began to clear, and I felt a little panicky. What was that scent?

Smoke. That's smoke. And gasoline. Get out of this car. Climb out the T-top.

I scrambled to my knees on the bucket seat. My boot heels snagged on the gear-shift on the center console behind me. I grabbed the window sill with both hands. The metal was warm. Acrid smoke flooded my nose and throat. A coughing fit doubled me over.

"Beautiful," the photographer called. "Beautiful, Cathryn. Work it, Cathryn."

The photographer who'd chased me now stood a few feet away, *videotaping me*.

"I need *help*. Help me, you cretin!"

"Come on, Cathryn, you can make it! You're a star, baby! And stars are always happy to perform! Think of the publicity you'll get! 'Wow. Look at Cathyrn Deen, doing her own stunts!'" He crept closer, the camera never wavering. I shoved myself headfirst out the window and tumbled to the ground. "Nice technique!" he called, laughing.

I staggered to my feet, but my left boot heel sank into the soft earth, and I tripped. I landed hard on my right side. Hair, face, right arm, right hip, right leg. Into the wet muck. What was this slick fluid on my hands? This smell? Oh, my God. *Gasoline*. The ground was soaked with it. And now, on my right side, so was I.

"Hurry, Cathryn! I think your catalytic converter's about to catch the weeds on fire! I want to see you *run* in that tight sweater and high heels! Raise your head so I can get a good shot of those beautiful eyes. Come on, hustle! Give your fans some jiggling tits to look at, doll!"

I scrambled out of the ditch on all fours. At that point my deepest desire was to reach the guy, wrap my hands around his throat and strangle him.

Behind me I heard a soft, sinister *whoosh*.

A fireball went up my right side.

Some victims of violent accidents say time seems to slow down. They say they felt disconnected, almost like a spectator. Not me. Imagine sticking your upper body into a hot oven. Imagine plunging your hands into the glowing coals of your backyard grill.

Imagine. That's how it felt.

You're incredible, Cathryn!" the photographer yelled. I would never forget the *thrill* in his voice.

I wasn't incredible. I was burning alive.

Roll. Get down on the ground and roll. I threw myself face down by the Trans Am, flailing, screaming, rolling. The heat retreated, the flames vanished. I went limp, gasping, peeing on myself, vomiting bile.

Four or five seconds. I was on fire for no more than four, maybe five, seconds, witnesses said later.

Shock began taking hold. Now, yes, I felt weirdly calm, pleasantly detached. *It'll take a week of spa treatments to get this smell off me*, I thought.

I heard sirens, I heard people still shouting. Some of them were even crying. One of them moaned, "Ohmygod, Ohmygod, *look at her*. I want to puke." Which struck me as incredibly *rude*.

I managed to lift my head. The photographer crouched less than an arm's length from my face, breathing hard, excited. I could see him through the smoke, I could hear him gulping for air, like a man about to come. Was *he* giving off that nauseating scent? It smelled like burned hair, and . . . burned . . . *meat.* He aimed the wide, black eye of his lens directly at my face. I looked into the glassy black mirror of that eye, the *world's* eye, and saw a grotesque, charred, sickening reflection.

And then I realized it was *me.*

Daddy and his sisters began entering me in beauty contests when I was old enough to toddle. As upper-class Southerners they generally looked down their noses at beauty competitions, which they considered lowbrow and tacky, but given my spectacular allure, they couldn't resist showing me off. "We're just honoring an old Southern tradition of exhibiting our prize livestock," one of my aunts told her friends. "You just watch. Cathryn will take more blue ribbons than a pretty sow at the state fair."

By the time I was six, I was a veteran with a roomful of trophies and tiaras. By the time I was eighteen, I was crowned Miss Georgia. I would have competed for Miss America, but I got my first movie role and handed the Miss Georgia crown to the runner-up, instead.

You don't spend your childhood on stage, duking it out with other ambitious little girls and their vicious stage parents, without learning to soldier on, no matter what. Once, when my music and costume had been sabotaged, I sang the entire theme song from *Annie* without accompaniment, wearing a plain black leotard and a skirt made from my aunt's pink cashmere scarf. I won the talent competition, and I won that pageant. I was four years old.

Strong Southern belle and Twenty-First Century steel magnolia, that was me. Coddled, blessed, praised, protected, then launched into the world of movies as a full-fledged glamour girl and sex symbol. Until now.

In the ambulance, I heard the paramedics talking about me.

I can't believe this is Cathryn Deen. Cathryn Deen. Do you know how many times I've jerked off to pictures of her?

Me, too. But not after this, man. Jesus. Look at her. Not anymore.

As my world faded to black, I hoped I'd die.

Thomas

At night, the Cove and the mountains around the Crossroads turn deep-green, almost black. You can feel the potential for evil in the darkness then, the surveillance of arrogant trees, the deadly lure of the cliffs, the subversive hollows, the drowning charm of the whitewater creeks, the hunger of wild animals slipping through the shadows, just waiting for you to become their next meal.

Around midnight I stretched out on the pew, too drunk to play another round of poker. The yard was lit only by the faintly illuminated café sign beside the Trace. The café's parking lot was empty. A few lights burned in the side dining room, where Delta and her quilting gang were stitching, gossiping and sipping sweet iced tea mixed with good mountain wine. The richest grapes thrive even in the wildest places. I watched the universe sprinkle its streetlights across the sky above Ten Sisters.

Bring it on, I told the evil. *I know you're out there.*

All those far-away threats, unknown. But here, in the light of the Crossroads, the world was safe and familiar, an old world, an illusion like all safe places, but still. As an architect, I appreciated illusions. Grief steals all the beauty in the world, then gives it back one piece at a time until the house you call your life is built on more hope than sorrow. So far, I'd only reclaimed a window here, a door there, hanging onto those small pieces of faith with my fingernails.

A brilliant, brief sparkle caught my eye.

Drawn down to earth, a star flashed and vanished over the western horizon.

Chapter 2

Thomas
Wild Woman Ridge

I had fallen in love with Cathyrn Deen's farm on my first day in the Cove, four years earlier. I arrived one rainy summer morning around dawn on a big Harley I bought when I left Manhattan. Just driving, looking for the next place to spend time among strangers who'd leave me alone while I drank and grieved. The North Carolina mountains swayed their hips and seduced me as I rolled down the East Coast intending to spend the summer chugging vodka on the beaches of Florida. I'd never suspected the Blue Ridge Mountains of the South could rival the Adirondacks of upstate New York for sheer, jaw-dropping scenery.

When my brother and I were kids, our old man took us along on his jobs at the Adirondacks' grand old resorts and turn-of-the-century "camps," those rustic log mansions created by gilded-age barons like the Vanderbilts. Our father, a master carpenter, was a tough S.O.B., not given to much sentiment and not all that likable. He bullied John for being overweight and called me a sissy because I had a knack for art as well as architecture. All in all, he did his best to make us spit in his face.

But he loved the memory of our mother, who died too young for me or John to remember, and we never doubted he'd throw himself in front of a runaway train to protect us. He respected his craft. To him, the historic camps of the Adirondacks epitomized it. Love him or hate him, we respected his dedication. He taught us to take responsibility for our thoughts, feelings and peckers, and he taught us to create whole worlds with a hammer, a saw, and our bare hands. He only had an eighth-grade education, so he couldn't put his appreciation for fine architecture into the sissy words he claimed to despise, but it showed in his reverence for the old places, his attention to every detail.

When I rolled into the Crossroads Cove that first day and saw the café welcoming me like an outpost in the wilderness, I thought of my old man and felt less alone. Smoke came from the café's chimneys, and cars already filled the parking lot, but I didn't stop for breakfast. Ruby Creek Trail, the old dirt road that crosses the Trace near the café, led me off the pavement and into the woods that morning.

I was just looking for an isolated place to throw down a sleeping bag. I didn't know it then, but I was following ghosts along a path so old the earliest French explorers had written about it in the 1700's. Before that, the Cherokees had carved its trail markers on rocky outcroppings. The petroglyphs that still remained—on boulders too big to steal—mesmerized me, and before I knew it I was deep in a fairytale hollow full of ferns, riding alongside Ruby Creek.

Lost.

I parked the bike and hiked up a ridge to get my bearings. When I reached the top I was surprised to find an abandoned pasture. Head-high pine saplings dueled with the tall grasses. Dew gleamed on sagging chestnut fence posts, worn gray by the weather. The pasture vanished around a curve in the forest like a green river going around a bend; I couldn't resist following it.

I walked for a long time before I crested a rise and halted. There, looking back at me at the far end of an alley lined with huge oaks and poplars, shimmering in the opalescent light of the sunrise, among old gray barns and fallen sheds and the faintest hint of flower beds in a forgotten front yard, gleaming pink and gold in the magic light, was a classic Craftsman cottage.

You've seen these bungalows in movies, you've seen versions of them in every neighborhood in America; they're the strong, small, proud children of efficiency and grace. Some are elaborate, and some are not; this one, hidden in the middle of a high-mountain farm, was the crown jewel of its kind.

I ran to it like a deranged lover, plowing through the weedy grass and the small pines. I bounded up wide stone steps and stood, awed, in the curving arch of the deep stone porch. I circled the house a dozen times, admiring the heavy, exposed rafters and their braces, that vaguely Asian touch that makes one think of a friendly pagoda. I caressed the thick stone chimney and foundation and pulled down a long tangle of vines that had climbed all the way to the roof, threatening to cover the wide, gabled dormer above the porch.

I didn't give a damn in anyone caught me trespassing or not. I cupped my hands around my eyes and looked through the windows at the maple floors and wormy chestnut wall boards, the built-in cherry cabinets and columned doorways. I chanted, "Look at that. My God, *look at that*," as if all the ghosts had followed me off the trail for a house tour.

Finally, dazed with appreciation, I stood back and gazed at the windows themselves. Stained glass bordered each one with intricate, geometric patterns. Sunlight glinted off coarse, pea-sized rubies and sapphires tucked in the soldered intersections. The house wore a necklace of hand-made windows decorated with local gemstones. My old man would have cringed at my artsy descriptions, but he would have appreciated the house as much as I did. It badly needed repairs. A fallen oak limb had gouged a hole in the roof. Several windows were cracked. Termites had ruined several rafters.

The house needed me.

The Nettie place up on Wild Woman Ridge, it was called. I found out when I went to the café and asked for information. A crowd of tourists cringed as I walked in the front door of the main dining room that day. The beard, the hair, the old jeans, the bloodshot eyes, the scarred biker jacket. I looked like trouble, I know. Someone slipped around back and warned Delta that a Hell's Angel had slithered into her dining room.

She came up front to see for herself. This sweet little woman grinned at me, handed me a steaming cup of coffee, and said loudly, so all the timid customers could hear, "Hoss, you look like you've been rode hard and put up wet. You better sit down with me and have a biscuit."

I loved her platonically from that moment on.

She sat across from me at a checkered table and answered every question I asked about the abandoned farm and its incredible house. Mary Eve Nettie had been a rebel, a maverick, an early feminist who kept her maiden name even after marriage, a legend. She'd inherited the farm from her parents, who'd made their fortune bootlegging the best homemade rum and bourbon in western North Carolina.

Mary Eve's parents built the farm's showplace home when she was a girl. Even then it was the talk of the mountains. The Netties picked a fancy, modern, Craftsman-cottage blueprint, "The Hollywood," out of a Sears and Roebuck catalog and mailed off a check for five-thousand-two-hundred-and-fifty-two dollars to Sears' Chicago headquarters—an astonishing amount at the time. Their extravagant mail-order purchase made them folk heroes to the entire mountain region, pissing off legions of Internal Revenue agents who couldn't prove the Netties hadn't earned the money panning rubies.

Sears shipped the entire three-bedroom bungalow by train from the company's northern lumber yards. Everything—including floorboards, mantels, cabinets, windows, doors, trimwork, and even the cedar shingles—arrived in North Carolina's Asheville depot in crates and stacks. Franklin Nettie, Mary Eve's father, trucked the materials over fifty miles of terrifying, high-mountain roads to the Crossroads Cove, where everything was transferred onto mule wagons for the rough trip by trail up to the farm on the ridge. Then Franklin and his crew of men assembled the house.

The finished cottage was a marvel of fine workmanship and detail. Mary Eve later embellished it in small, perfect ways, with handmade floor and counter tiles in the kitchen and stained-glass trim for the windows and front door. The bungalow was one of the few unsullied examples of a Sears Craftsman-style kit home. There wasn't another place like it in the country. I couldn't comprehend the neglect. A historic house like that, sitting empty. Uninhabited, ignored, left to rot. Sacrilege.

Clearly, Barnard Deen, the owner, a wealthy lawyer down in Georgia, simply didn't give a damn about his mother-in-law's mountain legacy. I camped out near the café and launched a campaign to buy the farm. I sent a dozen offers to Deen, each one more generous than the last.

Deen rejected all of them. He wouldn't even talk with me. After he died I tried to contact his heir, the famous Cathryn, with no success. Just more letters from attorneys telling me to forget it, and not to contact Ms. Deen again, and not to trespass on her property.

So, naturally, I had been trespassing and doing repairs at the farm, ever since. I'd spent many a night sleeping on the front porch among my hand tools and supplies. I'd watched thunderstorms roll grandly over the western horizon, where Hog Back Mountain, a neighbor of the Ten Sisters, filled the sky. I watched snow fall on the oaks; I'd watched the forest turn red and gold in autumn.

Everyone in the Cove knew the Nettie house and I were having an illicit affair, but they didn't mind. At the Crossroads, man-cottage love is tolerated.

In the meantime, I set up housekeeping next door on thirty acres I won at poker from Delta's brother-in-law, Joe Whittlespoon, aka the pot-farming "Santa" Whittlespoon. The Nettie place occupied one end of Wild Woman Ridge; the newly christened "Mitternich place" occupied the other end. I built a cabin on my land, and when I wasn't drunk, I planted a vineyard. I wasn't a farmer or a winemaker but I had a strong need to make new life take root on that ridge even if, some dark, drunken night, I ended my own.

🐾🐾🐾🐾🐾

Gruff and manipulative, Sheriff Pike Whittlespoon wasn't a lovable Andy Taylor of Mayberry, no, but a pragmatic officer of the peace for greater Jefferson County including the Crossroads Cove. He could track a lost kid across the roughest mountainside, sweet-talk an abused wife into testifying against her husband, or break up a meth lab with his bare fists. He and Delta had been married since they were sixteen—nearly thirty-five years—and he quietly worshipped the ground she walked on. He was a friend to his and Delta's sensitive, mullet-haired, ex-military son, Jeb, a fiercely protective grandpa to Jeb and Becka's likable kids, and a resigned defender of his unconventional older bro, Joe, the aforesaid hemp-scented Santa Whittlespoon.

At six-five and two-eighty, Pike outweighed me but couldn't look over my head without craning his. You could say we saw eye to eye on the justice system. He'd never clobbered me when I was drunk, and I'd never given him a reason to.

"Tommy-Son," Pike told me not long after my arrival in the community, christening me with both a *paterfamilial* relationship and an inferior rank, "if you ever get into that piece-of-shit 'vintage' truck of yours when you're drunk, and you attempt to drive that piece-of-shit 'vintage' truck of yours on my roads, I'll make sure you spend the next twelve months in zebra stripes, shoveling piles of Hereford shit at the county's 'vintage' prison farm."

Which is why I spent a lot of time sleeping in my truck under the café's oak trees.

I was outdoors at my cabin not long after sunrise that Sunday morning, sweating away my bleak Saturday-night mood and a full bottle of vodka. The twin handles of a post-hole digger felt righteous against the calluses of my hands. Blood, sweat, tears. Mother Nature's fertilizer. Blister by blister, I built my vineyard, an *homage* to the stained-glass windows of Frank Lloyd Wright.

I had just finished setting the last trellis post in the top-right geometric branch of the middle abstract tree in Wright's "Tree of Life" pattern. The original stained-glass window could be seen inside a turn-of-the-century home in Buffalo, New York. My version was six-hundred feet long, four-hundred feet wide, and could be seen by small planes and hang gliders. When I was done building trellises and planting grapevines, the *Nazca* lines of Peru would pale by comparison.

A rumbling noise crept through the fog in my brain. For a few seconds I ignored it, bending down to measure the precise depth of my newest post hole. When I was communing with the vineyard and fighting a hangover it took a lot to get my attention. But the rumble grew louder, and finally I looked up.

Pike's blue-and-gray patrol car roar out of the woods with the lights flashing. I dropped my tape measure. A fist closed around my chest, and for a moment I smelled terror and saw falling bodies on a Manhattan street. Doctors call this hyper-alert reaction 'post traumatic stress syndrome.' I called it 'smart.'

Pike slid to a stop within spitting distance of my sweat-dappled work boots. I set my post-hole digger aside and straightened my surveyor's tripod, giving myself a few seconds to breathe. "Don't cut me any slack, Pike. Just say it. What's happened to my brother? Or his wife or kids—"

"Relax. Your brother and his family are fine. Tommy-Son, why the hell don't you get a spare cell phone?"

I exhaled. "Delta, Jeb . . . Banger? All okay?"

"Fine. But Delta needs to see you pronto. She needs your help."

"What about?"

"Cathryn Deen."

"Let me guess. Cathryn Deen's business manager finally sent a *personal* reply to one of Delta's letters, and Delta's so shocked she wants everyone in the Crossroads to see it?"

The joke failed to register. There was something about the look on Pike's beefy, barn-board face that made me uneasy again. This was how John Wayne looked before he broke grisly news to the troops in *Sands of Iwo Jima*. If the Duke had to swallow his spit before he gave some hardened dog faces bad news, it was *really* bad. "Cathyrn Deen was in a car accident yesterday," Pike said. "Nearly burned to death."

The blood drained to my feet as he told me the gory details. CNN was reporting Cathryn would live, but she'd be badly scarred. "A shame," Pike finished. "What a looker. She favored Delta around the eyes."

Self-preservation kicked in. Cynicism makes a good antidote for caring too much. *If Cathryn Deen dies, maybe I can buy the Nettie place from her estate.* I'm not proud of that thought, but I admit it. "Why does Delta think I can do anything for her movie-star cousin?"

"You know how to pull strings in the great wide world. Get a phone call through to Cathryn's hospital room in California." Delta and Pike thought I could make miracles happen because I'd crawled out on a cliff once, up on Devil's Knob, not long after Jeb came home from Iraq, and talked Jeb out of jumping. When you're full of vodka and don't care about your own safety, it's easy to be a hero. I shook my head. "Pike, I'm sorry. But—"

"Look, you and me know Cathryn Deen's fancy husband isn't gonna let Delta talk to Cathryn's doctors. But will you at least try to help Delta out? She hates not being able to meddle in her kinfolk's troubles. Even if the kinfolk live on the other side of the country and haven't visited her in twenty years."

Across the deep-blue mountain sky, a hawk, hunting, sang its fierce and forlorn call as it glided like an angel on the high currents. No past, no future, just living in that glorious moment, suspended on thin air. Hawks are practical, they know the cosmic score. At best Cathyrn Deen probably didn't care about her Crossroads heritage or her grandmother's old farm, and might recoil at the idea of an obscure relative coming to her aid.

However, unlike a hawk, I had nightmares filled with regrets when I slept. Lots of karmic misery to pay back.

"Will you at least come and listen?" Pike persisted.

I nodded.

The hawk caught a perfect gust of air and floated, motionless, on the invisible palm of redemption.

🐾🐾🐾🐾🐾

Delta was not a crier. A woman who worked her butt off running a restaurant so successful *Southern Living* called it "a well-known jewel in the middle of the wilderness," who ruled over a rambunctious mountain family and a bearded drunk who slept with a goat under her oak, no, a woman like that wasn't going to break down and cry because her cousin's husband's cousin's lay in a Los Angeles hospital, maimed for life. "Life doesn't settle for 'simmer' just because you want to turn down the heat," Delta liked to say. That didn't make much sense, but it sounded profound.

"I intend to find out how Cathryn's doing," she declared. "That's all there is to it. And you're gonna help me, Thomas."

Delta, Pike, and the entire immediate Whittlespoon family stared at me in the crowded confines of the café's kitchen. A food-scented breeze curled around us. As usual, the wooden doors stood open and only the inner screened doors kept numerous cats, dogs, goats and squirrels from entering. A floor fan whirred even in the chill of the spring morning. Mouth-watering aromas wafted from a steam table filled with food. Cars and trucks crowded the parking lot. There were people who drove all the way from Asheville on weekend mornings, just for breakfast.

But they weren't being served, because Delta and all of her gang were all standing in the kitchen, giving me the pressure-wash of group power. In Southern terms, I was being *eyeballed.*

"You New Yorkers, you can get things done," Delta insisted. "You have ways."

"Contrary to popular belief," I said quietly, "Not everyone from New York has mafia connections or friends in show business. Delta, I've spent the past few years trying to get in touch with Cathryn Deen to buy the Nettie farm, with no luck. What makes you think I can get through to her hospital room now?"

She shook her apron at me. "You're my only hope! When I called that hospital in Los Angeles they wouldn't even tell me how she's doing! And when I said 'I'm *family,*' they told me I'm not on their list. I said, 'Well, let me talk to Cathryn's husband and I'll *get* on your list,' and they said, 'You'll have to go through his publicist.' What kind of husband needs a publicist to handle calls from his wife's *family?*"

Pike sighed and draped a long arm around her short shoulders. " Baby, Cathryn's daddy cut you and the rest of her mountain kin out of the picture twenty years ago, and since then all you've talked to are publicity people and lawyers and business managers every time you've tried to reach her. Now her husband's put up the same wall around her. This is nothing new. You can't help the girl, Baby. You just can't. She probably doesn't need or even want your help."

"But I don't *know* that." Delta flung a hand toward the small television attached to the kitchen's aging, beadboard wall between wire shelves stacked with pots and pans. CNN was showing a gruesome picture of Cathryn's burned Trans Am. "She's all they're talking about on the morning news shows! A member of my family is laying in a hospital bed on the other side of the country, in terrible misery, and she needs to know she's got kin who care!"

"If it makes you feel any better," I said gently, "I doubt she's aware of anything. Doctors sedate burn victims for the first few days after they're injured. Nobody who's been burned the way she has is conscious, at this point."

"But she'll wake up eventually, and when she does, she'll need her family. Her daddy's gone, her mama's gone, all those prissy old Atlanta aunts on her Deen side are dead or senile. I'm the last root left in her family tree! Thomas, you used to be an important architect in New York, and you were married to a rich wife who . . . well, you had big connections. You can find some way to get me through to Cathryn."

The mention of my old life didn't help matters. I turned away. Cleo scowled at me. "Don't be a quitter. Jesus believes in you, even if *you* don't believe in *yourself*."

"Jesus doesn't know me the way I do." I nodded my goodbyes and walked out. I was halfway across the back yard to my truck when Delta caught up to me. Small but stubborn, she blocked my way. "You can't hide from the world for the rest of your life!"

I looked down at her grimly. "I don't want responsibility for anyone's life but my own."

"Liar! If it weren't for you, my son'd be dead! You risked your own hide to stop Jeb from jumping off Devil's Knob when you were still just a newcomer around here!"

"Only because I have a particular aversion to people jumping off high places."

"I know about those pictures you keep in your truck! I've watched you look at 'em when you don't realize anybody sees you!"

I stiffened. "I should train Banger to 'bah' when he hears you sneaking up on me."

"You make yourself relive your wife and son's misery over and over, like if you just mourn hard enough somehow you'll travel back through time and change what happened to them. But you can't. You can't, Thomas. None of us can turn back time. What we *can* do is learn from our regrets and change the future." She grabbed my hands. "You know how it feels to be caught up in something so terrible it's like being down in a dark pit, not able to see even one speck of light at the top. That's where Cathryn is, right now, down in a pit. Be her light, Thomas. Be her light."

34

I stood there, my head bowed, my shoulders hunched. This is how it feels to be dragged from the cement shoes of a comfortable rut. The slow, steady strain on my legs became an excruciating amputation. My ankles pulled free from my feet. Bones snapped, cartilage tore, veins pulsed blood onto the soft brown clay of the yard.

"I'll make some phone calls," I told her. "But don't get your hopes up."

She squeezed my hands and smiled. "I already have."

Chapter 3

Cathy
Los Angeles, The Burn Ward

Unfortunately, nobody had had the foresight to let me die and become a legend. I could have joined Elvis and Marilyn in the Dead Icon Hall of Fame, but nooo.

"Cathryn Deen? Cathryn Mary Deen? Do you know where you are?"

I blinked slowly, wrapped in a cocoon of painkillers and sedatives, that cocktail of drugs given to burn victims for the first few days so they won't realize parts of their bodies have been deep-fried. I could barely remember my name, much less what had happened to me.

"Who?" I murmured.

If I could have seen myself, naked except for sterilized sheets and the huge bandages on my head, right arm, right torso, and right leg, my arms tied down, IV's and monitor lines everywhere, and a catheter between my thighs . . . if I could have seen my swollen, hairless head with the mass of bandages plastered to the right side, I would have willed myself to go back to sleep again. Permanently. My head was grotesquely swollen, and even the left side of my face, the side that would look normal again eventually, was raw-red.

Thank God I didn't know how I looked, yet. I heard myself mumbling in a weak voice. "Daddy? Granny Nettie? Mother?" They'd been visiting me. Daddy simply smiled at me. He'd never known what to say when I was hurt. That was the nanny's job. Granny Nettie said, "Eat, girl. Every time life gives you biscuits and gravy, eat and rejoice." In my dreams I stood in the kitchen with her, gazing out her wondrous stained-glass windows on Wild Woman Ridge, watching sunlight and shadows drape their smile on layers of enormous, blue-green mountains. *This is no place for skinny sissies,* those mountains whispered to me. The scent of lard, milk, sausage, flour, and butter filled my senses. Oddly comforting. *Everything will be all right, if you find what you really want,* Granny whispered. *Cheer up, I left a home for you. It's waiting.*

My long-dead mother, who I'd discovered was much prettier than the photos in my scrapbooks, leaned close and whispered, *Go home, yes. We'll see you again, some day.*

"Don't leave me." Too late. I was awake.

"Cathryn? Ms. Deen? I'm asking you again: Do you know where you are?"

My tongue felt swollen. I tested it, licking the front of my teeth. Helps your smile slide over your pearly caps. Looks sexy for the male judges. An old pageant trick.

"*Ms. Deen, do you know where you are?*" The voice was female and insistent. Not impressed by my teeth.

"Hell?" I finally whispered.

"No, it just feels that way. You're in the burn unit. I'm your primary physician. You're under the care of a large medical team."

"My entourage."

"In a manner of speaking. Now, listen carefully. I'll let you go back to sleep in a minute. We just moved you out of Intensive Care. It's been five days since your accident. We've deliberately kept you medicated for your benefit. The pain would be excruciating, otherwise. We don't want you to move around. You're hooked up to IV's. You have a catheter in your bladder. Until a few hours ago you had a feeding tube down your throat. Your current situation is a little . . . confining, I know. We don't want you feeling claustrophobic, so we're keeping you medicated. That will get better in the next week or so."

Of course, I thought. *I'll be fine. Probably just a few blisters.*

My vision was a little blurry, and when I looked upward I saw something puffy and red. I didn't know it at the time, but I was looking at the swollen underside of my eyebrows. I thought I was wearing some kind of pink-brimmed cap. I looked beyond it and found the source of the voice. It came from a white-swaddled shape hovering over me. The shape was masked and gloved, as if dealing with toxic waste. It might have come from another planet. It clearly had confused me with a serious burn victim.

"Get me to . . . a spa," I told the alien. "Just need a . . . mud wrap."

"Try to pay attention, Cathryn. There's lots of good news to report. Your eyes are fine, your lungs are fine, you are very lucky. Your burns cover slightly less than 30 percent of your body, which gives you an excellent prognosis for full, functional recovery. Your burns are primarily second-degree, meaning most won't need skin grafts, though there will be permanent scarring."

Scarring? *Scarring?*

"Your right hand suffered some deep tissue injury, so you'll need surgery to ensure joint mobility in your fingers. But that's very do-able."

Do-able. I was do-able.

"The worst thing I have to tell you is that you *do* have several areas of third-degree burns. In those places, the skin was destroyed and so can't renew itself. These areas include your right shoulder, on the right side of your neck and throat, and . . . on the right side of your face, from the corner of your eye and mouth to just behind your ear. Over the next few weeks we'll take skin from your undamaged left side, and your back, and graft it. It will replace the burned skin."

Okay. Essentially, I just needed a good exfoliant.

"The lower lobe of your right ear had to be amputated, but the rest of your ear is intact—though badly burned—and your hearing should be unaffected."

Wait a minute. This creature from another planet must be joking with me. I could have sworn it said I no longer had an ear lobe on one side. Guess I'd save money on earrings. The Oscars were in a few weeks. Would Harry Winston still loan me the twenty-carat tiers Princess Di commissioned not long before she died? I could wear one on my good ear, and one in my navel.

"Very funny," I whispered.

"I'm afraid this isn't a joke, Cathryn."

"Let me out of here. Have . . . work to do. Due in England on Wednesday. Photo shoot for Vogue, too."

"Try not to worry about your career, for now. You're probably going to be in the hospital at least six weeks. You'll be undergoing numerous small surgeries, and also, I'm afraid, regular debridement. Debridement is a procedure in which we change your bandages twice daily and remove dead tissue from your wounds. It's not very pleasant, I'm afraid. But don't worry about that right now."

Don't worry? "Gerald! Gerald. My husband. Tell him. I want out . . . of here. He'll handle this."

"He's very busy right now. Talking to the press, to your agents, all of that. Don't worry."

"I want him . . . here."

"I'm afraid we can't allow him, or anyone else, to visit you yet. The burn unit is a very sterile environment, Cathryn. Infection is a major concern for patients recovering from large-scale loss of skin. You won't be allowed to have many visitors, and the ones you do have will be covered in antiseptic surgical outfits like mine."

"Call him. I'll call him."

"You're in no condition to do that right now. Plus your husband has requested that you not be disturbed. We don't want any reporters trying to talk to you. You can't call out, and no one can call in without his permission. He doesn't want the media to harass you."

"But . . . I need my . . . my friends. My stylists. Judi, Randy, Luce. My people."

"I'm sorry, Cathryn. You have no 'people' here. Sometimes the burn unit feels like one of the loneliest places in the world. But you'll be all right. You get some rest. You've got a lot of work ahead of you."

She left. Other creatures from the toxic-waste patrol hovered over me. "We're going to help you go back to sleep now," one of them said. "We'll play your favorite music to keep you company while you drift off. Your husband says you love Gwen Stefani."

The creature put a CD in a sterilized boom box. *Hollaback Girl,* Stefani's hip-hop anthem, began to pound me like a drum. I couldn't really be trapped in a hospital bed listening to a thirty-five-year-old woman sing, *"This my shit,"* could I? I didn't love Gwen Stefani's music, Gerald just told people I loved it because his marketing people said she tracked to a young demographic who'd buy my cosmetics.

My favorite music? Bonnie Raitt, Rosanne Cash, the Dixie Chicks. Wise women with guitars. Gerald said they were too old and too feminist for my fun-loving image, and they probably didn't even wear makeup, much less encourage other women to wear it, but . . . where was he? And why wouldn't he even call me on the phone?

"I can listen," I mumbled. "I have an ear left."

"Go to sleep," a creature ordered, pulling a syringe out of a stint in my arm. "It's better if you don't think too much."

I shut my eyes. Aliens in antiseptic jumpsuits said I couldn't move, couldn't talk to anyone, that my right earlobe was missing, that parts of my skin would have to be replaced, and that I was lucky to be alive. Plus they made me listen to Gwen Stefani. No one who knew me, no one I trusted, was here. Not even my own husband and my family ghosts.

My people were gone. Even the dead ones.

Thomas

"Next time, ask me for something easy, Thomas," my brother said. "Like trying to get in touch with the Easter Bunny. And, by the way, I'm sending you a new cell phone. One with GPS tracking."

Since he was shouting, I moved the phone I'd borrowed from one of Delta's grandkids further from my ear. Even so, John's voice echoed off the unlined metal innards of my truck's cab. "Good," I shouted back. "When the satellite shows the new phone roaming around the barn behind the café, you'll know Banger ate it, too."

"I'd just like to be able to locate your body. Monica and the kids will be disappointed if there's nothing to bury. Did I mention she's planning a Jewish funeral for you?"

I liked my brother's wife. Her morbid sense of humor fit in perfectly with the Mitternich family brand. "Tell Monica I appreciate it from the bottom of my atheistic, gentile heart."

"She'll get all her family together and sit Shiva in your honor. Me? I'll just go to the nearest pub and raise a beer to Thomas Karel Mitternich, my self-destructive older brother, and then I'll find a kindly priest who'll lie to me and swear you aren't in hell for killing yourself."

"I love these cheerful conversations we have."

"Me, too, Thomas. But I digress. Have you completely lost your mind? Cathryn Deen's people will never let your pal Delta—or anyone else from the non-Perrier sipping, NASCAR-loving hinterlands—within so much as Jethro-yodeling distance of Deen's V.I.P room in a Los Angeles burn ward."

John had done his best to help me fulfill Delta's mission to call her cousin Cathryn, but he was right. Getting through the wall of privacy—or secrecy—Cathryn's husband put around her was impossible. It had been more than a week since her accident. John, a financial planner in Chicago, could follow a money trail to all kinds of information, but even he couldn't crack this code. Celebrities at Cathryn Deen's level of fame were either naked in the spotlight or invisible. Sadly for her, she was both, right now.

The bastard who shot the gruesome video of her trying to escape from her car, and then stuck his camera in her face while she was burning, was already selling the clip on the Internet. He'd dodged a criminal charge because his lawyer argued she was driving recklessly before he chased her. In a dangerous situation like a fire, the law says you don't have to risk your own safety to rescue someone else. How convenient.

So the video was available for a hefty download fee, and the major news channels were showing snippets of it in the guise of covering the controversy. In terms of debased human nature, the Christians-versus-lions smackdown at the Roman Coliseum had nothing over modern voyeurs. Delta was furious. So, on a quieter level, was I. I knew how it felt to see my loved ones exploited.

There was only one option left.

"I'm calling Ravel," I told John.

Silence. Then, very quietly and seriously, my baby brother said, "She'll eat your gonads with a side of lemon risotto and a nice cabernet."

"I know," I said.

"You don't deserve what she'll say to you."

"That's debatable."

"She wants blood."

"I've got plenty."

"Is Cathryn Deen worth it? A stranger, Thomas? Worth it? Why? And don't tell me this is only about that farm you want to buy from her."

I looked at the pictures on my truck visor. The slow, steady squeeze of misery eased for just a second. "Maybe, just maybe, this time I can make a difference in someone's life."

🐾🐾🐾🐾🐾

Two hundred and fifty million years ago Africa bumped into North America, buckling masses of metamorphic rock over layers of limestone, and thrust up the Appalachians. Throw in a few glaciers and eons of erosion, and now you had Devil's Knob, a craggy, treeless monolith protruding from Hog Back Mountain like a spike on the hog's side. I loved the primordial purity of the place. Touch the rock, and you were touching antiquity. Stand there, and you stood on eternity.

At 4,000 feet, Devil's Knob was one of the highest local balds. As I stood there, cradling another borrowed cell phone in one hand, I gazed north over the Crossroads Cove toward New York, approximately four states away. Barricading me from my old life were high ridges, deep hollows, forests of huge evergreens, rushing trout streams, secluded farms, ramshackle tobacco barns, placid black bears, herds of deer, flocks of wild turkeys, and the occasional liquor still alongside a marijuana patch.

Still not enough wilderness between me and my sister-in-law, but it would have to do. Ravel, Sherryl's sister, was no doubt lurking in her Trump Tower penthouse on Fifth Avenue, approximately seven hundred feet above sea level. I was at 4,000 feet. I needed to know she had to look up to me.

"Thomas, you sure you don't know anybody in the CIA to call instead?" drawled Joe Whittlespoon. Pike's older brother, nicknamed "Santa" for his obvious resemblance, sat a few feet away with legs dangling off the Knob's rocky ledge. He stroked his curly white beard with one hand and fingered a long cheroot of homegrown marijuana with the other. The sweet scent rose on a high breeze, mingling with the rich fragrance of pine and earth. A tie-dyed bandana hung from the bib of Santa's overalls. Rough rubies and sapphires, panned in local creeks, decorated the bracelets and rings he wore. Everyone in the county knew Santa was an old hippie who grew weed up on Hog Back, but he was Pike's big brother, after all. People in the mountains of the South had respect for their elders, especially those related to sheriffs. I had intervened on his behalf once when two beefy young entrepreneurs from Asheville tried to steal his harvest.

"I'm just saying," Santa went on, "that the CIA's got to be easier to deal with than your wife's sister. And better-tempered."

"I'm out of alternatives. Believe me, this is my last choice. I wouldn't do this for anyone but Delta."

"I warn you. Delta sees you as dough she can mold to her own purposes. There's an art to *kneading* people that way, and she learned it from the most irresistible force of nature the Cove ever saw, and I do mean Mary Eve Nettie. Mary Eve could spin people through her fingers like a magician twirls a coin. Godawmighty, that woman could make a man jump up and holler then lay down and moan. I ought to know. I was nineteen and Mary Eve was at least thirty-five the first time she flipped me on my back."

I stared at him. "You and Mary Eve—"

He nodded. His eyes became distant and tender. "That woman knew how to get what she wanted. And she gave as good as she got." Santa's phone suddenly vibrated in my palm, playing a few bars of The Grateful Dead's "Truckin'." Santa scrubbed a hand over his wistful expression then scowled at me. "Just remember, I warned you about Delta using you to get what she wants. She doesn't use sex to grease the skids the way Mary Eve did, but she's just as determined."

I looked at the incoming phone number. A 212 area code. Manhattan. Ravel. "Showtime." I let a few more bars of "Truckin'" play.

"Talk or jump off the cliff," Santa drawled. "Jerry Garcia isn't gonna save you from reality, son."

I put the phone to my ear. "Hello, Ravel. I appreciate you returning my call. If this weren't an emergency, I'd never ask for, or expect, your help."

"You fucking parasite." Her voice shook with emotion. It always chilled me to be hated so much. "There's only one reason I remain interested in your fate, Thomas. I keep hoping I'll hear that you've had the decency to blow your fucking brains out."

"Let's keep this simple. You got my message. You know what I want. You're a major stockholder sitting on the board of one of the biggest hospital corporations in the world. You can find out everything about Cathryn Deen's situation, right down to the name of the nurse's aid who cleans her trash can. I need that contact information, and . . . I'll do whatever you want, in return."

"I want you to suffer and I want you to die as miserably as Sherryl and Ethan did, you heartless, pathetic waste of human flesh."

"I'm not asking you to do me any favors. This is for some good people who need a break."

"Spare me your ludicrous attempts to deflect your own guilt by becoming a do-gooder for those white-trash hillbillies with whom you associate."

"Ravel, do what I'm asking, and I'll send you *the watch*."

Silence. After a minute I heard her crying softly. Then, "Ship the watch by private courier, insured, and when I'm holding it in my hand, you'll get the information you want. You emotionally manipulative bastard."

She clicked off.

"Well, that was easy." I tossed the phone to Santa.

He frowned at me over a plume of medicated smoke. "Delta

didn't expect you to bribe the Death Haint of Yankeedom with your keepsake."

The Death Haint. I liked how Southerners categorized the demons in our lives. You give a demon a funny name, the demon can't hurt you so much. I took my antique silver watch from my pocket and stepped to the edge of Devil's Knob. As I looked down into a maw of boulders, cliffs, and the greening tops of a hardwood forest far below, I popped the watch's lid and rubbed the pad of my thumb over the engraving one more time. The watch was one of my touchstones. I didn't have many left.

It had belonged to Sherryl's grandfather. Sherryl had had it engraved for me. *Thank you for giving me Ethan.* That summed up why our rocky marriage was worth it; it summed up everything that had been wonderful about waking up every morning. Our son. It was more than a trinket to me, more than a casual heirloom from my wife's family. Her sister knew that. It was the last gift Sherryl and Ethan gave me before they died.

And I had just traded it to help Cathryn Deen, a stranger.

Santa got up slowly, watching me. He was too stoned to stop me from taking a long walk off a short cliff, and he knew it. "Thomas," he said carefully, "I know why you come up here." He nodded at the phone I'd handed back. "Just like I know why you don't like for the outside world to find you too easy. I know why you go to the high places and look down and think about what it was like for your wife and son. But trust me. Some day you'll look up instead of down, and you'll see it all differently."

I closed the watch, slid it into my pocket, and stepped back from the edge.

All I saw was thin air.

🐾🐾🐾🐾🐾

Puffing with the effort, Delta climbed up a ladder to the low-pitched roof of Mary Eve Nettie's house and sat beside me in the glow of a setting sun. Gold, red, lavender, pink—the sky over Hog Back was a concentrated rainbow. Mist fringed the mountaintops, and the deepening blue-black night at the apex of the sky drew me to its infinite focus. There was no better view in the mountains than the one from Mary Eve's rooftop on Wild Woman Ridge.

A small herd of deer—mostly does with pregnant bellies but also some yearlings and young bucks with two-point antlers—grazed in the pasture near a weathered barn. A flock of wild turkeys pecked at the ground among the deer. I stored bags of corn in the Nettie barn, throwing out several buckets full every day to lure a crowd. I didn't hunt. I just liked the company.

"I expect Mary Eve likes the idea of a good-looking man sitting on her roof," Delta said quietly. "She's probably right out yonder in the pasture, looking at us right now. That big doe with the frisky eyes? Yep. That's her. Mary Eve always said she wanted to come back as a deer. Eat, sleep, screw and hang out with some good friends. 'Keep it simple but elegant,' she liked to say."

"I agree."

Delta patted my arm. "Your pocket watch is on its way to New York. Anthony picked it up an hour ago. He said he'll take extra-special care." Anthony Washington was the UPS driver out of Asheville. Delta insisted he eat every time he made the long trip to the Crossroads. For Delta's chicken and dumplings with biscuits he'd hand-deliver the watch to Trump Tower himself. "Thomas, I—"

"It's just a watch."

"No, it's not. Thank you, Thomas."

"I only did it because I want this house."

"You're a sorry liar."

"When Cathryn Deen's well enough, you tell her to sell her grandmother's house to me. That's the deal. Shake on it."

"Now, you know I don't do business with drunks who smell like my granddaddy's still. When Granddaddy McKellan poured off his makings the whole house smelled like a bar. Go and stick your head in one of the café's closets and take a big sniff. Corn liquor. Granddaddy was a conniving, adultering old dog who shamed the reputation of the McKellan family throughout these parts for decades. Plus he called me 'a fat little ugly girl' and told everybody I'd never amount to a hill of beans. You don't want to smell like his memory."

"It's just my new aftershave. *Eau de Vodka.* Don't change the subject. I want this house."

She thumped the roof with her knuckles. "Thomas, you don't need this empty house. You need a home."

"There isn't another house like this in the state. In the region. In the country. In the world. I could restore this house the way it should be restored. I have the money. I'm not poor, despite how I look to other people. There isn't much in the world I'm sure I can protect and preserve, but this house? I can save it."

"All this time," she said gently, "I thought you stayed in the Crossroads because you couldn't resist my cooking."

"I want this house," I repeated. "I sold my soul to my sister-in-law for you. All I ask in return is that you make sure Cathryn Deen sells this house to me."

"She *can't* sell it to you."

"Why?"

"Because after I talk her into coming here to live, she's going to need this house herself. Cheer up, though—I expect she'll welcome your help renovatin' it."

Delta patted my arm, knocked over the half-full bottle of vodka beside me and climbed down. I picked my jaw up off the roof's cedar shingles. My booze trickled off a gable, and I didn't even notice.

In the gloaming, she left behind only her Cheshire-cat grin.

Chapter 4

Cathy
Contact Is Made

"Any phone calls for me?" I murmured to the nurse.

"No, Ms. Deen, none today."

No calls. No people. No husband. No right ear lobe.

Hurt. Sleep. Hurt. Sleep.

Cry.

And to top it off, the nightmares had started. Every time I shut my eyes, I caught on fire again.

Two weeks after the accident I was still barely coherent, and could only describe my life in a few words. No drug stopped the pain completely, nothing clubbed my nightmares into submission, and nothing made me hungry enough to crave the chalky, high-protein milkshakes a burn victim has to eat constantly in order to fuel a body trying desperately to heal the leaking sieve of its own skin.

"Either you sip the shakes or it's back on a feeding tube, Ms. Deen," the nutritionist said, holding a straw to my mouth.

I sipped.

I had seen Gerald once, just once, for five minutes. He was dressed in the latest burn-ward fashion over his tailored suit: sterile cap, mask, gown, gloves. All I could see were his eyes, and I told myself I only imagined the repulsed look in them.

I just dreamed that, I thought. *Disgust and flames. Just another nightmare.*

I was still bound to my bed by tubes and bandages, and could move only my left forefinger to click a call button and a morphine drip. There was a television in the room, but the staff kept it on movies approved by Gerald. Despite being drugged, I was fairly certain I'd seen Leo and Kate escape from the *Titanic* about fifteen times already.

At night, when the TV was off, Gwen Stefani rapped endlessly about her shit. Now I know who sings the elevator music in hell. Alone in my bed in the dark, with just Gwen for company, I cried without using a single muscle in my roasted face, seeping tears.

Fat. I'll get fat from the high-cal shakes, I kept thinking. *I won't be a perfect five-foot-seven-size-four anymore.*

Since childhood, my entire life had centered on being beautiful, except when I visited Granny Nettie in North Carolina. Daddy did not like her and clearly wanted her memory forgotten. I returned from every Granny visit cheerfully sunburned, bruised from falling out of trees, several pounds heavier, and a good deal more opinionated about politics, women's issues, and religion. My Atlanta aunts loathed Granny Nettie and always urged Daddy to ban further visits.

See, I came from a mixed marriage. Daddy and his people were old-money flatlands Southern, from Atlanta and coastal South Carolina. Mother and her people were no-money mountain Southern, from the high Appalachians of western North Carolina. Mother died when I was only three, and Granny Nettie became determined to undermine Daddy's influence. The Deens openly regarded her as a redneck witch or worse. Her thick wrists were draped in funky bracelets studded with rough rubies and sapphires she'd panned in her creek at the farm. She raised milk goats and Christmas trees, could sing every song from *Cats*, had a number of boyfriends, some younger than herself, and openly admitted my Grandpa Nettie had been shot to death in 1967, during a blood feud with one of his Cherokee cousins over on the Qualla Boundary.

Can't get fat, can't get flabby, I thought in a daze, laying in bed. *Fat girls are not successful. Must perform isometric exercises to stay in shape. Squeeze and release, squeeze and release.* If only I could remember where my ass was.

I needed to talk to someone, anyone. I needed a voice in my good ear, telling me I would be all right. But Gerald controlled all contact with the outside world. Why? Was he ashamed of me? I'd make myself beautiful for him if he just gave me a chance. I'd call Luce, Randy and Judi and schedule a styling.

Yes! In a few months, after all the surgeries and other tortures were finished, I'd be ready for my close-up, Mr. DeMille. I had admired too many twenty-year-old faces on fifty-year-old actresses to lose faith in the power of plastic surgery now. Scarred for life, who, me? Nah. Delusion, thy blessing is an IV filled with reality-altering narcotics and hallucinations inspired by continuous showings of *Titanic*.

I cried every time the music swelled and the ocean liner, that unsinkable, legendary, beautiful ocean liner, sank.

Thomas

I had a hangover of epic proportions. Every time I glanced overhead, a fabric Rorschach test hit me between the eyes. A half-finished queen-sized quilt hung from its quilting rack in the ceiling of the café's porch dining room. On Saturday nights the Crossroads Quilters met there. Delta said the pattern was Pineapple. Abstract. Octagonal. Sunlight splashed off the jumble of colors. It made my eyes cross.

Delta didn't care. "Place the call," she ordered, staring at the speaker phone between us on a checkered tablecloth. "It's almost noon in California. I bet Cathryn's awake and about to have lunch. Good. People listen to me the most when they're hungry."

No surprise. Delta always smelled of flour and sugar, even on a weekday afternoon. An aphrodisiac for the spiritually hungry. Her skin was at that cusp of middle-aged softness, a friendly cushion around her bones. Her short, thick forearms were covered in freckles, and her hands were strong and quick. She was a human apple pie. I watched her distractedly smooth wrinkles off her chef's apron. Her fingers twitched toward the phone.

All I promised her was a phone connection. One call, a personal contact, and nothing else. That talk about Cathryn Deen moving here and living in her grandmother's house? Delta's naïve fantasy. The Nettie house is mine.

I blew out a long breath, took a reviving swallow of iced tea so sweet my tongue curled, then punched in the number Ravel's minions had faxed to the café. We'd be lucky if Delta didn't get ignored, insulted, rebuffed. I didn't want Delta hurt. People who believe in the goodness of mankind deserve protection from those of us who don't.

After two rings, we arrived on the other side of the continent. "Burn ward," an officious female voice said. "Security."

"I'm calling to speak with Cathryn Deen," I said officiously, in return. "I have my security code ready."

"Thank you, sir. Please punch it in now, then press the star sign."

I tapped a ten-digit number and the star sign. There was a click, then no ring at all, then another click. "Burn unit," a woman said.

"Gerald Merritt."

"Mr. Merritt! Sir, I'm so glad it's you. Your wife could really use more phone calls from you. Her psychologist asked me to tell you she's feeling very isolated. Like all victims of severe burns, she's struggling with a lot of emotional issues. As the head of her nursing team, I really have to question your decision to forbid any of her friends from calling. She needs contact with the outside world. Maintaining her public image seems like a high price to pay under the circumstances. What can I say to make you reconsider?"

This, I hadn't counted on. Lying about my identity to get Delta through to Cathryn Deen was one thing. Being asked for a decision on Cathryn Deen's phone privileges was another. On the other hand, her husband was obviously a major prick.

Delta waved at me furiously. *Gerald*, she mouthed, *is a mule pecker*.

Well, okay. We had a consensus.

I leaned closer to the phone. "I completely agree with your concern about my wife's need for more contact with her friends and family. My wife has a dear cousin in North Carolina. Her name is Delta Whittlespoon. From now on, whenever Delta calls, put her through."

"Wonderful! Delta Whittlespoon. I'm writing that down. I'll give you a direct number for Ms. Whittlespoon to use. Straight to your wife's room. Ms. Deen isn't able to pick up a phone, but, as you know, she can receive calls via a speaker. So when I put you through, don't wait for her to answer, just start talking."

Delta mouthed, *Yes!* and pumped one fist.

"Very good," I said crisply, hoping I still sounded like Gerald. "In fact, I have Delta on my other line right now. Let's transfer this call to my wife's room and—"

"You couldn't have called at a more crucial time. Your wife is having her dressings changed, and I'm sure she needs to hear your voice. A word of advice: Be prepared for her screams. Every patient screams during the debridement process. I'll tell your wife you're on the phone."

"Wait. Don't—" *Click*. I met Delta's horrified eyes. "I can't keep pretending—"

Delta grabbed my hand. "You have to. Cathryn needs you. She's being de . . . somethinged. It sounds terrible. "

"She needs her husband."

"Thomas, weren't you paying attention? He's not visiting her. He's not even calling her. He's abandoned her. She doesn't need a man like him; she needs a man like *you*."

"This is beyond insane—"

Click.

"Gerald," a soft, strained voice begged. "Help."

Inside, I stopped. Everything focused on the pain in that voice. Suddenly it didn't matter that I wasn't Gerald. I was here, and he wasn't. The mule pecker.

"Help," she repeated. "Help."

"Cathryn." I tried to speak softly, gently. I tried to blanket her with intimate sympathy. Common sense vanished. "Cathy, I'm here."

On her end, silence. Stark silence. Did my voice sound nothing like Gerald's? Maybe I'd used a nickname Gerald never used. *Cathy.* I kicked myself. Across from me, Delta hunched down to the phone and tilted her head, listening. We heard metal rattling on metal. Surgical instruments hitting pans. Rustling noises. A faint, low sound of distress. Cathryn. Moaning.

"Sorry, I'm not ignoring you," she whispered eventually. "I just had a moment of weakness while the nurse was. . . I couldn't think straight." Then came a sound I never expected. Her laugh. Low, torn. A war cry. "And I thought a bikini wax was painful." Another clattering sound. In the background, a nurse said, "Cathryn, take a deep breath. I'm going to scrub this raw area, now. It's going to bleed. That's normal."

"Oh, God," she whispered. "Nothing's *normal*."

My own breath knifed my throat. "Breathe, Cathy. Breathe. Slowly. You can do it."

She moaned again, then laughed again, but the laugh ended in a gasp. "Sorry. Being a . . . sissy."

"No, honey," I said. Honey. Delta smiled at me proudly. I frowned. I was in way too deep, but I couldn't bear to stop. "You're a strong woman, Cathy. You're a survivor. You're no sissy. Talk to me . . . honey. Tell me what's happening."

"They call this process . . .debridement. They ought to call it . . .torture." Another soft, wrenching sound. Another miserable chuckle.

"Always de bride-maid. Never . . . de bride. Ah! Stop, stop a second. Stop. Please. I'm freezing." Her teeth chattered.

"Okay, let's take a short break," the nurse said. "I'm going to tilt these lamps a little. I can't cover you with a sheet until we're done. There. Warmer? I know these lamps are awfully bright."

"Like sunning . . . at a really bad . . . nude beach."

Sweat eased down my forehead as I realized what Cathryn was saying. She was laying there naked, bloody, sections of her skin like raw meat. And she thought she was only sharing the intimate, humiliating misery with her devoted husband.

She should be. Where was the bastard?

"Gerald?" she groaned. "Please try . . . to visit . . . this week. I know I look a little charbroiled, but—"

"You're still the most beautiful woman in the world." I blurted it in a low, hoarse voice. As if I meant it.

I did.

She made a mewling sound. "Never thought . . . you'd say that again. I love you."

"I love—" *Don't do it. This is going too far.* "—you, too."

More broken sounds. I'd made her cry. She was crying because her husband said he loved her. Because she thought her husband had stopped loving her. I wanted to find Gerald and have a discussion. Mountain-style. I'd go hillbilly on his ass.

Delta reached over and pounded my arm for attention. *Me,* she mouthed. *Introduce me.*

"Cathy, I've got someone special on the line. This may sound a little odd, because it's been a long time since you saw anyone from your mother's family and friends, but a distant cousin of yours contacted me, from North Carolina, and—"

"Hello, Cathryn Mary Deen," Delta shouted. "Cathy Deen, I'm your cousin, Delta, and I was one of your mama's best friends, and the last time you came to visit your Granny Nettie, back when you were just a little girl, I dropped by with my little boy, Jeb, and we had a wonderful lunch with you and your granny. She was a great cook, and to this day I make biscuits by her recipe. And I just want you to know, Cathy—"

"Biscuits!" Cathryn said.

"Biscuits," Delta repeated. "I make and sell your granny's biscuits."

"Biscuits." Wistful, urgent, connected. The magic word.

"I'm sorry, Cathryn," the nurse interjected. "I have to start cleaning you, again. Try to relax. Take a deep breath."

"Quick, Delta, talk to me," Cathryn begged. "Talk to me about Granny Nettie's biscuits. About North Carolina. About her house. Is it still standing? Help me think about something besides being 'de bride maid.' Biscuits. Biscuits. You don't know what they mean to me. I want to know everything about Granny Nettie and her biscuits and you and there and—"

"Oh, lord, yes." Delta's eyes gleamed with victory. She launched into a fervent spiel about the café, its menu, the secret of good baking, the art of a flaky crust. A solar system in which there was no pain, no surgical tweezers plucking dead tissue off live nerves, no naked humiliation, no loneliness, no stranger like me pretending to be a loving husband. Delta handed her cousin's husband's cousin's daughter a soothing world that revolved faithfully around a large, golden orb, the eternal biscuit.

Cathryn didn't speak a single word after that, but her low sounds of distress and her pained chuckles punctuated Delta's stories along with the metallic clatter of the nurse's instruments and the low, sopping sound of bloody gauze dropping in a pan.

I sat there with my head bowed and eyes shut.

It makes no sense to say it, but I fell in love with Cathryn Deen that day. On a weekday afternoon at the cafe, in the fresh sunshine of springtime, while pretending to be her husband, beneath the psychedelic octagonals of a Pineapple quilt, and over the phone. I had been wrong about her. She was strong, she was smart, she cared about legacies and family. And I cared about her.

Every patient screams during debridement, the nurse had said.

Not Cathryn Deen.

Not Cathy.

Cathy

Funny the conversations you have with yourself while you nap in a drugged stupor after lying on a metal table, naked, under heat lamps, while a nurse scrapes the places where your skin used to be.

I'm a woman, now. Gerald called me a woman. He's never called me a 'woman,' before. Always a girl. A beautiful girl. A gorgeous girl. Maybe 'woman' is the only term that's true, now. The default endearment.

No, it sounded like a compliment. He sounded sincere.

That's not like him.

He called you 'Cathy.' So intimate. So sweet.

He hates nicknames. His classmates at boarding school called him 'Gerbil.'

His voice was so tender. A warm lotion. Deep, soothing, compassionate.

See? That's not Gerald.

He loves you. He said so.

Then why doesn't he visit? Why doesn't he call?

He did call. And he gave you a gift. Delta Whittlespoon.

Yes, you're right. He loves me.

❦❦❦❦❦

"Ms. Deen, we've got a package for you," a nurse said. "Overnight delivery, UPS, from a Delta Whittlespoon, in North Carolina. Would you like me to open it?"

"Delta!" I punched my morphine drip, waited for the pain to drift a little further out to sea, then lifted my head slightly. My right side, still thickly bandaged, felt like a raw steak covered in sponges. Physical therapists came in every day and made me lift various bandaged body parts. Heads? My specialty.

Swaddled in the usual antiseptic fashions, the nurse set a large cardboard box on my bedside table, snipped the tape, and opened the lid. My heart fought off an IV of anti-anxiety drugs and fluttered with anticipation. Delta. My cousin's husband's cousin. Even when not sedated and traumatized I had only a vague memory of a small, cheerful, dark-haired woman who'd visited Granny while I was there. Under the current mind-altering conditions, my brain recalled Delta only as an essence. She was a biscuit.

A loving, comforting biscuit. Wonderful.

The nurse held up a handful of something. "Music CD's," she announced. She shuffled through them. "Bonnie Raitt, Rosanne Cash. And . . . The Log Splitter Girls?"

"My new favorites!"

"The Log Splitter Girls?"

My foggy brain couldn't form an explanation. I frowned as I sorted through the many fascinating things Delta told me every time she called. Since she phoned twice a day like clockwork during my debridement sessions, and talked non-stop to distract me, I had a lot of details to sort.

One of Delta's neighbors, a woman, was a berry farmer. In her spare time, she and her partner wrote songs and played acoustic guitars in a girl group. The Log Splitters.

"They're lesbians," I finally told the nurse. "Lesbian musicians. Oh, and . . . berry farmers."

She laid the CD's aside. "Who'd have thought it? With a name like 'The Log Splitter Girls.'" Then she lifted two heavily taped, insulated containers from the package. "These appear to contain something perishable. One's wrapped in a cool pack."

"Cool. I like 'cool.'"

More snipping, and she popped the lid on a cup, held it near her face mask, and sniffed. "This is some kind of white goo. I'm a non-dairy vegetarian, so all I can say for certain is this gelatinous white goo smells like there's milk in it. Ugh."

My head craned a good two inches off the pillow. "Cream gravy!"

She set the cup down, popped the box lid, shrugged at the contents, and tilted them up for me to peruse. "Biscuits."

"Biscuits!" My entire body hurt with excitement. Sinking back on the pillow, I gasped, "Break biscuit into pieces. Dip pieces in gravy. Bring here."

"But it's all cold."

"Good. Nothing hot. Not anymore."

She put on fresh sterile gloves, fixed me a small dish of crumpled biscuit topped with globs of cold cream gravy, and brought it to me. I stuck my left hand into the dish, woozily grabbed a wad of biscuit and gravy, and, trailing IV's like some kind of sunburned cyborg, shoved the food in my mouth. The nurse gasped and threw a towel under my chin. Biscuit crumbs and dollops of cold gravy rained down on it. I chewed happily, crying.

Now I wasn't so alone. I had Delta Whittlespoon, and Bonnie and Rosanne and the Log Splitter Girls, and Granny Nettie's biscuits.

Soul food.

Chapter 5

Thomas
The Privy

You lied to Cathy Deen. Deceived her. She's probably figured it out by now. Probably thinks you're just someone else trying to exploit her. God. How did you let Delta talk you into making that call?

Half naked and hungover, armed with only a toothbrush and deodorant, I fought off a bestiary of regrets and a toilet full of wildlife. In primary colors.

Almost everything about the café was a remodel or an add-on, including the outside toilet that jutted from a nook near the side porch. There were bathrooms inside as well, but the The Privy Of Fine Art, as everyone called it, was a landmark and a plumbing-endowed museum of folk art. Visiting artists had covered its white plank walls with a whole zoo of abstract animals. A Noah's Ark scene roamed the ceiling, and a flock of purple turkeys lived in the narrow alcove where the toilet sat. Sitting in the cramped stall on a toilet painted with blue trout, while gazing at abstract purple turkeys, the average art lover was guaranteed a bowel movement in ten seconds flat.

On the wall above the sink, milky quartz pebbles had been glued in a rococo arch over an old medicine chest and mirror. On the wall over the urinal, dozens of arrowheads were arranged in a collage that pointed to a papier-mâché sun wrapped in rusting barbed wire. Thus, the simple act of urination could become an exercise in surreal contemplation.

The Privy Of Fine Art dated to the 1940's, when Delta's parents built the log grocery next to their farmhouse and installed gas pumps in their front yard. Back then, the Privy lured weary travelers with its flush toilet and electric lights, both of which were rare in the mountains. You could say the toilet was the Cove's first modern tourist attraction. Now, it was a quirky legend and a folk art inspiration. Over in Asheville, almost every art gallery sold works celebrating the Crossroads Privy. Photos, paintings, and even, once, a 3-D model sculpted from toilet paper.

I was in the Privy washing goat slobber off my face after a night sleeping with Banger in the truck, when Delta pounded on the rickety wooden door. The latch popped off the frame, which happens when you hit a sixty-year-old door decorated in pink-eyed green lizards. I thought about ducking into the toilet nook with the trout and turkeys, but since I was decent—in low-slung jeans, with an acre of brown beard covering my bare chest—I just stood there, scowling at Delta.

"I'd shriek and blush, but I have a hangover," I deadpanned.

"Cathryn got the care package. She loved it!"

"You're saying she didn't figure out that I was on the phone instead of her husband?"

"No! She's happy to believe everything you said! I'm sending her a package every week from now on. Biscuits, gravy and gifts. You have to help me think of other ways to cheer her up."

In Delta's view, people always cheered up, eventually. I dropped a tooth brush back in my shaving kit and said quietly, "Maybe I can find her a time machine on eBay."

"No, but you can find a phone and call her, again."

I went very still. "Let's not push our luck."

"There's nothing wrong with telling a good lie at a bad time."

"I'm reporting you to Cleo. She'll revoke your What Would Jesus Do? bracelet."

"What could it hurt to pretend you're Gerald?"

"It's not fair to her. If her husband's a bum, he's a bum. I might even make things worse for her."

"How much worse can they be, Thomas? She's a mess. She can still barely form a whole sentence—she's on a lot of medication—but she mumbled something about how wonderful her husband was for putting me in touch with her. Thomas, what is that cold-hearted bull hump up to?"

"Maybe he's there, maybe he's visiting and calling, and she's just confused."

"Even a drugged woman knows when her man's abandoned her. Thomas, please just—"

"No. Eventually she'll find out, and she'll be hurt that a stranger invaded her life and took advantage of her trust. She'll think I'm some kind of con artist." I hesitated, looking down at Delta grimly. "And maybe she'll think you are, too."

Delta gasped. She'd never thought of it that way. "Oh, Lord."

"I'm sorry. You don't know how much I'd like to help her." After a second thought, I amended, "Because I want the Nettie house."

"Have you seen the gossip magazines this week? All those awful headlines! 'Scarred For Life. A Career Up In Flames. Horror On the Highway Leaves A Dream Girl In Nightmare.' It's all about horror and tragedy and mutilation, and they make it sound as if Cathryn's worthless, now! And all the TV talking heads are debating 'the culture of beauty' and 'the culture of fame' and 'the culture of celebrity,' but I don't think any of 'em would recognize the culture of *decency* if it crawled out of their ten-dollar martinis and bit 'em on the behind! They're all showing pictures from that sleazy photographer's videotape at the same time they're turning up their noses and pretending to be appalled!"

"Nothing that's sold as 'news' surprises me," I said quietly. "It's about selling melodrama and making money. And propaganda for the political cause du jour."

"There are comedians on some of the morning radio shows making fun of her. Do you know what one lowlife said? He said, 'Put a bag over her head. No sense wasting a good piece of tail.' Why do you men talk that way?"

"I don't talk that way. Pike doesn't talk that way. Or Jeb, or Bubba. Or my brother. Don't paint us all with the same brush."

"I know, I know! But I just don't understand the ones who do talk that way about women!"

"They're idiots. They run their mouths for the same reason apes hoot and beat their chests. Because they feel vulnerable around the female of the species, and they want her to be submissive." Trying to lighten my diatribe, I clutched my shirt to my bare pecs. "Speaking of vulnerable and submissive, I could use a little privacy, here."

"Do you feel threatened by women?"

"Absolutely. But my old man raised my brother and me to let girls hit us and never hit back. That rule is both literal and metaphorical and includes a laundry list of other rules of gentlemanly behavior."

"Good for him! I wish I'd known him. A good man. A gentleman. Men should be respectful of women! We're all they've got!"

"Women can be just as cruel as men. This obscene treatment of Cathryn isn't about sexual politics. It's about jealousy and money and power and the usual suspects. Society puts extraordinary people on a pedestal. Then it knocks them down."

"That doesn't mean it's fair."

"Do I have to say it? 'Life isn't fair.'"

"How is she gonna feel when she comes out of her cocoon and realizes she's the newest sick joke? And that there are people out here who are *glad* she got hurt. Folks who are making money off what happened to her! I can't believe that photographer got off without any charges. Sure, she was speedin', but he was *chasin'* her!"

Delta shook her head and walked out, slamming the door. I donned my shirt, then spent some time finding a new spot to screw the latch eye back into the pock-marked door frame. Her words rang in my head. I hated what was happening to Cathy, and I wasn't fond of my fellow men, especially their willingness to fly commercial airliners full of innocent people into tall buildings filled with other innocent people. Maybe I should take up the ministry. I could preach on the evil nature of Man. *Hallelujah.* But I doubted the faithful wanted to hear what I had to say.

Why did God give Cathy every gift a person could want then snatch it all away like a bad joke? Why did He allow children to die in goddamned horrible ways? Why had God, the universe, sheer bad luck—whatever we want to call it—come crashing down on Cathy Deen just as it came down on Sherryl and Ethan? Yes, give me a chance to preach. I'd tell people God didn't care.

If God even existed, if He had a plan for Cathy and for me, He'd have to give us a hint what to do next.

Cathy

A banner day in Crispy Actress Land. I could sit up. Well, halfway up. And instead of being naked I got to wear a lovely, chic hospital gown in a fetching style that covered the relatively undamaged side of my body, which was now peeling like the mother of all sunburns. If I weren't taking enough steroids to supply an entire major league baseball team, the itch would have been unbearable.

I slowly spooned Delta's latest supply of cold gravy and biscuits into my mouth while gazing at the thousandth re-run of *Titanic*. I had other movies to watch, but I'd developed a strong affection for icebergs and water. Everything wet and cool. There are no fires in *Titanic*.

A nurse came in. "Wouldn't you like that food warmed a little?"

"No, thanks." I had also developed a small quirk about hot food. I wouldn't eat it. Heat, in any form, could not be allowed near my body. So far, I'd been able to fake out the shrinks on staff. They kept warning me that irrational fears were common among burn survivors, that all manner of oddball ideas and reactions were normal. I kept mumbling that cold cream gravy was considered a delicacy in the South. *Hah. I have them fooled.*

"You have a visitor," the nurse said. She took my dish.

Gerald, I thought. *Finally.* I lifted my left hand toward my face, instinctively checking makeup and smoothing hair, but the hand would only go so far before it hit the end of a tether. Occasionally it dawned on me that maybe my arm was tied down so I couldn't rip off my bandages or find out what my face felt like. Plus I was still the bionic woman, hooked to various IV's. "How do I look?" I asked the nurse brightly.

She stared at me over her mask. "Better every day."

Hey, *that* sounded good.

She opened the door, let an antiseptically uniformed stranger in, and left us alone together. I blinked and frowned. The stranger stayed across the room, as if I might be contagious.

This wasn't Gerald. This masked and gowned person had female legs and wore mascara. She carried some kind of paperwork in a clear plastic envelope. What I could see of my visitor's face, around her eyes and forehead, beneath the sterile cap, was whiter than my bedsheets, and glistened with sweat. But her eyes didn't waver. Shark eyes.

Oh, God.

"Either you're an agent," I said slowly. "Or a lawyer."

"I'm a lawyer, Ms. Deen. One of Mr. Merritt's attorneys."

"I don't know you."

"We haven't met, before. I'm a . . . specialist." *Oh, God.* She ventured a few steps closer as she slid a document from her envelope. "First, Mr. Merritt has authorized me to relay the following personal message to you." She cleared her throat and read:

Cathryn, you and I had a partnership based on who and what you were. The basic contract of our marriage thus has been voided. You chose to drive

*recklessly. You chose to drive that embarrassing lowbrow sports car despite
my repeated entreaties to consider your public image. You chose to leave your
security people behind with complete disregard for protecting yourself and my
investment in your future. I'm sorry, but you have violated my trust and now
you must accept the consequences.*

The lawyer tucked the note back in the envelope and looked at me
firmly over her mask. "Pursuant to the California statutes regarding no-
fault, uncontested conditions and the arrangements of your mutually agreed
upon pre-nuptial contract, Mr. Merritt is filing for divorce. I've notified
your attorney. Here's a copy of the filing." She placed the plastic envelope
atop the bed pan on my tray table. "Have a nice . . . sorry."

She left.

The man who swore to love me forever before God, an ordained
minister, and five hundred of our closest friends at a million-dollar ceremony
overlooking the ocean on a private Hawaiian beach now decreed me a
worthless investment.

*Maybe he's right. It was all my fault, that accident. I'm ugly, and I
deserve to be punished.*

After a while I realized I was moving my good hand just a little, gently
patting what I could reach of myself, which was only my left hipbone.
There, there. It'll be all right.

Even I didn't believe me.

Thomas

Easter weekend was the unofficial start of spring tourist season in the
mountains, and the café was a mad house. Wonderful aromas rose from
the pans of a big steam table. Squash casserole and mashed potatoes with
heavy cheese, meatloaf and creamed corn, turnip greens filled with chunks
of ham, to name a few selections. "Jesus didn't rise from the dead so all
these people could go camping!" Cleo yelled as she grabbed full plates and
headed back to the dining rooms.

Delta grinned as she stirred a large pot of collards. "The Lord
understands the need to commune with nature and eat my food."

As I cleared a full bus pan and began loading the dishwasher, Pike
walked in. He tossed his sheriff's Stetson atop a stack of clean pots and
began helping Becka and Jeb pack big pans of peach cobbler into a box.
Someone at the new golf club in Turtleville was holding an Easter picnic.

Who knew Jesus had risen on the eighteenth green?

"Texas Hold 'em, nine sharp Saturday night at my office," Pike announced to all of us in the poker gang. "Complimentary chocolate Easter bunnies all around." Pike's "office" was an old construction trailer out back. Its main features were a poker table, an old *Coca Cola* cooler full of beer, and a wooden porch across the back, where his guests could spit, smoke, and take a no-frills manly piss into a stack of firewood. In other words, it was perfect.

"How much money did I win from you last week?" I asked.

Pike grunted. "Two hundred and fifty thousand dollars and fifty-two cents. You take another IOU?"

"No, and I want two chocolate rabbits. Up front."

"Somebody turn that TV up," Delta ordered as she slid a big pan of biscuits from the oven. "*Entertainment Tonight's* coming on. Sometimes they mention how Cathy's doing. She won't watch it. I told her I'd report back to her if they say something stupid."

"They ever say anything on those gossip shows that's not stupid?" Jeb put in, then dodged as his mother threw a biscuit at him. He caught the biscuit and retreated to a corner to eat it. Biscuits were never wasted at the café, even when used as weapons. At lunch and dinner Delta served them with fresh butter and honey. At breakfast she dished them out with cream gravy. Cream gravy with pieces of spicy sausage in it. If there is a God, he serves that in heaven. *Sans* sausage for the kosher angels and vegans.

"Thomas, those dirty tables won't wait for you wake up from your hangover," Delta called as I methodically arranged more dishes in the dishwasher. "Get a move on."

"I'm not paid to take all this pressure. In fact, I'm not getting paid at all."

"You get free food and the fellowship of people who love you just the way you are. That's what you get, Mister." She held out a biscuit.

A black hand intercepted it. "Why, thank you, Miss Delta," said Anthony, the UPS man, who had just wandered in the back door. "Bite my crumbs, white boy."

"You're in uniform. Isn't it against the rules to eat my biscuit while on the clock?"

"I made my last delivery in Turtleville thirty minutes ago. I'm heading home to Asheville as soon as Delta packs my take-out. I promised my wife a café dinner tonight."

"We could use another hand at poker this weekend. Hey, there are chocolate bunnies in the pot."

"Ask me next Saturday. My wife's going to visit her mother in Detroit."

"Maybe I'll save you a biscuit. Or maybe not. Depends on whether I ever get my share."

Delta threw a dishrag at me. "Hush. Here's *ET*." She clicked a remote and the kitchen TV suddenly blared the show's opening theme. One of the perky blonde hosts appeared on screen. "Big news in the tragic story of Cathryn Deen tonight," she announced. "Her husband of one year has filed for divorce, and we've just learned that an infection has sent Cathryn back to Intensive Care. Doctors are calling her condition serious."

Delta froze. So did I. When she turned to look at me, she had tears in her eyes.

"She's going to die," Delta said.

I shook my head. "Not if I can help it."

Cathy

Now the whole world knew Gerald had left me.

The malaise that settles on burn survivors a few weeks into treatment is bad enough without being deserted by a loved one. Medical teams work on you as if you're a lab animal, the drugs steal the time of day, you have no mirrors, you begin to think you don't exist. Top that off with brutal rejection by the man who vowed to love you forever, and suddenly, you evaporate.

I felt . . . gone.

I lay there in a stupor that pre-Easter afternoon, my ICU cubicle quiet and dark, my mind wandering between painful memories of Gerald and weirdly colored dreams where odd animals slid up the wall then burned to ashes on the ceiling, when a man spoke to me out of the ether of my speaker phone.

"Cathy," he said quietly, "my name is Thomas, and I'm going to tell you how the sunset looks today over Hog Back Mountain, from the front porch of your Grandmother Nettie's house."

The voice was deep, resonant, and vaguely familiar. Had I heard it somewhere before? I associated it with comfort. "Hello, Thomas," I answered, without opening my eyes. No need to ask for a formal introduction. I knew that voice, somehow. "I'm not having a good day."

"I know, honey."

"Can't figure things out. Why me?"

"I used to believe bad things only happen to other people. But they don't."

"Did I deserve this? Can't see what I did wrong."

"You didn't do anything wrong, Cathy."

Maybe I was just imagining this voice. Maybe an angel was speaking to me. You shouldn't ignore an angel. "How can you be sure?" I asked.

"I'm an expert on guilt."

"Tell me why."

"My wife and son died in an accident. There were things I could have done differently that might have saved them. Or at least saved my son. I was supposed to babysit him that morning, but I had a deadline to meet. My wife and I fought over whose schedule was more important. I insisted she take him with her."

"Oh, Thomas. I'm sorry."

"I always believed the people I loved were protected by some magic bubble, just because I loved them. If there is a God, He wouldn't let anything terrible happen to me or mine. I was a good person. I'd never deliberately hurt anyone, so why should God hurt me? Then something bad *did* happen, something so awful I couldn't have imagined it. Everything I believed about fate and luck and fairness went out the window. Ever since, I've felt as if I were standing in the ruins of a house I've lived in all my life. Logically, I know I can rebuild it, but it'll never be the same. I don't know where to start."

"Empty. So empty. I understand."

"I'm not a minister, I'm not a philosopher, I'm not a therapist. But I've spent a lot of time trying to understand why people suffer. Buddhists say the point is not to explain it, but to embrace it and see what good can come out of it for yourself and others."

"Buddhists see . . . silver lining."

"You got it. And Muslims believe suffering is a divine test we all have to take. Do we meet it with hope and patience and courage? They say without suffering there would be no way to salvation."

"Islam . . . not for sissies."

"Right. No wiggle room, there."

"Episcopalians . . . best finger food."

"What?"

"I was raised Episcopalian. Because . . . my aunts said . . . Episcopalians are more respectable than Unitarians and . . . serve better hor d'oeurves."

Thomas, my mysterious confident, made a sound. Through the fog of drugs and apathy I realized it was a chuckle. *I made him laugh.* Imagine. Maybe some part of me was still charming.

"Talk," I urged. "Keep talking."

"Okay. Let's see. Now, Catholics will tell you God works in mysterious ways, and that in order to understand the nature of suffering, we have to be obedient. Not submissive and helpless, but from the root of the word, *obedire*, from Latin. *To listen.* My old man sent my brother and me to Catholic school. So I can tell you for a fact that if you don't listen to a nun, she'll demonstrate the meaning of the word 'obedient,' and you *will* suffer."

I managed a little smile. "Funny," I whispered.

"Not so funny when Sister Angela threw erasers at my head. She had an arm like Roger Clemons."

"Astros."

"You know baseball?"

"Clemons, Roger. Cy Young winner, throws a mean slider. My father used to take me to games. The only hobby we shared."

"Let's go to a game when you're well, again. Deal?"

"Deal. Until then, tell me something hopeful."

"When you lose everything," he said slowly, "you go blind. All you can do is sit in the dark and wait for the light to come back. It seeps in, here and there, just enough to keep you alive. Your job is to have faith that the light will grow stronger."

"I'm blind. So blind right now."

"I know, but don't give up."

"Why not?"

"Because we have a date for a baseball game."

"Okay."

"I hear you smiling."

"Lopsided. The bad side hurts."

He was quiet for a few seconds. Then, gruffly, "I said I'd tell you about the sunset from your grandmother's porch. You ready?"

"Yes. Sunset. Help me see its light."

"I'm sitting on the stone steps. They're deep-gray granite with white quartz veins. The center stones are worn from foot traffic. The outer stones are tinted with green moss around their edges. Tiny, yellow wild flowers are blooming around the foot of the steps and in-between the stepping stones that lead from the porch. I clipped the weeds in the front yard with a swing blade, so sunshine can reach the smallest wildflowers. The whole yard's a delicate shade of gold."

"Ah!"

"The huge oaks around the cottage have finally greened out. But they're still in their spring spectrum. The leaves are pale lime and apple green, tender. By June they'll be dark green. The oaks have got to be over a hundred years old, all of them. Two people couldn't link arms around the trunk of the biggest one. They make a natural canopy over the house. The roof could use a little more sunlight—it gets some algae on it in spots, during wet summer weather—but the trees are worth it. Even during the worst heat of August, the yard and the cottage are cool and shady.

"There's a huge old dogwood in the yard, and it's covered in cream-colored blossoms right now. The fringe trees bloomed white over a month ago, around the time the crocuses came in. You should see your grandmother's yard when hundreds of tiny, purple crocuses bloom in a thin layer of snow. It's as if someone scattered the blooms on a white blanket. The wild azaleas are in bloom right now. There's a whole thicket of them in the edge of the woods along the pasture. Flame orange. They're so bright they almost glow in the dark. And the jonquils. The jonquils are blooming. I don't know how many your grandmother planted in the edge of the front yard originally, but they've multiplied over the years, so now there are hundreds of them. They cover a good acre or more. Beautiful, egg-yolk yellow trumpets. Everywhere. And there are a pair of giant forsythia shrubs. Enormous. The size of small elephants. Covered in yellow blooms."

"You . . . know all about flowers and shrubs. Are you a gardener?"

"No, but I've done some work that required me to have a basic knowledge of landscape design."

"You must be a poet at heart. The way you describe things. So pretty."

"No. I'm just fascinated by details."

"Then keep giving me details. I love them."

"All right, let's see. Later in the year, the Rose of Sharons in your grandmother's side yard will bloom. They're twelve-feet tall and a good eight-feet wide. The blooms will resemble big trumpets, like hibiscus. Soft pink. You should see the bees they draw. I'm looking straight down the alley of the front yard, into the river of pasture that runs down the hill. Picture a golf fairway, only turning green with tall grass and lined with the old chestnut posts of pasture fence. I cut the old barbed wire off the posts. It was rusty and broken in places, just a hazard for all the deer who graze around here.

"The alley of pasture draws your eye straight to Hog Back Mountain, which is an extension of the Ten Sisters around the Crossroads Cove. It's a big hump of a mountain, with a dip on the left end, then a smaller hump, left of the dip—that's where the name comes from, obviously, because looking at the outline you can imagine the top silhouette of a hog's head and back. The lower ridges of the mountain are filled with hardwoods, but the top ridges are covered in dark evergreens, so you see this patchwork of different shades. Deep blue shadows fill the hollows and coves on the mountainside, and a white mist rises in the evening, like now."

"Magic," I whispered.

"There it goes, the light's fading. The golds and blues and pinks are being absorbed into the trees, and the balds, and the earth. The mountain's shadow is stretching right up the alley of pasture and trees toward us, until, in a few more minutes, the cottage will be part of the mountain, just like the sunset. It's a helluva thing, watching the sun set over Hog Back. It makes you feel like the whole universe is safe inside the mountain until morning."

"Safe," I whispered.

"I'm going to send you pictures of your grandmother's home. Pictures of everything and everyone around the Cove, too. Look at them, memorize every detail, believe what you see. This is a special place. Promise me you'll get well and you'll come here and see the sunset from your grandmother's porch. Promise me, dammit. Don't give up."

"I promise," I whispered. "Keep talking, please. I'm being . . . absorbed by the mountain. I like it."

"Good. Get some sleep. Fight off that infection. You can do it."

His name is Thomas, I thought as I drifted off, *and I love how he sees me. He must have beautiful eyes.*

Thomas

I tucked the phone into my back pocket and leaned against the curved stone arch of Mary Eve's front porch. On that porch in the middle of the woods, I felt her beside me. *Okay, Mary Eve, I kept your house alive. Now you help me keep your granddaughter alive. Deal?*

The last ray of light winked at me over Hog Back.

Chapter 6

Thomas
Baptist Stone Monkeys

In the midst of Cathy's downturn, three men drove their rented sedan into the café's parking lot, armed with cameras. I happened to be at the grocery buying kerosene and canned food—the staples of life at my cabin. The strangers asked everyone where Cathryn Deen's grandmother used to live. Delta wasn't on hand to marshal a diplomatic or at least *unified* response. She was at her house doing chores; she and Pike lived at the end of a shady lane that ambled into the foothills behind the café.

"The Nettie house burned down years ago," Delta's brother, Bubba McKellan, told the visitors without looking up from his potter's bench.

"It was sold to a couple of bikers out of Nashville," said Cleo, as she tossed empty tomato cartons into the dumpster behind the café. "They've turned the whole farm into one of those survivalist schools. Got a lot of guns. And big, mean dogs. Praise Jesus."

"A bunch of nudists rent the house," said Becka, while sorting mail at the window of the post office, located inside Jeb's gem shed. "Outsiders can't get within shoutin' distance. Those nudists are tough-skinned when it comes to folks violating their privacy."

Naked survivalists living in a burned house. Naturally, the visitors weren't convinced. They walked up to me as I was loading a case of Spam alongside canned vegetables, kerosene, a ten-pack of toilet paper, a case of vodka Jeb picked up for me at the state's ABC liquor store in Asheville, and a five-pound bag of stone-ground grits produced by an old mill over in Turtleville. Once you adopt grits as part of your diet, you're a Southerner. It alters your genetic code.

The visitors grinned at my eclectic grocery list. "Dude, you look like a man of the world," one said. *Dude*, eh? The others looked at me as if they expected my albino cousin to appear at any moment and start picking a banjo. After nearly four years in the mountains I could affect a decent mountain drawl—or, at least, a hokey, movie-of-the-week imitation. Good enough to fool ignorant asswipes from somewhere else.

"'Shore nuff," I said drily. "What can I do for y'all?"

"I bet you hunt and fish all over these mountains. I bet you know where to find every old farm and abandoned house."

"Well, let's just say I shore nuff know where some bodies are buried."

They paled a little, then laughed. The lead asswipe said, "Okay, dude, how would you like to make fifty bucks just for taking us on a hike?"

"Fifty bucks! Boy howdy. You must really wanta find some place special, huh?"

"You ever heard of the actress, Cathryn Deen?"

"Why, sure! I seen a movie or two of hers. Boy howdy."

"We understand she used to visit her grandmother around here. A woman named Mary Eve Nettie. We're . . . fans of Cathryn's. We'd like to see her grandmother's house."

"Why, there ain't much to see."

"Probably not, but we'd love to get a few snapshots. How about a hundred dollars for you to guide us to the place?"

"Whee, doggy. A hundred dollars!" I ambled over to their sedan. "Tell ya, boys, I'm not sure this here city car could make it up the trail to the Nettie place. Might have to take you in my truck."

"No problem, dude."

I peered at the sedan's back seat. "Got you a pile of camera gear, there! Looks pro-fessional to me! All for a few snapshots! Mighty impressive! You boys work for one of them grocery-store gossip papers or something?"

"Something like that. Then we have a deal?"

"Shore nuff. Load that gear in the back of my truck and I'll take y'all right now."

"Cool!"

I waited until they'd loaded about, oh—conservative estimate—ten thousand dollars' worth of cameras, lens, flash units, and tripods into my truck alongside my groceries. Then I said, "Hold on a minute, I got an idea for how to make more room back here for y'all to sit."

I fetched a vintage tire iron from beneath the front seat of my vintage truck, and I walked back to them without smiling, and said in my old man's deadliest, streetwise, Brooklyn voice, "Get outta my way or I'll splatter your fucking brains all over the parking lot."

And then, within the course of a few dedicated seconds, as they yelled and dodged and begged and ran, I reduced their camera gear to a gleaming pile of junk.

It would make a perfect new sculpture for The Privy of Fine Art.

I named it 'Privacy.'

🐾🐾🐾🐾🐾

I stood before Judge Benton Kaye at the courthouse in Turtleville. Judge Kaye was the only black man in Jefferson County, except for Anthony the UPS driver. Short and chunky, with a face that hadn't been helped by a landmine in Vietnam and a stint as a part-time professional boxer during law school, you'd think the judge would have some sympathy for a disenfranchised outsider like myself. Especially one who played poker with him on Saturday nights at the café, and who had designed and built a gazebo for his wife, Dolores, at her heritage plant nursery.

Instead, Judge Kaye pointed his gavel at me, handle-end first, his fist wrapped around the head so that the gavel stabbed the air like an ice pick, and he said sternly in an accent that belonged to a Corleone, "Those photographers will go back where they came from and tell people we're all a bunch of violent, inbred rednecks. Including *me*. I don't appreciate the irony of that."

"I understand, Judge. I promise you it won't happen again. They won't be back. In fact, I'm guessing they won't set foot in the entire state of North Carolina again."

"Your guard-dog attitude wouldn't be motivated by self-interest, would it? Everybody knows you want the Nettie place all to yourself."

"Yes, I want the Nettie house. I'll always want the house. If Cathy Deen ever agrees to sell it, I'll buy it. But it's not just that. Her privacy's been exploited enough. I'm not going to let photographers take pictures of her grandmother's farm, too."

"Good intentions are no substitute for the rule of law. I take it you have no remorse for terrorizing three poor, harmless parasites of society and destroying all their equipment?"

"That's not true, Judge. I do have remorse. I wish I'd taken one more swing at the 400 millimeter lens. I only cracked the casing."

Benton laid his gavel down. He looked at the court reporter over his reading glasses. "Mrs. Halfacre, rest your fingers for a minute. This is off the record."

Mrs. Halfacre grinned and put her hands in the lap of a canary yellow dress suit with pink Easter chicks embroidered on the lapels. Benton looked down at me grimly. "There's something I've wanted to ask you for four years. You're under oath now and I expect you to answer me and answer me truthfully."

"There's truth and there's facts. But I'll do my best."

"After nine-eleven, is it true you tried to join the army?"

"Yes. Several times. They rejected me. Something about being over thirty and a little too eager to kill everyone named 'Mohammed.'"

"Have you ever considered anger-management therapy? Your sessions with Dr. Smirnoff and Dr. Absolut don't count."

"Therapy is for people who have unrealistic anger and guilt. My anger and guilt are based entirely on reality."

"I've read what you did on nine-eleven. There's nothing realistic about your guilt."

"I was supposed to keep my son that morning. My wife and I argued, as usual, over whose time was more important, hers or mine, and I insisted she take him with her. As a result, they both died. Nothing can change that fact."

"I see. We're supposed to see into the future and base all our decisions on every possible outcome, including massive acts of terrorism. What you regret, Thomas, is the brutal pettiness of unknowable fate. Something neither you nor anyone else can ever overcome."

"That doesn't mean I can't try."

"You're looking for someone to punish. If I could place Osama Bin Laden in front of you right now, hand you a gun, and allow you to shoot him, would that give you closure?"

"You'd have to fill a stadium with the people who should die along with him."

"Care to name names?"

"Let's just say it starts with everyone who stood to benefit politically and economically from nine-eleven, and everyone who's made money off it since."

"I didn't realize you're one of our resident conspiracy theorists."

"There's never been a war in the history of the world that wasn't started by the wealthy for the wealthy."

"As a Jersey boy who joined the Marines voluntarily in 1966, I'm insulted that you believe patriotism can only be a façade for cynical self-interest."

"There are patriots and there are politicians. Not necessarily one and the same. True patriotism is about home, family, and community, not killing innocent civilians on the other side of the world for big corporations."

"'Community' is this entire country. This way of life."

"When invaders set foot on the coast of North Carolina I'll rip their necks open and piss down their throats. Not before." I looked at Mrs. Halfacre, whose chicks were fluttering. "Excuse my French, ma'am."

Benton steepled his chin on his fingers. "What happened to that man who wanted to kill everyone named Mohammed?"

"He's seen too many pictures of innocent Iraqi women and children we killed."

"We?"

"If we truly believe 'we the people' are the government then yes, we killed them."

"If Eisenhower had worried about accidentally killing civilians during the invasion of Normandy we'd all be speaking German now."

"If Eisenhower were here he'd repeat what he said when he left the White House. 'Beware of giving corporations and the military too much power.'"

"Let me see if I understand this, Thomas. Somebody killed your wife and son. You don't know exactly who's responsible, you trust no one's version of the facts, you want to punish legions of faceless villains, and so . . . you blame yourself and attack camera equipment."

"I blame myself for sending my wife and son to die for the sake of my morning work schedule. As for attacking camera equipment, well, it's a start."

"To be honest, then, Cathryn Deen's privacy is of no real consequence to you."

"Your Honor, you took a long walk to reach the wrong destination."

"Show me the truth, the way and the light, then."

"If I can save her life, and if there is a Heaven, and if my son is there, maybe I'll get to be with him when I kill myself."

Silence. The only sound was Mrs. Halfacre's gasp.

Benton slowly lowered his hands to his gavel. "You . . . see Cathryn Deen as a way to earn Brownie points with God?"

What did he expect me to tell him? The truth? That I didn't believe in Heaven, never expected to see Ethan again, and considered God a bad joke foisted on humanity like a cheap drug? That I loved Cathy? Purely and simply loved her. A woman I'd never met. No, if I admitted that in open court Mrs. Halfacre's chicks might shit on themselves. I shrugged. "I'll accept karmic credit wherever I can get it. I'd like to go back on the record now, please."

Benton sighed. "Mrs. Halfacre, remove your hands from your heart and start typing."

"Dear Jesus," Mrs. Halfacre said. "I don't care what everyone whispers about you, Mr. Mitternich. You're not crazy in a *bad* way."

"Why, thank you." I gave her a slight bow.

Benton picked up his gavel. "Thomas, you're going to pay full damages to those photographers, and I can't let you off without serving time."

"You're going to miss me at poker. Who else lets you win?"

"You just sealed your fate." He raised the gavel. "Full damages, six months' probation, and two weeks at the county farm."

Rap.

🐾🐾🐾🐾🐾

So there I was, doing hard time. Pike didn't let criminals off easy. Jail meant a work detail. It also meant enduring an old-fashioned, zebra-banded jumpsuit.

"My, my, Tommy-Son, don't you look 'vintage,'" Pike said drolly, the first time I stepped out of a cell.

As a new member of the Jefferson County chain gang, I debated leading an escape to The Lucky Bean coffee shop across from the Jefferson County courthouse, located on the shady square of tiny Turtleville, the county seat. Turtleville perches on the rocky banks of Upper Ruby Creek, so a cool river mist rises along main street most days. In the summer it's great; in the winter, it's bone-chilling; now, in the spring, it turned my cheap cotton jumpsuit into a cold, damp glove. April is way too cold for water-based convict labor, and a zebra-striped jumpsuit is even more humiliating after it gets clingy. I and my two fellow inmates—Bert, the chronic check bouncer, and Roland, the recidivist speeder—shivered on scaffolding halfway up the courthouse's two-story brick entrance. We were pressure-washing the stone gargoyles over the main doors.

"Tommy-Son, work on that gargoyle's left ear again," Pike ordered from his comfortable place on a dry bench below the scaffolding. "It's still green. Looks like he's got an ear infection."

"He's made of limestone, and the surface of limestone is porous. He needs to be sealed with a good stone primer."

"I'll mention it to the city council. They'll be glad to know you're offering positive input for the civic good. Proof that our rehabilitation system works."

"Does that mean I'm a trustee, now? Can I take Bert and Roland across the street to buy some lattes?"

"Some what?" Bert drawled, wrestling a pressure wand as it pelted the gargoyles' stone perches.

"Coffee with milk in it, you podunk know-nothing," Roland explained. He dragged a compressor further along our scaffold. "I like mine mocha-flavored."

"Nobody's going to get coffee of any kind," Pike said, scowling up at me.

"I want to know something," Bert said. "How come we got monkeys on a courthouse in a town named Turtleville?"

Roland shook his head. "They're not monkeys, you idjit, they're stone demons."

"I'm a Baptist, so I'm callin' them monkeys. Baptist stone monkeys."

"They're gargoyles," I intoned in a professorial way. "It's from the Old French *gargouille*. In medieval times they were used as part of the rain spouts on cathedrals. Now they're mostly ornamental."

"All righty, then," Bert said, "but how come we got ornamental gargles on the courthouse in a town named after turtles? Shouldn't we have ornamental turtles, instead?"

"Turtleville was named by the Cherokees, idjit," Roland said unkindly. "My grandma was a Cherokee, and she said it was Turtle Town back before the white men came. Cherokees thought highly of turtles. They said the world rides on the back of a big turtle."

"Don't tell the Baptists that. They'll want to put a sticker on the science books."

Roland looked at me. "What do you think, Mitternich? Did the world come about through evolution, Genesis, or turtle power?"

I smiled thinly. "I believe in the theory of random chaos. In other words, 'Shit happens.'"

Bert and Roland guffawed. Bert aimed his nozzle at the *Jefferson County* carved into the arch on which the Baptist stone monkeys sat. "All righty, you wise-ass Yankee, answer this trivia question: Who's the county named after?"

"Thomas Jefferson, I assume. Our third president, and noted architect."

"Wrong. It's named after Amos Jefferson. Our first pioneer goat drover, and noted lady's man. Three wives—all married to him at the same time—and nineteen children." Roland called down to Pike. "Sheriff, ain't both you and Delta kin to ol' Amos?"

Pike grunted. "Everybody whose family goes back more than two generations in Jefferson County is kin to him. Whittlespoons, McKendalls, Netties, you name it. All kissin' cousins twice removed, or something."

Cathy, too, then, I thought. She was always on my mind. Descended from Amos Jefferson? Maybe fate intended that I be liked by Cathy and the local goats. "Goat drover, huh?" I said. "So I assume Banger harks back to a pioneer goat who ate pioneer cell phones?"

Bert and Roland chortled.

"Quit jabbering and work," Pike called. "Tom, you're a bad influence on your fellow criminals."

I concentrated on the gargoyle's gangrenous ear. A fine mist of water splashed back and soaked my beard. "If I can't be a good role model, at least I can serve as a warning."

Pike didn't laugh. He didn't believe in random chaos or personal excuses. I was on his shit list.

I finished the gargoyle's ear and turned off my compressor. Bert and Roland were still working. "Thomas," Delta called. I looked over the end of the scaffold.

She and Dolores Kaye stood below, gazing up at me proudly.

"I brought you and the rest of the gang some blueberry pie. The Log Splitter Girls sold me their last reserves of home-grown blueberry preserves from the harvest last fall. In your honor."

Roland and Bert grinned at me. "You da man!" Roland whispered. "Those lesbians don't part with their last batch of berries for just anybody."

"Thank you," I called down. "Any news?"

Delta nodded. "Cathy's fever's gone. They got the infection under control. She's out of Intensive Care and back in the burn ward. She says send more biscuits. She hasn't said another word about her husband. It's like something or somebody cheered her up. Maybe I'll tell her about those camera-totin' yahoos you scared off. She needs to know there's some place in the world where a good man will still stand up for a woman's defense."

Cathy's fever broke. A fist eased inside my chest. I smiled.

Pike and Delta stared up me. "Why, look there," Pike quipped. "He's got teeth."

Delta set a covered pie dish on the bench, tweaked Pike's cheek—the lower one, not the one on his face, when she thought nobody was looking—and headed for the coffee shop. Dolores Kaye smiled up at me solo. Picture a black, gray-haired, dread-locked-bun Aunt Bea in L. L. Bean mud boots, stretch-waist jeans, and a sweatshirt with a gardening slogan.

Roses aren't just red.
Violets aren't just blue.
Visit Kaye Heirloom Nursery
And see the antique hues.

"Thomas," she said, before she turned to follow Delta, "I've ordered some more *vidal blanc* vines for you. My treat."

Even a chain-gang convict could have a fan club.

Cathy

I never thought I'd be glad to get back to the burn ward, but it was practically cheerful compared to Intensive Care. My first goal was to learn more about the mystery caller who'd coaxed me through the infection.

"Someone named 'Thomas' called me a few days ago," I told Delta.

She yipped. "I shoulda known!"

"Another cousin of mine?"

"No, honey, not even a distant cousin twice removed by marriage. He's not from around here, but he fits in good. A few years ago, he saved my son's life. It's a long story. I'll tell you about it when you feel like listening."

"Saving lives. He's had some practice, then. I thought so."

"Well, well. I guess you and Thomas had a nice talk."

"He talked. I mostly listened."

"He lives on the property next to your granny's place! And he truly loves her funny old house. He keeps an eye on it. Well, more than keeps an eye. Let me tell you all about him—"

"No, I like the mystery."

"But don't you want to—"

"No. I picture him being . . . grandfatherly. Maybe in his late fifties or early sixties. A little balding, a little on the paunchy side. Widowed, he said. His wife and child died young. He must be lonely."

"Honey, you don't have to picture men as sweet, harmless daddies or granddaddies in order to trust 'em."

"Oh? All my life, men have wanted me because of the way I looked. I never knew how easy my life was because of their interest, the breaks they gave me, the perks. Everything I believe about myself was built on a false foundation. Now I'm ugly, and men don't want me. No more free lunches. So . . . I don't want men. Not the way I used to. I need for any men in my life to be . . . neutral. Please."

She sighed. "Okay. I'll just say this much: He's not a mule pecker, like Gerald."

"That's good to know."

After our conversation ended, I lay there finessing my mental image of Thomas. He lived in a placid little house with white shutters on the windows and bird feeders in the yard. He had a garden, a sweet, lazy dog he'd adopted at a humane society, and a pair of fat housecats. He watched baseball games via a satellite dish—one of the big ones, out in the yard, not the newer ones that could be mounted on the roof. Framed pictures of his wife and son decorated his bookshelves and bedroom dressers.

He wore khakis with suspenders because of his pot belly, Minnetonka moccasins with worn spots where his knobby bunions prodded the leather, and golf shirts with his church's name stitched over the left breast. He had bought the shirts when the church sold them to raise money for a new sanctuary. He was kind, and thoughtful, and he would never deliberately try to hurt anyone, including me.

❦❦❦❦❦

"Cathryn? Are you ready?"

The psychiatrist stood beside my bed, holding a large hand mirror with the mirror side turned away from me. Behind him, several nurses and therapists watched me warily, like game wardens ready to tranquilize a cornered bear. My good hand gripped the bed rail so hard my fingers went numb. *They've got this all planned out. They'll grab me if I try to run. Shoot me with a dart gun. I'll wake up in a cage with a tag on my good ear.*

"Ready," I lied.

The doctor slowly pirouetted the hand mirror and held it up to my face.

I looked at the thing in the mirror. *The thing.* The thing still had beautiful green eyes, high cheekbones and a lush, lovely mouth. It still had a perky, tilted nose and creamy skin on the good side. But the other half of the thing's face looked like a bad horror-movie mask, as if a special effects artist had slopped some latex onto the skin in weird rivulets and puffy patches and painted it in creepy shades of pink, red, brown and fish-belly white. The imaginary latex pulled at the right corners of the thing's mouth and eye, distorting them just a little. The thing had a slight, permanent smirk.

Scar tissue slithered its tentacles upwards into the thing's scalp. The thing's head was still bald on that side but had been allowed to grow a soft brown stubble on the unburned side. The thing's hair looked even worse than Demi Moore's shaved head in *G.I. Jane.*

And the thing's right ear—well, the special effects people would simply *have* to come up with a prettier one. The ear looked as if they'd poured latex into a mold but stirred the rubber before it hardened. When they took the ear from the mold they accidentally tore off the bottom lobe. No, this deformed ear simply wouldn't do.

"Cathryn?" the shrink said gently. "How are you feeling?"

I'm fine, but that thing in the mirror wants to die.

"I'm seen enough for today. Now I'm going to eat some biscuits and gravy."

I pulled Delta and Thomas's latest care package to my chest, tore off a chunk of biscuit, jabbed it into the gravy, then popped the chunk into my mouth. Chewing violently, I stared at the psych squad. Eventually they put their dart guns away and concluded I was safe to leave alone. They exited the room, taking the mirror with them.

I dropped the biscuit on my stomach and cried. Recently I'd insisted on seeing everything that been written and televised about my accident.

A bad idea. The jokes, the exploited video, the gleeful nastiness of people. One movie critic had called me "pop-culture royalty with a tragic, Icarusian belief in her own infallibility."

Since I'd never gone to college (I was starring in the successful Princess Arianna movies by then,) and had spent most of my teenage years achieving bored "C's" at a private Atlanta prep school, I had to look up Icarus on a hospital computer. Icarus, of course, was the reckless Greek whose homemade wings melted when he flew too close to the sun. "Like Icarus," the critic said, "Cathryn Deen was a victim of her own hubris."

I had to look up "hubris," too.

Shaking, I touched the grisly textures on the right side of my face. I stroked a shivering fingertip over the rough crest of flesh that had been my ear. The *thing* wasn't just in the mirror. The thing was me.

I'm never going to let anyone photograph me again, I'm never going to North Carolina and let Delta see what I look like, and I'm never going to show this horrible face to Thomas.

I wanted him to remain my safe, grandfatherly fantasy.

And I wanted to remain *his* fantasy.

Beautiful.

PART TWO

Most urgently, women's identity must be premised upon our "beauty" so that we will remain vulnerable to outside approval, carrying the vital sensitive organ of self-esteem exposed to the air.

—*Naomi Wolf*

I, with a deeper instinct, choose a man who compels my strength, who makes enormous demands on me, who does not doubt my courage or my toughness, who does not believe me naïve or innocent, who has the courage to treat me like a woman.

—*Anaïs Nin*

Chapter 7

Cathy
The Phantom of Hollywood

"Heads up, One. The kitten is at the doorstep. Repeat. The kitten is at the doorstep."

"Copy, Two. The door is open. Watch for coyotes. Multiple coyotes in the street."

"Copy, One. We're turning in."

My code-talking bodyguards were as serious as Secret Service agents, and just as well-armed. I sat between two of them in the backseat of a small limo with windows so deeply tinted it felt like a cave inside. Outside, the bright May sun gleamed on the palm trees and expensively watered begonias of my mini-mansion in the Hollywood Hills. I was free of the hospital, finally. Now I could be a prisoner in my own home, instead.

"Sorry, Ms. Deen," one of my bodyguards said, as he threw a thin black blanket over my head. "Just to be on the safe side. These windows aren't completely opaque."

"No problem," I said from under the blanket. I liked being covered.

As we rolled through the open gate of the twelve-foot stone wall that surrounded my home, security people blocked a small herd of paparazzi who leapt out of vans and cars. My attorneys had gotten a restraining order against the guy who videotaped the accident. For the next twelve months, at least, I didn't have to worry about being ambushed by him. But I was still a meal ticket to the other "coyotes" in the paparazzi pack. They wanted one thing from me: the first, priceless photograph of my scarred face.

My mission in life was to keep any of them from getting it.

Ten seconds later, the gate closed behind the limo, and the bodyguard pulled the blanket off of me. Weak with relief, I gazed out at the Italian cypress and Mediterranean elegance of my sunny courtyard. "I want out."

"Just a few more seconds, Ms. Deen. Let us pull into the garage, first. We suspect there are photographers stationed on a rooftop up the hill. If you get out now, they'll spot you."

I nodded and sat there stiffly, fighting an urge to claw the windows. Sweat slid down my forehead. I was swathed in a scarf, sunglasses, a long-sleeved shirt, and baggy trousers. Not to mention wearing a tight therapeutic mask over my entire head. Picture support hose, for your face. I looked like I might knock over a convenience store. Under my clothes I wore a custom body stocking of the same material. These would be my second skin for months to come. Hopefully, the pressure would force my healing skin to form flat scar tissue instead of the Freddy Krueger variety.

The limo pulled as far as its length would allow into the cool, quiet confines of the five-car garage. I looked at my collection of cars and shivered. Only the Trans Am was missing. Thieves had filched parts of its burned hulk from an L.A. warehouse. The steering wheel had shown up on eBay.

I didn't want it back, anyway. I'd never drive a sportscar again. Or *any* car. I didn't even want to *ride* in cars now. The quick limo trip from the hospital had filled my mind with images of being chased, of crashing. Of burning. I added cars to my growing list of phobias.

"*Senora* Cathryn! Welcome home!" Bonita and Antonio Cavazos ran up to me as I tottered from the car. My legs were weak, my nerves were raw. I nearly fell into the Cavazos' arms. The middle-aged couple managed my house from top to bottom, inside and out. They supervised maids, cooks, and gardeners, and lived in a small guest house near the pool. Now it would be just me and them. The fewer people who saw me, the better.

"Did you have all the mirrors in the house removed?" I asked.

They looked at me sadly, and nodded.

Yes, it was neurotic of me, but I couldn't stand looking at myself. Not only my face, but my body. A serpentine pattern of scars ran down my neck, shoulder, and right arm. They made a patchwork of weird textures and colors, as if my skin had melted then re-formed. There were splotches of scar tissue on the side of my once-perfect right breast. I had puckered scars on my right hip, and a network of scars trailing down my leg like infected vines. If I looked in a mirror again would I see another vision that hinted at my doomed future? I shuttered to think how much worse it could get.

"No mirrors," I emphasized dully.

"No, no mirrors. Come inside, *querita*," Bonita soothed. I walked slowly, limping a little, holding her and Antonio's arms. My legs shook. When I finally stepped into the mansion's cool, stone and red-brick interior, I was so exhausted I couldn't muster the energy to cry when I saw the main rooms.

Empty.

Gerald had left the house but taken all the furniture.

"But we had one of the guest suites decorated in all your favorite styles," Bonita assured me, crying. "Come and sit on your balcony and I'll bring you something cool to drink, and you can look out over the city."

"*Gracias.* Antonio, are the new awnings up?"

He nodded. "Just as you asked. Every patio and every balcony is covered. Awnings. Side panels. And see-through curtains across the front. You can sit outside anywhere, and no one can watch you. I even told them to install a cabana beside the pool."

"*Gracias.*"

I wasn't just worried about photographers. I couldn't stand the sun. Some sections of my healing skin were super-sensitive and easily sunburned. I itched constantly. My right hand, bound by scar tissue that needed several more small surgeries to stretch the skin as it healed, felt like it was covered in a rubber glove. Heat that hand in the bright L.A. sunshine? No way.

The Cavazos helped me creep to my bedroom, a lovely cocoon in warm blues and sage green with a touch of pink silk here and there. The furniture was a mix of English and French country pieces, the wood golden, the styles simple. The bed was a big four-poster with a lace canopy. Light filtered in through tall, arched windows. Double doors opened on a private balcony, now completely covered in the tent-like awning. Off the bedroom were a large bath and sauna, an exercise room, and even a small kitchen. I'd told Bonita and Antonio to have the gas stove removed. No flames. Only a microwave remained.

"Your friends sent a gift," Bonita said. On a vanity table sat a box from Delta. Bonita and Antonio left the room, softly shutting wide doors behind them. The silence felt overwhelming. Loneliness filled me, so deep my bones ached.

I shucked my scarf, my sunglasses, my shirt, my pants, my shoes, and stood there in nothing but the ugly body stocking. Slowly, I pulled the face mask off, and dropped it on the cool, tiled floor.

I opened the box. Delta's biscuits, with soul-sustaining cream gravy. And a large manila envelope. On the envelope was written "Welcome Home, Cathy" in neat, blocky script, as if a draftsman had outlined the words for a blueprint.

Inside were the most wonderful photographs. I recognized the scene instantly. Granny Nettie's house, and her barn, and her pasture, and Hog Back, and deer, and turkeys, and spring flowers, and a sunset.

And a note. Simply signed, "Thomas."
Welcome home. It's waiting for you.
I hugged the pictures to my chest and cried.
I wasn't brave enough to go.

🐾🐾🐾🐾🐾

My new life as a Hollywood recluse settled into a daily routine. Though I still underwent small procedures, I was able to return to some semblance of a normal life. It was just that my definition of "normal" had changed.

I had no past and no future. I lived like a vampire in a four-million dollar bat cave, avoiding uncurtained windows and never venturing outdoors except late at night. Over my pressure suit and head mask I wore hoodies, scarves, sunglasses, and hats. I looked like a bag lady with a Gucci logo.

I spent my time waiting for the next package of biscuits, gravy, and photos from North Carolina. There were weeks when the thought of them was all that got me out of bed. I read self-help books that didn't help, watched the safe and cheerful Food Network, slept, cried and taped Thomas's photographs all over my room, photos of the home I was too terrified to visit. One picture had a hand in it, pointing to a flower. *That must be Thomas's hand. A nice hand. Surprisingly lean and virile-looking for an aging grandpa.*

Not only would I never meet Thomas in person, I might never leave my house again. The beauty of being rich and eccentric is that, for a price, almost everything and everyone you need will come to you. Doctors, therapists, nurses, security guards. I became the queen bee of a pay-per-visit hive in the midst of west L.A.'s most protected mansions. A recluse among recluses. My gates had gates.

The sight of a match flame or lit stove on television made me queasy. Even the Food Network sometimes ambushed me with flaming desserts. I couldn't watch *Cops* because the highway chases made me hyperventilate. When forced to go back to the hospital for outpatient procedures—stretching, sanding, nipping, all of it painful and humiliating—I rode in service vans to hide from the photographers who always lurked outside my gate. So far, I had been dirty laundry, a couch that needed new upholstery, and termite control. During the trips I shivered and sweated and prayed not to crash and burn.

My divorce from Gerald would be final by autumn, a few months away. The pain of his abandonment went deep but the pain of my own stupidity went even deeper. How could I have been foolish enough to marry such a cold-blooded huckster? I was thirty years old when I fell in love with him. I waited until I was a grown-up to tie the knot with someone. I'd intended to marry one time only—a smart, mature partnership for a lifetime. Instead, I'd fallen for a man who treated me like a champion Persian. Something to show off and sell.

Gerald forged ahead with Flawless as if nothing had happened. The notoriety of my accident actually helped launch the company. I began to realize he'd isolated me at the hospital because he wanted the public to forget the real me. He wanted women to look at my face in the ads and be inspired to buy the products, not think of my flame-grilled skin.

He wanted me, the real me, to be forgotten.

And I was all too eager to go along.

"The irony is," I told Delta during one of our phone calls, "the last time I talked to my husband, right before he sent the lawyer with divorce papers, was the time I felt most loved and accepted by him. When he called to introduce you to me. He was wonderful."

"Almost like you were talking to a sweet stranger," Delta said in a sly tone.

"Yes."

"Why don't you come for a visit? These mountains will do your heart good. No photographers, no gates, no walls, no curtains. Thomas will take you up on Wild Woman Ridge to your granny's house. You need to meet Thomas."

"Oh, I can't travel for a long time, yet. Don't believe what you read in the tabloids. I'm not a recluse, I'm just devoting myself to my therapies. The doctors think they can fully restore my face. There are amazing new treatments and some plastic surgery techniques you can barely imagine. I'm going to be just fine in a few months. My agent is already fielding all sorts of new offers."

Lies, lies, lies.

❦❦❦❦❦

My agent sat on the hearth of my empty living room. I sat in a lawn chair where Gerald's sofa used to be, wearing my face mask, a lovely Versace scarf and a sweat-suit.

"Aren't you hot in that outfit?" my agent asked, shivering in my sixty-degree air conditioning. "How can you stand that . . . that ski mask?"

"It's therapeutic. The more I wear it, the more my skin grafts will heal smoothly. My face is going to look fabulous in a few months. Really."

"Cathryn, I'm sorry, but it's time to deal with reality."

"Absolutely! You said you have a long list of offers to discuss with me. So let's discuss."

"I'm not saying I recommend these offers, but I'm duty-bound to tell you about them."

"Let's start with movie roles. I'm willing to take something small, classy, maybe an indie film by some up-and-coming director. Hmmm. It'd be so much fun to go to Sundance for an indie premiere. I love Utah in the snow season. All those frosted Mormons."

My agent stared at me. "Movie roles? No. There aren't any movie offers."

I knew there weren't, just as I knew my face would never look fabulous, or even semi-normal, again. But I had to keep up the façade of pride. Pun intended. "Oh, all right, we can work on the movie angle later. What else have you got?"

"A tell-all book deal about your accident. Movie rights to the book deal. Talk show appearances about your accident. Larry King and Oprah— Oprah wants you first, though. She never takes Larry's leftovers."

"I don't want to talk about my accident. I want to act."

"Okay, well, I do have some offers in that regard. Not movies, but solid guest parts on television."

"All right, so I'll jump-start this new phase of my career on the small screen, first. Maybe it would be good to star in my own series. I'm thinking classy. Romantic comedy. HBO or Showtime. One of those well-written series that smart people watch."

My agent looked away and cleared her throat. "Here's what you can choose from: a stoic burn victim whose husband was murdered by his ex-wife on *Law & Order*. A courageous young doctor with burn scars on *ER*. An idealistic prosecuting lawyer who had acid thrown on her face by a vengeful ex-con on *Boston Legal*."

"You're kidding . . . right? What am I, the new poster girl for fried skin? When casting agents type 'Singed Actress' in their data bases, my name will pop up?"

"Look, I'm just the messenger."

"Don't you have any better messages?"

"Last but not least, you have offers from at least a dozen major magazines. All of them want exclusive rights to your first post-accident photographs. *Vanity Fair* is guaranteeing you the cover if you'll pose nude for Annie Leibowitz."

Pose nude? Naked and scarred? *Look at the freak.* I stared at her. Inside, another small part of me withered and went into hiding. "Have you lost your mind?" I said softly. "I can still act. I'm a good actress. I was going to be the new Elizabeth Taylor in *Giant*, for God's sake."

"Well, sweetie, now you're the post-Richard Burton Liz. You're Elizabeth Taylor settling for a chance to play Wilma's mother in the live-action remake of *The Flintstones*. I'm sorry."

"I still have my talent, my personality."

"You were valuable because of your looks. You were special. Without the face, you're just another actress. You can't even distract people with a sexy body. You can't wear a low-cut dress anymore, or go sleeveless."

"I'm not just a bunch of parts. Women are more than the sum of their parts."

"Not in this business. Not in any business where men like to watch. Television, movies, video games. Take a look at the perky little reporters on the cable news shows. Size six and under thirty-five."

"That's just the news business."

"Oh? You think Rachael Ray is a star on the Food Network just because she's a good cook?"

"What about Paula Deen?" I shot back. "She's older and motherly and gray-haired and . . ."

"She's a great cook. You can't even make spaghetti."

"All right, all right. But couldn't I play character roles? Look at all the successful, pizza-faced men playing strong roles on television—"

"Women get wrinkles. Men get character lines. Yes, that saying is true, Cathryn. There are double standards. Women get fat. Men get 'love handles.' Women get dumped for younger wives. Men get . . . younger wives. Men control most of the choices. They control most of the money. In ways that don't always seem obvious, despite decades of progressive work in women's rights, men still call the shots. And we women go along with it. We're traitors to our own kind."

"I never knew you felt this way. Do you hate men?"

"No, individually, they're just fine. But group them together and they're dick-wagging tyrants. And women let them get away with it. We want to please them. We don't want to be the ugly broad or the fat chick or the flat-chested bitch they ignore. We know they want to look at pretty women. Pretty, young-looking women. All the rest of us are just the support system for the breeding stock. Or the butt of the joke."

"That's not true! Look at all the women who are successful because of their brains and hard work."

"They're the exception to the rule. Tell that to every fat, homely, or just ordinary-looking female who's ever cursed the system." My agent's expression became distant, angry. "Growing up in Minnesota, I wanted to be a figure skater. My parents spent everything they had on my training. I was a true athlete, Cathryn. I had the chops to pull it off. But when the important coaches started picking out the girls who had the best chance of becoming champions, the ones most likely to make it to the Olympics some day, they wouldn't even give me a try. Not because I didn't have the talent, or the heart, but because I wasn't pretty enough."

"You could have taken up speed skating. Or ice hockey. Or . . ." Suddenly I realized how clueless I sounded. "I'm sorry," I finished wearily. "Remember that old TV commercial where the model said, 'Don't hate me because I'm beautiful?' And everyone hated her just for saying that? I never understood why. I thought it was a joke. I didn't ask to be born beautiful. I realize it gave me a lot of advantages, but I didn't ask for them. Now I can understand why other people resent those advantages, but does that mean I shouldn't get a chance to prove myself?"

"Cathryn, my Jewish grandmother used to say, 'Luck is a bouquet of roses, *bubelah*. Some people get it in one big bunch. Other people get it a single flower at a time, until one day they go—Ah hah! I have a whole bouquet!'"

"I worked hard to earn my roses!"

She sighed. "I know, but you started with so many more of them than the rest of us ever get. All you had to do was gild the lily. The rose.

Whatever. Cathryn, be happy with all the roses you've already been given. Maybe there are some more out there, waiting for you to find them in places you never looked, before. Your career—the one you want—is over. Get out of L.A. Go somewhere far away from this business. Forget about the life you had. Get a hobby. Marry a nice guy and have some kids. You're rich, you have no money worries, you can start a charitable foundation or something. You're a good person. A smart person. You can do something new with your life." She stood. "Or you can play a burn victim from now on."

When I said nothing, afraid I'd cry, she squeezed my shoulder on the un-burned side, and left.

I went back to bed.

🐾🐾🐾🐾🐾

Scheduling a hair-and-makeup consultation with Luce, Randi, and Judi was one of those useful, turning-point moments I would look back on later, much later, as a character-building experience. But at the time it simply added another straw to the towering heap of Last Straws I was already carrying. The sword of Damocles isn't really a sword, it's a thousand deceptively harmless needles hanging over a person's head and dropping, like water torture, one shivering razor point—or one feathery straw—at a time.

"Hi, folks," I sang out as the trio walked into my bedroom suite. I stood there with a desperate façade of nonchalance, dressed in a slender black t-shirt and slacks, sans face mask, my incoming hair a short, dark, inverted bowl that gave me a vague resemblance to Moe of *The Three Stooges*. "Welcome to the lair of the Phantom! Come and work your magic on me!" My tone was perfectly cheerful. I'd spent hours practicing.

The three of them stared at me in horror. Judi murmured, "I'm so sorry for you. I had no idea it was this bad." Luce cried and nodded. "We thought the rumors were all lies." Randy literally backed toward the suite doors, one hand on his heart. "I need a little air," he said. When a black guy looks ashen, you know it's bad.

So much for my cosmetic support group. Their outright *pity* was a shock I hadn't expected. I waved them off. "Thanks for coming, but let's re-schedule, okay? I'm having a lot more surgery on my face, you know. I won't look like this the next time you see me. We'll look back on today and . . . *laugh* at how y'all reacted. Okay?"

They escaped as quickly as good manners and hyperventilation would allow. I wandered to a desk in one corner and deleted the three of them from my address book. No, there wouldn't be any styling sessions in the future.

That night I crept outdoors. Los Angeles glittered under a beautiful, lonely moon. I sat by my pool and put my bare feet in the water, watching the moonlight reflect on the water, and crying from frustration. I couldn't bring myself to look at my reflection in the water.

I rummaged among my prescriptions and found a bottle of pills I'd stopped using weeks earlier, as the pain became manageable without them. I poured the capsules into the palm of my burned hand, counted them, then put them back in the bottle one at a time, listening to the soft tap of each highly controlled opium derivative. Click. Click. Click.

Wash them down with a bottle of bourbon and they'd take away the pain permanently. A thought to keep in mind.

❦❦❦❦❦

Shattered Recluse—
Cathryn Deen Hides From Public
In Heart-Breaking Shame.
Curtains, Cover-Ups And Cold Meals—
Rumors Of Star's Quirks Increase.
Most Beautiful Woman Now Most Tragic Eccentric.

Most of the time the tabloids screech half-truths, wild exaggerations or outright lies. Unfortunately, in my case, they got it right. Judi, Luce and Randi couldn't resist talking about me to friends who talked to reporters.

Only the weekly care packages from Delta and Thomas stopped me from swallowing the bottle of pills. One particularly depressing day I pulled out a couple of photos, stared at them, and did a double-take.

"In this picture, Cathy, you're napping in the pasture," Thomas had written on the bottom of a photo. A small, gold-and-white calf snoozed in the sun. In the second photo the calf was being chased by a baby goat. Thomas wrote, "Here you're frolicking in the hay with Ellen. She's named after Ellen DeGeneres. You and little Ellen are just good friends."

A Greek shipping heir had once named a yacht after me. A famous chef had named a dessert in my honor. But no one had ever named a cow after me, before. The little gold-and-white calf had big, dark eyes and a nose that looked so small and delicate I could cup it in my palm.

She was beautiful. I put the pictures on my nightstand, in front of the pills.

Thank you, Thomas, for enough light to keep me going a little longer.

Thomas

I didn't start out to name a calf after Cathy. It just happened that way.

There's nothing more fun on a hot summer day than the smell of cow manure and blood. Throw in a few fat, buzzing flies and an audience of suspicious women, and you've got the makings of a bad reality TV show. *Survivor: Crossroads.*

I sat on the barn floor at Rainbow Goddess Farms—the queendom of our local, lesbian berry farmers, Alberta Groover and Macy Spruill, who were also known by their musical *nom de ovaries*, The Log Splitter Girls—with my big, bare, male feet planted firmly on either side of a cow's vagina. Around me, watching intently, were two-dozen women and children. They worked and lived at the place, which was a combination commercial farm, commune, co-op and unofficial shelter for battered women.

Thus, I was surrounded by a spectrum of women ranging from those who didn't *need* men, to those who didn't want men, to those who didn't trust men, and finally, to those who thought all men should be castrated and forced to watch *Thelma and Louise.* Some of my spectators were armed with hoes and shovels. If anything went wrong with the bovine birth about to occur, I just hoped they wouldn't kill me in front of their kids.

Yours truly, Cow Midwife. I'd just dropped by to borrow some more camera gear for my newest round of photos to send Cathy. Alberta and Macy instantly recruited me to act as their human forceps. A victory for brute masculine strength.

"Now, Thomas. Take this baby by the feet and pull gently," ordered Alberta. Both she and Macy crouched beside me on the heels of their manure-stained work boots, peering at the pair of tiny, bloody, mucous-covered hooves peeking from a raw, heaving vortex of cow twat.

I leaned in close between my bent knees, carefully wrapped my hands around the calf's tiny feet, and pulled. The mother, a gold-and-white Guernsey milk cow, grunted wearily, so tired she couldn't deliver without help. It was her first pregnancy, and labor had gone on for too long, even though the calf was turned correctly and simply should have slipped out.

Pull, that's it, pull, that's it!" Alberta chanted. Females push babies out, males pull them. I did my sex proud.

A gooey, bloody, placenta-draped calf squirted into my lap. I grabbed it in a hug. It uttered a soft bleat and began wrestling. Instantly my hands and arms were covered in gore, my jeans were stained, and my beard filled with blood, mucous, and placenta. The audience applauded, cheered or went "Eeeew."

"Good pulling. We'll take it from here," Macy said. She and Alberta scrubbed the baby with old towels. As its soft, golden hide began to dry it revealed a milkshake splash of white on the calf's back and front legs and a broad dollop of white on its face. A truly beautiful bovine.

I got to my feet and watched, swaying a little. My head buzzed. I had been in the delivery room when Ethan was born, had stood by Sherryl's head, coaching, watching in awe as our tiny, perfect son eased into the world. He seemed to smile from the moment he was born. Surely he'd had cranky days and crying bouts during his three years of life, but I couldn't remember anything but his smile, now.

"Why did we need a man to help?" one of the women whispered behind me. "I thought no men were allowed here. With all that hair and beard, this guy looks like a psycho Wookie."

"Ssssh," someone whispered back. "That's Thomas Mitternich. You know. The one with the wife and son. Who died in . . . you know. Nine-eleven."

"Oh, my God. You mean that's the alcoholic who intervened when LaRane's ex-boyfriend and his biker friends tried to run her off the road?"

"Yep. That's him. Mr. Nice Guy. Get this: he's straight, and he's celibate."

"No way."

"Way."

Their conversation came to me through a hazy fog.

"It's a girl," Macy proclaimed, peering between the calf's hind legs. In deference to me and the handful of male children on hand, the other women stifled their high-fives and applause.

Alberta looked up at me, smiling. "Tom, in honor of your midwifery, you get to name her."

A dark rim began to crowd my vision. "All right," I mumbled. "Cathy.

I name her 'Cathy.'"

"Ohhh-kay." Alberta scowled. She and Macy looked at each other askance, then shrugged. Macy turned to the audience. "We hereby christen our new heifer, our sister of the nurturing breast, 'Cathy.'"

Applause.

I had named a milk cow after Cathy.

I walked gingerly out of the barn, holding my arms away from my sides. I tried to concentrate on the farm's sunlit spring fields, the Log Splitters' big log house, the barns where Cathy's four-footed sisters produced organic milk via the warm hands of milking women. I tried to notice the free-range hens who laid politically correct eggs, the shelter-rescued dogs, cats, rabbits and pot-bellied pigs, and the nude statue of a goddess in the herb garden, carved by chainsaw from a ten-foot-tall oak log. But all I could think about was the viscous coating of birth fluids beginning to dry on my skin, to tighten, squeezing my breath out of me. *Don't go there. Breathe. Don't look down.*

But the horror, the compulsion, was too great. I looked down at myself, my hands spread in blood-stained supplication. Suddenly I was back in lower Manhattan, covered in drying blood and the dust of the dead, searching for Sherryl and Ethan.

Wrapped in death, again.

Time for a drink.

Chapter 8

Cathy
The Seclusion Worsens

Beauty opened all the doors; it got me things I didn't even know I wanted, and things I certainly didn't deserve. So sayeth Janice Dickinson, one of the first supermodels, who appeared on *Vogue* covers an incredible thirty-seven times during a career that peaked thirty years ago. Now, at fifty-something, Janice was a reality TV star with a vocabulary that might make a Marine blush. So sayeth Janice: *I'd rather be an honest bitch than some ass-kissing, sugarcoating, namby-pamby, wiping-ass motherfucker.*

Me, too, I thought. *If I could just muster the energy to get angry about something.*

All three of Janice's memoirs were scattered around me on my bed, along with a laptop computer, self-help books, books on phobias and panic attacks, feminist manifestos including *The Feminine Mystique* and *The Beauty Myth*, a Bible, a book on Zen Buddhism, and *Gone With The Wind*.

Scarlett was the ultimate beauty queen. Put her at a microphone, ask her about her interests, and she'd smile that deadly smile and say in a soft, lilting voice, "I plan to devote my life to achieving world peace." But you just knew she was thinking, *Screw world peace. I want money, Tara, and Rhett with a stiff one. I want Ashley to kiss my feet and do my hair. And as for Melanie? Bite me, you holier-than-thou bee-atch.*

Across from the foot of my bed, on a giant, flat-screen TV, a flabby but well-hung man and a hard-faced woman with stretch marks on her thighs were engaged in lathered, fast-pumping, doggie-style sex. On another large TV, Mary and Half-Pint were getting a stern but adorable lecture on life from Little Joe, I mean Pa, via *Little House on the Prairie*. Porno and *Little House* had only two things in common: No one caught on fire, and neither remotely resembled real life.

Perfect. I wanted nothing to do with real life. I'd been Googling the biographies of the great recluses, my soulmates. It came as no surprise when I discovered that money is the great emancipator for the mentally unhinged hermits of the world, the smooth wall between a homeless man hiding from his demons in a storm drain and Howard Hughes hiding from his in a Las Vegas hotel he owns.

I lay in the center of my bed, propped up on pillows, dressed only in my fake-flesh-colored pressure suit and glorified ski mask, drugged into a meditative state, with a remote phone set plugged into my good ear through a small hole I'd cut in the side of the mask. I held one of Janice's books to my chest, idly watched the porno movie, and ate one of Delta's biscuits.

Framed photos of Granny Nettie's farm decorated the entire room now. I'd taped Thomas's latest ones to my bed posts. I went back to reading Janice's book. I was fascinated by the feverish determination of her survival, the gleeful anger with which she observed the world. I wanted to understand how people did that: Get angry. I couldn't manage to get angry at my circumstances, just more and more depressed. I was searching for landmarks on a lonely road with no map. Hello, fellow travelers.

Let it be known that in my pre-grilled life I had been the Goody Two-Shoes of modern womanhood: I didn't smoke, do drugs, drink heavily, or hook up with casual acquaintances for unprotected sex and Howard Stern interviews. I read books with lots of pages and small print, occasionally went to museums, and could listen to opera without falling asleep. I never posed nude and I never flashed my breasts or ass on film. Not that I have an entrenched moral resistance to all forms of public nudity, it was just that my aging Atlanta aunts would have voided my membership in the Junior League, and it would have broken Daddy's conservative heart.

All in all, I had been a wholesome person.

Now I was a flash-fried porno watcher, reader of lurid tell-all's and suicide-victim-waiting-to-happen. I had way too much pride to admit my bizarre fears to anyone, even my doctors, who, of course, knew I was hiding a Pandora's Box of twitchy ideas but could do nothing about it without my permission. Oh, no. I wasn't going to let some shrink chronicle my personal trip down the rabbit hole. What if Homeland Security decided to round up all the quirky people some day, post-apocalypse? They'd Google the term "nutzoid," and there I'd be in the database of not-so-private medical records. Off to the internment camp with me, you betcha.

I knew I should be grateful to be alive, grateful to have the best medical care money could buy, grateful to be so rich I never had to work another day in my life, grateful for biscuits, grateful for Thomas and his photos. But I wasn't grateful, at least not on a sincere, joyous level. I wanted my old life back. I felt guilty for not feeling grateful to be alive and rich, and I felt guilty for having been a pampered princess who somehow brought the wrath of bad karma down upon herself.

Suddenly, an answer dawned on me.

I need to bribe God.

Some people promise to do good works if God will save their lives or the lives of loved ones. My prayer request was simpler: *Please, God, show me how to be happy with the way I look now.* What could I give up that epitomized my vanity, my wealth, my very sense of self?

"I've got it," I said, sitting up in bed one afternoon. "*Haute couture.*"

I ran to the dressing room off my bath suite. Past the sauna, past the massage nook, past the personal beauty salon complete with waxing station. I threw open a pair of twelve-foot-tall double doors, flicked a switch, and gazed at row upon row of designer fashions.

If God would just let me feel beautiful again, even if it was just a delusion, I'd donate everything to charity. My Valentino's, my Chanel's, my Donna Karan's, and even my beloved Vera Wang's. I began grabbing innocent, unsuspecting gowns off the racks.

Hours later, I carried what I thought was the last of the sacrificial couture into the empty living room. I spread each gown on the floor. The huge room looked like a designer version of a murder scene. Instead of chalk outlines, Yves Saint Laurent and Versace showed where the bodies had fallen.

Suddenly God spoke to me, or I spoke to myself and He just listened in.

Cathryn, I notice you kept the dresses with high necklines and long sleeves.

Well, Sir, those are the ones that will hide some of the scars on my neck and right arm.

You're planning to put on a beautiful gown and go out in public? This is news to me. If you truly felt confident about your new look, you wouldn't worry so much about hiding your scars.

What are you insinuating, Sir?

That your effort to come to terms with your scars is a little half-hearted. What you really want is a miracle. I'm not going to give you that miracle. You want to be beautiful again. Not just feel beautiful. Be beautiful. No can do.

"Then you're not getting the rest of my dresses," I said bitterly, and went to bed.

🐾🐾🐾🐾🐾

Bonita cried the next morning when she saw the designer fashions thrown everywhere. "Everything? You want to donate *everything* to my sister's mission school?" Bonita jokingly called her nun sibling "Sister Sister." I'd given large donations to Sister Sister's convent in the past, but never something like this.

"Everything. You contact an auction company, sell all of this, and send Sister Sister the money. Wait a minute. *Almost* all the money. I want a part of it to go to my cousin in North Carolina."

"There must be one or maybe even two-million dollars' worth of designer gowns here."

"At least. Now that I'm grotesque and infamous I expect these gowns will sell for twice what I'd paid for them."

"Bless you, but—"

"Just tell your sister to have her fellow nuns say a prayer for me."

"A simple prayer? This may qualify you for sainthood."

"I'll settle for a few prayers asking God to give me a makeover. Or at least a clue about what I should do with my life."

She hugged me and left to call Sister Sister in Mexico.

I set my bottle of pills out on the nightstand every day, now. Got them out, counted them, put them back.

Every day.

Chapter 9

Thomas
Cora And Ivy Arrive

That fall, when Anthony delivered a check from Cathy for a quarter-million dollars, everyone in the Cove took a sharp breath and swallowed their own spit. I walked into the front yard of Delta and Pike's big log house—a ten minute stroll along a winding drive behind the café—and found a Saturday afternoon community barbecue had turned into a gape-at-the-check party. Several dozen people—in other words, the majority of the Cove's residents—came over to have a look. The heady scent of smoked pork mingled with the sweet September air and the fragrance of money.

"She says it's to cover all my shipping costs for biscuits and gravy over the months," Delta yelled above Billy Ray Cyrus singing *Achy Breaky Heart* on a boom box. "And to cover your photography costs. I get half and you get half, she says. I told her I don't need it and besides, family doesn't take payment for sending biscuits to family. So then Cathy said, 'Give your half to a local church, then,' and I told her, 'Oh, boy, after he gets this, the pastor of Crossroads Cove Methodist is going to tell the pastor at Turtleville First Baptist to kiss his ass,' and Cathy said, 'Just tell the pastor to pester God on my behalf. I don't think God's listening to me.'"

A little out of breath from yelling, Delta took a minute to recover while I studied the hand-written check. Cathy's signature was elegant and sprawling, but tilted precariously at odd angles. A handwriting expert might say she seemed desperate for direction.

Don't tell my heart, my achy breaky heart, Billy Ray sang.

"What are you going to do with your half?" Delta yelled.

I shook my head. Thanks to John, who managed a few good investments I'd made, and thanks to my cheap lifestyle, which was one degree short of pioneer living, I didn't need money. I'd rejected the government's nine-eleven compensation, donating all of my share, over a million dollars, to charities for children. I didn't want the government's hush money; I wanted to know what really led to that day, a futile hope. Money doesn't buy amnesia. Cash wouldn't make me forget the terror in Sherryl's and Ethan's voices the last time I talked to them. Cash doesn't buy off guilt.

Cathy's trying to make up for something, I thought. *Cathy, you haven't done anything wrong. Trust me. I'm an expert on the subject of culpability.*

"You hang onto my half for now," I told Delta. "Tell Cathy I'll find a righteous use for the money. Sometime that might bribe God to give her a call."

Thomas

A few weeks later I still hadn't thought of a way to spend Cathy's money. Delta regarded me as a slackard. One chilly October morning, as I slept off a hangover in my truck, she poured a stew pot full of water and ice cubes on my face. I opened my eyes, blinked away the cold water, brushed ice cubes off my beard, and gazed up into Banger's pink nostrils. His tongue descended. He licked my nose.

I pushed him away and sat up, holding my head. My hangover was deep, broad, and pounding. "Okay, he's awake, we can go," a voice said, accompanied by snickers. I squinted over the side of my truck. Delta disappeared through the café's back door, swinging her empty pot. Six young faces peered back at me from close range. The oldest was Bubba's teenager, Brody, fifteen. The youngest was Jeb's baby, Laura, eight. All of Delta's grandchildren, nieces, and nephews stood beside my truck, watching me with unsympathetic glee. "See ya," Brody said. "We gotta catch the bus. Aunt Delta told us to make sure you woke up after she doused you."

I managed a thumbs up. The six of them headed for the school bus stop by the Trace, lugging back packs, cell phones, iPods and laptops. It was a Friday. Fridays were "casual electronics" day in Jefferson County schools.

Or something like that. I couldn't think. My head throbbed.

"Bah," Banger said, and nibbled my shirt. Pieces of my cell phone were scattered on my beard. I pushed him away again. My hand connected with cardboard. I tore Delta's message off Banger's collar and tried to focus. She had written only one word, in big, angry letters.

BACKSLIDER

I crawled out of the truck. The frost was on the pumpkins and the hardwood forests of Ten Sisters had turned into an impressionist's landscape of red and gold. My outdoor bedroom required an extra blanket over the sleeping bag. And now, apparently, an umbrella. I staggered to the Privy, washed up, then made my way back to the truck. I slumped in the front seat, pulled the visor down, and touched the pictures of Ethan and Sherryl.

Today was Ethan's birthday.

He would have been eight years old.

For his birthday I'd plant another row of grapes in my 'Tree of Life' vineyard. I drove up the Trace halfway to Turtleville then turned left on a winding side road called Fox Run Lane. A big green sign welcomed me to Kaye's Heirloom Plant Nursery. Dolores and the Judge lived in a handsome little Victorian overlooking the grounds. They'd converted a small barn into a shop and offices. Thanks to the Internet, UPS, and the post office, Dolores did a brisk business shipping roses all over the country. Her rose beds covered the nursery's terraced hillsides, rimmed in hogwire fence to keep out rose-loving deer. In summertime the roses exploded in a cacophony of colors so beautiful it lured drive-by rose gawkers from all over western North Carolina.

Inside the shop Dolores stocked bonsai and orchids, but also sold upscale gardening knickknacks and handcrafted items made by some of our locals. Her shop was a favorite of the Asheville ladies-who-lunch. It wasn't uncommon for sleek sedans or SUV's full of salon-tanned women to head straight from the café to the nursery. Women don't like to admit it, but they prefer to shop in packs, like wolves. I waited until a carload of lunch ladies left before I walked in. My public persona tended to make strangers sidle one hand into their purses for the pepper spray.

"You look awful," Dolores said helpfully.

I leaned on the counter by her cash register, inhaling rose potpourri that soothed my stomach. "I love it when you flatter me."

"Your *vidal blancs* came in, but I'm still waiting for the *baco noirs* you ordered. I hope you're not intending to be 'all vine and no vinting.'"

"Beg pardon?"

"It would be a shame if you just plant these wonderful hybrids for fun and don't make wine from the grapes. *Baco noir* makes a luscious red. The plants do well at these elevations. You could start your own small winery, Thomas. There are little boutique wineries all over these mountains, now."

My Frank Lloyd Wright-inspired vineyard was more about creating order in my personal universe than creating a good glass of wine. A way to distract myself during my waking hours. Maybe Ethan could see it from Heaven.

"I'll keep that in mind," I lied.

"Backslider." She looked at me sternly.

"Ah hah. Word gets around."

"I know it's your son's birthday today. Delta told me. You think your son would want to see you like this? You think you're the only person in the world who ever suffered a tragedy in their lives?" Dolores jerked her head toward several lovingly framed pictures of her and the Judge's grown daughter. She'd died in a car accident on a Florida highway along with her husband and their new baby. Dolores and the Judge had been devastated. They moved to the Crossroads to escape the memories.

"Believe it or not," I said quietly, "I'm fully aware that the world is full of grief and suffering. I've never claimed to be special, and I don't ask anyone to feel sorry for me."

"Thomas, of course you have the right to mourn, sure, but you have to keep moving, keep reaching out. I understand what you're going through. When Benton and I first came here we wanted to sit down and die. We didn't know what to expect from the lily-white mountain culture up here. Maybe we only moved here to confirm that the world was a mean, cold place full of people who didn't want us around and didn't care about our loss. But guess what? Here came Delta Whittlespoon. She showed up on our doorstep the day we moved in. Saying in the way only Delta can put it, 'Hello, Black People! Have a biscuit!' Or words to that effect. She and Pike and their family welcomed us and made sure everyone else did, too. Delta dragged us out of our despair day by day. We'll never forget that, and we'll never stop trying to pay her back by paying her *forward*, if you know what I mean. We aren't going to let you just sit down and give up."

"I appreciate your concern but—"

"I don't want to speak in religious slogans, like Cleo at the café, but I believe God puts us here for a reason. There are people who need you, people whose lives would be terrible without you. But you have to make an effort to find those people and to recognize them when they find you."

"I wish I believed that."

"You do, deep in your heart," she said flatly. "Or you'd have killed yourself by now."

I couldn't talk about this subject anymore. I stepped back from the counter. "Now about those *baco noirs*—"

"Sssh." She spotted something out the window beside the cash register. "One of my girls is here. She hand stitches those fabulous silk throw pillows over there on the wicker chair. I provide the material, she does the rest. The women who just left? They bought ten pillows at thirty dollars each. This girl's one of the most creative fabric artists I've ever seen."

Dolores called all her craftspeople her 'girls and boys.' She needed to mother people. Or in my case, to club them with tough love. From my angle I couldn't see anything out her window except the front grill of an aging blue sedan with a primer-colored hood. "I'll be out back, loading some mulch in my truck."

Dolores clucked disapproval at the person I couldn't see. "She's stoned, again, I bet. I should tell Benton. But I don't know what would be worse, leaving her in charge of those little girls or leaving them without even an aunt to raise them."

I wasn't interested in gossip—or being sucked into any discussion that involved children. I started toward the back, pulling on a pair of work gloves I kept in my pocket. "I'll be outside," I repeated.

"The girl's name is Laney Cranshaw. She only moved here a few weeks ago. From way over in Raleigh, I think. Her sister's dead, she's raising her two nieces, and she hasn't got, to put it politely, a vessel to urinate in or a window to throw said urine out of."

I tugged the last finger of my gloves into place. "I'll be out—"

"She and the little girls are living in a tent in the state park. It's only a matter of time before the park rangers make them leave. I've tried to talk to her about it—this community is willing to help her—but she's got a chip on her shoulder a mile wide. I suspect she's afraid to have anyone in authority look too closely at her background. Or at her drugs."

"Here's some advice for you. *You can't help people who don't want to be helped.*"

"People always want to be helped," she shot back. "They just don't always want to admit it."

We heard footsteps on the shop's small wooden porch. "Sic 'em, Dr. Phil," I said drily, and walked out the reconstituted barn's back door.

I was shoveling mulch into the truck's bed a few minutes later, when small, quick footsteps crunched to a halt on the gravel walkway behind me.

"Hagrid!" a small voice trilled in a heavy mountain drawl. "You went on a diet!"

I turned slowly and looked down. The most wonderful little face looked up at me. Dark eyes flashed beneath long, glossy black hair. She clutched her hands over the heart of a faded Powerpuff Girls t-shirt. A tiny yellow butterfly fluttered around her pink sandals and little-girl baggy jeans.

The butterfly was charmed.

So, against my will, was I.

"Hagrid?" I said gently, not wanting to scare her—though she hardly looked nervous, gazing up at me in Harry Potter-inspired wonder. "I'm afraid I'm not Hagrid. I'm his . . . skinny cousin. Herman."

"Herman! Have you seen my owl? I sent her off with a note for my teacher. I can't come to school tomorrow because Ivy and me have to help Aunt Laney move our tent to a new campground. I'm in the first grade."

I put a hand over my brow and scanned the sky. "I haven't seen any owls lately, but I'll keep an eye out. What's her name?"

"Mrs. Jones."

"That's an interesting name for an owl."

Peels of little-girl giggles rose in the air. "Mrs. Jones is my teacher. My owl is named Arianna."

"Oh. That's a great name for—"

Princess Arianna. Cathy's first starring role, when she was only nineteen, had been in a whimsical sword-and-dragon film titled Princess Arianna. The film had been a surprise hit, and she'd made two sequels, Princess Arianna and the Dragon, then Princess Arianna and the Wizard, which were also box office successes. The trio of films had become perennial favorites for children and also for the Spock-ears crowd at fantasy and science-fiction conventions. Cathy had been, hands down, the most ethereally va-voomish princess ever to grace a sword-and-sorcery potboiler.

Not that I was all that familiar with Cathy's films. Chick flicks, mostly, and the Princess Arianna shtick was cheesier than old brie. Delta, however, owned all of Cathy's films on tape and DVD. She popped one into a TV in the café's quilting room every Saturday night. I couldn't help but watch as I wandered through on the way to poker.

"That's a beautiful name for an owl," I finished gruffly. "I bet you've seen all the Princess Arianna movies."

"Oh, yes! I love Princess Arianna! We used to have the tapes, but one of Aunt Laney's boyfriends busted 'em."

All my fatherly feelings coalesced in a single clump of protectiveness. "I know a place where you can watch Princess Arianna's movies on Saturday nights. For free."

"Where?"

"Let's go inside and talk to Dolores about it. She'll tell your aunt—"

"Hey! Leave her alone!"

A righteous, pre-teen dynamo bounded out the back door and ran down the path. My first impression focused on fuzzy, red-brown hair around blue eyes in a round-cheeked, light-brown face, with freckles. She planted herself between us and the smaller girl then stared up at me with obvious fear but also stony determination. "What do you want, mister?"

The little one peered around her and smiled at me. "Ivy, his name's not Mister, it's Herman! He's Hagrid's cousin. It's okay."

"I told you not to talk to strangers."

"But he's not a stranger! He's Hagrid's—"

"He's not Hagrid's cousin. He's not from a fairytale. He's hairy and he's a stranger."

"Ivy, don't be so mean!" The smaller girl squirmed forward. "I'm Corazon. My daddy was Mexican. My name means *heart*, in Spanish. You can call me Cora." She tugged on her sister's hand. "And this is Iverem, but you can call her Ivy. Her daddy was an African-American. She's twelve. I'm seven."

"Stay away from us," Ivy warned me between gritted teeth. "I know where to kick men so it hurts. Come on, Cora." She began tugging her sister up the gravel path. "I told you not to talk to strangers."

"But he's not—"

"Iverem is a Nigerian name, I believe," I said. Ivy halted and turned, staring at me, her eyes wide. Cora gaped at us both. "I once worked with an architect from Nigeria," I went on. "She was a good friend of mine. A very smart and strong person. When she married, she and her husband gave their children Nigerian names. I helped them do the research. *Iverem*. Doesn't that mean 'blessings?'"

From the look on Ivy's face I scored major points, but then her eyes flattened and she retreated. "Bullshit artist," she hissed, and led Cora back inside. Cora disappeared while looking back at me and waving.

I sat down on the truck's tailgate. My hands shook, and not just from the hangover. Epiphanies can be delicate, painful, and needle-fine. Dolores was right. People always want help, they just won't admit it. Especially when they're young and suspect the world is full of monsters. The tougher ones are defensive, and the gentler ones build fairytales around themselves.

On Ethan's birthday, here, suddenly, was a gift I could give him. The hope of a happier life. Not his, or mine, but theirs. Two small strangers named Cora and Ivy. Feeling illuminated, as if light glimmered briefly through the pores of my skin, I glanced at one of the shop's back windows. Dolores stood there, watching me.

Pay it forward, she mouthed.

At that moment, I thought of the perfect way.

Chapter 10

Cathy
The Darkening Ruby

First, Thomas named a cow after me. Then he turned me into a landlord.

Dear Cathy, thanks to the money you sent, you're now the proud owner of a 'tenant house,' he wrote. *Around here, that's what people call a rental property. Yours is a small cottage on Fox Run Road. You're renting it to Laney Cranshaw and her nieces for one dollar a month, with all utilities covered by you, the landlord. You also furnished it, including a TV, a DVD player, and an entire collection of your Princess Arianna movies and the Harry Potter films. Before this, the Cranshaw trio lived in a tent at the Turtleville camp ground. They're broke.*

Living in a tent. I re-read that line several times from the comfort of my bed with silk pillows. Living in a tent, with winter approaching.

Delta told Laney you bought the property as an investment and don't care about making anything other than a token rent payment from tenants, that you just want someone to maintain the cottage. Laney doesn't have any clue I set this up. Delta's acting as the liaison because Laney is suspicious of 'do-gooders' in general but Delta convinced her you're on the level. As Delta put it to her, 'Why would a movie star with millions of bucks in the bank need to charge anybody rent?

Good point. I blinked slowly, eager to concentrate but a little woozy.

I'd just come back from a day at the doctor's. Plastic surgeons were still working on my hand, where scar tissue had to be snipped and stretched so I could move all my fingers smoothly. I balanced the letter on a gauze mitt big enough to catch a baseball.

Remember the pictures I sent of Kaye Nursery? Thomas wrote. *Your property is just up the way from there. Four pretty acres with a house, a small yard, beautiful woods, and a branch of Ruby Creek. My half of that check you sent covered everything, including closing costs. Can't beat mountain prices. Enclosed are pictures.*

I prowled through the latest care package from him and Delta, found a big envelope, and slid the photos onto the lap of my robe. The top one showed a delicate little house with white-board siding, old-fashioned red-and-white metal awnings, and red shutters. It was shadowed by large sourwoods whose leaves had turned a deep red and a maple that had gone a bright, sunny yellow. It was adorable. Thomas, sweet, grandfatherly Thomas, had picked a house girls and elves would love. I approved.

The cottage has a history. I like that about it. And the history is tied to your grandmother. Her grandfather, Parker Nettie, built it for his second wife's brother, Samuel Barkley, (according to Delta, who knows every family tree in the entire Crossroads orchard.) Samuel used it as a mining cabin back in the late 1800's, when there was a small gem-mining frenzy around the Cove. The frenzy fizzled out in a few years, but there were (and still are) plenty of semi-precious gemstones in the creeks, and a few rare finds of jeweler-quality rubies and sapphires. They're all composed of the same mineral—corundrum—but the color is the telling point. Rubies are red corundrum and sapphires are blue, green, yellow, lavender and you-name-it. Color and clarity define the quality. Do you know what gives corundrum its color? The impurities in the mix. Think about that, Cathy: The most beautiful gems aren't the purebreds, but the mutts.

Mutts. Rubies. Me. Maybe I just needed more impurities in my minerals. Thomas always found odd, endearing ways to say I wasn't ugly now, no matter what. But he hadn't *seen* me.

Delta says your grandmother—and your mother—were expert gem panners. They had an eye for the raw stones—it's a talent, since gems in the rough look like ordinary gray rocks. Delta says they were both 'gem dowsers,' meaning they could sense where the best stones could be found in a creek, much like a water dowser claims to 'feel' the presence of an underground stream. I understand your mother died in childbirth when you were just two years old. Delta has some great pictures of her from their girlhood friendship here in the Cove. You should see her and Delta in overalls, panning in the very same creek you now own. They couldn't have been more than ten years old. I'll make copies and send you some.

Mother, in overalls, up to her knees in a mountain creek? I had only seen pictures of her in ball gowns and slim Chanel suits, looking like Jackie Kennedy on Daddy's swank, older-man arm. Shuffling Thomas's photos of the cottage I'd just bought, I halted suddenly. Two little girls looked back at me.

Here are Laney Cranshaw's nieces. Ivy is twelve, Cora is seven. They have different fathers, and their mother died a few years ago. Their aunt's had some problems and life hasn't been easy for the three of them. Even so, Cora's a hopeful little angel. Ivy is smart but very suspicious. Pike checked into some background. The girls spent time in foster care a couple of years ago, after one of the aunt's boyfriends molested Ivy. To Laney Cranshaw's credit, she called the police on him herself. But the damage was done.

I have to be very careful around Ivy. She spooks easily and doesn't trust men—who can blame her? And she's very protective of Cora. Last week she punched a kid's lights out when he teased Cora for believing in fairytales.

I read and re-read that last part, feeling more depressed and angrier on their behalf each time. I'd had a privileged childhood, but not a particularly happy one. Daddy was doting but distant; my aunts were crusty socialites who exhibited me as if I were a piece of heirloom silver. Maybe I'd inherited my aunts' cold-blooded attitudes. Daddy's sisters—who were all older than he, and done with childbearing by the time I came along—clearly liked golf and their lap dogs far better than their own offspring.

"Any fool can breed—it requires not one lick of common sense, elegance, wisdom or good fortune," my Aunt Emiline once told me over her martini and cigarette. "But smart females protect their physical assets, choose their mates for practical partnership, and only breed when it suits them. Then they raise their brood unsentimentally and shoo the ungrateful little darlings out into the world the moment they turn eighteen. If you plan correctly, Cathryn, you can be done with children—and husbands—while you're still young enough to do whatever you please."

Sometimes I wondered if my aunts weren't glad, secretly, that my mother had died young. They got Daddy, their handsome baby brother, to themselves again, (his society girlfriends were no threat,) and they could raise me like a pretty doll, without motherly interference and sans all serious maternal responsibility.

At any rate, I grew up with no avid desire to produce children. When

I was twenty-two-or-three, drinking wine on a movie set with a raucous bunch of women on the crew, I listened in relief as a sizable cross-section of the sisterhood confessed to not desperately wanting babies. Ah hah. The secret society of happily childless women was not so secret.

Now I held up Thomas's photo and studied Cora and Ivy more closely. I didn't want children, and yet, here they were . . . my children. At least by virtue of living in a house I now owned. Ivy stared back at me with a solemn frown, her eyes sharp and blue, her complexion mocha, her hair a reddish-brown cloud around her face and shoulders. She was a little chubby, her features not quite symmetrical and not quite either/or, white or black. Grim self-defense radiated from her smart, steely eyes.

I'd give her straight hair like Beyoncé, with some gold highlights, I thought, *and put her in a brown velvet jumper with a short-waisted burgundy jacket, with some fun turquoise jewelry to pick up the blue in her eyes. And I'd find some way to make her smile. I'd promise her she'd never have to live in a tent, again. And that no one would ever again lay an unwanted hand on her, ever.*

As for Cora . . . she beamed sunshine into the world. That smile, that innocence. A miniature Jennifer Lopez with straight black hair so fine it floated around her happy face as if electrified by her energy. I'd feather-cut that hair, put some rhinestone barrettes in it, dress her in a pale gold dress with cream piping and rows of tiny pleats across the bodice. And I'd do everything in my power to keep that innocent shine in her eyes.

Dolls. I'd dress my two living dolls in charming finery—just as Daddy and my aunts had done to me—and tell them how pretty they were . . . no, I'd tell them it wasn't important to be pretty, not to take that too seriously, to be happy with their bodies and their faces and to enjoy life's biscuits.

I groaned. What should *anyone* tell little girls? To ignore the pressures, the commercials, the sexy billboards, the magazines? To not idolize the latest stick-sized teen pop singer with implants and an eating disorder? To ignore an entire culture devoted to making them feel bad about their looks so they'd shop obsessively for the perfect makeup and clothing to transform them into a beer-commercial image of femininity?

I thumped the picture with my bandaged hand. "No thong panties until you're eighteen," I told Ivy and Cora. "If skanky underwear is so wholesome and cute, then why don't we see little boys in bikini briefs with 'Hot Stuff' on the front? We don't sexualize little boys for entertainment, that's why! But girls are fair game.

"You don't have to buy into that hype, you know. You don't *have* to turn yourselves into pint-sized beauty queens and miniature hoochies! You can . . . you can play softball, if you want to! I wanted to play softball, you know, when I was thirteen I tried out for the team at my private school, and I made it! But my father wouldn't give permission. He said I might get hurt—ruin my precious looks with a few scars, you know—or have a tooth knocked out. Well, so what if I took a few stitches or needed a new tooth or two? I loved that game. I loved the feel of the ball hitting my glove, and I loved whacking the ball with a bat. I even loved chasing line drives by Tiffany Moskowitz. The toughest batter in the history of girls' slow-pitch." I bounced the photo on my gauzy mitt. I was nearly yelling, now. "You girls play softball if you want to! And ice hockey and basketball and . . ." my voice trailed off.

I was yelling at two small strangers on a piece of photo paper.

I slumped, then laid the photo aside. Who was I to give advice on not caring about pleasing people, about following your heart? If a magic genie popped out of the empty Perrier bottle beside my bed and offered me three wishes, my first one would be: *Make me beautiful, again.* I sank back on my pillows. After a while, I wearily raised Thomas's letter and finished reading.

Here's Ivy's drawing of a water sluice similar to the kind Samuel once built on Ruby Creek. She found an old schematic in a pamphlet on local mining history. Ivy has a natural eye for form and structure. She loves to read and sketch, and she's a math whiz. Her suspicious nature is a tough nut to crack, but the girl's got a lot of potential if she just gets half a chance. As for Cora, well, Cora loves animals, and has always wanted pets. The Log Splitter Girls run an unofficial animal shelter at their farm, so they gave Cora her choice of cats. See the next picture.

I lifted one more photo from the stack. There stood Cora on the cottage's front porch, smiling a huge smile as she hugged a placid-looking kitten. But I wasn't prepared for what perched on the porch rail next to Cora's right shoulder.

A rooster. A ratty-feathered, one-eyed rooster.

The half-grown calico in the picture is her pride and joy. Cora's named her in your honor, Princess Arianna. Which is also the name of Cora's invisible owl. Speaking of birds, some redneck threw out a half-dead rooster on the road. Delta says he's a fighting breed, and it looks like he went down for the count one time too many. He's missing one eye and quite a few feathers. But he's good-natured and tame, which may explain the end of his career in the ring. Cora has decided he's a magic owl in disguise, and she's named him Herman, in my honor. Don't ask why. It's a long story.

Herman the pacifist rooster. And a cat named after the character who made me famous in my first movie. A *cat* named after me. And an owl, too. Lest we forget, I was already the namesake for a Guernsey calf.

By the way, Thomas finished, *Cora sent you a ruby she found in the creek. Look in the box.*

I rummaged until I found a glittering little cloth bag with a ribbon tie. I opened it and tenderly deposited the contents on the palm of my good hand. A rock. It was a small, garden-variety rock. Even I could recognize a plain yard rock. I looked back at Thomas's letter.

It may look like an ordinary piece of quartz from the driveway. But to Cora, it's a ruby. If you could see how Cora sees the world, you'd know that, by God, that little hunk of quartz must be a ruby at heart.

I curled my good hand shut around the stone. Scattered around me on the bed were wads of torn paper. My finalized divorce papers. Gerald had sent another pretty, shark-eyed woman attorney to deliver them, as if demonstrating how he needed beauty around him in all aspects of his life. She'd been waiting when I came home from hand surgery. The doctors couldn't do anything else for my face, but at least my fingers could close smoothly around Gerald's throat. I didn't have two good hands to use at the moment, so I'd ripped the papers apart with my teeth.

Never piss off an actress who still has uncapped incisors.

My dreams were in pieces. I no longer trusted magic, good luck, the kindness of strangers, the adoration of men, or God's grace. But thanks to Thomas, I could still wield a princess wand. I could turn a tent into a real house and give two little girls—and a cat, and a one-eyed rooster—a sanctuary. I could give Cora and Ivy something I'd taken for granted as a child. Security.

I laid Cora's ruby by my pill bottle. A photo of Gerald and his new girlfriend stood nearby.

Thomas

Ms. Deen is asking the two of you to manage a trust fund for Cora and Ivy, including full college scholarships for both girls. She wants to leave a legacy far more positive than the current media portrayal of her as a reclusive failure.

Delta threw the lawyer's letter down on the café's sunny table.

"Thomas, I'm fifty years old, and you're going to drink yourself to death in a year or two, but Cathy acts like we'll just naturally outlive her. She's planning things as if she's not going to be here to supervise them herself."

Frowning, I skimmed the letter again. "Maybe she just likes to cover all the possibilities."

"Maybe she just intends to lay down and die," Delta insisted. "Look at these headlines." Delta spread several grocery-store tabloids on the table. "'Friends Worried About Star's Mental Health.' 'Neighbors Glimpse Frail Cathryn Only At Night.' 'Star's Divorce Now Final; Could Be Last Straw.' What can we do, Thomas? Oh, sure, when I call her she says not to pay attention to the gossip, but could all of these magazines be lying?" She pounded a tabloid with one flour-speckled forefinger, leaving white fingerprints on Brad and Angelina.

I pushed the gossip rags aside. I wanted to take Cathy by the shoulders and look into her eyes and say, *Fight back. The evil can't get you, if you don't let it.* Except I wasn't much of a role model for that advice. "I'm not sure what else we can do to help her."

Delta sighed. "I've offered to visit, and I've invited her to come here and live at my house until she's ready to be on her own. Why don't you talk to her again? Just let her keep thinking you're a sweet old man calling her to chat."

"I could share my philosophy," I said grimly. "Advise her to move to the Crossroads and stay drunk for a few years."

"Maybe she should. Look at the progress you've made, Thomas. You only sleep drunk in your truck once a week or so, now, and the local betting pool has lowered the odds on you killing yourself to one in a hundred. I shouldn't tell you this, but it used to be one in five."

"I'm honored."

"If you could talk to the old you, the one who barely made it through each day, what would you say? What kept you going?"

"I have a rule. If my hand trembles when I pick up the pistol I keep at my cabin, I'm not sure enough. Doubts will mess up even the most carefully planned suicide. It's hard to shoot straight if your hand shakes. I don't want to screw it up."

Delta slowly sat back in her chair, her mouth open in horror. "Dear Lord," she whispered.

I nodded. "You asked."

Her shoulders sagged. "Well, thank goodness, women don't shoot themselves."

113

"No, they swallow pills."

My tongue froze on the last word. Delta and I stared at each other. Delta said in a chilled voice, "Cathy's planning to kill herself."

I pulled a new cell phone out of my jeans' pocket. John had laminated a tiny picture of a goat's head on the back, inside a red circle with a slash across the goat's face.

I made a call.

Chapter 11

Cathy
Decision Time

It was after midnight. I came in from sitting by the pool. There's nothing like swilling a two-hundred-dollar chardonnay straight from the bottle. I had a pint of the finest aged bourbon waiting for me, next. Bourbon is the drink of morbid Southerners everywhere. The julep in the mint julep. The rebel in the yell. The moonlight in the magnolia. I was ready to go, and bourbon—along with the pain pills—would take me home.

My hair was nicely moussed and fluffed. It had finally grown out enough to hide my deformed ear, and I'd lacquered its dark curves into place. I'd done my makeup, at least on the unburned part of my face. My famous eyes looked big and sultry, though bloodshot. I was dressed in flowing silk pajamas—deep red, like a ruby. Over them I wore a gorgeous, kimono-like red robe. When the medical examiner's office leaked details of my suicide, they'd have to mention how elegant I looked. Gerald and his new girlfriend wouldn't be able to upstage me at my funeral.

"*Cobarde!*" Bonita yelled at me. *Coward.*

My trusted housekeeper stood in the middle of my bedroom suite, crying but furious. She shook my bottle of pills at me. "I found these hidden in your nightstand. My daughter died of an overdose! You know that! How could you consider doing such a thing to yourself! Have you not thought of how it would hurt the people who care about you? How dare you!"

115

In all the years she and Antonio had worked for me, Bonita had never pried into my personal belongings before. Who'd alerted her to the pills? No one knew about my stash. "Those are prescription," I insisted.

"Oh? The doctors stopped giving you these months ago." She tapped a fingernail on the bottle. "I see the date on this. You've been saving these up for . . . you know! Ah, *querita*! A million nuns could say prayers for you but it won't save you if you take your own life!"

"Episcopalians don't go to hell. We go to the country club."

"You admit it, then. You were going to kill yourself!"

"I kept the pills in case I had a headache."

"A headache? Oh, don't lie to me. My daughter used to lie to me. I should have seen the signs. And I should have done this for my daughter." She ran into my bathroom.

I followed her as fast as I could, weaving a little and holding onto furniture. When I heard the rush of water being flushed down the commode I yelled again, "They're prescription!"

Too late. I staggered into the commode room and watched my suicide dose swirl toward the Pacific. Bonita slammed the commode lid and faced me. "I know you can buy more," she said grimly. "The drug pushers in this neighborhood drive Mercedes and call themselves 'friends,' and hand out pretty pills in nice containers, but they're no better than the lowest street dealers. If you do business with them, Antonio and I will quit working for you. We'll leave."

"You can't leave me!" I sobbed.

She grabbed me in a hug. "We don't want to leave you, *querita*. But I won't risk walking into your room one morning and finding you dead from pills!"

"I just want to . . . stop hurting."

"I know, I know. Sssh." She helped me to bed, shoved all my books aside and held my hand as I huddled under the covers. "What am I going to do with my life?" I moaned. "I'm not good at anything besides being ornamental. I'm afraid of everything and everybody now, except you and Antonio. Who gave you the idea to look for pills in my room?"

"I'm not telling you."

"No one knew. No one."

"Maybe they guessed. Friends who have thought the same sad thoughts as you. Someone who knows how it feels to be in despair. You can't blame your friends for caring."

Delta? I thought. But she was the most cheerful, stable soul in the universe. No. She'd never had a suicidal thought. Thomas? A sweet, grandfatherly stranger who sent me photos of sunsets and flowers and close-up pictures of Granny Nettie's stained-glass windows? Thomas, who said to me at the hospital, *I used to think bad things only happened to other people. But they don't.*

He knew tragedy. He knew despair. Maybe he knew *me* better than I thought.

Thomas.

Thomas

My newest cell phone rang at five a.m. and scared me out of a nightmare. I had been choking in a cloud of dust, looking at my hands coated in ash and dried blood. Watching the towers fall, again. Unable to move.

"John?" I said the instant after I put the phone to my ear. "What's wrong?" By then I was already standing, naked, beside my bed. A raccoon and two possums scurried out the open door of my cabin, leaving an overturned trash can and empty Spam cans in the cold autumn moonlight.

"Thomas?" Cathy's voice. "It was you, wasn't it? You called my housekeeper earlier tonight. You told her to look for pills in my bedroom. You assumed I want to kill myself."

I inhaled sharply and dragged a hand over my face. "From the tone of your voice, I must have been right. You had pills. You intended to take them. Correct?"

"Prescription pills. Perfectly legitimate. You had no right to scare an employee of mine."

"Oh? Dead is dead, whether a doctor wrote the prescription or you bought it off a guy on a street corner."

"I'm not suicidal."

"Yes, you are."

"Are you psychic?"

"No, but I know how tempting it is to give up and die."

"If I do, I'm sorry, but it's none of your business."

"Yes, it is."

"You send me pictures, you've called me once on the phone. I appreciate your friendship, but you don't know the real me."

"I know you intended to take those pills. You might as well admit it."

"I am not going to admit anything. Why do you care so much? Have you got ulterior motives? What do you want from me?"

Everything, nothing. More than I can say. Keep it simple. "All right, if you really think I'm only interested in what you can do for me, I'll lay it on the line. I want to buy your grandmother's house."

Stunned silence. "My grandmother's . . . are you saying you've worked you way into my life over all these months because you want me to sell you her farm?"

"No, that's what *you're* saying. But since we're on the subject, you *should* sell me the farm. Why, not? You don't care about it, you don't want it. You and your father abandoned it."

"That's not true. He had someone maintain it. It was well-cared-for. He told me so. When he died a few years ago his business manager assured me the farm was in good shape."

"He lied, then."

"My father was *not* a liar."

"I'm afraid in this case he was. Look, you don't want the house? Great. Sell it to me. I'll buy it from you, restore it, cherish it."

"I see. It's true, then. You've been nice to me to get my house."

"No, you don't see, Cathy. Come here, and I'll show you. Then you'll see."

"I can't—" her voice caught. "I'd like to, but I just can't visit. You don't understand my problems."

"Yes, I do. I know how it feels to shut your eyes every night afraid you'll see and feel things you never wanted to remember. I know how it feels to go through every day wondering how you'll put one foot in front of the other. There's no easy way to overcome that. But you're not a coward. I know you're not. Anybody who could grit her teeth and make jokes while a nurse scrapes her raw skin . . . you're as tough as they come."

"How did you—you never talked to me during—" I heard her gasp. "That was you on the phone that day at the hospital. Not Gerald. You."

"Delta was desperate to get through to you, and I helped her. I didn't start out to deceive you, it just happened that way."

"You."

"Yes, me. And what I heard that day convinced me you've got the guts to survive. Don't give up now."

"After what I've learned tonight, why should I believe a word you say?"

"Do you care about your grandmother's legacy?"

"Yes. Despite what you think, I love her house, my memories of her, the freedom I had when I visited her . . . I love that place."

"Then believe this, if nothing else: If you kill yourself, I'll burn her house to the ground. Understand? If you die, everything you love—and everything she left for you to love—dies, too. I swear to you. If that's what it takes to keep you focused on living."

I heard her inhale sharply. "You're even crazier than I am."

"I've had years to practice."

"Everything I thought I knew about you is wrong. You're a sociopath. And an arsonist."

"You don't have to believe in me. I believe in you. Stay alive, come here to visit, and prove me right."

She hung up.

I looked down at myself. At least I had stopped her from taking the pills. I had saved her life, for tonight at least. That victory gave me the biggest erection of my life.

🌿🌿🌿🌿🌿

"You threatened to burn her grandma's house down," Delta repeated slowly, baring her teeth on each word. "To burn it. You threatened a woman who's been burned. You threatened to burn down her granny's house. *Thomas.*"

Surrounded. I stood in the café kitchen the next morning being eyeballed by Pike, Jeb, Becka, Bubba, Cleo, Santa. The entire Whittlespoon clan seemed to have come together in an impromptu jury, with me as the defendant. They were armed with paring knives and stew pots.

"Maybe it wasn't the best tactic," I admitted grimly, "but it got her attention. I wanted to make her mad, to shake her out of her depression for even a second, to make her think. The hardest thing to do when you're that miserable is to think clearly. You have to grab those quick moments of insight and hold onto them. I hope she does."

Silence. I couldn't tell if anyone understood my argument. Pike scowled. The others stared at the floor. Delta shut her eyes and stood with her hands on her hips, her head bowed.

Finally, Jeb raised his head and squared his jaw. "Tom's right. He did for Cathryn Deen the same thing he did for me when he crawled out on that cliff and talked me out of jumping. I won't tell y'all what he said. It's private. But he made me see the light."

What I'd said had been fueled by more vodka than anyone suspected. And it went something like this: *Jeb, goddammit, either jump or get out of the way so I can. You have a family to live for. I don't.* The fact that Jeb took that grim quip as an insightful bit of wisdom—a shared fate, a promise of brotherhood—had been pure good luck. Someone had been watching over Jeb and me that day. I wasn't sure I'd get that lucky, again. What had I accomplished last night? What if I provoked Cathy to shut me *and* Delta out?

"What if she won't take my phone calls anymore?" Delta said loudly.

"I'll call her and apologize. Right now. I'll do whatever it takes to calm her down."

"No. You've done enough damage. I doubt she'll ever listen to you, again. I'll call her. If she'll talk to me, I'll let you know what she says." She threw a biscuit at me. "Get out of my kitchen."

I nodded, grimly palmed the biscuit for Banger's breakfast, and walked out.

Cathy

My head pounded from the wine. My eyes were grainy from crying all night. Yet I felt oddly clean, as if I'd detoxed through my tears. Most amazing of all, I was mad as hell. Finally.

"Delta?"

"Cathy, I'm so glad to hear from you. About last night—"

"Does Thomas Mitternich run around the Crossroads without any kind of ankle bracelet or parole officer or keeper?"

"Thomas? Why, he's the sweetest . . . you sound different. Are you okay, honey? I'm sorry if he upset you. He was just trying to help."

"Upset me? He accused me of being suicidal."

"You sure you weren't?"

"He admitted he lied to get access to me from the start. And then he threatened to destroy my grandmother's house. He's obviously not who I thought he was."

"So you *were* going to kill yourself."

"I had a bottle of prescription pills. Prescription."

"Uh huh. Well, well. Thomas does have good instincts. And I have to say, it's good to hear you soundin' mad as an old wet settin' hen."

"I won't let him blackmail me with my grandmother's heritage."

"What are you planning to do?"

"First of all, I want to learn all about him. Starting with his full name."

"Mitternich," she said quickly. "Thomas Karol Mitternich. His daddy's people were Dutch, way back, from upstate New York. I don't know about his mama's people. She died when Thomas and his brother were little."

"Mitternich. Spell that for me, please." As she did, I typed it into my laptop. Thomas Mitternich. "All right, I gather he's not a native North Carolinian? Did you say he's from New York? How did such a maniacal Yankee end up in your community and win your friendship?"

For a moment there was silence on Delta's end. Then she said quietly, "I can tell you what I know about Thomas, but it'd be better if you read the whole story. Type his name into that, what is it, 'Google.' That's it. You do a Google search on Thomas Mitternich. See what the newspaper reporters wrote about him a few years ago."

I frowned. "He has a public record?"

"You could call it that. Just . . . go and read about him. It'll open your eyes a lot better than me jabbering about him."

"All right," I said slowly, bewildered.

"And Cathy?"

"Yes?"

"It's good to hear you sounding lively."

"I don't have any choice. My life has been invaded by this man."

"You might want to visit here as soon as you can, you know, so you can judge him for yourself. We never know what he's going to do next."

"Oh, don't you worry. I'll do whatever it takes to protect my grandmother's farm."

"Good! You stay riled up. Go and read about Thomas on the Google, and then come here and kick his butt. And honey?"

"Yes?" I was already clicking feverishly on the Google search button. I thought I heard her chuckle, but I was too busy tracking down information on my new nemesis, Thomas Mitternich, to ask what amused her so much.

"I'll have some biscuits ready when you get here," Delta said, "with extra gravy."

Chapter 12

Thomas
The News Articles

Heroes of 9/11:
Ordinary Citizens Showed Extraordinary Courage
Atrium News and Features

When they married, Thomas Mitternich, the son of a Brooklyn carpenter, convinced his wife, Sherryl, an heiress from New York's venerable Osken family, to leave New York's tony upper east side for the historic neighborhoods of lower Manhattan. The area offered the best of both worlds, he told her: old-fashioned charm with breath-taking views of skyscrapers, most notably, the World Trade Center.

Mitternich, 34, an award-winning young architect specializing in the preservation of historic buildings, kissed Sherryl and their three-year-old son, Ethan, goodbye the morning of September 11 as Sherryl put Ethan in a stroller. Sherryl had a 9 a.m. meeting with event coordinators at *Windows on the World*, the renowned restaurant at the top of the WTC's North Tower. She was planning a surprise birthday party for her sister, Manhattan socialite and business woman Ravel Osken Cantaberry. Pushing Ethan in the stroller, she'd walk the few blocks between the Mitternich condo and the twin towers

The Mitternichs loved living on the tenth floor of a former office building dating to the 1890's, which Thomas himself had restored for well-known Manhattan developers Schmidt and Roman. Working at home that morning, he could easily see the World Trade Center's main towers, north and south, from his office windows.

As Sherryl and Ethan headed for the condo's elevators, Thomas tucked Ethan's favorite toy—a vintage, metal dump truck Thomas had bought and restored—into his hands. Ethan smiled and asked if his father would take him and the dump truck to play in the park later. Thomas said sure.

When American Airlines Flight 11 struck the World Trade Center's North Tower, Thomas heard a muted boom and felt a tremor shake his drafting table. He looked up to see smoke boiling from the North Tower's top floors. He rushed down to the street and headed for the WTC on foot, while repeatedly trying to contact Sherryl via cell phone.

By the time he reached the WTC complex, panicked evacuees crowded the area. Thomas doggedly followed fire, police and paramedics toward the North Tower. Dust and smoke now clogged the air. Debris littered the streets, striking people as it fell. Horrifically, the debris included human body parts. Thomas was splattered with blood and tissue when a torso struck the pavement directly in front of him, disintegrating on impact. Shards of falling glass gashed the young architect's head, and a fist-sized chunk of metal glanced off his left shoulder, fracturing his collar bone.

Bleeding, injured, but determined to find his wife and son, Thomas made his way into the skyscraper. There, in the chaos of the lobby, his cell phone rang. It was Sherryl.

"I'm not sure which floor we're on," she said. "There's a lot of smoke, and it's getting hot. We're trying to make our way to the stairs."

"I'll find you, I swear, I'll be there as quickly as I can," Thomas told her. In the background, he heard their son crying. "Tell Ethan I'm not going to let anything happen to him. I promise."

He heard his child scream "Daddy," before the phone went silent.

Thomas raced up a stairwell as far as he could before being blocked by people descending—many hurt, bloody, and burned. Two firefighters from a ladder company were struggling to transport several badly injured office workers. "Your wife and son probably came down a different stairwell," one of the firefighters told Thomas. "The South Tower's been hit, too. It may collapse. This one, too. You've gotta get out of this building. You can't go any further up the stairs."

Unable to do more than pray his own family had escaped down a different stairwell, Thomas helped the firefighters carry victims to safety. He returned with the firefighters three times to assist other wounded evacuees, despite his own injuries.

He was carrying a young woman to paramedics on the street when the North Tower collapsed. Like many people that day, he stared in disbelief while the massive skyscraper imploded. Paramedics had to wrestle him into their ambulance as a tidal wave of choking dust filled the street.

He was determined to return to the tower, searching for his wife and son, even in the ruins.

❦❦❦❦❦

Firefighters Laud Civilians Who Came To Their Aid
PSR Northeast News

Thomas K. Mitternich has been named an honorary NYFD firefighter for assisting firefighters in the rescue of his fellow citizens on 9-11, and for extensive volunteer work at "the pile," as Ground Zero is known, in the weeks and months since. Mitternich continues to work exhaustively at the site, aiding searchers and coordinating information for survivors and their families.

Mitternich's wife and son remain missing.

❦❦❦❦❦

Photo, DNA Evidence Confirm Worst Fear For 9-11 Hero
North Press Correspondents

For Thomas Mitternich, one of the civilian heroes of 9-11 and an inexhaustible volunteer at Ground Zero ever since, it was the day he'd been dreading for over seven months.

The New York City Medical Examiner's Office, using DNA analysis and dental records, has confirmed the remains of Mitternich's wife, Sherryl, and son, Ethan. Adding to the tragedy, photography experts have conclusively identified Sherryl and Ethan as among the dozens of victims who lost their lives when they jumped from the towers. A cameraman at the scene snapped a picture of a woman clutching her small child as she leapt from a blown-out window of the North Tower. The woman is Sherryl

Mitternich. The child is Ethan.

"We don't classify the 9-11 jumpers as suicides," a spokeswoman said. "They had no choice. It was either die from the smoke and heat, be killed when the building collapsed, or jump. They knew help wasn't coming."

It is estimated that Sherryl, Ethan and other victims who leapt from the highest floors of the North Tower fell for as long as ten seconds before hitting the streets or plaza below. Although death was instantaneous on contact, experts admit many of the jumpers likely remained conscious during the fall.

Workers at Ground Zero last week presented Mitternich with a heartbreaking artifact recovered from the ruins: The mangled form of an antique toy truck he had lovingly placed in his son's hands that doomed morning.

Cathy

'The jumpers likely remained conscious during the fall.'

That one quote kept running through my mind. After I read the online articles about Thomas and his family, I lay flat on my back on the cool tile floor of my curtained balcony, dizzy with information overload. Thomas wasn't a grandfather, he was only in his late thirties. In grainy news photos that accompanied the articles I saw a tall, lean man with brown hair, solemn eyes, and a haunted expression. A man who was suffering. Yes, he wanted my grandmother's house, but he wasn't the kind of man who'd cheat or scheme to get it. And yes, he had saved my life. And he deserved better than the things I'd said to him. Infinitely better.

Slowly I got to my feet, pacing the shadowed space. The heavy canvas curtains moved slightly in a rare breeze, a dry puff of Southern California's baked air. Shards of light streaked the floor, then vanished as the panels shifted. I paced through the streamers of light, then in the dark they left behind.

His wife and son jumped. They were going to burn alive, so they jumped. He couldn't save them. Sherryl Mitternich took their son in her arms, and jumped. Jumped. And she knew she was jumping, and she had time to think about it all the way down. Holding her terrified son in her arms. If I were Thomas, one thought would never leave my mind. *Daddy, why didn't you save me and Mommy?*

I groaned and put my face in my hands. *If I don't get out of this house,*

I'm never going to have a life, again. I won't deserve to have a life. I'll never prove anything to Thomas. I'll never deserve his respect. Look what he's been through.

I rushed to the curtains. For months I'd never opened them, never stood there in the day light. Now I shoved them aside and grasped the balcony rail. The hot light of an L.A. afternoon washed over me. I looked wildly at the mansions on the hills below me, their manicured gardens peeking from under awnings and security fences. Every shrub might hide a long camera lens attached to a photographer.

"You don't scare me," I said aloud. "Go ahead and take a picture."

The voice was willing, but the knees were weak. They wobbled, and I feared I'd pitch over the rail from the unsteady force of my own panicked thoughts. I staggered into my bedroom and sat down at a desk.

My hands trembling, I typed in "Crossroads, North Carolina" on a satellite map search. No matches. Good. Delta's beloved mountain cove wasn't known in the stratosphere. How many places on Earth were *that* hidden? Sweating, I typed in the café's address. To the satellites and the post office, the Cove must exist only in the vicinity of greater Turtleville.

A satellite image filled my laptop's screen. Yes.

Forest. Nothing but forest and a few gray splotches where bald rock protruded from the green mountains. Zoom in once. A few tiny clearings appeared, scattered in the wilderness. Zoom in again. There was Turtleville, with its tiny streets, perched on a small river and served by only a few roads. And way over to the right, tucked among a ring of gray balds and blue-green vastness, was a small valley. The Cove!

I hovered a fingertip over the little houses and barns and fences. "That must be where Delta and Pike live, and that's got to be Jeb and Becka's house, and that's Bubba and Cleo's place, and way up there, that must be Santa's place. Delta's right. He does a good job hiding his marijuana patch."

Zoom in a third time.

A road. One tiny road. It must be the Trace. There. The café. And around it, a cluster of buildings, like wooden sperm snuggling up to an egg. The Crossroads Café. The center of comfort in my life. Delta and the café. The home of my biscuits, spiritual and otherwise. Now, having found the landmarks I needed, I could find Thomas and, next door, my grandmother's farm.

I guided the map to the northwest, holding my breath. When I saw two small islands in the sea of woodland, side by side but separated by a swath of green, I zoomed in one last time.

"Granny," I said softly. Her barn was clearly visible, but everything else was hooded in trees. The roof of her house could just be glimpsed through the giant oaks around it. Hidden.

No one could see me there. I could walk outdoors. I could sit under the trees, lay in the grass, dance in the pasture like a wild deer, and no one could take my picture. Not even satellites.

I moved the map a little and studied Thomas's clearing. Just the tiniest cabin. No shade trees, no major outbuildings, but . . . what was that geometric pattern in his pasture? I squinted. It looked like abstract trees, or maybe a pair of abstract arrows with a third one in the works. I sketched it on a notepad with a pencil I grabbed.

Whatever it was, it was beautiful. Ethereal. But it seemed to point next door. Toward my grandmother's house. Toward my heritage. Toward me.

I turned the laptop off and sat there, hugging myself, rocking.

You are going to North Carolina. You are going to prove you can take care of yourself without anyone's help. You're going to find out what you're made of, prove that you've got more to offer than a face. You are going to live at Granny's farm. You are going to be strong. You are going to show Thomas you won't give up on life, either. You are going to make him respect you as much as you secretly respect him. Or you are going to die trying.

PART THREE

A woman has got to be able to say, and not feel guilty, 'Who am I, and what do I want out of life?'

—*Betty Friedan*

The thing women have yet to learn is nobody gives you power. You just take it.

—*Rosanne Barr*

Chapter 13

Thomas
Thanksgiving

Cathy left Los Angeles without warning, the day after Thanksgiving. There it was seventy-five degrees and sunny. In the Cove it was thirty degrees and snowing. We didn't get serious snow more than a couple of times each winter, and usually not before January, but that fall the north wind howled down off Ten Sisters and Hog Back with a post-turkey-day vengeance.

"Her housekeeper will only say Cathy's 'moving,'" Delta told me in the café's kitchen, wringing a dish towel in lieu of her hands. "Cathy ordered her not to tell us where. The housekeeper says Cathy wants to disappear but let the paparazzi think she's still living in Los Angeles. She'll get in touch with us as soon as she's re-settled. What in the world do you think she's up to, Thomas?"

"If we can't find her, all we can do is wait."

Delta pointed sadly at a cardboard box on one of the kitchen's linoleum countertops. "I was just fixing her next box of biscuits. With turkey and dressing and pumpkin pie thrown in for the holidays."

"I know." I nodded at the manila envelope in my hand. "I was planning to send her pictures of the house covered in snow. Even though she thinks I'm a arsonist and a sociopath, I hope she can't resist the photos."

Delta looked away furtively. "Oh, I expect she's forgiven you. Or changed her opinion for the better, at least."

I arched a brow. "What have you done?"

"I just told her your full name. And suggested she Google you. Does it tickle when somebody Googles somebody? Sounds like it ought to."

The weight of a long, cold winter of memories settled on my shoulders. "You know I don't like—"

"She needed to see who you really are."

I shook my head and walked out on the café's front porch. Snow fell in large, soft flakes, hiding the mountains, even making it difficult to see the Trace. There wouldn't be any dinner customers, not tonight. The broad pasture of the Cove was a pure blanket of white. The November afternoon was fading into a silver, snowy white-out. I smelled wood smoke from chimneys, the clean scent of snow, the aroma of food. A cozy night for people and animals to gather together around warm hearths and full tables. A night for eating comfort food and for making love under soft, heavy quilts.

I hunched my shoulders, went to my truck, and drove home to the cabin. I needed to be alone, to study the inside of my own head and come to terms with solitude on a cold night. I'd pushed Cathy too hard, and it didn't help that Delta had clued her to my history. Cathy had enough on her plate without my hypocritical motivation speeches. *Architect, restore thyself, first.* She was probably out of the country, hiding in some European ski resort or on a private island, some place tropical. Contemplating killing herself where I couldn't intervene.

Cathy

"Are you certain there's an intersection somewhere in this valley, Ms. Deen?" my driver asked. "I can't see anything in this blizzard."

"Look for a group of buildings on the right." My teeth chattered from nerves. No, not nerves, terror. And exhaustion. I'd left my home in Los Angeles at dawn, L.A. time, in a delivery truck. I left California two hours later in a private jet. I left the Asheville airport at two p.m., East Coast time, in a full-sized black Hummer pulling a U-Haul trailer full of high-tech camping gear and accompanied by a second Hummer so my driver and bodyguards could leave the first Hummer at Granny's farm and return to civilization without me.

Team Pioneer Cathy, I called my group.

Pioneer. Right. I was dressed in wool with a GorTex vest over insulated fleece longjohns, my feet encased in heavy wool socks and waterproof hiking boots, my hands covered in wool gloves, and a colorful Aztec-design ski mask hiding my head and face. I looked like an overstuffed piñata, but at least I wouldn't have to worry about freezing to death in Granny's unheated house. I planned my journey into the wilds of the Blue Ridge mountains like an Arctic explorer planning a trek to the North Pole.

The only unpredictable element in the plan was me. After months of seclusion I took my fear of cars, fire, and publicity on an excruciating cross-country tour. I had so many bottles of tranquilizers in my purse it rattled when I reached for a tissue. Yet even with drugs to sustain me I'd suffered periodic panic attacks all day, and I was having one right now. In the old days I'd often joked, "Oh, I'm having a panic attack," and had assumed people who suffered from them just felt jittery. Now I knew better. It was as if someone shut off reality, oxygen and clear thought. I wanted to run, to escape—from what? To where? My heart raced, and a surreal and sinister kind of disconnect rose inside me, short-circuiting calm thought, putting me on automatic pilot. An attack lasted fifteen minutes on average, evaporating as quickly as it came, leaving me drained.

"Are you all right, Ms. Deen?"

"When you s-see the café, the grocery, the other little buildings," I said between chattering teeth, "that's the Crossroads. The actual intersection is on the f-far side of the café."

"It's four p.m. here. If we don't reach your grandmother's farm soon, it'll be dark. Are you sure you don't want to turn back to Asheville for the night, Ms. Deen?"

For a moment I hesitated. We'd just spent a hair-raising hour on a narrow two-lane climbing up and over the mountains that surrounded the Cove. Think 'roller coaster with no safety track.' Almost every curve was framed by sheer drop-offs on one side and craggy, perpendicular mountain rock on the other.

If you give up now, you'll never try again.

"I'm sure."

"All right. I'll radio the lead Hummer and tell them to keep going."

As he called the bodyguards at the head of my two-Hummer caravan, I wrapped my trembling hands tighter around the cold metal canister of a small fire extinguisher. It was my security blanket, just as the Hummer reassured me, a little, with its hard-to-roll-over-and-catch-on-fire attributes.

If this hulking, high-tech vehicle couldn't get me up to my grandmother's farm in this blizzard, I'd call the Pentagon and ask for a refund on my taxes. They'd designed Hummers to climb mountains, ford rivers, and roll across battle fields without losing so much as a lug nut off a wheel. It had better make it to Wild Woman Ridge.

"There's your café," the driver announced. "Looks pretty empty. No customers on a night like this."

I pressed close to the back seat's passenger window and peered through the snow. The café. *Oh, yes, it's adorable, and friendly, and everything I thought it would be.* Even in the fading light and whirling snow, with the parking lot empty and only a single light burning on the sign by the gas pumps, the Crossroads Cafe was a reassuring icon in my crazed journey.

You could stop right here, I told myself. *Go inside, surprise Delta, get a hug. She's a hugger, no doubt. And then she'd give you biscuits and gravy, and invite you to spend the night at her house.*

No. That would be taking the easy way out. I couldn't ask for help from Delta—or Thomas—I couldn't go back to Asheville and stay at a nice hotel, I had to make it all the way to my grandmother's house. If I walked into the café I'd be admitting I couldn't make it on my own. Even Delta would be embarrassed. *City girl shows up in a Hummer with bodyguards,* people would whisper. *In a blizzard, toting a fire extinguisher.*

I took another anti-anxiety tablet, trying to swallow it with a bone-dry mouth. The pills improved the brain's serotonin level. I must have enough serotonin to relax a rabid grizzly by now. Were there grizzlies here? No, just black bears. Harmless. All they'd do was raid the house, steal my food, and growl at me. *City grrrirl.*

Dread filled me again as the café and its world faded into the snowstorm. "There's the intersection," my driver announced. "We're, uh, turning onto that . . . trail?"

"Yes!" I craned my head to look between the front seats. "That's it! Ruby Creek Trail!" Thomas had refreshed my childhood memories with detailed and affectionate descriptions of the wilderness road to Granny's house, so I was fairly certain I could find the place. "Now all we have to do is follow Ruby Creek for about twenty minutes. When we come to a fork in the trail, take the trail to the left, up the ridge. It winds around and eventually comes out of the forest beside my grandmother's front pasture. We should be able to see the house from that point."

"Ms. Deen," my driver said, "Are you sure no one's been eaten by wolves around here, lately?"

"Not lately."

Yet my stomach curdled with fear as my Hummers and U-Haul turned off the civilized Trace onto its wild country cousin. The smooth ride became a bumpy one. The snowy, darkening forest closed around us. On the right, as we descended into a long hollow filled with towering, Christmas-like firs and rhododendrons, Ruby Creek appeared beside us, its shallow currents bubbling between snow-covered boulders.

I pressed close to the window. Granny Nettie had taken me panning for gemstones there! I'd found some small, gray baubles with just a hint of color peeking through. She polished them for me on her own grinding wheel. Even though they turned out to be little more than purplish pebbles, I had taken them home to Atlanta and kept them in my jewelry box. After she died I asked Daddy to have our jeweler make Granny's rubies into a bracelet for me. He said he would, but then he lost them. Or said he did.

I cried into my Aztec-inspired ski mask as the creek followed me to my grandmother's home, now my home, polishing the magic of things I had lost, or that had lost me.

❦ ❦ ❦ ❦ ❦

Twenty years after I watched my grandmother's odd and lovely little house disappear through the back window of my father's Mercedes for the last time, I stepped down into the ankle-deep snow of her front yard and looked up at the house again. It was shrouded in whirling snow, its low-pitched roof and thick, exposed rafters hidden in shadows, its lovely stained-glass-rimmed windows dark and frosted. It wasn't quite real, more of a mirror vision than actual stone-and-wood.

Four wide stone steps led up to the deep veranda. Snowflakes eddied beneath the broad shallow stone arch that shouldered the veranda's rustic eaves. That archway dressed up the bungalow with a kind of Arabian flair. I remembered being very small the first time I visited Granny, feeling awed by the entrance. I thought I had found the cottage of a sorceress in the wild woods. Maybe I had.

Abracadabra. Granny, I'm here. I'm back.

"Ms. Deen, do you want us to break the door lock?" one of my bodyguards said, shouting as if snow had volume.

I shook my head. "Let me look for the key, first."

My legs trembling, I held onto a snowy ledge of the thick stone walls that framed the steps. The security people dodged around me, beaming their flashlights along my path, stomping ahead of me to test the veranda's stone floor for ice. My heart in my throat, I halted before the broad front door. I recalled it being made of dark wood, with a beautiful horizontal rectangle of stained glass near the top. "This door looks like solid cherry," one of the men said to another.

"It is," I told them.

Aiming a small flashlight at the glass panel, I almost cried with happiness when I saw the intricate scene that had enthralled me as a child: a kaleidoscope of meandering creek, a glass collage of trees, and a background of sparkling green mountains. My grandmother had made this exquisite glass design herself.

It held the whimsical secret of the door key. Granny had taught me the poem so well I'd never forgotten it.

Third mountain to the left
Look due west of its crown
That's where the door key
Can always be found.

The bungalow's walls were covered in hand-cut cedar shingles stained dark brown. With the forefinger of my gloved hand I traced an imaginary line from the peak of the third stained glass mountain on the left to the nearest shingle beside the door frame. Holding my breath, I gently put my finger beside the shingle's bottom corner and nudged it sideways. Just as it had when I was a little girl standing on a milking stool to reach it, the shingle swung to the left.

And there, behind it, hanging on a small nail, was the door key.

Granny's voice might easily have been mistaken for a wisp of wind under the veranda eaves, but I swear I heard her whisper. *See? You never forgot this house, and this house never forgot you.*

Team Pioneer Cathy unpacked the U-Haul, did a quick reconnaissance tour of the yard and barn, then went over the house from the tip of its small, unfinished attic to the bowels of its stone-walled cellar, their heavy footsteps echoing on the empty hardwood floors. I stayed in the living room with all my supplies, opening boxes and unfurling a sleeping bag on a cot in the corner by the fireplace. I set battery-powered lanterns along the hearth and on the broad mantel. I was too nervous to notice many details, just an overwhelming impression of dark wood, stone, and windows with no curtains. Elliptical pools of high-tech lamp light made weird patterns on the wood-paneled walls and ceiling. Wind moaned in the chimney. An aging piece of plywood had been bolted across the front of the fireplace.

I kept eyeing that prohibitive screen. A fire would have been so warm, so cheerful.

So terrifying.

No fires. This house would be a flame-free zone. I patted my ski mask. I'd rather shiver.

I pulled a hammer and nails from the boxes, along with several wool blankets. I nailed them over the windows. I remembered the house filled with sunlight during the daytime, cozy furniture, paintings, whimsical pottery, and lit at night by flickering yellow light from beautiful old kerosene lamps. Without my grandmother's furnishings in it, the house felt like a wooden mausoleum. I'd save a thorough exploration for morning.

Team Pioneer Cathy returned from securing the perimeter. "Where are the light switches, Ms. Deen?" the leader asked.

"There aren't any. My grandmother never installed electricity."

"Bathroom?"

"Chamber pots and a wash stand. For serious business, she used an outhouse."

"Ms. Deen, we did a quick survey of the yard. There's no outhouse. Not even a pile of debris where one used to stand."

I shook my head. "It's out there somewhere. My father rented this house to tenant farmers after my grandmother died. They lived here up until a few years ago. There has to be a relatively new, intact outhouse."

"No, ma'am."

Another unfriendly surprise, like the plywood-barricaded fireplace. Ohhh-kay. I'd improvise. "Well, I've got my handy-dandy portable chemical toilet in a box here, somewhere. I'll set it up and find the outhouse later."

"Ms. Deen, do you have any idea where to find clean, running water? There's only a small hole in the wall over the kitchen sink. Someone covered it with a piece of wood."

I frowned. "There should be a pump-handled spigot." I made pumping gestures. "You know. Old-fashioned. Pump the handle, water eventually comes out. There's a rain cistern outside with a pipe that runs straight to the kitchen wall. You can see it from the kitchen window. I used to climb the cistern and sit in the water. Just like the girls on *Petticoat Junction*. Remember that show? I watched all the re-runs."

"Maybe there used to be a cistern, but it's not there now. And from the looks of the patch on the kitchen wall, there hasn't been a faucet of any kind over the sink for a lot more than a few years."

My heart sank. Thomas had been right. My father lied to me about taking care of the farm. Daddy wanted to make certain no one, including me, preserved the homeplace of Mother's embarrassingly backward mountain family. "Well, I've got plenty of bottled water to drink," I said cheerfully. "And plenty of snow to melt for washwater. There's also a well out in the yard, with a pretty well house . . ."

Their shaking heads told me that was gone, too. I took a deep breath. "I'll have someone drill a new well. In the meantime, please tell me there's still a small pond on the far side of the barn. It was spring-fed, and my grandmother raised catfish there." Nods. "See? I have a pond. Plenty of water."

The men looked doubtful, but they helped me unpack a few boxes of food and water, and set up my toilet in one corner of the living room. They screwed a heavy-duty latch bolt on the back door to replace its flimsy hook-and-eyelet, and, finally, made sure all the windows were firmly latched. "We could nail these shut," one said.

The thought made me see woozy stars for a second. How would I escape in a fire? "No nailed windows," I said. The men looked disappointed. "Please change your mind and come back to Asheville, Ms. Deen," the leader urged. "When I worked for Halliburton in Iraq I saw bunkers in the desert that were more modern than this place."

"My grandmother lived here happily all her life. My grandfather died young, and after my mother left home to marry my father Granny stayed here all alone. When I visited she left the windows open and never locked the doors. She felt perfectly safe." *And so did I.*

"Did she die of natural causes?"

"She died of a stroke while leading an anti-Reagan rally in Asheville. Look, I appreciate your concerns, but I'll be fine. Now, get going. You've got a thirty-minute drive on a snowy trail just to reach the paved road in the Cove. And then an hour on the mountain road. Get out of here before dark. Save yourselves! Just kidding. Remember, I've got friends in the Cove, if I need help."

Not that I'll ever ask for it, I added silently.

Team Pioneer Cathy sighed, gave up, rummaged in the boxes, and presented me with a surprise gift: a shotgun and two boxes of shells.

"How sweet," I said. "Thank you, guys. Whatever I kill first, I'll have it stuffed and send it to you."

At least they didn't have to teach me how to use the gun. One of my aunts had been a champion skeet shooter, and she'd taught me the basics of gun etiquette. Of course, I didn't have her accoutrements, but does a gal really need a diamond bracelet with an NRA charm, a shaker of martinis, and a custom shotgun with a monogrammed mahogany stock?

I shooed Team Pioneer Cathy onto the veranda and then waved them goodbye. But as the spare Hummer's taillights disappeared into the snow and the darkness, my chirpy assurance faded and reality set in. Talk about living off the grid. The cold mountain night crept close around me, leaned over my shoulder, sniffed me like a meal, and whispered, *Fire didn't do you in, but ice just might.* The wind whipped wet flakes through the holes of my mask, planting cold, wet kisses on my eyes and mouth.

I looked around fearfully. Was this adventure a call to self-sufficiency or an idiot's guide to self-destruction?

My hands shook as I turned off my flashlight to test the full effect of aloneness atop Wild Woman Ridge. Oh, yes, this was the darkness I remembered from my visits as a child. Not just dark, but dark-dark. Dark-of-the-womb dark. No streetlights, no road sounds, no sirens, no distant glow of city lights, no nothing. Just me and my scars and my phobias and my proud notion that I would show Thomas Mitternich a thing or two about strength of character.

A little door opened in my brain. The hinges creaked. Diaphanous spider webs stretched tight on the door knob. A sign over the door said, *Primitive Superstitions, aka Creepy Shit You Don't Want To Think About.*

These ancient Appalachians brimmed with ghost stories, witch stories, hauntings and risings, spirit panthers screaming in the forest, spirit lights dancing in the hollows, encounters with Beelzebub. The kind of stories suburban kids tell each other over flashlights at a pajama party, only these were worse, because here in the mountains they were based on real history.

And their sources were buried nearby.

Oh, God. I'd forgotten about the Nettie cemetery in the woods behind the house. Dozens of Netties, going back to the eighteen-hundreds, were all buried in a pretty clearing where my grandmother had planted so many jonquils the graves became a sea of fragrant yellow blooms every spring. There were pioneer-settler Netties under pitted, fading tombstones, modern Netties under fancy granite pediments, baby Netties under cherubs, even favorite Nettie dogs and cats and one very special goat under flat rocks with their names chiseled on them.

The only two Netties who weren't buried there were the two whose spiritual surveillance I needed most: Mother and Granny. Mother was buried in the Deen section of an Episcopal church in Atlanta, and Granny was buried in the graveyard of the Methodist church in Turtleville. Daddy and I were in Europe on vacation when she died, so Daddy said there was no way we could get home in time for the funeral and no way he could plan an old-fashioned burial in the isolated Nettie cemetery. Or perhaps he didn't want to honor a custom that he saw as archaic and even primitive, like the Nettie heritage in general.

"Granny? Mother?" I whispered in the darkness. "I realize spirits don't have geographic concerns, but I really wish you were within walking distance right now, because at the moment I'm recalling some fairly lurid details about our dead-Nettie heritage."

Hadn't the ghost of Granny Nettie's brother wandered the hollow of Ruby Creek with a grisly head wound, searching for the rival who had murdered him over a woman? Hadn't Granny turned from her kerosene kitchen stove one sad morning in 1946 to see a small, playful handprint in the biscuit dough on her kitchen table, the kind of handprint my mother's elder brother, Lucas Nettie, liked to press into the pristine dough to tease her, only little Lucas had died the week before, of meningitis? Hadn't she seen Grandpa Nettie standing in the pasture hours after he was shot dead? Hadn't she seen the Cherokee spirit of her mixed-race great-grandmother floating along the deer paths of these woods, moaning for the full-blooded relatives the army had sent on the Trail of Tears?

Granny had related those stories to me with matter-of-fact sincerity and no trace of morbid concern. "There's a difference between ghosts and spirits," she explained. "Ghosts are just lost souls, but spirits let you know they're around for a reason. To teach you something and to comfort you."

At the moment I didn't feel comforted by any possible ectoplasmic sightings, no matter how Granny categorized them. I stared into the black portal of the front yard, hearing the skeletal fingers of the big oaks click and rustle in the wind, sensing generations of my mountain kin in the shadows, waiting for me to cut and run.

I don't want to see dead Netties.

Above my head, something growled.

I leapt inside the doorway, switched the flashlight on quickly, grabbed the unloaded shotgun, then wobbled the flashlight toward the veranda's rafters. Two beady black eyes stared down at me. A small raccoon was overnighting the storm in a nook of the rafters. He growled again. No, not a growl; okay, it was more like a frightened chuckle.

I sagged a little. "At least you're not dead and not a relative."

I backed slowly into my new home, shut the door, locked it, loaded the shotgun, set it on the hearth next to my cot, stuffed several pillows behind my sleeping bag so I could prop up, then crawled into the bag still fully clothed, including a fur-lined parka. I pulled the bag all the way up to my nose. Peering out, I waited sleeplessly for dawn.

Pioneer Cathy had arrived.

Thomas

As the snowy post-Thanksgiving night settled in, I lay on my bed in the firelight of my cabin, wondering where Cathy was and still kicking myself for provoking her to leave Los Angeles. My cabin, or, as I called it, Chateau de Vodka, felt claustrophobic that night. If I calculated the physics of my own saliva just right, I could spit all the way from one end to the other. *That* small. When the cell phone buzzed on the kitchen table, I finished poking a log in the fireplace, tossed back a double shot of vodka in a coffee mug, rolled across the bed and picked up the phone without ever taking a full step.

Pike drawled in my ear. "Thomas, did you see anybody turn up Ruby Creek Trail as you were heading home?"

"No. Nobody and nothing. Why?"

"Aw, Falter Perkins was out 'taking some fresh air'—meaning he was turkey-hunting out of season, in the snow, so the game warden couldn't see his tracks—and he swears he heard heavy trucks—or something that sounded like heavy trucks—pass by on the creek road. This would have been right before dusk."

"I left the café before then. Didn't see anybody headed that way."

"Oh, well. Ever once in a while some ignorant yahoo tries to use the creek road as a short cut to Turtleville. They get to the fork and realize they're in the middle of the mountains with not even a road left, much less a town. Only an idjit would head out that way in the snow and the cold, with it getting dark."

I stood up. Vehicles on the creek trail worried me. "I'll go over and check," I told Pike.

"Are you nuts? Your piece-of-shit vintage truck doesn't have four-wheel drive. You'll get stuck and then it'll be *my* butt out in the snow giving you a ride home. Delta and I are just about to get in bed with a pumpkin pie, a bottle of Apple Jack and a copy of *Playboy*. Snowy weather and holiday leftovers brings out the beast in that woman."

"Don't worry about me. I'll break out my vintage snow chains." I said goodbye and tossed the phone back on the table. I started pacing. Three strides one way, three strides back. Hamsters on tread mills had more options. Outside, snow filled the gloom with cold crystals of isolation. I pictured Cathy on a private beach somewhere, hiding from prying eyes in a cabana, distrustful and alone, watching a distant ocean on a white-sand shore.

Her grandmother's house was my best hope of keeping her alive and in touch. So what if I was overprotective? No one but me would know I'd made a crazy trip out in the snowstorm to check on the place.

No one but me.

🐾🐾🐾🐾🐾

Damn. Tire tracks on the road up to the Nettie house. The falling snow hadn't quite filled them in. They made broad parallels in the beam of my truck's headlights. What the hell was this invader driving—a tank?

I downshifted for traction as the truck followed the tracks up a slushy path to the broad knoll of the farm. Firs and cedars, heavy with snow on their evergreen boughs, leaned over the trail. They whacked the truck's windshield and grabbed at its heavy-duty wipers. The aged wipers fought back and won.

Good craftsmanship was built to survive. I pulled a vintage World War II pistol from a cloth sack on the seat. Good craftsmanship would also give trespassers a need for clean underwear.

I switched off the headlights as the truck crested the knoll. I rolled down my window, hung an arm out, and used a flashlight to creep along the final yards until the trail left the woods. On my left appeared the leaning chestnut posts of the front pasture. I guided the truck along that fence line until it reached a corner. I was now at the edge of the barn yard. Fifty yards further and I'd come to the shrubs and walkway of the house. I parked the truck, tucked the gun inside a deep pocket of my sheepskin coat, snugged the brim of an old fedora low over my eyes, and moved through the falling snow with just a pinpoint of flashlight in front of my boots. I followed the mysterious tire tracks to a hulking black Hummer under the front oaks.

Whoever owned this gas-sucking suburban Panzer meant business. North Carolina tags. Buncombe County. That meant Asheville. A rental, maybe? The photographers I'd chased off months ago? Maybe they thought they could sneak past us hicks in a snowstorm and prowl around Cathryn's property to their hearts' content. Maybe photographers had sniffed out her departure from Los Angeles and were stationing themselves anywhere they might ambush her, no matter how remote the chance.

I'd do a little ambushing of my own.

I circled the house, noting the faint glow behind the covers someone had placed on the living room windows up front. The windows of the dining room, kitchen, and two bedrooms were dark and curtain-free, as always. I halted by each, glancing inside quickly. Dark, empty rooms looked back. All right.

For the past four years I'd treated the Nettie house as my own private stomping ground. I wasn't a thief, I wasn't a vandal, I was a volunteer caretaker. I'd jimmied every window open, picked the front door lock, wandered the house at will. I knew what was stored in the attic, and in the cellar. I knew which windows creaked when I opened them, and which floorboards squeaked under my feet.

I knew how to slip inside silently.

There was no lock on the screen door of a tiny, covered porch sandwiched between the back bedroom and the kitchen. The blueprint for this Sears bungalow called it a sleeping porch; it was just six by eight feet, and Delta said Mary Eve had only bunked there on the hottest summer nights. Both the bedroom and kitchen looked into the porch via small windows. I'd recently repaired the sash weight on the window of the bedroom side, so I knew it would open without a sound. I popped the latch with the blade of my pocket knife, then eased the window up. Sticking my head into the dark room, I held my breath and listened.

No sounds came from the front of the house. Good. I might catch the trespassers asleep. Latching my hands atop the window frame, I levered myself inside, settling lightly on the bedroom floor. The house was solid; the joists strong. The wide maple floorboards had been fitted as seamlessly as jigsaw pieces.

Solid craftsmanship doesn't squeak when you walk on it.

Moving one slow step at a time, I entered the house's central hallway. It gave me a clear view straight to the living room up front. Through the doorway I saw an odd assortment of stacked boxes near the front door, with a single small lantern giving off a white glow. The rest of the living room was steeped in darkness.

I walked up the hall, listening hard. No snoring, no conversation, no rustle of book pages turning, no low melody of a CD player or radio. Briefly I touched the gun in my coat pocket, but left it there. The old man had taught John and me the hard rules about handguns and rifles, the first one being, *Only fucking morons pull a piece on somebody if they don't intend to shoot,* with the second rule being, *Don't be a fucking moron.*

I passed the kitchen and dining room doors on the left, and the front bedroom door on the right. Two more soft steps and I'd stand in the living room doorway. Just stand there and confront whoever had had the balls to set up housekeeping in this very private, very special place.

One step. I picked up my foot to take the next one.

I heard a soft, well-oiled click behind me. Something hard prodded the middle of my back. I froze. A husky female voice said calmly, "You have to ask yourself one question. 'Do I feel lucky?' Well, do ya, punk?"

A woman. A woman . . . quoting Clint Eastwood in a *Dirty Harry* movie. I knew that throaty voice. Goosebumps scattered up my spine. It couldn't be. Could it?

"Hello," I said quietly. If we were quoting schlock lines from movies, I'd do my part. "People of Earth, I come in peace."

"Go ahead," she answered. "Make my day."

"What we've got here is a failure to communicate."

"I shot a man in Reno, just to watch him die. This is a gun against your spine."

"I thought you were just happy to see me."

"Turn around. Slowly."

I pivoted inch by inch, my hands lightly spread by my sides. My heart raced, my head buzzed with a strange mixture of concern and exhilaration. Finally, in the shadowed hallway, I looked down at the oddest sight—a slender creature in a furry parka, her face and head hidden by a colorful ski mask, staring up at me with big, fearless green eyes, while pointing a shotgun at the center of my chest.

Cathy.

I knew how I must look to her, tall, bearded and shaggy, my face hooded by the fedora, a hulking figure in the heavy sheepskin coat. It would be entirely understandable if she pulled the shotgun's trigger. *Keep it light. Keep it casual.* "Of all the gin joints in this town," I said in a Bogart-ish tone, "why did you have to move into your grandmother's house without telling me?"

Those amazing green eyes swept over me, studied me, narrowed, widened. She took a step back. The shotgun wavered, lowered. Her soft, full lips parted in an *oh* of amazement. "Thomas?"

Now it was my turn to stare in surprise. She'd seen no recent photos of me and had only heard my voice what, three times by phone? "How did you know?" I asked.

She tilted her head. Her eyes became solemn, reserved, but shimmered with tears. "Your voice is special," she said. A pause. "You had me," she quoted gruffly, "at hello."

❦❦❦❦❦

The emotional simplicity of that night, when Cathy and I met face-to-face, or rather, face-to-ski-mask, for the first time, defies easy description. In philosophical design terms a house isn't just walls and a roof, it's the spaces those walls and that roof enclose. There's the miracle of basic physics, the magic of perfect joinery, but also the zen of defined air. Call if 'flow' or 'feng shui' or just good architectural instincts, but when a design is right it makes you take a deep breath, slowly and evenly, then exhale and relax. You don't have to think. You're part of the house, now. The house tells you what to do.

Our design was right, Cathy's and mine. Our house made it easy.

"No need to explain anything tonight," I said after she lowered the gun. "Mind if I lay down on the floor of the back bedroom before I faint? I'm not accustomed to being threatened with a shotgun." *Or falling deeper in love at first sight.*

"You're staying?" she asked, tilting her head.

I nodded. "Even you change your mind about shooting me, I'm not leaving you alone here tonight."

She pondered me another second, those amazing eyes giving my motives an unfettered once-over, then she nodded. "You shouldn't go back out in this snow. I'm surprised you made it here at all. Do you have four-wheel-drive and snow tires?"

"No, I have a nineteen-forty-five Chevy truck with a can-do attitude and nothing left to lose."

She put the gun aside, brought me some blankets and a bulky backpack, and said, "That's full of bagged granola. It's all I have. I'm afraid it'll make a crunchy pillow."

"No problem. I have a crunchy head. Thanks. See you in the morning."

I went into a back bedroom and lay down in the dark on the blankets, with the granola under my head, and stared at the ceiling in wonder. *She's really here.* I heard her move around the living room, I heard her scuff the old wood floors as she climbed into her makeshift bed. A comfortable silence folded into the shadows, security radiated from the togetherness.

For the first time in twenty years, the first time since Mary Eve Nettie's death, her house nurtured life inside it. Mine and Cathy's. Together.

It was as simple as that, that night.

Cathy

Thomas won me when I stared at him over the barrel of a shotgun and he looked back without anger, fear, or any other discernible emotion except an intense need to make certain I was safe. I knew how ridiculous I looked in the ski mask, but he didn't laugh.

He won me with his determination to save me from myself, he won me with his haunted hazel eyes and with his penchant for saying the right wise-ass thing at the right moment. He smelled of fragrant woodsmoke that made me want to burrow under his beard and listen to his heartbeat, and he had the perfect touch of insanity. After I almost shot him, he said in perfect accord with the horror of near-death, "Mind if I lay down on the floor of the back bedroom before I faint?" and when I gave him several wool blankets and a brand-new backpack full of bagged granola for a pillow, he nodded *adieu* and left me alone as if nearly being shot were no big deal.

I loved him. I didn't know him well enough to believe any different. I loved his deep, gentle voice. I loved his compassion. I loved his wicked sense of humor. I loved him for suffering for his wife and son. I loved him for saving me from swallowing a bottle full of pills, I loved him for braving a snowstorm to check on my house, I loved him for admitting he wanted the house, not me. Honesty is a powerful aphrodisiac.

Was there chemistry, was there sex underneath the surface? Absolutely, at least on my side of the equation. But my sexual circuits had been scrambled for months, and I didn't trust them. Every time I touched myself with my scarred right hand I lost interest. I thought of scars, not orgasms. When I thought of a man, any man, touching me, I winced. So, for me, Thomas was the distant thunder of a storm I wanted to avoid.

Chapter 14

Cathy
The Next Morning

Still fully dressed and wearing my ski mask, I crawled out of my sleeping bag, tiptoed to the hall doorway, tilted my head, listened to the sound of Thomas snoring—I love to hear men snore—and then I walked to the corner of my living room where the portable commode sat out in unsheltered glory, and I looked down through the seat into a bucket of pristine, bright-blue chemical water, and I thought about the noise it would make, and I said to myself, "Maybe I'll just pee in the yard," so I walked outside.

The moment I stepped off the veranda's stone stairs, I halted in wonder. I was on the set of an old-fashioned Technicolor movie. The sky was so blue, the snow was so white, my breath made perfect silver clouds in the air. The expanse of white pasture and the snowy alley of forest led my eyes straight to the frosted backbone of Hog Back Mountain. I turned slowly, taking in the huge oaks of the yard, the weathered barn with its snowy tin roof, and finally, the house. Roofed in a perfect layer of snow, it looked as if someone had made it out of dark gingerbread with white icing.

There were no ghosts, no, that morning there were spirits, comforting spirits everywhere, welcoming me to the cold, clean vista of my new life.

Be real. The only comforting spirit around here is alive and asleep in your back room. Once planted, that thorny thought refused to evaporate. I hiked to a cluster of wild rhododendrons, uncovered my necessary parts, squatted grimly, melted some snow, re-dressed and kicked fresh snow over the spot the way dogs fling dirt with their hind feet. I marked my territory.

Thomas walked out onto the veranda as I reached the bottom steps. No coat, no hat, just a vision of faded flannel and worn jeans and heavy boots, long legs, great shoulders, glossy brown beard, a foot-long brown ponytail, and those haunted, warm eyes. He nodded solemnly. "Morning."

"Good morning." I pointed over one shoulder. "Those rhododendrons are mine."

"I claim the Rose of Sharons."

I nodded back. We passed each other politely, like commuters headed in opposite directions on the subway stairs. I went inside, he went to see a man about some shrubs.

I felt immediately and eminently comfortable with him, and yet excruciatingly aware that he had not yet seen one single, scarred part of me. Or even an unscarred part. Even my hands. I was wearing gloves.

I intended to keep it that way.

"I made breakfast," I said when he walked back into the living room. I held out a protein bar. "Low carb."

He tucked it in his shirt pocket. "Hmmm. Reminds me of the processed meal bars mom used to make. Let's go down to the café and share the recipe with Delta."

"We need to talk about that. I want your word that you won't tell Delta or anyone else I'm here. I'll make my debut when I'm ready."

"All right. You have my word. But give me an estimated time of arrival."

"When my protein bars and crunchy granola runs out."

"That could take years."

"Thomas, I appreciate everything you've done for me. But I need to be alone up here. This is probably the only place in the world where no one can find me and where I can find out if I'm more than a pretty face. Do you understand? It's nothing personal, but I don't want your help again. Or Delta's."

I expected an argument, a defense, a call to lean on his broad shoulders. Instead he blew out a long breath. "Good. If I leave now I can get down to the café for breakfast. I mean, in addition to eating your delicious protein bar. Just let me grab my coat and hat." He walked down the hall while I pivoted to gaze after him, open-mouthed. He whistled as he went.

Be careful what you ask for.

I frowned and began opening boxes. Protein bars, lots of them. Bottled water. Instant coffee. Why, *that* would be tasty with cold water. He walked back into the living room, his coat in place, his hat in his hands.

"There are boxes full of your grandmother's housewares in the attic," he said. "Your father hired someone to clean out the house when she died, but Delta and a few other friends rescued most of the little things, and stored them. The basement is in good shape. It doesn't leak, there are no critters living in it, and there's plenty of shelving for storage. You'll find cases of your grandmother's canning jars down there, and an empty coal bin, but not much else. The barn is empty. You can park your Hummer in it if you want to. You'll find some bags of corn in the feed crib, and an old bucket. I throw out corn for the wildlife whenever I'm here. If you do it regularly, you'll get deer and turkeys in the front yard every morning and every evening."

"Does the raccoon always hang out in the veranda rafters?"

"Most nights. His name is Fred, but he'll answer to Louise, BarFace, Fuzz and 'Hey, Thing.' He likes leftovers. You can leave them on the edge of the steps and he'll thank you for it."

"I'll set out my best china for him."

"Now, about heat."

"Heat?"

"The fireplace is safe. I pried that plywood off it during the summer, cleaned the chimney, even built a few small fires in it as a test. It's well-designed. Pulls a strong draft. There's an old stack of firewood in the barn. Oh, and the Franklin stove your grandmother had in the kitchen for heat? Delta rescued it when your father sold off the household goods, and it's in the corner of the enclosed porch room at the café. She fires it up every night in the winter. Uses hickory chips. Customers love it. I can find Delta a replica and you can have the original back."

I had gone very still during the heat discussion. Cold needles scratched my forehead. When I didn't say anything, Thomas drew a deep breath. "Sorry. I should have thought before I suggested—"

"I don't . . . build . . . fires. Ever."

"I'm sorry. But Cathy, you have to try. You'll freeze up here."

"Not as long as I have GorTex and wool."

"How about a propane space heater?"

"Nothing with a flame. Discussion closed. Okay?"

Maybe it was the strain in my voice or the twitch beside my left eye. He let the subject drop. "If you have an emergency," he said gently, "Call Delta. If you don't show up at the café within a couple of weeks, I'll drive up here and see if I can find your body."

Oh, he was good. Nonchalant, business-like, with just a fine, spicy edge of sardonic wit. He restored me. I clucked my tongue at him. "Don't sound so hopeful."

"As one loner to another, I understand the consequences. You gotta do what you gotta do, even if it's self-destructive."

"If you discover my gnawed corpse in a wolf's den, please don't naturally assume I threw myself into its jaws in a fit of suicidal despair. Don't burn this house down out of spite. I recently changed my will to leave it to you."

He went very still. His eyes pulled me apart, looked inside my loyalties, assessed the enormity of what I'd just said. "You're not kidding." His voice was stunned.

"Not kidding. No."

"Cathy, that's not what I—"

"Spare me your slavish gratitude. My point is, you won't burn this house down if it belongs to you, will you?"

Slowly, he exhaled. His jaunty expression returned. "I'm sorry, but you and I made a deal. You die, the house burns."

"That's not how your original threat went."

"I just amended it."

"You're serious. You're really serious."

"You bet. If you kill yourself deliberately, or even if you're just careless—say, you stub your toe and fall off the back steps with fatal consequences, or a rabid squirrel bites you, or you're hit by a meteor—whatever. This place is toast."

"I came here to protect it from you."

"Good. Go ahead and do that. Stay alive."

"You don't think I can live here, do you? You don't think I have the ovaries to thrive and survive."

"The what?"

"Men have balls, women have ovaries."

"On the contrary, I know how tough you are. That's why I respect your decisions and won't insult you with patronizing advice."

"Oh, really? Even if you secretly don't think I can actually survive in your beloved mountains? But I *am* my grandmother's granddaughter."

"Good. Live up to her legend. She made it through some rough winters on this ridge, alone. She chopped firewood and shoveled coal, she hunted deer and turkey for food, she grew her own vegetables, she raised chickens and goats. By all accounts she was a strong woman who survived a lot of hard knocks and never gave up her faith in what was beautiful."

"She was a farmer/artist," I countered. "She panned for rubies and made jewelry."

"All of the above and then some. She appreciated the simple act of survival."

"Exactly how seriously do you rough it in Zen-like purity over at your cabin, Mr. Mitternich?"

"Me? I've got no electricity, no indoor plumbing, and I use a fireplace for heat. Under a lean-to on the back side, there are three cords of firewood I chopped myself. My fireplace puts out approximately a five-foot radius of heat on a cold night. In this weather I sleep under five blankets, and I'm wearing thermal longjohns. Do you think you could live like that?"

I shifted guiltily inside my GorTex, wool, and chem-pak foot warmers. "I think you'd be surprised."

"You can always go down to the Cove and stay with Delta. She has a big house, a nice guest room, you'd have lots of privacy and all the comforts of home. Plus biscuits."

"So much for respecting my decisions and not patronizing me."

"I'm giving you information. What you do with it is up to you."

"You refuse to picture me living in my grandmother's house and being happy here."

"It's a quiet place. Some day, when you're ready, you'll want to be part of the world again. You'll leave."

"What about you, Thomas? How long are you planning to hide in these mountains?"

"Four years ago I bought an old motorcycle and left New York with no aim other than to end up dead somewhere. Instead, I ended up here. The jury's still out on my future."

"If you owned this house, what would *you* do with it?"

"Restore it. Clean it, refinish a lot of the wood, but otherwise leave it as-is. Fill the house with Craftsman-era furniture."

"And live here?"

"I don't think of it in terms of living in it. I just want to make certain it's protected."

"So what would you do with it?"

"Get it listed on the historical homes registry. Turn it over to a conservation group who'd preserve the land and use the house in some dignified way."

"Doesn't the house deserve to be a home, again? Not just restored, but modernized for comfortable living? That would be the best of both worlds, it seems to me."

"Modern living is overrated. And I'm not looking for a home."

"I see. You wouldn't put in electricity or plumbing?"

"No."

"Not even a nice flush toilet?"

"I'm a purist."

"I guess this quells any thoughts I had about hiring you to design my renovation."

It was hard to see his expression through a beard, a mustache, and the low brim of a fedora, but I was pretty certain he lost a little color. "Renovation?"

"Delicately and discreetly done. I promise you."

"I'll supervise. For free."

"I'll think about it and get back to you."

My heart sank at the concern in his eyes. I'd never competed with a house for a man's attention before. I sagged a little. "Thomas, I'm not going to do anything without your input. If it weren't for you, this house might be in ruins now. Thank you for taking care of it. Let's talk more about how to restore it after I settle in."

His eyes, which had been grim, softened. "You play fair. Thank *you*."

"In your experience, do most women *not* play fair?"

"Aw, just when you and I were getting to be friends again."

"All right, all right. Gender politics can be debated another day." When he looked at me with a thoughtful frown, I squinted at him righteously. "I know a few big words. I never went to college because I was making multimillion dollars as an actress by then, but I can spell my own name and even count to ten without using my fingers."

"Speaking of your fingers, are you going to wear gloves all the time? Not to mention that ski mask?"

He prodded me where it hurt. I couldn't joke about my scars with him. "It's time for you to leave," I said quietly.

"Have you not been outside with your face uncovered since the accident? Not even once?"

My heartrate picked up. "I've had . . . publicity issues."

"Not anymore. Not here. This is private. You're among friends. If you don't free yourself from—"

I began backing up. "I'm not a building you can restore. Sorry."

He took a step toward me. He held out a hand. "The Parthenon. The Roman Coliseum. The Liberty Bell. All are more interesting because they're not perfect anymore. Give me the ski mask, Cathy."

Alarm burst my veins and flooded my bones. My heart drummed a spot above my left breast. I took two more stumbling steps backward, my hands up, warding him off. He didn't grab at me, he didn't lunge, he simply advanced, his hand out stubbornly. "Take off the mask, Cathy."

"Get away from me!"

"I know you've got the guts to take that thing off."

I backed into the living-room wall with a force hard enough to jar my teeth. "I'm not a sideshow for people to stare at!"

"If you accept how you look, everyone else will, too."

"I won't make it easy for people to exploit me anymore! We live in a culture of sensationalism, an oozing, decadent society where selling photos of misery is considered good ol' free enterprise and nothing's sacred anymore! Including my scars! I asked to be a celebrity, but I didn't give up the right to treated with respect!" I slapped his extended hand.

"Not that many years ago people brought their kids to public hangings for entertainment. Society hasn't changed, Cathy. Its ability to share its worst impulses has just gotten more efficient."

"That's why I came here! I don't want to be the victim of anyone's worst impulses again!"

"You can't live your life worrying about that. Let the hyenas have their pound of flesh. Then they'll get bored and leave you alone. Screw 'em. I know how it feels to be dogged by reporters. Everyone who lost loved ones on nine-eleven became a go-to interview for the media. Some of us still are, whether we like it or not. What's my opinion on the Iraq war? Do I think we can achieve peace in the Middle East? Do I hate the President? Do I love the President? What do I think of the plans for Ground Zero? How do I feel about politics? Would I like to run for the Senate against Hillary Clinton? *Goddamn.* After I came here, they couldn't find me easily so they quit trying. It's safe, here. Trust me." He didn't waver. "Give me the mask."

Do we act on impulse or is impulse the excuse for our subconscious to break free? By now I was in the grip of a full panic attack, gasping for air, my thoughts short-circuited, my reactions frenzied. I just wanted Thomas to leave me alone, to let me breathe. I slung the glove off my right hand, grabbed the bottom of the ski mask, dug my scarred fingers deeply into the hot, confining wool, then dragged the mask up and off my head. I shoved it into Thomas's hand.

Cold air washed over my face. My damp hair feathered my scarred temple and cheek, clung to the striated pink rivers along my jaw, revealed the grisly right ear. Humiliation, anger and grief vibrated through my muscles. If I could have unhinged my chattering teeth to scream obscenities at Thomas, I would have.

Instead, locked inside the lost world of myself, I stared up at him with ferocious misery, scouring his eyes for any hint of repulsion. I couldn't find it. I couldn't find anything except calm scrutiny. My ugliness turned him into a poker-faced cipher. Oh, he was good at locking up his own reactions.

Slowly, never taking his eyes off my face, he reached into his coat, brought out his pocket knife and flicked the blade open. With a few swift, surgical movements of his hands he sliced my ski mask into pieces. He threw the pieces onto the hearth. Then he closed his knife, returned it to his pocket, and nodded to me. "I'm going to get a scrap of paper and a pen from my truck. I'll write my phone number down for you. If you need anything, call me."

He turned and walked out of the house. I wanted to scream, I wanted to cry, I wanted to hit him or punch the walls or curl up on the floor with my arms around my head. I didn't feel free, I felt exposed. He had looked at my face, and now he was leaving.

I grabbed the shotgun and followed him outdoors, where I stationed myself on the snowy walkway. The brilliantly blue morning bathed my face, the sunshine warmed the ruined skin that had not felt full sunlight since the day of the accident. My scarred self was a battery of conflicting energies, and I was being charged.

My eyes fell on a gatepost at the edge of the front yard. I remembered a picket fence around a flower bed when I was child. Now, only one wooden sentinel remained to guard my grandmother's irises and daylilies from hungry wildlife.

Thomas had laid his cell phone atop the post.

I took aim at it.

Returning from his truck with the piece of paper in one hand, he halted when he saw me with the gun. "Don't do—" he began. I pulled the trigger. The recoil nearly knocked me down; the sound was a thunderclap that shook my scalp loose from my skull.

But his cell phone, the innocent, symbolic victim of my bitterness toward life in general and the outside world in particular, lay in satisfying bits on the snow. Its pieces flew over approximately fifty square feet of my yard. I would find one later, embedded in an oak.

Thomas studied the carnage with a frown. "My brother's not going to believe this."

"Get off my property."

He sighed. "Okay. Plan B." He pointed to his right, toward the barn, the woods, the road to the creek trail. "My land is that way. "Keep the sun over your right shoulder, walk down the ridge to the creek. Cross the creek, go up the next hill. I'm in the first cabin on the left. Well, the only cabin. Look for the vineyard in the clearing. It's an unusual pattern—"

"Tree of Life," I intoned grimly. "Frank Lloyd Wright. I know. I did my research. I saw it on the satellite pictures. It's pointing right at me."

"Well, don't come over and shoot it."

"You've seen what you came here to see. Now just leave. Leave."

Thomas looked at me a long time, and I made myself stand there and take his scrutiny. "I know you hate me right now," he said. "And I know you don't believe me. *But I like what I see.*"

"Liar."

After he drove away my legs folded under me and I sat down hard in the snow with my head bowed. In my coat pocket was a thin wool scarf. I pulled it out and raised it toward my hair, intending to drape my head and hide the burned side of my face. Old habits die hard. I almost had the scarf in place when the first small sounds and sensations began to register. A winter bird chirping. The low whisper of the wind in the forest. The air on my face. The warmth of the sun. Seductive.

I looked around furtively, like a cat peeking out of a doorway. Forest, pasture, sky, house. Me. Alone. Safe. I'd dreamed of privacy and freedom here. Thomas had pushed me out of the nest in that direction. All I had to do was practice being comfortable in the open. My hands shaking, I lowered the scarf to my lap. I brushed my hair back, turned my face up to the sun and shut my eyes.

Oh, God. The freedom felt so good.

Chapter 15

Thomas
One Week Later

I'd told Cathy I'd come looking for her body if she didn't show up at the Cove in a couple of weeks, but halfway through that grace period I was ready to risk being shot by her again. The snow melted but the weather turned bitterly clear and cold. I paced my cabin's floor at night, thinking about her without so much as a fire in her fireplace. I didn't get much sleep that week, and I didn't take a drink. Not one. My seven-day sobriety record was solely and completely inspired by the thought that I had to be on alert if Cathy needed me.

Apparently, she didn't.

And I felt guilty not telling Delta the truth. "You sure Cathy sounded fine when she called you?" Delta demanded every day. This time, it was early on a Saturday afternoon, just after the lunch crowd cleared out at the cafe. "Cathy's okay," I answered. "As I keep saying, you'll hear from her when she's ready." I wish I felt as sure as I sounded. I stood on a ladder along the café's front porch with bundles of twinkle lights in my hands, looked down at Delta's worried expression with a pang of remorse, and nodded. "I promise."

"Can't you trust me with a little more information?" Delta tossed one end of a pine garland to Becka, who waved an industrial stapler with maniacal intent as she and Cleo dragged the serpentine greenery into place along the porch's rail. "Like where is Cathy?"

"She swore me to secrecy. She has her reasons. You'll see."

"I just don't understand why she'd call you but not me."

"Trust me, you'll understand eventually. She needs her space."

"She needs biscuits!"

Santa walked out of the café's front doors wearing a floor-length brocade coat trimmed in fake mink and a matching brocade-and-fake-mink Santa cap. He made a chunk of spare cash every holiday season playing his namesake at private parties and corporate events in Asheville. "I'm doing a Victorian Kris Kringle thing for the Asheville chamber," he explained. "I haven't got the under-robe done yet, but what do you think so far?"

"Looks good with the camo pants and the *Rolling Stones* sweatshirt," I said.

"Right on, Rudolph," he said drily, and went back inside.

I helped Delta and the family decorate the café every Christmas. This was no small chore. By the time they were done each year, the restaurant and all related buildings glowed like a carnival at night. Synchronized reindeer pranced along the roof, and plywood cut-outs of angels, snowmen, carolers, and Santas in sleighs, outlined in multi-colored twinkle lights, paraded along the roadside as if a strange caravan were headed down the Trace. Best of all, Jeb and Bubba parked Bubba's 1970 Chevrolet *Impala* in the pasture nearby, outlined it in lights, put sequential strings on the wheels so it appeared they were turning, and arranged lights on the car's side to read NASCAR ROCKS.

It was a work of art on wheels. People came from all over to admire the NASCAR Christmas car and the Cove's kitschy light show. I was proud to be part of it.

Delta continued gazing up at me as if I'd betrayed her. "Thomas, don't take this as an insult, but you haven't gotten drunk in a week. You haven't slept under the tree in your truck, either."

"It's been twenty degrees at night. I could freeze my . . . I could freeze."

"That hasn't stopped you in winters past. This strange behavior of yours has something to do with Cathy, doesn't it? And I noticed you suddenly have a new cell phone."

"Didn't come in the mail!" Becka, our postmistress, called smugly.

"I'd have known!"

"That's right. You didn't get it in the mail from your brother this time, you went over to Turtleville and bought it." Delta shook a wreath at me. "What is going on?"

I hung a string of twinkle lights on rusty nails along the porch eaves while I contemplated a diplomatic response. Luckily, Pike roared into the parking lot at that moment and slid his patrol car to a stop next to us, spraying fine gravel. Delta yelped and shook the wreath at him.

He rolled the window down and looked at us grimly. "I just got a call. Laney Cranshaw's in jail over in Chattanooga. Drunk and disorderly at a bar near the aquarium. Got in a hair-pulling slap-fight last night with her boyfriend. Tennessee's keeping her 'til tomorrow. All right, who's volunteering to go pick up Ivy and Cora? Why, thank you, honey." He nodded at Delta. Then he peered up at me, an evil grin widening his face beneath the bristle of his crewcut. "Why, thank you, Tommy-Son. That little Cora sure does dote on you. Too bad Ivy wants to gut you with a dull fork. Y'all have fun now, you hear?"

He waved at us and drove off.

Delta frowned at me as we walked to my truck. "Just tell me this much. When you talked to Cathy last week did she say anything about coming here to visit?"

"Yes."

"*When?*"

"That I can't tell you." I tossed a Christmas bow to Banger, luring him from the cab of my truck. If I left a window down and parked beside a picnic table beneath the oaks, he always hopped up on the table and climbed inside the truck. "There's barely enough room for me, Delta, and two girls on the seat of this old truck," I told him.

"Bah," he said as he hopped out. I waved Delta into my truck's rump-sprung passenger seat with the *élan* of a royal coachman. She poked me on the arm. "When is she coming here? When?"

"Soon."

I hope.

❦ ❦ ❦ ❦ ❦

"We're not going *anywhere*," Ivy insisted, standing in the living room of the cottage on Fox Run. She glared at Delta and even more so at me. "I can take care of Cora. We don't need any help. Especially from a man."

I have this effect on girls of all ages, I thought grimly. Ivy and Cathy would make a good pair.

"Oh, hon," Delta began. "You don't have to take care of your baby sis alone—"

"We're not leaving this house," Ivy repeated. "Don't worry about Cora. I'll watch out for her. I always do."

"You aunt's gone a lot?" I asked gently.

"No! That's not what I meant! She's here all the time!"

My heart twisted. Ivy was streetwise. She'd never admit their aunt deserted them regularly. It would be grounds for another stint in foster care.

"Honey, nobody's saying you don't know *how* to take care of your baby sister," Delta soothed, while I stepped back. "But why don't y'all come with me just for the night? Y'all can help out at the café. I'll pay you a dollar an hour for wiping off tables and stacking plates in the kitchen. Then we'll have some ice cream and banana pudding, and some hot chocolate, and we'll watch TV, and then y'all can sleep in one of my guest beds. It'll be fun!"

Cora, who had dodged both Ivy and Delta to run to me, looked up at me worriedly. "What should we do? I can't leave Princess Arianna and Herman."

Herman, the rooster, had a nice coop and fenced pen in the backyard. I'd built it for him. I'd even installed a small heat lamp. "I just checked on him," I told her gently. "He's sound asleep. His good eye's shut." I nodded at Princess Arianna, the cat, who was curled up, purring, on the couch. "She's fine, too. We'll leave her in the house with plenty of food and water and her litter box."

"Okay, then I'll go to the café. Do you wipe tables for a dollar an hour, too?"

"I've graduated to being a busboy. You can be my assistant."

"Okay!"

Ivy's mouth flattened. "We don't need any help," she repeated.

"Well, I do," Delta said. "I need lots of help. And I'm not ashamed to admit it." She nodded my way. "Thomas needs lots of help, too. He's the most helpless man I know, especially when he's trying to avoid telling me what he knows I want to know. Isn't that right, Thomas?"

She threw down the gauntlet. I gave her a little *Matrix* hand gesture. Palm up, fingers together, extend, curl. *Bring it on, Biscuit Queen.* "You know, I do need help with something," I told the girls. "Cathryn Deen's coming to visit us soon. I'm sure she'd like some special, homemade Christmas ornaments. Ivy, you have an eye for design. Cora, you know how to put magic in everyday things. Can you two help me make some ornaments this afternoon?"

"Oh, yes!" Cora squealed. "The real Princess Arianna's coming here? Oh, boy!"

"Ivy? Will you trust me and Delta? I give you my word you and Cora can come back here as soon as your aunt gets home."

"Promises are easy to make," Ivy said. "My aunt makes promises all the time."

"Do I look like your aunt?"

Cora, missing the point, burst into giggles. "No, you have a beard!"

"I will never break a promise to you, Ivy." I looked at Delta. "Can I be trusted?"

Delta scowled. "Ivy, this man is like a bank vault. You put your faith in him, he'll give it back with interest. Come on over to the café and make some Christmas ornaments for my cousin Cathy and don't worry about it."

Ivy frowned and chewed her lower lip. "Cathryn Deen lets us rent this house for diddly. So I guess I owe her a few Christmas ornaments. Okay."

"Good! Pack your overnight bags and let's get going."

"Hurray!' Cora squealed. She bolted from the living room with Ivy following slowly, casting shrewd looks at me as she went.

When we were alone, Delta swung to face me. She grabbed me by the beard. "Thomas Karol Mitternich, were you lying just now? Is Cathy coming here for Christmas?"

"It's a possibility. That's all I can say."

She punched me on the arm.

I just smiled.

Cathy

Cathryn Deen's Body Found Frozen In Ravine— Empty Gas Can, Uncharged Cell Phone Seen As Clues In Embarrassing Death

I didn't want that headline on my obituary.

"I can make it to the Cove before hypothermia sets in," I kept telling myself as I staggered through the hollow along Ruby Creek that Saturday. My breath punctuated the frigid air with quick white puffs. My legs were rubbery. Bundled up in sheepskin, wool, leather, and mink ear muffs—in other words, a walking PETA target—I'd left the farm two hours earlier. *That's what you get for lazing in bed all those months in L.A.*, I chided as my lungs struggled to support my legs. *You're not ready for a mountain aerobics course.*

The Hummer's bright-yellow emergency gas can bounced from my left shoulder. I'd fashioned a carrying strap for it from a ball of twine I found in my grandmother's attic. The useless cell phone bounced in my back pack. From my coat pocket I pulled the wrinkled satellite photos I'd printed out when I was still in California. Okay. Here was the creek, and there was the Cove. And here was the intersection of the Trace and the creek trail. And if I headed to the southeast right now, that would be a left turn off the trail at this point, I could cut the corner and reach the café sometime before my toes turned black from frostbite.

I stuffed the maps back in my pocket, took a deep breath, and climbed down a steep hillside toward the creek. *Ah hah.* A little known fact: Creeks have water in them. I found a shallow eddy with a sandy bottom, waded through ankle-deep water fringed with ice ledges, and hoped my high-tech, waterproof hiking boots actually were.

They weren't.

As cold water squished through my heavy socks and puddled between my toes, I climbed the hill on the creek's far side and went doggedly southeast.

I distracted myself by practicing my speech to Delta.

Hi, cousin, nice to meet you. Yes, I realize it appears that I'm an idiot who ran out of gas without ever driving anywhere and who let the cell phone discharge without ever placing a call for help. But things were going so well for me until then.

🌺🌺🌺🌺🌺

Prior to my emergency hike to the Cove I'd spent the week happily playing house at Wild Woman Ridge and exploring my land. The glory of being alone, unseen and unsee-able, gave me exactly what I'd hoped to find at Granny's secluded home—freedom and security. First, I prowled the forest of young pine trees beyond the back yard and found my grandmother's orchard—gnarled apple trees, fig trees, a half-dozen stately pecans, and a fringe of tall blueberry shrubs desperately reaching through the evergreens toward sunlight. I made notes to myself. *Clear pines from orchard. Get book on fruit and nut trees. Learn how to make pecan pies.*

I found a concrete pad where the well house used to be. *Have new well dug. Have two or three new wells dug. Need lots of water. Irrigation, fire protection. Sprinklers!* I had already decided to install a sophisticated sprinkler system throughout the house. *Thomas, I'm sorry, you can tell me how to hide the heads so they don't disrupt the architectural purity, but I am going to have sprinklers.* And all the wood paneling had to come off the walls so fire-retardant siding could be installed behind it. I wasn't going to live in a wooden house without safeguards. One of the first things I did was unpack a box full of fire extinguishers. There was now one in every room, including the closets.

I scrutinized forlorn spaces in the small, sunny kitchen, where Granny had reveled in her refrigerator, an ancient model that ran on kerosene, and a slightly more modern stove that ran off propane. Daddy had sold the stove and the amazing fridge along with everything else of value. *Install electric fridge,* I wrote in my notes, *and microwave.* I wasn't sure my nerves were up to a conventional stove and oven, even a non-flaming electric model. But I could stand a microwave.

I loved the kitchen, where a window over the sink looked out on the side pasture and barn. Tall white cabinets rose to the ceiling, and the countertops were covered in finely fitted ceramic tiles painted in bright splashes of color. *Granny made these.* She'd had them fired at a kiln in Asheville. As a boy, Delta's brother, Bubba, had helped Granny cement the tiles in place. Granny had inspired him to learn pottery-making.

The kitchen floor was done in large, red-clay tiles embedded with flat white stones. As a child, the stones had looked like random specks to me, but now, with no table and chairs to break the effect, I realized in astonishment that each tile displayed a constellation. All twelve signs of the zodiac were there, and the Ursas, major and minor, and Orion and Andromeda, and others.

I took off my shoes and walked the sky in my sock feet.

Note regarding kitchen floor: clean it and re-seal it, buy a glass-topped table so you can see through, no rugs to hide the universe!

I hauled several dozen boxes down from the attic and unpacked a treasure trove of Granny's belongings. My favorites were her dish cloths and tablecloths, hand-embroidered with all sorts of whimsical homages to famous painters—Picasso and Van Gogh, Georgia O'Keefe and Frida Kahlo. The Kahlo—Frida's colorful self-portrait, oh, boy, could that woman have used a little wax job between those eyebrows—included a quote.

"I paint self-portraits because I am so often alone, because I am the person I know best."

I laid that dish cloth on a box and looked at it a long time. "Granny, were you lonely here?" I said into the absolute silence of the cold house. I didn't want to think of my grandmother that way—I wanted to revel in her independence, I wanted to embrace the notion of being alone the rest of my life.

Surely she approved.

I unpacked her grand blue-and-red enamelware pans, her black iron skillets, and her crockery canisters for flour and sugar. I filled the kitchen cabinets with her vessels; I lined the counter with the crockery, with her hammered aluminum bread keeper, with a funny old cookie jar in the shape of a hula dancer. I set a wonderful kerosene lamp on the counter by the sink, though I'd never light it, and I hung a pair of her tablecloths in the window as temporary curtains.

Facing the fireplace in the living room was a floor-to-ceiling wall of built-in cabinets. Their cherry wood was dark and a little dull from years of neglect and decades of smoky fireplace residue, but the cabinets made a grand show, regardless. I found a box full of old, framed photographs and set them on a few shelves. Mother. Grandmother. My long-dead grandfather, young and handsome and probably trouble. Relatives I didn't recognize. Pet dogs, cats, a goat. *The* goat? "Bah Ba Loo," was written on the back. The one from the cemetery? I hadn't ventured out there yet. I made a mental note to check for a Bah Ba Loo headstone.

But the shelves still looked bare.

Waving a flashlight, I went downstairs. The basement was cold and tomb-like, like all dark basements, but I could picture it with the warm light of a few good fluorescent bulbs on the heavy stone walls. The walls were lined with thick plank shelves, and on those shelves was a veritable museum of old jars. Not only were there cases of canning jars, there were large, two-gallon pickle jars.

"Granny's milk jars," I exclaimed. She'd had a milk cow. Twice a day she brought in a bucket of fresh-squeezed moo juice. She poured that raw, creamy fresh-milked milk into the recycled pickle jars, then covered their tops with cheesecloth. As the heavy yellow cream floated to the top she'd strain it off.

That raw milk, and the raw cream from it, had been the most luscious-tasting treat in the world. I remembered riding down to the Cove with her in her truck. She'd sold her extra milk and eggs to the café.

Besides the milk jars were dozens of cobalt-blue bottles—some of them soda or medicine containers, others the squat, hard-working jars that once held the most ubiquitous cure-all a cold ever met: Vicks VapoRub.

I picked up an empty jar and tried desperately to get a whiff of mentholated memory off it, but the scent was gone. Why had she kept these? I wracked my brain. The bottle tree. She'd had a bottle tree in the front yard. It was a post she'd set in the ground, bored with holes all up and down the length of it. She whittled small, bare tree branches into odd configurations, then wedged one end into a hole and hung a blue bottle from the tip. Her bottle tree had been a glorious blue light-catcher, casting strange pieces of rainbows onto the flowers, the yard and my face.

I toted all the jars upstairs. Milk jars, Vicks jars, soda bottles, canning jars. Jar World. As soon as I had time I'd build a bottle tree for the blueware, but in the meantime I set all the jars in front of the living room cabinets and gazed at the raw potential.

I sat next to Martha Stewart at a dinner party once, and I asked her the secret of simple décor, and she leaned over to me and whispered profoundly, like Orson Welles in the opening of *Citizen Kane*, just one solemn word.

"Grouping."

I grouped.

When I finished, my cabinets gleamed with fascinating jar themes. I brought in a few twigs, some sprigs of wild holly to adorn a jar here and yon, and voilà. A masterpiece in found glass. I set a battery-powered lantern in their midst at night in lieu of deadly candles, and shards of reflected light scattered across the living room.

The ordinary can become extraordinary with just the smallest effort to see beyond the surface. I touched my face from time to time. Yes, it should be a lesson. Not one I was ready to believe, though.

A marvelous built-in china cabinet filled one wall of the small dining room, too. I polished its glass windows and their stained-glass rims until they glimmered like calm water. When I found Granny's blue willow china, I polished that, too, slaving at it over a bucket of water I hauled from the cow pond. When the china was pristine, I arranged and rearranged it in the cabinet.

Then I took one coffee cup and saucer, and one small plate, and I formed some empty boxes into a kind of table, with a folding camp chair beside it. I put the earless Van Gogh tablecloth over the boxes, filled my cup with bottled water, neatly dumped cold, vacuum-sealed chicken alfredo onto the plate and, using a plastic fork from my camping supplies, I *dined*.

Best of all were my grandmother's quilts, stored carefully with paper tucked between the folds. There were only four, all double-bed size. I remembered her having many more. These were all that had escaped Daddy's cold-blooded dispersement of her belongings. I shook my head over them, hugged them to my chest.

I put one of the quilts over my sleeping bag and used the other three as drapes for the living room windows. The old curtainrod holders were still in place. I brought in several interesting tree limbs from the forest floor, perched them on the old holders, draped the quilts just so, and I had colorful curtains instead of wool blankets.

My house. My house. It was still a dark, barren enclave in so many ways; it still had no furniture, but now it had memories on the shelves and at the windows. I had put a touch of makeup on it, just enough to bring out the light in its eyes.

Such musings and decoratings kept me busy for an entire week. But eventually I sat on my cot in the corner next to the boarded-up fireplace at night, tired and chilly and bundled in an increasingly grungy set of clothing, wondering what I should do next. I went out one morning and circled the Hummer with its keys in my hand, as if I'd cornered it in the wild and didn't want to spook it. Somehow, some way I had to shore up my courage enough to drive again. I had not driven a car since the accident. Even the thought of driving made me queasy. My heart raced, my hands shook. I looked at the Hummer and saw the Trans Am. I dropped the keys, picked them up, hurried back inside. Shame filled me. It was bad enough to be a maimed misfit, but to be held hostage by these fears was the ultimate humiliation. I paced the living room, hands on hips.

My plan had been to call Delta eventually, tell her I was here, swear her to secrecy, invite her to visit, then beg her to be my liaison with the real world. I'd give her money and lists, and she'd send supplies. I'd also tell her what kind of furniture I wanted, and she could buy it for me. But who would deliver it? Who would tote and fetch and unload in perfect, trustworthy secrecy?

Thomas would. But only if I promise not to alter so much as an antique nail in this entire house.

Damn.

While I tried to come up with a way to be a totally self-sufficient hermit yet also go shopping, I fell in the cow pond. It was late afternoon on the sixth day. I had issues with the pond because its smooth, silver water reflected my face, thus I refused to look directly at the water while scooping my bucket into it. The ground around the pond was frozen hard, and a rim of thin ice covered most of the water, making it difficult to tell exactly where the pond ended and the shore began. I was bent over, scooping water at a hole I'd knocked in the ice, while looking at a hawk perched in the bony fingertip of a tall poplar tree, when I stepped on ice instead of earth.

The ice collapsed, and I went into the frigid water headfirst. Sputtering and flailing, weighted by a heavy coat and hiking boots, I crawled out like a soggy teddy bear. By the time I reached the house, I was shivering so hard I could barely shuck my clothes. I dried off with a wool blanket and swaddled myself in a dry outfit but still couldn't get warm. Night was falling, and a little thermometer I'd set on the porch rail said the temperature was only heading south.

If I can just warm up I'll be fine. I just need to re-start my personal thermostat. I looked out the window at the Hummer. I had the ovaries to sit in it with the heater running, at least.

As a cold, golden sunset faded over Hog Back, I climbed into the Hummer carrying blankets, bottled water, and several protein bars. I cranked the engine and turned the heater on low. *Just for a few minutes,* I thought, as the seductive heat surrounded me with blissful comfort I hadn't known for days. I tried the radio and found WTUR-AM, the Voice of Turtleville Since 1928. Somewhere in outer space, WTUR's earliest farm reports and gospel singings were well on their way toward the universes next door.

Porter Wagoner serenaded me. "It's good to touch the green, green grass of home." A song about a man dreaming of the old homeplace on the eve of his execution. My kind of music. I made a mental note to climb in the Hummer the next night, Saturday, and listen to the Grand Ol' Opry live from Nashville.

My grandmother's eclectic tastes had included a pure love for that show. She'd adored its bluegrass and hillbilly music, its soap-operaish country tunes and Patsy Cline ballads and even the slick, orchestrated tunes that had crept in by my childhood. When I visited, she and I listened on a battery-powered boom box in her living room. The boom box sat atop the aging wooden console of a hand-cranked radio her grandfather had ordered from Sears in the 1920's.

"I remember first appreciating the Grand Ol' Opry when I was a teenager during the Depression," she told me. "I snuck out of a church social to go to a roadhouse down on the creek. I drank homemade gin with a Jewish bootlegger from Chicago and listened to Bill Monroe and his Blue Grass Boys on the radio. Can you imagine singing along to 'Blue Moon Of Kentucky' with a bootlegger who translates the lyrics into Yiddish? It was a night I never forgot."

She never forgot that night, and I never forgot her colorful story about it. She linked me to that time and those people as if I'd touched them myself. Yes, I would make listening to the Grand Ol' Opry my new Saturday night hobby. Maybe Faith Hill or Garth Brooks or Travis Tritt would suddenly burst into Yiddish. You never know.

The warmth, the music, the soft glow of the Hummer's dashboard lulled me as night closed in. Irresistible. I snuggled down in the seat, cuddled a blanket to my breasts, and shut my eyes. Just a nap. Just a short, warming doze.

The next thing I knew, I was blinking sleepily in the bright sunshine of morning. The Hummer had grown suspiciously cold and quiet. I lurched upright in the seat and tried to crank the engine. All I got was the sound a large cat makes when it tries to throw up a furball.

I looked at my wristwatch. "Oh, my God." I'd been sleeping in the Hummer, with its engine running, for more than twelve hours. The gas tank had been only a quarter full when my bodyguards and I arrived; now it was empty, and to top off the misery, the battery seemed dead. I climbed out, trying not to panic. "Okay, so it's not like I was planning to drive anywhere soon. No problem. I'll decide what to do about it later. I can always call for help by phone."

I went inside the house, ate a tasty breakfast of protein bars, brushed my teeth, spent the morning polishing the windows in the bedrooms, then sat down on the hearth to call Bonita. I checked in with her every day around noon, East Coast time. We had an agreement. If she failed to hear from me, and couldn't get me on the phone in return, she was to alert Delta that something was wrong.

I pulled my cell phone from a pocket and started to punch the speed-dial number for Bonita. Then I peered at the phone's display and realized it was blank. That's when I remembered I'd forgotten to plug the phone into its charger in the Hummer. Which now had a dead battery. "Oh, my

God," I said again, this time loudly.

Bonita would call Delta and tell her I was missing. Delta would tell her sheriff-husband, Pike, and he'd organize a search team involving most of the local citizenry of greater Turtleville and maybe even the entire Jefferson County, and my fervent dreams of living here as an anonymous hermit would be finished.

I could almost hear Anderson Cooper reporting the story on CNN: *Tonight we bring you the shocking truth about Cathryn Deen's whereabouts. We'll tell you how the actress once called 'the world's most beautiful woman' was found wandering the wilderness of North Carolina's Appalachian mountains. We'll tell you about her bizarre new lifestyle without heat, plumbing or furniture, her decorative jar-arranging and her mysterious references to a Jewish bootlegger who once sang, 'Bloy Levone Iber Kentucky'* . . .

My only hope was to hike to the Cove before that happened.

Thomas

Architecture is a language, an art, a method for drawing castles in the air. I believed in it passionately and understood its concepts completely. But until that Saturday afternoon at the café I'd never realized how the structure and supports of my chosen discipline could build a bridge between the small, delicate spaces that separate people, too.

"These are your load-bearing walls," I explained to Ivy, maneuvering small squares of cardboard on a checkered table in the café's main dining room. "If you fold this piece of cardboard like so, atop the walls, now that, see, is called a 'pitched' roof."

"Like the roof most houses have," she said, her chin on her folded hands as she avidly scrutinized the tiny cardboard house we were making with the help of silver duct tape and glue made with flour and egg whites.

"Yes, a standard residential roof."

"A roof for Tinkerbell's house," Cora put in. "That's a fairy house."

"You betcha. Okay, what are these areas on the sides called?"

Ivy frowned a moment, then brightened. "The gables!"

"Where the fairies sit to get out of the sun," Cora added.

"Right! Now let's add something to the roof design for more interest." I dabbed some homemade glue on the roof and stuck two sugar cubes there. Using an olive fork as a tool, I molded a dab of raw biscuit dough atop each cube, forming tiny, peaked roofs. "What are these structures called?"

"Houses for the fairy's pet birds," Cora said.

"Dormers!" Ivy said.

I nodded. "Right on both counts."

The girls and I studied the strange little house. It would need a lot of glitter and miniature plastic holly to approximate some kind of Christmas ornament, assuming it didn't fall apart, first. But even grim-faced Ivy looked pleased when I said, "I hereby declare that Ivy and Cora's first house design has met all the building codes for cardboard, egg paste, and sugar cubes." I set it aside with a flourish. "Next," I said solemnly, taking more cardboard in hand, "I'll show you how to build a miniature Craftsman bungalow just like the one up on Wild Woman—"

"Speakin' of the Nettie house, Thomas, I need to talk to you right now, please."

I looked up quickly. Delta stood at the door to the kitchen, her face pale, a phone in hand. She pointed to it then gestured for me to keep quiet and come quickly. "You girls practice your pitched roofs," I said. When I entered the kitchen Delta grabbed me by one arm. "Cathy's housekeeper called from California. She's scared to death, so she confessed everything. How could you not tell me Cathy's been up here at her granny's place all week! I ought to skin you alive and fry you for bacon! Thomas, Cathy didn't call the housekeeper this morning! They have a strict routine where they talk at the same time every day! Something's wrong!"

A chill went down my spine. "Keep the girls occupied. I'm going to the Nettie place."

"I'm calling Pike. He'll organize a search and rescue—"

"Not yet," I said as I headed out the kitchen's back door. "Keep it to yourself until I have a chance to search the farm. If we spook Cathy by over-reacting she'll never trust us again."

"But she might be hurt or—"

"Don't say it," I ordered, then ran for my truck.

🐾🐾🐾🐾🐾

I called Cathy's name until my throat was sore. I went through the cottage, the woods, the barn—nothing. In the Hummer I found empty protein-bar wrappers, empty water bottles, a jumble of blankets, and the keys still in the ignition. A quick try confirmed that the Hummer wouldn't crank.

God. I pounded a hand on the hood. "What were you doing out here, Cathy? Did something or someone scare you out of the house?"

I made one more circuit of the farm, calling her name hoarsely. This time, as I went past the barn, my attention fell on the iced-over pond. Something odd caught my eye. I dropped to my heels beside an area where new ice hadn't quite thickened to an opaque sheet. Something—or someone—had made a large hole in the ice within the past twenty-four hours. Now it was slowly re-freezing. A limp brown finger protruded from the white surface. I grabbed it and tugged.

One of Cathy's leather gloves pulled free.

She's in the pond.

I cannonballed into the pond's center, shattering the inch-thick ice and landing on the mushy bottom in waist-deep water. The pond was only a few strides across and shallow around the rim. I broke up the ice with my fists, dropped to a crouch, and searched every square foot with methodical sweeps of my arms and feet.

No corpse. Thank God.

Gasping, already numb from the cold, I crawled out and searched the area around the pond and barn for more clues. As I staggered, teeth chattering, into the farm's graceful old driveway, where a hummock of brown winter grass made a median in soft, sandy loam, I saw a footprint heading away from the farm. It was the smallish track of a shoe with a heavy grid. Like a hiking boot. A woman-sized hiking boot.

Heading down the driveway.

Dripping icy water, I stumbled to my heater-less truck. My fingers were too stiff to close around the steering wheel. Once I reached the hollow where the farm's drive intersected Ruby Creek Trail, I got out and searched the dirt again. There. A footprint. And there.

She had left the farm on foot. I found tracks along the trail for nearly a mile, then none after that. She turned off the trail, but which way? Toward the Cove? Was she trying to take a short cut? Or had someone chased her into the woods? She was probably lost at best, and at worst . . .

Driving with my palms, shivering so hard I had trouble keeping my foot on the gas pedal, I headed back to the Cove as fast I could push the old truck without bouncing down an embankment into the creek. I needed dry clothes and warm hands, then I'd call in reinforcements and head back to the woods.

Hang in there, Cathy.

Cathy

When I wandered out of the woods and saw the café in the distance, framed by huge mountains in the crisp winter sunshine, its roof welcoming me with funny, life-sized cutouts of prancing reindeer, tears welled in my eyes and I patted myself over the heart. I had a sense of direction. Finally.

"Heat up some biscuits, Delta," I shouted into the wind. "The prodigal actress is home from the hills!" My feet were wet and freezing, my legs wobbled, the straps of the gas can and backpack had rubbed sore spots on my shoulders, but by God I'd survived a journey across a thousand miles of uncharted wilderness—or at least seven miles up and down along the steep skirts of Hog Back—without falling off a cliff, getting lost or having to cannibalize a finger or two for food.

Now if I could just sidle up to the café without anyone noticing, slip inside and talk to Delta in private, I'd preserve some shred of dignity. Delta wouldn't tell anyone I'd been an idiot.

I made my way with soggy, shivering stealth along a privet hedge bordering a large garden plot decorated with last season's scarecrows. I hurried behind some sheds and an old barn where a sign offered SWAP AND THRIFT, then under magnificent old oaks as big as the ones at my house. I spied a few cars in the café's parking lot and several pick-up trucks out back. No sign of Thomas's ancient, bottle-nosed rust-hog. Good. While I was proud to show off my hiking instincts, I didn't want him to know about the Hummer and the cell phone.

Creeping up behind a storage shed, I peeked at the back doors and windows and delivery porch of the café. What a gently cluttered, friendly and serviceable place. The yard included an old picnic table and weathered Adirondack chairs, the porch was stacked with old vegetable crates, and a fading *Drink Coca Cola* sign hung over the main kitchen door. Several fat cats appeared from behind shrubs, purr-owing at me sweetly, and a couple of fat dogs peeked out a dog entrance in one of the back doors of the buildings that bordered the café, and then . . .

The goat arrived.

He came trotting from the general vicinity of the shade oaks to my left, a shaggy white menace wearing a leather collar like a dog. Banger! Thomas had sent pictures of him. But he never mentioned Banger was a *guard goat*. Banger glared at me with sinister, marble-glass goat eyes. His jaunty goatee bobbed as he broke into a lope. Stubby horns curled back from his forehead like rockers on an up-ended rocking chair. He lowered his head as he neared me, shaking that horny pompadour at me.

"Oh, shit," I whispered.

I dropped my gas can and ran for the café's back doors. He cut me off. I dodged between two trucks. He followed at a gallop. I sprinted along one side of the café, hoping to find a side door or maybe a trellis to climb. I rounded a corner and saw a bump-out on the side of the building—some added-on little storage room or something. To my delight, when I reached it, a large, colorful sign on the door welcomed me.

THE PRIVY OF FINE ART
Sit Down, Wash Up, Open Your Mind

The Privy. Thomas had sent pictures of it, too. A bathroom and a sanctuary. Thank you, God.

I jumped inside and slammed the door shut behind me just as Banger reached it. *Wham.* Fumbling in the shadows, I found a light switch. *Flick.* I spotted an aged hook-and-eye latch. *Click.* The door was rickety, and the latch was none too reassuring, but I felt safe enough to utter threats. "Beat it, Goat of Satan," I said through the door. "Or I'll turn you into a gyro sandwich."

Banger butted the door another time or two, then stopped. I listened until I heard his evil little cloven hooves wandering away on the pea gravel. Sagging with relief, I turned around.

Wildly colored trout and turkeys gazed back at me.

"This is Noah's Ark on drugs," I said in awe. Then my attention went to the electric heater gushing warmth high on the wall, the sink with plenty of paper towels, soap, hot and cold water faucets, and—in a narrow, purple-turkey endowed nook to one side, the beautiful, wonderful flush toilet. With plenty of toilet paper.

Warmth, warm water, soap, a comfortable place to pee. Heaven.

I'd be recuperated and presentable when I defied Banger again on my way to find Delta. I allowed myself one glance in the mirror over the sink, winced, then hung my coat over the glass. I laid out a pair of sunglasses and a long wool scarf on the counter next to the sink. I'd don the dark glasses and wrap my head and neck decorously, aiming for a sophisticated look circa 1960, say, Audrey Hepburn in *Breakfast at Tiffany's*, only showing a hint of my *Phantom of the Opera* scars.

I shucked boots, socks, wool pants, heavy undershirt, flannel overshirt and mink earmuffs. Dressed in a lacy white bra and the snug, stretchy bottoms of my gray longjohns—which sported a handy removable crotch with Velcro fasteners—I grabbed a handful of paper towels. With one raucous tug the crotch piece of my longjohns joined the pile of clothes in the floor. I glanced down at my small brunette triangle framed in a gray cloth keyhole. My pubes had a front seat window at the car wash.

I filled the sink basin with delicious, warm, soapy water then washed myself as contentedly as a wren in a birdbath. Except for avoiding the scars down the right side of my body—a habit I'd perfected—I almost felt relaxed.

Afterwards I lounged on the trout-decorated commode seat, still dressed in nothing but the bra and crotchless longjohns' bottoms, with one chilled foot propped on the opposite knee. I rubbed some pink back into my toes while I let my socks dry a little more. Suddenly I heard several sounds outside in quick succession: A loud engine, silence, a slammed car door, and heavy feet on gravel, heading my way.

I didn't even have time to yell. My invader slammed into the bathroom door. The latch popped out of the frame. The door swung inward and bounced off the opposite wall.

Thomas nearly fell inside.

Soaked, shivering, dripping water from his beard, his hair, and all his clothing, he brought a whirl of icy air with him. He kicked the door shut then hunched over the sink, trying to grip the rim with splayed hands.

By then I was frantically scrambling for my gray stretch top and flannel shirt. Not to mention the crotch piece of my longjohns. A dilemma—what should I cover first—my exposed groin or the scars that framed the right side of my body from head to foot? Thankfully, since I was tucked in the folk-art nook of the commode, I was the last thing he noticed.

When he finally turned and saw me, he uttered a hoarse sound that was either pure frustration or relief or both. His teeth were chattering too hard to let him speak. He flung a bare hand atop my bare shoulder. I didn't know if he was patting me in appreciation or thumping me in disgust. Either way, the icy stiffness of his hand alarmed me. Clutching my clothes to my flimsy bra and naked groin, I stared at him in dawning fear. "What did you do?" I asked. "Take a dive in the creek? Your skin is blue."

He studied me as if I were a mirage while struggling to tug something from his coat pocket. Finally he produced a sodden brown glove. My heart sank as I recognized it. "Oh, no. You went to the farm to look for me. You thought I drowned in the pond?"

He nodded.

Screw modesty. I tied my flannel shirt around my waist like a skirt to hide my pubes. Trying to ignore the fact that my breasts were barely covered by the bra and that every ugly rivulet of scar tissue could easily be seen along the right side of my face, neck, arm and torso, I used my undershirt to towel Thomas's wet hair. He hunched forward helpfully, his face inches from my breasts, and when I muttered, "Enjoying the view?" he chuckled. The castanet rhythm of his teeth made an interesting accompaniment.

I shoved his coat off his shoulders, revealing an old New York Giants football jersey underneath. The coat landed with a heavy, wet thud. I jerked my coat off the bathroom mirror and flung it around his shoulders. Then I grabbed his shaking hands and guided them into the basin full of warm water. "When you're warm enough to talk, you can yell at me for causing you even more trouble," I told him. "But I didn't ask you to worry about me. Ever." He pulled his hands from the water, holding mine, then brought my hands to his chest and shook his head at me.

Sign language. *It's hopeless. I can't help myself.*

I looked up at him in abject wonder. Where had he been all my life, and why couldn't I have found him before I turned into a scarred bundle of neuroses? Ice-cold water dripped off his beard onto my fingers. I wound my hands around the beard's soggy mass and tugged hard. "It's a marvel you didn't drown from the weight of this . . . pelt. I gave up my ski mask at your request. Now you give up this furry albatross. You might as well. It's going to turn into a chunk of hairy ice if you don't."

He frowned, shivered, shook his head, but I tugged on the beard again and he finally shrugged. I squatted by my back pack, prowled through the protein bars, then stood holding a huge pocket knife. I flicked a six-inch steel blade open. "Boy Scouts would knock over old ladies for this baby," I intoned. I twisted his beard into a fat tourniquet just below his chin and sawed it like a thick rope. When the last strands parted I raised eighteen inches of sodden brown beard like a victory scalp. He looked at it forlornly.

I snorted. "If it's any consolation, you still have plenty of beard left. Shape it up, give it a nice henna rinse, and you could pass for a liberal arts professor or a roadie for Lynyrd Skynyrd. Especially with the ponytail."

"'F-Freebird' r-rocks."

"Ah hah. A Lynyrd Skynyrd aficionado, I see. I'm impressed, Yankee."

After tossing a pile of wet beard in the trash can I ran more hot water in the sink. "Keep your hands in that. I'm going for help at the cafe. I'll be right back."

His gaze went to my bra, then back to my face. He was very good at pretending not to look at my scarred arm or the puckered, discolored flesh that swarmed from my armpit downward, disappearing where my right hip was covered by the longjohns.

"Yes, I really should put my shirt on before heading into the café," I said grimly. "In the meantime—" I waggled my pronged fingers from his eyes to mine—"Put your eyes right up here, buddy. Right here." He arched a brow but complied. I whipped the flannel shirt from around my waist, put it on, buttoned it, grabbed my trousers, pulled them on, jammed my bare feet into my damp hiking boots, then plucked my crotchpiece from the floor. I tucked it like a bib into the collar of his drenched football jersey. "A souvenir for you. Maybe it'll wick up some of the water dripping off what's left of your beard."

Just a hint of a wry smile began to pull at one corner of his mouth. His lips were starting to lose their blue tinge. He had a good, wide, full mouth. "This would be more fun . . ." he said slowly, his teeth clicking, "if it was one of those movies . . . where we get naked to share . . . body heat."

I picked up my scarf, the scarf I had planned to use to hide the scarred side of my face when I met Delta. Instead I dried Thomas's face with the soft woolen ends, then wrapped the scarf around his neck. He was gallant to flirt, but then he was a gallant man. I shrank back inside my ugly skin. "Sorry, but this is one of those movies where I have to out-maneuver a crazed goat to bring you some towels and dry clothes instead."

"D-damn," he said.

❧❧❧❧❧

Banger gave the chase his best effort, but I made it to the back steps of the café a good stride ahead of his evil little horns. Bounding onto the cluttered porch with him right behind me, I jerked the kitchen's screen door open then the white-washed wooden door behind it. With no warning and not so much as a 'May I come in?' I bolted inside. The door slammed shut behind me, and Banger's head thudded on its bottom panel.

Three people popped their heads over the top shelf of a prep bar, gaping at me. It's not as if a coatless, disheveled stranger in rumpled hiking clothes should provoke alarm when she leaps into a kitchen unannounced.

I stared back at them while I caught my breath. Thomas had sent me so many pictures of Delta's family that I knew all three of them on sight: Little, brown-haired Cleo, fortyish and freckled, with her gold cross pendant and 'What Would Jesus Do' bracelets; big, solemn Jeb, with a military tattoo on one forearm and a head full of dark hair he wore in an unashamed mullet; and his wife Becka, a tall redhead with four tiny gold hoops in one year and three diamond studs in the other.

But from their startled looks they not only didn't know who *I* might be, they expected me to pull a gun and rob the place. "Hello," I finally managed between breaths. "I know this may come as a surprise, but I'm—"

My voice trailed off as Delta rushed into the kitchen. She didn't see me at first. Her head was cocked to one side and she was deep in conversation on a portable phone. "I told Thomas I'd give him time to go look for her up at Mary Eve's place," she was saying, "but he's been gone too long and I'm not waiting another second. Pike, she may have fallen off a cliff for all we know. She might be lost in the woods, freezing! You call out everybody you can muster. Get the forestry service helicopter! Get the tracking dogs! Cathy's a city girl, and she's about as helpless as a kitten, a little, newborn kitten—"

"*Delta,*" I said hoarsely. Seeing her in person for the first time was more emotional than I expected. "Meow."

Her head jerked up. She stared at me. "Nevermind!" she shouted into the phone, "She's right here!" She rushed me with her arms out. The phone fell in a pot of beans. "Cousin Cathy!"

"Cousin Delta. I'm so sorry I scared you—"

"All that matters is that you're alive, and you're okay, and you're here!" *Whoomp.* She grabbed me in a hug. The scent of flour and butter filled my nose. She was a head shorter than me. Her dark, graying hair enveloped my chin, as soft as a sable brush. Her body was plush but strong. It was like being hugged by a human biscuit. She rocked me from side to side. She patted my back. I threw my arms around her and pressed the good side of my face into her hair. She turned me into a smiling, teary sauce of cousin-hood. She was the biscuit. I was the gravy.

Delta stepped back, crying and smiling, and took me by the shoulders. "Let me get a good look at you!"

"Thomas is in the Privy. I'll explain later. Right now I need some towels and—"

"One look. Just one." She grabbed my face. Her quick hands caught

175

me off guard. I started to turn away. Delta stared only at my eyes, studying them intently, while her smile broadened and a look of sheer satisfaction came over her face.

"We favor each other around the eyes!" she exclaimed. "Just like I've always told people! We really do!"

Caught in her charm, I could only sigh with relief and nod. I should have known Delta would see me just the way she wanted to. We were family.

We favored.

Thomas

Cathy might not think of herself as a movie star anymore, but her presence at the café created a hum of excitement that was almost tangible. Most of the immediate Whittlespoon clan—a good twenty people, counting children—suddenly showed up in the kitchen that Saturday afternoon. So much for keeping Cathy a secret. They performed halfhearted prep work for the dinner menu while craning their heads toward the swinging doors that led to the public areas, hoping for any sound that hinted Delta and Cathy were about to emerge from the café's front dining room.

Everyone wanted a look at her. Scars and all.

Ivy and Cora couldn't concentrate on building more cardboard Christmas cottages, and neither could I. We sat in the side dining room aimlessly gluing sequins to pine cones. I was distracted by my stiff new overalls and sweatshirt with the John Deere tractor logo, the only emergency outfit available in my size at the Crossroads Grocery and General Store. The strange sight of my beardless chest caught me off guard every time I looked down at myself.

My skin felt as if it had been shaved by icicles then heated with a blow torch. I owed that sensation to the memory of Cathy tenderly caring for me in the Privy. Also to the memory of her breasts in the low-slung bra, and the peek I'd stolen when she turned just-so to pull her pants up. She'd never been nude in one of her films, so I naturally wondered if she had tattoos or birthmarks to hide. That's my excuse and I'm sticking with it. I'll say this much: No tattoos, no birthmarks, and those crotchless longjohns treated me to a front and back glimpse of world-class feminine assets.

"Maybe Princess Arianna and Delta are done talking now," Cora whispered across the table to me. "Can we go meet her?"

"Not yet. She and Delta have a lot of catching up to do. Like I told you, they haven't seen each other since Cath—Princess Arianna—was about Ivy's age. And that was twenty years ago."

Ivy scowled toward the closed double doors to the café's front dining room. "Aw, she probably doesn't want to meet a couple of dumb hick kids, anyway."

"Hey." I leaned forward and looked at her somberly. I didn't talk down to Ivy. She was a smart girl and nobody should patronize her. "You designed a house earlier today. I don't know anybody else your age who could do that. And I was impressed by your understanding of architectural terms. If you're interested, I'll help you build a model out of popsicle sticks. That's how my old man—my father—taught me the basics of structural design."

Ivy shrugged, but her mocha freckles took on a pink tint and she flicked a sequin into the air with jaunty brown fingers. "Laney says I waste time reading books."

"It's never a waste of time to read a book."

"You think Cathryn likes to read? Nah. She's pretty, she doesn't need to."

"So it's okay for pretty girls to be dumb?"

"Yeah. They get lots of attention just for batting their eyes. People think they're smart just because they're pretty. Especially if they're pretty and white." Her eyes narrowed. "They've got it made."

"I bet Cathy disagrees with you. She reads books; she's not dumb."

"What does she look like in person? Is she still pretty?"

"Yes, she is. Only in a different way than before. But she doesn't think so."

Ivy's eyes flickered with instant interest. "She doesn't?"

"No. She feels ugly right now. People have been mean to her about the way she looks since her accident. Don't forget that, when you meet her. Be careful what you say."

Cora, wide-eyed and worried, said urgently, "We'd never be mean to Princess Arianna on purpose! I'm gonna go tell her so, right now!"

She moved fast for such a little girl. Before either Ivy or I could stop her she was out of the chair and at the double doors. She tugged them open and bounded inside. But when Ivy and I reached her she had halted only a foot beyond the doorway. She stared at Cathy with her mouth open and a horrified gleam in her nut-brown eyes.

"What in the world?" Delta said. She and Cathy had been having a sit-down heart-to-heart at a table in the front dining room over hot tea and cheese biscuits. Cathy got to her feet quickly, tugging at the scarf she'd taken back once I reached room temperature. It didn't quite hide the right side of her face, and she knew it. The effect had to be unnerving for a child, especially one like Cora, who put a protective filter between herself and even the smallest sorrows. Delta gave me a how-could-you-let-this-happen? scowl.

"You must be Cora," Cathy said nervously. Cora didn't move or make a sound. Cathy slumped. "Cora, it's okay. You don't have to say hello or anything. I know I look kind of funny."

Cora leapt toward her like a dark-haired hummingbird. She grabbed a chair, pushed it close to Cathy, clambered onto its seat, and reached up. With one little hand she pushed the scarf aside. Cathy froze. Cora gently laid the hand on her burned cheek, patting it with feathery care. "I know what happened," Cora whispered. "This is where Pereforn breathed on you, *isn't* it?"

In the Princess Arianna movies Pereforn was a dangerous, fire-spewing dragon. Cathy studied Cora with relief and then tenderness. "He breathed on me, yes."

"You're still a beautiful princess, anyhow."

"You think so?"

"Oh, yes! And I'm so glad you're here!" She perched on the toes of her tennis shoes and held up her arms. Cathy swept her into a hug. "I have your ruby in my purse," she told Cora, her voice breaking. By now Delta was wiping her eyes and my throat felt tight.

Cora squealed. "You do?"

Cathy set her down gently. "Absolutely. It's brought me good luck."

"Aunt Laney said it was just a rock."

"Nope. It's magic."

"Wow."

Cathy's gaze went to Ivy, who stood there looking awkward and defensive. "Ivy?"

"Iverem."

Cathy clicked on an internal switch. That megawatt smile I mentioned? That stunning charisma? She aimed the beam at Ivy, full-blast. "I have the sketch you sent me. Of the panning sluice. I found a frame for it at my grandmother's house, and so I framed it and I'm displaying it on my living room cabinets. Among my jar collection. It looks great there. It's nice to meet you, Iverem."

Ivy didn't stand a chance. Transfixed, she took a dazed step toward Cathy, then another, stopping at the end of the hand Cathy held out. The left one, unscarred. I noticed Cathy tucking her right hand behind one hip.

"You can call me Ivy." She squeezed Cathy's hand. A semi-shake, tentative and awed. I could almost see the thought on her face. *Cathryn Deen shook my hand. Mine. I'm famous, now.* "You have a jar collection?" Ivy asked. "Is there something in the jars?"

"No, I just like the, uh, empty jars. That's kind of weird, right?"

"No, and anyhow, I like weird stuff."

"Me, too. Cool."

"Cool."

Delta and I traded a look. She put a hand to her heart, smiling. *Cool,* she mouthed.

Behind me, a herd of feet exploded out of the kitchen. Delta's smile faded. So did Cathy's. She pulled her scarf back into place then sidled toward the doors to the front porch. "Stampede?" she joked weakly.

"Oh, honey, you've gotta meet the rest of your distant kin *some* time, and it might as well be now," Delta soothed urgently, grabbing her by one arm. I raised both arms to barricade the door, but they swarmed around me. "It's no use," Pike growled, clamping a hand on my shoulder. "This is like a Baptist river-dunking ceremony. Cathy has to get her Whittlespoon baptism over with in one fell swoop. Just say 'Amen,' and step aside."

The entire herd surrounded Cathy with kindly but obsessive scrutiny. She plastered a smile to her ashen face as Delta introduced each family member in colorful detail. Cathy's anxious gaze went to me. Sign language. *They're staring at my face.*

All I could do was nod. *So let them.*

"Thomas, people will remember this day a hundred years from now," Delta whispered to me. "The legend of Cathy Deen has begun."

"Lord, thank you for bringing Cathy to be with us," Cleo announced, looking heavenward. "But excuse me while I get this room warmed up for the dinner crowd." She hurried to a hearth on one wall, squatted on the heels of her running shoes, pulled a long-handled butane lighter from her jeans' pocket, fiddled with a control for the fireplace's pilot light, then clicked the lighter.

The logs ignited with a loud *whoosh* of orange-and-blue flames.

Cathy bolted out the front doors and staggered to a porch rail. She vomited over the side with ragged, humiliating force, splattering a neat coil of garland on the ground below, waiting to be stapled along the balustrades.

"Somebody get a wet dishcloth," Delta ordered, then went to Cathy and held her forehead while she vomited again.

I grabbed a pile of paper napkins off a serving table and started out the porch doors, but both Becka and Cleo stopped me.

"What's worse than puking all over the Christmas garland in front a bunch of strangers?" Becka asked.

"Having your new boyfriend wipe the puke off your face," Cleo answered. "Amen."

"I'm not—" I began.

"Like hell you aren't," Becka said drolly.

They took the napkins from me, and I let them.

Chapter 16

Cathy
At Delta's House That Night

I woke in the dark, humiliated but starving, fixated on the scents of cornbread and beef stew somewhere in Delta's house. On the pine chest of Delta's guest room an antique clock chimed ten times.

Ten o'clock? Had I been sound asleep since late afternoon? After my spewing debut Delta had carted me to her house quickly, insisted I down several teaspoons of some homemade stomach remedy she called "herbal butter," then gave me clean clothes and steered me to bed. All I remembered was hearing one of my own delicate snores before I fell asleep.

Now I reluctantly pushed aside the soft caress of a flannel sheet and an aged quilt pieced from dresses Delta's grandmothers had owned when gas cost twenty-five cents a gallon and every civilized flapper wore a bell-shaped *cloche* hat pulled so low over her brow she had to tilt her head back to see. If I weren't starving I might have stayed in that heirloom cocoon for the next several years.

I shuffled into a softly lit hallway, trying to ignore the fact I was dressed in tube socks, flannel pajama bottoms that didn't quite reach my ankles, and one of the café's logo sweatshirts. *The Lard Cooks In Mysterious Ways*, its slogan said in big pink script. I smoothed my hair over the scarred side of my face, cleared my throat to see if anyone responded, and when no

181

one did I padded toward the back of the house, where I vaguely recalled seeing a big, lovable kitchen. As I passed an open bedroom door I peeked into its shadows. Cora and Ivy snuggled in a double bed under quilts. Two housecats snuggled with them.

"Sleep the sleep of innocence restored," I whispered. I felt maternal and amazingly profound.

I found the kitchen and stood just outside the entrance, an archway lined with family photos, while I watched Delta at the stove. She hummed as she worked. How could someone be so happy about the simple task of making a meal?

There are people nobody notices, but the world revolves around them. They're the quiet ones, the strong, peaceful ones, who form the unbreakable hub for a bunch of fragile spokes. True families aren't bred, they're spun together. And at their center, at the center of the infinite wheel of every family of every kind, blood or otherwise, there is a hub, that person, those people, who hold the wheel together and keep it turning.

Once upon a time I'd thought I was a hub simply because I paid a lot of people to orbit around me. Now I made a soft, mournful sound at the truth: I wasn't even an outer moon of a forgotten sun. Delta turned quickly from her stove. "Why, our newest Crossroads resident is awake and lookin' pink again," she said kindly.

"I really put on a show today, didn't I?"

"Yep. You're a legend, already. I mean it. I told Thomas so. Legends don't have to be perfect. In fact, the more warts they have, the better. Gives the gossips and the historians plenty to explain. You've got more warts than a frog's butt. I mean that in a good way."

"Gee, thanks." Formerly a princess, now a frog's ass. Maybe some prince would come along and transform me with a kiss. It wouldn't be Thomas. I'd never vomited in front of a man before.

"Have a seat," Delta urged again. "The stove won't bite."

"Put a leash on it, just to be sure."

"Aw, come on. It's tame."

I inched into the kitchen, squinting in the lights of a wagon-wheel chandelier over the long, pine-slab table and keeping an eye on her six-burner, professional cookstove. Delta set a blue crockery soup bowl filled with stew on a placemat. "Try a spoonful of this while I get you some hot cornbread."

I stared at the blue gas flame beneath the stew pot on the stove, then quietly shifted my place setting to the opposite side of the table. I sat down slowly, darting more glances at the burner. You never know when a stove might jump away from its berth and try to fry you. It happens in cartoons all the time. The aroma of the soup seduced me and I finally looked down at it. "You cooked all evening at the cafe and now you're cooking for me. I would have been happy with just some more of that herbal butter and a biscuit."

"Aw, it's no trouble. I cook like other people breathe. I don't even have to think about it. So you liked my home remedy, huh?"

"I know this is a strange thing to say about butter, but it even *tasted* soothing."

"Butter is good for the soul." She pulled a small black-iron skillet from the oven. A golden cap of cornbread puffed over the rim. The smell was delicious. I grabbed a spoon and shoveled a quick appetizer of beef stew into my mouth. "I've never been so hungry in my life," I said when my mouth was briefly sans stew again. "I haven't had an appetite like this since before . . . since last spring. Can you teach me how to make that butter remedy? It's like an appetite stimulant and a tranquilizer rolled into one."

Delta pursed her lips as she sliced the cornbread then scooped a steaming triangle onto a plate beside my bowl. "It's a secret recipe. Santa makes it." Her tone was too casual. "He keeps me supplied, but only for serious medical emergencies."

Santa. The pothead of Jefferson County. My hand halted with the cornbread halfway to my mouth. "Are you saying you gave me *pot* butter?"

She cocked her head and widened her eyes as if shocked. "You're in the house of the county sheriff. A man sworn to uphold the law. All I gave you was an old-timey mountain remedy made from medicinal herbs."

After a moment of slow—very slow—pondering, I stuffed the cornbread into my mouth and shrugged. Okay, I was stoned. No wonder I was hungry despite the sinister stove watching me.

Delta settled across the table from me with a big bottle of Biltmore chardonnay and a pair of wine glasses painted with uneven blue polka dots. "My granddaughter made me a whole set," she explained as she poured wine.

"Beautiful." I lifted a glass and studied it intently.

Delta began chuckling. "Don't stare at the dots so hard."

"The sky over Hog Back is almost this exact shade of blue. And Ivy's eyes were that blue when she was trying to decide whether to like me, today. And in the Privy, Thomas's skin was blue. Blue is the universal color of deep personal connections, don't you think? If Jesus were a color, He'd be blue."

"I think I gave you too much butter. Five hours later and you're still able to see Jesus in polka dots."

Delta sipped wine while I finished two bowls of soup and the entire skillet of cornbread. The meal absorbed enough illicit herbal remedy to lift me from my philosophical daze. Depression settled in. "I used to be so comfortable as the center of attention. Now I make a fool of myself when someone lights a gas log."

"Aw, come on," Delta said. "Take your glass of wine and let's go sit in my sunroom. Pike added it on the summer after my mama and daddy died. They died of heart attacks within two months of each other. All that summer Pike and me worked on the sunroom. I bet I cried over every nail. All that sorrow, going into something productive. Now it's my favorite place in the house. At night it's a good, quiet room for contemplating life."

I followed her wearily into a spacious glassed porch filled with plants and wicker. An electric space heater hummed in one corner. We settled in cushioned lounges with the wine on a small table between us. The room looked out over the Cove's enormous pasture. A half-moon hung in the clear winter sky over the mountains. Frost glinted on the winter grass. I peered into the silvery darkness. "Where's Thomas tonight? After watching me throw up he retreated to his cabin, right?"

"No, he's playing poker with Pike, Jeb, the Judge, Dolores—the usual gang. Pike has a little trailer out back of the café. It's got a table, some comfortable chairs, a fridge, some deer heads and stuffed turkeys. That's where the card sharks go every Saturday night."

So Thomas had stayed nearby. I could go see him, if I wanted to. Discuss blue dots with him. That cheered me up.

"The rest of us hang out in the café's side room," Delta went on. "Drink wine, shoot the breeze, hold our weekly quilting bee. We finish a quilt every couple of months, give it away, then start another one. The quilt-in-progress is on a quilting frame we pull up to the ceiling during the week. You'll see. Do you sew? We've always got room for another quilter. No experience needed."

I looked at her dully. "I don't think I'm going to be part of the gang around here. After what happened today—"

"You threw up. Who cares?"

"I didn't just throw up, I panicked. I embarrassed myself, I ruined your decorations, I upset you and your family, not to mention being the reason Thomas jumped in the pond at my grandmother's house. I have . . . disabilities, Delta. Phobias. Quirks. My skin crawls when people look at me. I freak when I see an open flame. I'm too scared to drive a car. All I want to do is find a way to live up at Granny's place with as little human contact as possible, so I won't keep making a fool out of myself."

"You got off to a bad start is all. Look, you just need a plan. A *recipe* for easing yourself out into the world again. Let's start by talking about your granny's house. You should put in electricity and plumbing. She'd want you to fix it up however it suits you."

"You think so? She could have upgraded the house, but she didn't. Why?"

"It suited her. She grew up with it that way. But that doesn't mean she'd want you to keep it the same."

"It's a vintage design. There aren't many of those Sears kit houses left. Especially ones that haven't already been remodeled. If I change anything, it would be like boring holes into a Ming vase to turn it into a lamp."

"Mary Eve was into Zen and all that stuff. She'd say change is good."

"Thomas loves the house the way it is. He's taken care of it devotedly. I'm not comfortable betraying his vision of the place."

"It's your house, hon, and you need to claim it."

"Maybe Thomas is right. He says I'll want to leave some day, go back to the so-called real world. I should give this house to him then, in pristine antique condition. He's just waiting for me to leave."

"If you think Thomas wants you to leave, you're more stoned than I thought. Give him half a chance and you'll have him on your doorstep all the time." She winked. "And elsewhere."

"I've got to stand on my own two feet without needing a man's help. Besides, what man wants to touch a woman who looks like this?" I pointed to my face.

Delta frowned at me. "If women sat around waiting to feel perfect about themselves before they got laid, all the ugly-as-mule-peckers men would be awful lonely. They'd never get any action."

I took a deep swallow of wine. "A little cellulite and sagging skin isn't bad. But my scars are . . ."

"Cathryn Mary Deen! You listen to me! By the time she died your granny had an ass like the backend of a fat hen, big freckles, liver spots, an appendix scar and big knuckles from arthritis, but she *still* got more pecker than any woman in ten counties. Men adored her. It's about attitude. If you think you're sexy, men will too. You gotta stop using your old standards and learn to see what's right about yourself, not what's wrong."

"I don't know how to do that."

"You think you're the only person who's ever had to rethink everything they know about themselves? Let me tell you about my son. Jeb was in the National Guard. He got called up at the start of the Iraq War. He only spent about six months over there before he nearly got killed by a mine. He came home a stranger. He'd seen terrible things but he couldn't talk about 'em. He slept with a pistol under his pillow. He cried when he tried to touch Becka. We found out later he killed some Iraqi women and children by accident. Poor Becka and the kids were scared to death of him and for him, and so were Pike and me. He disappeared one night during a thunderstorm, and we all nearly went crazy. Thomas and Pike trailed him up to Devil's Knob. Jeb was going to jump. Thomas had to crawl out on a ledge and coax him back. Whatever Thomas said to him out on that cliff—neither one of 'em will tell—it made a difference. Jeb started to get better. Now he's okay, but is he the same? No. The fun-loving, laughing boy I raised is gone forever. It breaks my heart."

"Thomas saved his life?"

She nodded. "Thomas has a knack for knowing what to say to somebody in despair, doesn't he?"

"Yes."

"So look at it this way: You're returning the favor."

"No, I'm just frightening him into a new attitude. He's afraid to turn his back in case I do something awful to the house. Remove a nail. Polish a splinter the wrong way."

"He could use his splinter polished, that's for sure." She poured more wine in my glass and then hers, took a long swallow and waved her glass at me. "Here's a little secret for you. The Log Splitter girls? Well, their names are Alberta and Macy, really. Alberta and Macy have their eye on his sperm."

"Why?"

"They've had two children together already, with the help of a man around here who shall remain nameless." She leaned close to me and whispered, "Santa." I nearly spit my wine. Delta settled back and went on, "And they want to have a third child, but they'd like a little diversity in the gene pool so maybe folks won't notice that the two they've got already look a lot like a certain dope-growing old hippie. They're real fond of Thomas so they've set their sights on him. Call him a 'metrosexual,' I guess because he's respectful and doesn't dog their commune of hard-luck women. Anyhow, they'd love to get him on the receiving end of a specimen cup and a turkey baster."

I downed most of my glass of wine at that point and held it out for a refill. "Is he interested?"

"No way. He's scared silly of ever being responsible for another child, even if nobody asks him to help raise it." She poured my wine. "But all you have to do is see him with Cora and Ivy to know he's cut out to be a daddy. He's a natural." She paused, frowning at me as she set the bottle down. "Please tell me you weren't planning to have babies with that mule pecker."

"Who?"

"Gerald."

I hesitated. My relationship with Gerald sounded so cold-blooded, now. "We had an agreement. Oh, all right. A pre-nup. Babies were in the contract. Two. The timing had to be mutually agreed upon. I had my attorneys amend it to say if I got pregnant unexpectedly it was my choice whether to have an abortion or not. I'm pro-choice, but I doubt I'd ever choose that option for myself. So I wanted it clearly stated. Gerald wasn't happy about the option, but he agreed. You know, I suspect he'd secretly had a vasectomy, anyway." I gulped some wine. "Mule pecker."

"You can put all that intimate stuff in a contract?"

"You can put anything in a contract if you're stupid enough to love and trust a man."

"Don't go painting with a broad brush, now. You picked one rotten apple off a tree full of good ones."

"I know, I know. I don't want to hate men. I just don't want to ever depend on one, again."

"Well, well, that double-edged dilemma's really gonna work out." She stared into her wine glass for a long time. Then, "Before Jeb was born, Pike and me nearly divorced. We were only in our early twenties, but we'd been married since we were sixteen. Felt like we'd been together our whole lives already, and after . . ." Her voice trailed off. She shifted in the lounge chair, drank more wine, stared into the moonlit winter pasture. "I'm gonna tell you something very few people know. Even Thomas doesn't know this." She looked at me with tears already gleaming in her eyes. "We had two children who drowned."

"Oh, Delta."

"Pike, Junior, our first-born, and Cynthia, our little girl. He was six and she was four. They went on a Vacation Bible School outing to the French Broad. The river, the big one, you know, east of here. I wouldn't have let 'em go without me, they were so little, but Santa's wife—he was married, then—she was one of the chaperones. She was young and flighty. I should have known better. She turned her back and they wandered off. It took . . . two days . . . before their bodies were found downriver. We figure Cynthia fell in and Pike, Junior tried to save her."

"I'm so sorry."

"I thought I'd die. Me and Pike both nearly lost our minds and our hearts and our souls. What happened broke up Santa's marriage. His wife wasn't a bad girl but I hated her from then on without any hope of forgiveness. She left here and never came back. Died a few years ago. Left us a letter that said she'd never forgiven herself. So *her* life was ruined, too."

Tears slid down Delta's face. She kept her gaze on the moon light. "Pike and I didn't know which way to turn. Who do you blame when there's nobody to blame? I accused him of blaming me for letting the kids go on the trip, he accused me of blaming him for not being a good provider—by that I mean, he was working long hours at a lumber mill halfway to Asheville and working part-time as a sheriff's deputy, and I was working at the county high school in the cafeteria and helping my parents take care of two sets of grandparents who were getting old and needy. So to Pike's way of thinking, I let the kids go on the river trip because I was worn out and needed a rest, and that was because he didn't make enough money for me not to work. It was just crazy, sad talk, made no sense then or now."

She held her wine glass to her cheek for a moment, as if it were a child's face she could cuddle. "We didn't touch each other for nearly two years. Pike took to drinking and smoking dope with Santa. They'd disappear for whole weekends doing God knows what. And me? I screwed a couple of men who came through here to go fishing. How do you like that for a confession?"

I wiped tears off my face. "It must have made sense at the time."

She nodded. "My babies died in a way I couldn't bear to think about. I didn't care if I lived or died, either. My husband didn't want me anymore. So what difference did it make?" She sighed. "Pike knows about those men. We got past them a long time ago."

"What brought you and Pike back together?"

"Your granny. She stood by us, she kept saying we'd be okay if we could just remember why we loved each other. Your mama was gone by then, I mean, she was down in Atlanta being a career girl and working as a paralegal at your daddy's law firm. Mary Eve was lonely and she had time on her hands, so she'd show up at our house nearly every day—well, hell, it wasn't a house, we were living in an old trailer back here in the woods—she'd come by every day and bring biscuits and talk to me. When my Grandma and Grandpa McKendall died, they left me the café. Nobody thought I could make a go of it. My own mama—my mama was a mean piece of work—she said I didn't deserve it, I was no business woman, that I should sell the place to her and Daddy, and she wouldn't let Daddy loan me the money I needed to get started. The cafe wasn't anything but a sandwich shop then. There wasn't even a stove in the kitchen.

"Mary Eve loaned me the start-up money. She told me to follow my heart. She said if I went around listening to everybody who said I had odd or stupid ideas I might as well sit in a corner and suck my thumb the rest of my life. She said, 'The Lard cooks in mysterious ways, and it's up to you to make a meal with what He gives you.'

"So I started cooking. Cooked eighteen hours a day for months, feeding anybody who came by. People needed my food, they liked my food. And I felt alive again, just a little. Then one day I looked up and there stood Pike. He'd kept his distance since we barely spoke anymore. But there he was. He walked into the kitchen and said, 'You need a dishwasher?' and I said, 'I could use your help, sure,' and he went over to the sink and rolled up his sleeves and started washing. There was no big moment when we made up. There were lots of small ones. Then one night after closing we walked into the trailer, and we went in its tiny bedroom, and we made love. And slowly but surely, we were okay. Jeb was born a little over a year later."

I was crying long streamers of tears by now, and Delta reached over and patted my hair, comforting me for her sorrows as well as my own. She pried my scarred hand free from my wine glass and squeezed it hard. "I feed people," she whispered fervently. "I feed them with my heart and my hopes, and I nurture every hungry part of them. That's what I do. I feed their souls. That's the only way to keep going when times are bad. For them and for me. To know I'm here for a reason. That I can make a difference in other people's lives. Just like your granny did. And just like you will, and Thomas will, when you finally figure out the way."

I swung my feet off the lounge chair, sat facing her, and bent my head to hers. "I'm going to try my best not to disappoint you," I sobbed. "I love you, cousin."

189

Apparently, those were words even stoic Delta couldn't resist. She began crying hard, too, and only managed to say, "I love you, too, cousin," between ragged breaths.

Of course, in the midst of our full-fledged mutual breakdown we heard a back door open and shut, followed by two sets of heavy footsteps in the house. We quickly straightened up, scrubbing our eyes with our sleeves, wiping our noses, clearing our throats, and trying to breathe normally. We made snorting sounds in unison.

"We'd be more delicate if we weren't drunk," Delta said with a broken laugh.

"At least you're only drunk. I'm drunk and stoned."

"Sssh. Here comes Pike. And Thomas."

The men's tall frames filled the sliding glass door from the sunroom into the kitchen. They were backlit by a lamp on the counter. I hoped they couldn't see our faces in the dark sunroom any better than we could see theirs silhouetted against the light.

"Everything all right here?" Pike drawled. From the tone of his voice, he knew it wasn't.

"We're just talking about food." Delta answered, her voice a wobbly treble. She hoisted the nearly empty wine bottle. "And wine."

"And wine," I echoed, nodding. To be honest, I said it this way: "An' vine."

Thomas leaned against the door frame. He sank his hands into the pockets of his borrowed overalls. Their soft denim clung to his long legs. The lamp highlighted the broad cut of his shoulders above the narrow bib straps. He had shoved the sleeves of his borrowed sweatshirt up to his elbows. His forearms were thick and graceful. The side of his throat, above the sweatshirt's round neckline, made a clean, strong line against the lamplight. Who knew overalls could be so erotic? "Stomach better?" he asked gently.

"Just fine, thanks." *Jus' fine, tanks.* I looked at Delta. "Off to bed. Goodnight, cousin."

She draped an arm around my neck and hugged me. "Goodnight, cousin. You need any help?"

"Nah. When I was in the Miss Georgia pageant? Had vertigo from an ear infection. I walked on four-inch highheels in a thigh-cut green maillot with a big sash across my boobs saying Miss Atlanta. Damned sash wasn't pinned correctly on my shoulder strap, so I had to walk just-so or poof! The banner'd fall off. I was so dizzy from the ear thing I felt like I was on stilts on a trampoline. But I made it. I nailed that swimsuit competition. Hah. This?" I waved a hand at myself, meaning my current tipsy circumstances. "Piece of cheesecake."

Delta laughed. "Okay, Miss Atlanta, you teeter off to bed. Thomas, give the gal a no-questions-asked escort down the runway, please-sir."

"I'll make sure she gets to the end of the runway, but I can't guarantee she won't waggle her wings and trip over her landing gears."

I stood. I had never been a sloppy drinker; I could hold my liquor. But my face was swollen from crying and I was dressed like a homeless person at a pajama party, so my goal in life at that moment was to make it through the lighted part of the house to my bedroom with as much speed and *élan* as possible. "Outta my way, please. I'm cleared for take-off." I gave Delta's slightly graying dark hair a pat. "I'm going to give you gold highlights."

She laughed. "Will it hurt?"

"No pain, no gain. Beauty is as beauty does. Life is a box of highlights. Or something. Goodnight."

"Goodnight."

I started past Pike. I couldn't resist a big, middle-aged daddy figure. "Goodnight, Cousin Sheriff. You know, growing up, I watched re-runs of *Gunsmoke* with my aunts." I patted his chest. "You look like James Arness. You know. Sheriff Matt Dillon?"

"Thank you, Miss Kitty," he drawled.

"You're welcome."

I avoided looking at Thomas as I continued on to the kitchen. "No need to walk me back to the saloon, Festus."

He caught me by one elbow as my tube socks slipped on the kitchen's smooth tile floor. "Why, shucks, Miss Kitty, but I disagree." We headed down the hallway toward the guest rooms, his hand bolstering me like a warm steel brace. "You okay?" he whispered. "Were you crying with Delta or was Delta crying with you?"

"A little of both. We're okay."

"Good."

I cupped a furtive yet dramatic hand to the side of my mouth. "Pike and Delta are listening. The girls are right down there in that room. Sssh. The ears have walls. I mean, the walls have ears."

He smiled. "You're the one talking, not me. Here's an irony for you. You're drunk, and I'm sober."

"What are you like when you're drunk?"

"Quiet, too quiet."

"Not me." I wobbled to a stop outside my bedroom door. "I'm *Chatty Cathy*. Remember those dolls? The ones with the string in their backs? Daddy bought me all of them. New ones, old ones. Did you know Maureen McCormick was the voice of the 1970's dolls? That's right, Marcia Brady. Marcia, Marcia, Marcia. I had blonde *Chatty Cathys*, brunette, redheads. I even had the black one. Daddy and I picked it out as a Christmas gift for our housekeeper's daughter—yes, we had a black housekeeper and her name was 'LaRynda' but I called her 'Mrs. Washington' because Daddy said it was respectful but you know, he made her wait for the bus outside in the rain and snow, see, there was a special bus route through the neighborhoods of Buckhead—that's where we lived, near the governor's mansion—where the black maids worked, oh, yes, it was all so old-school and lily-white, anyway, I picked out the black *Chatty Cathy* for LaRynda's daughter, who was my age, but when I gave it to her she said, 'I want a white one, like you have,' and I said 'How come?' And she said—her name was 'Sharon'—Sharon said, 'Because black girls are ugly,' and I said, 'How come you think so?' And Sharon said, 'Because everybody says so, nobody even sees us when they look at us, but everybody says *you're* pretty and everybody sees *you*.'

"So anyhow, I traded with her and I got the black *Chatty Cathy* and she got one of my blonde ones. But you know, that's *sad* and I'm so glad things have changed. But even now, do you think black women get enough respect for their beauty? I don't." I took a breath as I looked up at him solemnly.

"Where's that string?" Thomas said drily, turning me so he could look at my back. "I'd like to tie a knot in it."

"Nobody's pulling my strings anymore. No strings attached. I'm nobody's puppet."

"I think you've almost exhausted your string analogies for tonight."

"I'm babbling. I know it." I shut my eyes, took a deep breath, then backed toward my open door, hugging myself. "I discharged my Hummer's battery, ran out of gas, made you jump in the pond, threw up at the café, now I'm high and I can't stop talking. I'm so nervous. You make me incredibly nervous. You're not like any other man."

"I'll take that as a compliment."

"Even worse, I have nightmares and I'm afraid to go back to sleep. Will you sit with me a little while? This is not a comeon."

"I love it when you talk dirty."

"Good. Come and sit."

I wandered into the bedroom with him behind me. He turned on a lamp and left the door open. That charmed and depressed me. He was a gentleman or disinterested or both.

You don't want a man, you want a memory. A boyfriend said that to me when I broke up with him for no apparent reason. He was right. I could have any man I wanted, so there was very little challenge about it. I got bored easily. Now, unfortunately, I wanted a lot of memories with just this one man, Thomas Karol Mitternich, but I was trapped in fears and scars—both his and mine. "There's a chair," I said, as if he couldn't see it. "Take it to my side of the bed, please." Then I climbed under the covers. As he pulled the chair around I worked my quilt and sheet like a bird works a nest. *Put your face right side down, puff the pillow a little, right arm casually curled up, right hand tucked under the pillow. Yes! Your scars are hidden.* I laid down on my right side with the scarred side of my face burrowed just-so into the pillow. Now I looked like the old me. As long as I didn't move.

Thomas sat down slowly in the chair, watching me with a quizzical frown. "What are you doing? Getting ready to lay an egg?"

"Posing. That's what my whole life has been about. Tilt this way, glance that way, suck in my stomach, catch the light just so. I have to learn new poses, now. If I work at it, I can angle the bad side of my face away from people most of the time."

"There's no bad side. There's just your face. Don't do that. You'll get a crick in your neck."

"Better a crick than to be stared at in the wrong way." I shifted a few more times. Finally, mired in the bed like a damaged Greek statue half-buried in the ashes of Pompeii, I could relax. The illusion was in place. "I was raised to be a geisha," I explained. "To be ornamental. Like a prize piece of livestock. Don't tell me it isn't better to see me this way. 'A work of art.' That's what people used to call me. When I was a girl artists were always asking my father if he'd let me pose for them. He was so proud. And he'd tell me, 'A thousand years from now, collectors and historians will admire paintings of you. Your beauty will make you immortal.'"

Thomas scowled. He pushed the chair aside and sat down on the floor close to my head. The antique bedstead was so low he could gaze right at me. He propped his arm on the bed and steepled his head on his fist. Cocooned in the intimate light of a single lamp, we were separated by so little space I could feel his breath on my cheek.

"You're still beautiful," he said, his voice low and husky. "Of course you are. It's amazing to look at you. But it has nothing to do with whether you qualify to be the new Mona Lisa."

"I wasn't fishing for compliments. I just . . . I know what I'm good at. I want to show you."

"You don't have to bury half your face in a pillow to impress me."

Tears welled up. I blinked them away. "There's a branch of Daddy's family that still owns a plantation on the coast of South Carolina. They have an old slave cabin there; they use it as a guest house. They call it 'the servant quarters.' Servant, not slave. Sounds so much kinder, doesn't it? Happiness is all in how you see your place in society, in my opinion. I'm a geisha. Or at least, I was. And I was happy to be one. I just want you to know that."

"If it makes you happy to peek at me from a strategically doodled hollow in a fluffed-up pillow, so be it." He paused. "But you look like your head's being swallowed by a big marshmallow."

I chortled. Amazing. He could make me laugh. "I'm just drunk enough to cry and laugh at the same time. Not to mention . . . do you know about Santa's pot butter?"

"Oh, yeah. That explains a lot."

"Go. *Go.* Save yourself. I'll talk to the ceiling for a few hours, then I'll go to sleep."

"You'd rather talk to the ceiling than to me?"

"No, I love talking to you. It's like safe sex. Sex without touching."

"Hmmm."

"Nothing personal. I don't want you to touch me. Don't want anybody to touch me. The scars. I can't stand the idea of being touched."

He unfurled his fist, angled a rakish forefinger at my quilted shoulder, and gave me a sly look. "I don't know if I can help myself. I might poke your shoulder at any moment."

"Please, this isn't a joke."

He lowered his hand and looked at me gently. "I'm not going to touch you, I promise."

"It's terrifying to not know where my power base is, anymore. Before, it was a given. Men wanted me. Any man, anywhere. I knew where I stood. It wasn't always a fun thing, you know? To know everything about yourself is judged through a lens of sex. Men were shy or nervous or defensive or . . . at the opposite extreme, like Gerald, confident but also possessive and arrogant. But here you are, 'None of the above.' I don't have a framework for you. They didn't teach us about men like you in geisha school."

"I'm one of a kind."

I smiled at him. He smiled back. My smile faded. "What was your wife like?" I whispered.

He went very still. The light left him. His gaze shifted away from me, seeing her. "Smart, pretty, very rich. We met during college. Not *at* college, at a sports bar. I was working there. Bartending. She was slumming. Home from Harvard. Her family had bought the block. In a sense, she was my landlord."

"Your wife went to Harvard? That's not just smart . . . that's *Harvard.*"

"She got a degree in law. Top of her class."

"Did she go into practice?"

"Only for a year or two. Then we had Ethan, and she stayed home."

"Was she happy to do that?"

"She thought so, at first. She was the rebel in her family. I think marrying me was a way to flip them the bird. But she and her sister were close, and her sister kept trying to lure her back to the fold. Marrying beneath her socio-economic class sounded a lot more romantic than it was."

"But you became a very successful architect at a young age! How could anyone not be impressed by you?"

He smiled sadly. "Are you flirting?"

"No, for once in my life, I'm having an honest conversation with a man. I'm sure I'll regret it in the morning."

"It'll be our secret."

I studied him for a moment. Then, "Your marriage was rocky, but you were glad to have a son."

"Absolutely."

"I won't lie and say I can imagine what it feels like to lose—"

"I don't like to talk about him." Thomas drew back a little. "Nothing personal. I have my own nightmares."

Should I tell him about Delta's children? No, she would have told him herself if she thought it would help. She'd confided in me. But it was private. But maybe . . . "Delta understands what you've been through, more than you know. That's all I'm going to say."

Thomas tilted his head and scrutinized me. I saw the reference sink in. "Her first two children. I've heard about them."

I groaned. "Not from me, you didn't."

"Pike told me."

"Whew."

"Around here the secrets travel in smaller circles, but they do get around. That's all right. It's among friends."

"Okay, let's just be friends."

He eyed me as if challenged. "Just friends, all right. I've got an idea. We'll be born-again virgins. It's all the rage with the young folk, I hear. First, I'll tell you when I lost *mine*. Virginity, that is."

Dread slithered up my stomach. I didn't trade virginity stories. Not with anyone. Or if I did, I made mine up. But I didn't want to lie to Thomas. "Oh, let's not—"

"I was sixteen. She was seventeen. She had a lisp and a convertible VW bug." He arched a brow. "Yes, an older woman with a speech impediment and a soft-top."

"Good choice." I said nothing else.

A few long seconds ticked by. Thomas clucked his tongue. "I showed you mine, now you show me yours. Lost-virginity story, that is."

"Boring. Just boring. No point in—"

"No gory details needed."

"Why, *suh*," I said in a slurred drawl, "no gentleman insists on such information from a lady."

He frowned lightly as he studied my face. "What's wrong, Cathy? What happened to you?"

I went very still. I wanted to look away from him, but I couldn't. *He already senses something. You might as well talk. He shared intimate, humiliating moments with you at the hospital, he's seen your scars, he's seen you half-naked in the Privy. Talk to him.*

"I was thirteen," I admitted. "He was in his forties. A photographer. My father hired him to create a professional portfolio for me. It happened in his studio one afternoon. And no, it wasn't rape."

As Thomas absorbed the information his eyes went cold. For an unnerving moment I thought I'd made a big mistake by confessing. Then he said very softly, "Any time a man that age talks a thirteen-year-old girl into sex, it's rape."

"I was worldly. Infinitely confident. Already an expert at flirting with grown men. And well-aware that I had a lot of sexual power. I thought being wanted by an older man was an . . . honor. A victory for me. 'Look how much I can control men.' Later I realized how naïve I was, and that he had controlled *me*, not the other way around. It was a hard lesson to learn." Even now, prickles of shame stung my face. "I've never told anyone that story before."

Thomas shut his eyes for a moment, and when he opened them they were still angry, but also gentle. "Thank you for trusting me."

"What do you really think? Don't be gallant. Tell the truth."

His jaw tightened. He raised a hand to touch my face, halted when I flinched, lowered the hand to the quilt. "I meant exactly what I said. You were just a kid, and you were molested. The bastard should have been castrated. That's what I think. Case closed."

I searched his eyes. *He's being honest. My innocence is that simple to him.* "I like how you see me," I whispered.

"No wonder you have a love-hate relationship with photographers."

"I used to pride myself on using them more than they used me. Not anymore. They got the last laugh, Thomas. I'll never forget looking into a camera lens while I nearly burned to death. I'll never forget the joy in that photographer's voice. I don't ever want anyone to take my picture, again. Ever. I don't even want to pose for a driver's license."

"If you spend your life hiding from photographers, then they *will* get the last laugh. Don't worry about being photographed. I'll help you deal with it."

"The way you dealt with those photographers who came here to find my grandmother's farm?"

He arched a brow. "You know all my secrets."

"Delta told me. And she told me about you going to jail."

"Not just jail. The chain gang. Hard labor. Come on, I want some sympathy."

"You pressure-washed gargoyles."

"No, I pressure-washed *Baptist stone monkeys.*"

"What?"

"That's a bedtime story for another night."

"Thomas, why were you willing to go to jail for me? I'm not being coy. I really want to know."

He stood slowly, bending over me with immaculately timed care, not to startle me. I drew a deep breath anyway, shifted awkwardly, dislodged my perfect halo of pillow, and turned the bad side of my face to the light and his eyes. He kissed me very lightly, very slowly on the mouth. The kind of kiss that made me shut my eyes instinctively to absorb the sensation. The night seeped in between us, the shadows filling in the soft amalgam of empty unknowns.

Thomas drew back just enough to look down at me. "Does that answer your question?" He turned out the light and left the room.

I had a spot on the center of my stomach, halfway between my navel and my pubes. My sweet spot. The right man's slow, concentrated fingertip on the sweet spot would slowly reduce me to a boneless puddle of receptive languor. Thomas stroked my sweet spot without laying a hand on me. Amazing.

For the first time since the accident, I put the scarred hand between my legs and rubbed myself to an orgasm. Then I fell asleep easily, and for once, I didn't dream of fire, but only of warmth, and Thomas.

Chapter 17

Thomas
The Next Morning

I woke on Delta and Pike's living-room couch in a haze of turbulent feelings from the night before. One hand instinctively slid deep inside the voluminous tent of my overalls. I was dreaming about touching Cathy, and touching myself in the process, before I remembered where I was, right about the moment I heard Cora whisper, "He must have an itch."

My hand retreated to the outer Siberia of the coffee table, knocking over an empty water glass I'd left there. I sat up. Cora and Ivy stood at the far end of the couch, peering at me from under neon-orange yarn caps, like miniature hunters. They were dressed and wearing their coats. Apparently they'd come to say good morning and goodbye, and had gotten more than they bargained for. Ivy frowned at me shrewdly; Cora smiled without a clue.

"Good morning," I said. When caught in the act it's always best to pretend you aren't doing anything intimate.

"Our aunt's here," Cora said wistfully. "We gotta go."

"Cathy's already gone home to her grandma's house," Ivy informed me. "The sheriff took her. She told Delta that everybody should stay away. She said she has to sink or swim. That nobody can hand her a life jacket, because she's got to make it *herself*." Ivy's stony façade cracked a frown. "But I don't even think she can sew. She talked to our aunt about making some curtains for her. Aunt Laney said yes."

Cora's smile dwindled. "Aunt Laney promised to call Delta and Cathy next time she's in jail. They said she had to promise."

"That's a good idea." I swung my feet off the couch and sat up. "I'm going to give you my cell phone number so you can call me, too."

Cora brightened. Ivy didn't. "What if Banger eats your phone again?" Ivy inquired coolly.

"Then call Banger, and I'll listen to his stomach."

Cora giggled. Even Ivy had to crack a smile. "Cathy gave us her number, too."

"Good."

"She put that quilt over you."

"What quilt?" I looked down. I now wore the quilt from the guest bed. It had sprouted patches of hair. Brown hair, like mine. Ivy pointed at them. "Cathy trimmed your beard. We watched."

I felt my chin. The sawed-off stump of my beard was now a neatly rounded topiary. "How does it look?"

"You're handsome," Cora said.

"You've got an Adam's apple," Ivy said with a shrug.

"Now, don't go flattering me." I folded the quilt carefully, catching my beard scraps. Cora spotted one of the cats and bounded out of the room to tell it goodbye. When I looked up I met Ivy's shrewd stare again. She sniffed at me. "You were in Cathy's room last night. Sitting on the floor by the bed. I went to the bathroom, and I saw you. Why were you sitting in there on the floor?"

"We were talking in low voices. It was easier to hear from that spot."

"Men don't go in women's bedrooms just to talk. Were you gonna put some moves on her?"

Ivy desperately wanted to know the rules in a world where men seemed to break them. At the moment she didn't need a lesson in respecting other people's privacy. I cleared my throat. "Sometimes men and women just talk."

"Bullshit. I saw you kiss her."

"That's all it was. A kiss. Cathy needs a friend right now, not a boyfriend."

"So you weren't trying to get in bed with her? Trying to talk her into it? What if she put some moves on *you?*"

"Now, just wait . . ."

"Don't you want her to?"

"You know, I don't mind answering questions, but some things are private."

"You *do* want her to. Men always want women to put the moves on them."

There was no easy way to discuss basic sexual biology versus the rules of civilized courtship, especially not with a twelve-year-old who hadn't seen much evidence of the latter. I set the quilt aside and looked at Ivy somberly. "You know what? It's as simple as this: Most men are nice to women, and most women are nice to men. They treat each other with fairness and respect. They make each other feel good, not bad. If someone makes you feel bad, get away from him."

"So if a man's not nice to me, and I don't run away fast enough, I was *asking* for it?"

Jesus. I shouldn't be surprised that a kid like Ivy still hadn't come to terms with being molested. After all, Cathy still harbored doubts about her own experience as a girl. What could I say that wouldn't sound clumsy? "Ivy, nothing was your fault, and nothing you said or did was 'asking for it.' Now listen. I can't tell you to forget what happened to you. And I can't promise you that no one will ever try to take advantage of you again. But let's get something straight between you and me. You're safe around *me*. You and Cora. *Always.* In any circumstance, no matter what. And if you and Cora ever need me, if you're ever in danger—anytime, anywhere, for any reason—I *swear* to you, all you have to do is call me. *I will not let anyone or anything hurt you.*"

Her blue eyes widened by tiny degrees during my short speech. Now the dark pupils became wide apertures of a camera set to catch any small lie in me. *Men see everything through a lens of sex*, Cathy had said. But so do women, even the half-grown ones. I wanted Ivy to focus on the basic truth, to snap the image of the one simple guarantee a male can offer a female of any age: *I won't hurt you, and I will protect you from other men.*

"You understand?" I asked again. "You believe me?"

For a few seconds I wasn't sure she'd answer at all. Then her eyes narrowed and the shield went back in place. "Yeah," she said drily. "Sure." She shrugged and headed toward the door, then halted. Ivy looked back at me with wary respect. "She kissed you. Cathy kissed you on the top of the head, while you were asleep. She'll put some moves on you one day. Don't worry."

"Thanks. That's good to know."

"Bye."

"Bye."

After she left I sank back on the couch and exhaled. My simple life was getting more complicated by the day.

In the kitchen, Jeb, Becka, Bubba, and several of their respective kids gazed at me with fervent curiosity as they shoveled breakfast into their mouths around the big table. Delta pointed at a stove full of biscuits, center-cut bacon, cream gravy, salmon patties, and scrambled eggs covered in cheese. Just her usual low-cholesterol Sunday breakfast to gird the family for a morning's work and worship. "Help yourself." She shrugged into a coat and grinned. "Thanks to the wine, I overslept. It's nearly seven. Cleo got the café kitchen up and running for my lazy butt. Time to go make the donuts."

"Pike drove Cathy back to the ridge?"

"Yep. Took some gas, a battery charger, and I packed her a box of food that'd feed an army for a week. Plus I sent along a big air mattress so she doesn't have to sleep on a cot. She'll be fine." Delta pointed to a note on the counter. "Cathy and I made a list of things she needs right away to make the place livable. Thomas, she's trying her best to honor your idea of how her house ought to be outfitted, but you need to back off. First thing, I'm calling Lewey over at the propane company to set her up with a tank and a generator. Then she can hook up some extension chords. Have a little space heater and some lights. A microwave. It's a start. She agreed to go shopping with me next week. To get some furniture."

I grabbed the note. "I'll take care of this."

Delta grabbed the list back. "Haven't you ever heard that country song? 'How Can I Miss You If You Won't Go Away?'" She stuffed the note into her coat.

I grimly followed her outside into the gray half-light of the cold December morning. "I'm not trying to control how she renovates the house. I'm trying to offer unconditional support and friendship."

Delta arched a brow. "She needs to be on her own for awhile. And you've got issues you haven't settled yet. You need to quit drinking for good, not just a week or two. You need to get straight in your mind what you want to do with your life. You need to make peace with that truckload of self-blame you carry around. You need to bury what happened to your wife and son, Thomas, and say *Amen* over the past. Otherwise, you're just gonna drag Cathy into your misery, and she's got plenty of her own misery to still figure out."

"I'm not trying to hurt her. I'm trying to help her."

"You're trying to get her in bed." Delta headed up the tree-lined driveway that led to the café's backyard, pumping her plump arms and short, plumb legs energetically, daring me to keep up with her righteous attitude.

I fell in beside her, chewing my tongue. "This is not a fourth-grade crush."

"I wish it were. Don't go adding sex to this complicated recipe, mister. Turn your burners on low, let things simmer."

"She needs me. And I'm glad to be needed. There's nothing wrong with that."

Delta shook her head. "Making love too soon's like trying to bake biscuits in an oven that's not hot enough yet. Oh, sure, you can get the dough to rise and the crust to brown, but inside? Still raw."

"I doubt I can get Cathy that close to my pilot light, so don't worry."

"Thomas, whether you realize it or not, when you're around her you give off heat like a steam table. Good, sweet, sexy heat. And she inches as close to you as she can get without admitting she loves the warmth. But if you burn her—" Delta swiveled to shake a finger at me as we walked—"if you burn so much as a single hair on her head, she's gonna have a hard time trusting you again. Now, 'fess up about something. How come you've dodged women since your wife died? No bullshit, tell me the truth."

I halted. So did she, peering up at me like a dark-haired owl. "I didn't want to start a new life. Didn't want to find someone new. I wasn't ready to move on."

"You're a handsome man, you've got money, you're not too long in the tooth. If you splashed on a little cologne and washed your truck, you could go over to Asheville any weekend and hook up with wild, tattooed, dope-smoking college students from UNC."

"Male, female, or art majors?"

"Go ahead and joke. But nobody would fault you if you went lookin' for love in all the wrong places, if you know what I mean."

"I thought women appreciated a man who prefers his sex with a side helping of love."

"Sure we do. I'm just asking. Are you ready to have a love life, again?"

"Cathy needs me."

"You didn't answer my question."

"I'm taking the idea of having a life one day at a time. It's a new concept for me."

Delta threw up her hands. "Here's Cathy, wandering in the wilderness, scared of stoves, throwing up when people look at her, and you want to offer her a guiding hand when you don't know which way you're headed yourself! Talk about the blind leading the blind! Oh, yeah, you and her should just go to bed together. That'll make it all work out!"

"All I did last night was sit *beside* her bed and talk to her."

"Must have been some mighty intense pillow talk, that's all I can say. 'Cause she wanted out of here as fast as she could go this morning."

"Not before she covered me with a quilt, trimmed my beard, and gave me a kiss on the head. My dastardly plan to seduce her seems to have backfired. She's treating me like a new puppy. Delta, amazing though it may seem, women are not the only ones who can go years without a good . . . companionship."

"Who says women can go years? I can't even go for days. Ask Pike."

"I promise you, even a handsome, fully functional, worldly pervert such as myself is capable of profound romantic patience."

"You take matters 'in hand' a lot, am I right? Oh, heck, why be coy? I hope you jerk off all the time."

I scowled at her. "Never fear."

"Good. Keep the pipeline primed and let Cathy settle in and stand on her own two feet. I'll keep an eye on her, don't worry. In the meantime, go find yourself a hobby. Go Christmas shopping. Hey, go up to Chicago and visit your brother."

"Look, I don't—"

"You're trying to pretend January isn't coming." All the good humor and patience fled from her face. She stared up at me grimly. A chill went through me. January was always my low point. Worse than Ethan's birthday, worse than the anniversary of nine-eleven. Delta knew it.

"Maybe this time I'll stay in control. You have to admit it I'm doing better."

"*Better's* not good enough, Thomas. You know I'm right. If you get through January then you'll know you're ready to move on with your life. Until then you need to keep clear of Cathy. You don't want her to get used to depending on you now, only to have you go down the drain after the first of the year."

I hung my head. "I'll make you a promise," I said finally. "I'll keep my distance, but I need to stay involved. Please. Let me take care Cathy my own way. Give me that list."

Slowly, warily, she handed over Cathy's to-do list. "Just how are you going to accomplish this without showing up in person?"

I gave her a rueful smile. "I'll have a small army of minions do my evil bidding. Women who can't resist my slightest whim. My harem."

"Oh, my lord," she said wryly. "You're calling in the lesbians."

PART FOUR

It is amazing how complete is the delusion that beauty is goodness.
—*Leo Tolstoy*

A man has every season while a woman only has the right to spring.
—*Jane Fonda*

Chapter 18

Cathy
The Log Splitter Girls

I woke to the sound of trucks coming up Wild Woman Ridge. Lots of them. For a few sleepy, horrifying seconds, as I staggered from my sleeping bag and quilts atop the gelatinous comfort of Delta's loaned air mattress, I thought the entire press corp of *The National Enquirer* had found me. Images of my scarred face swam before my eyes in full color next to the latest pix of fat/thin/high actresses getting divorced/detoxed/nipped-and-tucked. I'd be a prize catch in a media buffet that fed on fallen women. But when I pushed back one of my homemade quilt-drapes and stared out the living room window I saw several late-model pickup trucks, a van, and a big flat-bed hauling a tractor and pulling a trailer loaded with a robin's-egg blue portable toilet.

The toilet had been on my wish-list to Delta. Okay. But what was this crowd for? I hadn't asked her to send strangers. In fact, I'd spent quite a bit of time telling her how few people I wanted to meet. So what had she done?

Sent a work crew, the portable toilet, and a tractor.

As I tugged hiking boots onto my socked feet, I hopped to another window and peered out. The light was dim; what uncivilized time was it? I checked my wristwatch. Did these people have an aversion to business hours? Only the first rays of cold winter sunshine had begun to slant into the yard. One pale glimmer hit the driver's door of the lead pick-up, a big, hulking, burgundy model with a dual cab and a jacked-up chassis. I squinted and read: RAINBOW GODDESS BERRY FARM, Macy and Alberta Spruill-Groover, Crossroads, North Carolina. Macy and Alberta. The Log Splitter Girls.

"The Log Splitter Girls?" I said, astonished. "They raise berries, sing lesbian folk music, *and* deliver portable toilets?"

By the time I made it outside, wrapping my head in a scarf and puffing white clouds in front of me in nervous dread, nearly a dozen women, all dressed in burly workclothes, stood in my yard. I stared at them, and they stared back.

Two stepped forward. Though they were swaddled in matching quilted jackets and matching yarn caps, there was a definite personality difference. One smiled at me between long blond braids above an ankle-length khaki skirt while the other frowned at me under poofs of curly red hair above camo hunting pants. Both had the ruddy outdoorsiness of pioneer women. I felt like a show pony among mustangs. Recalling a photo on their CD, I realized who each was. Blonde braids: Macy. Red curls: Alberta. Seeing them in person, I refined that image. Macy: Smiling, sympathetic and friendly. Alberta: None of the above.

"We're late," Alberta grunted. "Your porta-shitter wasn't ready to be loaded when we went to pick it up."

Colorful. And she made it sound as if the portable toilet's tardiness was my fault. As if I'd been a poor mother. I looked up at the boxy blue outhouse on the flatbed and scolded it loudly, "Bad porta-shitter. Bad."

Macy laughed, and the other women either smiled or at least only stared at me curiously, as if they'd never expected an ex-movie star to say "porta-shitter." Alberta, however, grunted again and thrust out a hand, then scowled harder when I squeezed it with my left hand instead of shaking it with my scarred right. "You need a job done. We're here to do it. This is our farm's down-time, so we've got the hours. The cash income'll make a big difference to our women. Nicer Christmas presents for their kids, money for savings accounts. They'll earn every penny you pay. We can give you two full weeks before Christmas, sun-up to sun-down. Macy handles our accounts. She'll negotiate our rates with you. I'll expect a check from you for all our labor and materials on each Friday. Thomas said you'll pay top dollar for top-quality work. That's what our crew will give you. If you think there's any chore around here a female crew can't handle, admit your ignorance right now and we'll debate it."

She halted, waiting defiantly, as if I were dumb enough to step into that snake-pit of gender-baited politics. Besides, I'd stopped listening at the words, *Thomas said.*

"Thomas sent you?"

"Yep. Delta told him you had work that needed doing, so he called us. You got a problem with that? You don't want 'our kind' doing the job? For the record, Macy and I are the only card-carrying lesboes in the group." A sardonic smile curled her upper lip. "The rest of these women are 'normal.' Nobody'll hit on you, steal your jewelry, or snap a picture of you when you're not looking. All these women live and work at Rainbow Farm because it's a safe house, you get it? They don't want the world to find them *or* you."

Thomas sent his friends to keep an eye on me, I was thinking in a separate universe from Alberta's. *Maybe he wants to make sure I don't do anything he doesn't want done to the house.*

"Welcome to my home," I announced grimly, ignoring Alberta and addressing the group. "It's not a museum; it's not a historic site. It's a sweet old house that needs a makeover. I know what I want done and how I want it done. If that suits you, let's get to work. If you disapprove of my plans, don't call Thomas and rat on me. I'm going to renovate this place the way I see fit, and that's that."

"Are you paranoid?" Alberta asked. "Thomas gave us your to-do list. That's all. Do you think we'd toady up to him and sell out a sister? God."

My face grew warm. "Well, whatever."

Macy added gently, "Thomas isn't even here. He's gone to Chicago to visit his brother. That's a big step forward for him. This is the first time he's left these mountains since he arrived four years ago."

"Ah." A shock. Thomas, my fellow recluse, had left our mutual ridge. I'd never driven a man out-of-state by kissing him before. Surprise and a strange, sinking sensation of dread chilled my skin. Thomas wasn't at his cabin. Thomas wasn't nearby. Thomas was several states away. Fear trickled down the center of my stomach, and I knew I'd have to go inside an take a pill. Oh, my God. He'd truly become my safe place, my sanctuary, along with this farm. This was not good.

Suck it up, Alberta can probably smell weakness like a buzzard smells roadkill. Look at that sneer. She's practically circling overhead with her beak sharpened already.

I cleared my throat. "All right, as long as we all understand the deal, then . . . good. Who'd like a cold cup of instant coffee and a protein bar?"

Silence. Alberta scrutinized me as if I were a puzzle missing a few pieces, and Macy bit back a worried smile. Behind them, one of the women raised a hand. "If that's what they serve for breakfast in Hollywood," she said politely, "it's no wonder all the women out there look like sticks with eyeballs."

"I'll set up a campfire kitchen under the trees," Macy said. "How do you feel about a breakfast of herbal tea, tofu-and-turkey sausage, and homemade wheat bread covered in fresh farm butter and homegrown strawberry preserves?"

"Screw the protein bars."

Everyone laughed and relaxed, except Alberta. She faced the crew like a drill sergeant. "Get moving, team. Greta Garbo's not paying us to flap our labias in the breeze. We're on the clock."

Labias? Greta Garbo? So I was the recluse of the vaginal silver screen? Oh, this was going to be fun. Alberta's obedient lackeys headed for their tool belts and tractor keys. Fingerlings of sunlight spread the good news to the yard, the trees, the frosted air of morning: The Log Splitter Girls and their coven were here to work some magic.

Apparently, Thomas had left me on my own, for my own good. Just as I'd asked him to. Damn.

Thomas

I missed Cathy, I missed our small haven in North Carolina, and I dreaded seeing my brother's three boys, who I'd avoided for the past few years because all three reminded me of Ethan. Like him, they had eyes the gold-brown color of some ancient Viking's wooden cudgel, square jaws, wavy brown hair and the female-luring divet of a dimple in one cheek. We Mitternich men all looked Anglo-Euro-Slavic in a ruddy, lanky, swarthy, Dutch-tulip-farmer way, as if Don Quixote had fathered children with a Flemish milkmaid. The old man had been lean and compact, built for the steerage cabin of an immigrant ship, but our mother had been elegantly plush and six inches taller than him, according to family photos and memoirs of a distantly Russian heritage. The old man said her people had been expert horsemen in the czar's service, which might mean Cossacks or might mean nothing but wishful debates around a beer cooler at a family reunion.

But when I stepped out of a taxi in front of John's six-bedroom mini-mansion in a gated community with its own private stables and riding trails, the first thing I saw among the manicured hedges of the snow-dappled front yard were all three of my nephews atop their expensive hunter-jumper ponies. Mother's Cossack heritage must be true. Here were our family horsemen, riding the sodded-lawn tundra of affluent suburbia.

Jeremy, Bryan and David all stared back at me in descending orders of age and recognition. My nephews were dressed in protective riding helmets, jodhpurs, knee-high black riding books and neon-orange vests over their quilted coats. If they fell off the ponies, they'd bounce. David, six, and Bryan, nine, craned their helmeted heads and began backing their ponies away from me. "Mom!" David yelled into the wireless cell-phone remote attached to his ear. "A stranger is here! A real hairy stranger!"

"Dad!" Bryan called via his remote. "Some guy with no car is in the driveway!"

But Jeremy, the oldest at twelve, remembered me. "Chill out," he told his younger brothers. Then, into his remote, "Mom, Dad? Uncle Thomas must have caught an earlier plane. He's here already."

"At ease, guys," I said as I started up the driveway. One of Cathy's scarves fell from my coat pocket. I'd swiped it that day at the Privy. She always carried extras. The ponies snorted. David and Bryan stared as I bent and scooped the mystery cloth back into my pocket. Even Jeremy backed his pony up.

"My hand warmer," I lied.

The mini-mansion's double-front doors sprang open. A tall, portly, thirty-five-year old suburban dad with a receding brown hairline and a penchant for expensive ski sweaters loped out, followed by a plump, beaming soccer mom with salon-blonde hair, diamond-bedazzled fingers, and a *Happy Hanukah* apron over her Christmas sweater. They both wore natty wireless cell phone earpieces. The John Mitternich family was always outfitted like an Uhura fan club at a *Star Trek* convention.

"I don't believe it," John shouted as he grabbed me in a hug. "You trimmed your beard and you came to visit! It's a holiday miracle!"

"Our very own non-Confederate rebel has returned to civilization," Monica noted, alternately hugging me and curiously prodding a *Possum, The Other White Meat* patch Bubba and Jeb had super-glued to the shoulder of my coat one night while I was passed out in the bed of my pick-up. They still guffawed over it.

John wiped tears from his eyes and hugged me again, rocking me back and forth and patting my back. "Good to see you, good to see you," he said hoarsely. "I knew if I kept sending you phones I'd finally get through to you."

"Well, you know what they say in the Christmas movie," I deadpanned over the emotion in my throat. "Every time a hillbilly hears his cell phone ring, an angel gets a beer."

Cathy

Behind every inoffensively sweet woman there's an iron-willed enforcer—usually a husband or boyfriend, but it could be a sister, mother, or girlfriend—who does most of her dirty work. What would Glenda the Good Witch be without the Wicked Witch of the West? What would Melanie be without Scarlett? Just a pair of perky Pollyanna's whose angelic do-gooding hinted that they secretly felt superior to the Munchkins and the Rebels. In order to be noble, a good girl needs an enemy, a cause, a rallying cry. Her goodness has to stand strong against true villainy. Joan of Arc wouldn't be much of a legend if she'd said at trial, "Oh, never mind that vision thing I mentioned," and the English had just threatened to singe her eyebrows and revoke her passport.

I'd never had to play the wicked witch before, because I hired people—mostly men—to be the Wicked Witch for me. Thus, I could reign supreme among my people as The Lovable, Nice and Beautiful Star of Oz. If you're beautiful and famous you're expected to be one extreme or the other—a bitch or a saint. Now that I wasn't beautiful, maybe I could choose a middle ground. Alberta was belittling but effective. Macy was motherly and completely non-threatening. Delta was both lovable and commanding. I wanted to be like *her*.

Okay, I still had some kinks in my self-empowerment themes. But I knew that what happened between me and the Crossroad's ultimate female tough guys, The Log Splitter Girls, would be a test of my ability to fit in with the reality of my new life, to find out if I was more than just a pretty face.

I needed a chair and a whip.

My relationship with Alberta rolled farther down the ravine of crankiness every day. She clearly didn't respect me, didn't expect much backbone from me, and, no doubt, saw me as a main competitor for Thomas's valuable sperm. Our tense working environment wasn't helped when I overheard her referring to me as "Little Red Hiding Hood," when I wore a red scarf over my head. A lapsed Catholic, she openly joked to Macy and their crew that the Pope ought to name me, "Sister Cathryn of the Mental Disorder," after I diligently placed fire extinguishers near Macy's portable camping stove and after I insisted that the crew move my new electric generator, with its propane-guzzling combustion engine, an extra thirty feet from the house.

"I've never known a generator to sneak across a yard and burst into flame," Alberta told the crew loudly. "But we're not getting paid to use common sense, so move it." Turning to me, she delivered the final coup de grace. "By the way, I know you're so rich you don't care about the cost, but nobody in her right mind powers a house on a generator fueled by propane. It costs a fortune and you'll have to get the tank refilled about once a week. You should at least have ordered diesel. And I just want you to know that when you fire up that generator, it's going to sound like a cement truck idling in your yard, day and night. You'll never have another quiet minute here." She sniffed. "But I guess, being used to the background noise of a city, it doesn't bother you to make an unholy racket."

I stared her down, indulging in a quick imaginary laser attack with my eyes. When I finished burning a large, neat hole in the center of her forehead, I said between gritted teeth, "Get me a *diesel* generator and build a shed around it to muffle the sound of its engine."

She arched a red brow. "My crew doesn't have time to 'build' you a shed for your new generator this week. But I'll have Turtleville Mini-Barns deliver a pre-fab shed tomorrow, and I'll have the diesel generator installed inside it, then my crew will line the walls with insulation." Her short, ruddy curls bounced with evil delight as she nodded at her own brilliance. "That way, the generator will be trapped inside a cage made of sound-proof and fire-proof walls. It won't be able to hop across the yard and attack you."

At that point I thought about shooting her, but didn't want to spend the holidays in jail.

🌑🌑🌑🌑🌑

Over the next few days I had to admit Alberta was a born leader, or at least a born drill sergeant. She ran a tight, efficient crew and supervised every detail to a perfectionistic fare-thee-well. By midweek my rutted farm road had been scraped and graveled all the way down the ridge to the creek trail. A sturdy metal gate hung discreetly between two handsome beech trees where the farmroad meandered along a rocky incline. No unwelcome visitor could get around that natural barricade of rocks and trees if I padlocked my gate.

A new water pipe protruded neatly over my kitchen sink. Its gravity-fed spigot released a hearty stream of sweet, clear, ice-cold water from a hundred-gallon drum outside. The drum sat atop a tall wooden platform, a cute miniature of that *Petticoat Junction* water tank I mentioned. An in-flow pipe sprouted high on the drum's side, nosedived to the ground, disappeared at a right angle beneath the raw earth of a newly filled trench, then made a bee-line to a cute little well house the Rainbow women built of weathered wood and old tin roofing salvaged from one of the farm's collapsed tool sheds. Inside the well house, a small electric pump vacuumed water up the deep, narrow pipe of my newly-bored well.

"You got great underground water up here on this ridge," the well driller proclaimed. "Easy to tap into, got real good flow, plenty to irrigate with."

"Enough to give me excellent water pressure for a sprinkler system?" I asked.

"Well, sure, ma'am, like I said, plenty for irrigation."

"No, no. I mean an indoor sprinkler system. I plan to install one this spring."

"You planning on watering plants indoors, ma'am? You mean, like a greenhouse?"

"Safety sprinklers. In the ceiling. In case of fire."

"Like they have in department stores and motels?"

"Yes, a commercial type of sprinkler system."

"You're gonna put sprinklers in the ceiling of your house?"

"Yes."

He pointed to the cottage. "That nice little one-story house with lots of windows to jump out of."

"Yes."

He tugged the brim of a "Get 'er Done" tractor cap lower on his forehead, shuffled his work boots, and hunched his shoulders in a camo hunting jacket. "Ma'am, don't take this the wrong way, but . . . why don't you just buy extra fire insurance and put in some smoke alarms?"

"Oh, I'll have smoke alarms and other back-up systems in addition to the sprinklers."

At that point, Alberta, who'd been listening with her hands on her hips and her eyes set on permanent roll, slithered up to my well driller and fake-whispered to him, "She's also planning to build a *moat* around the house. With a fire-proof drawbridge made of steel."

My gullible well driller went wide-eyed. "Well, ma'am," he said to me, "when you go to filling your moat? Your new well sure will get a workout."

As he headed for his truck I lasered another imaginary hole between Alberta's eyes. "That wasn't funny. He believed you. He'll tell people I'm building a moat."

An evil little smile crooked her mouth. She nodded at my ever-present scarf-hood, at my ever-present gloves, and at the fire extinguisher I was just about to place inside the new well house. "Yeah, we wouldn't want folks to think you're peculiar." Chuckling, she walked off.

"Smug, fearless *bee-atch*," I muttered.

Don't ever assume lesbians are endowed with a special brand of wisdom, compassion, or sensitive insights into the suffering of their fellow travelers on the path to an alternate reality. They're just real people, after all.

Behind my house, the orchard emerged from among the stumps of chainsawed pine trees, and an old walking trail to the family cemetery was cleared of overgrowth. But best of all, a big, diesel-powered generator hummed gently inside a pretty mini-barn at the edge of the backyard. Beside it, looking like a large silver suppository on metal legs, stood a tank of diesel fuel. Alberta's crew ran a cable from the generator to an outlet box on the cottage's back porch; then they fired up the generator, plugged several orange extension cords to the outlet box, and snaked them through the house.

This wasn't the cheapest or most efficient way to power a home, but it meant I didn't have to install wiring and have the power company ruin the scenery with lines. They'd have had to put in power poles or underground lines all the way from the Trace up the creek trail and then up the ridge to my house. This way, except for a network of extension cords taped along my chestnut baseboards, the ridge's non-electrified integrity remained unspoiled. A thick, orange, outdoor extension cord curled across my back yard and slithered under a wall of the new well house. Electricity brought water to my kitchen sink. Water so cold it made me wince every time I splashed some on my face, but still, I had water and I hadn't yet ruined Thomas's precious house.

I hope you're happy, I told him. I tried not to think of him being so far away, in Chicago. I had to take a pill whenever I did.

Delta drove up one afternoon for the farm's official lighting ceremony. She and I hadn't been furniture shopping yet, but she'd already orchestrated the delivery of a small fridge, a microwave and a queen-sized mattress and box springs with a utilitarian metal bed frame. As a housewarming gift she and Pike brought me pillows, flannel sheets, a comforter, and a beautiful quilt in a log-cabin pattern, made by the Saturday-night quilting club at the café, which included Alberta and Macy. I tried to picture Alberta doing something as delicate as needlework, but couldn't. We put the bed in the front bedroom of my three-bedroom house. "I remember sleeping in this room when I visited," I told Delta. "I remember that it had been my mother's room." It seemed so big when I was little, but the queen bed left barely enough space to walk around it and fluff the covers. "How did people sleep comfortably on cots or double beds in bedrooms this small, especially without central heat and air conditioning?" I made the mistake of saying that aloud in Alberta's presence.

Alberta snorted. "They had other priorities. Like putting food on the table and keeping a roof over their children's heads."

She strolled out. I looked at Delta. "Never ask a rhetorical sissy-girl question around the queen of the Amazons."

"Aw, Alberta's all right. She's just had a hard life, that's all, and she doesn't trust anybody who hasn't."

I gestured grimly toward my hooded face. "I need to be even *more* maimed to qualify for her respect?"

"Oh, hon." Delta hugged me. "It's not what hurts you that makes you respectable. It's how you get over it."

"So I still have a lot to prove. At least to Alberta."

Delta shrugged. I reached for the boxy metal bar of a multi-unit power strip attached to one of the orange extension cords. Delta set a small silver office lamp on a plastic crate by my new bed. A loaner until we went shopping. I plugged its cord to the extension cord then slowly put my hand on the lamp's switch. I looked at Delta. "This is going to be the first time ever that this house has been lit by an electric lamp."

She looked heavenward. "What's that, Mary Eve? Oh, okay, I'll tell her." Delta smiled at me. "Your granny says, 'It's your house now, so let there be modern light.'"

I pushed the switch. The white, pragmatic glow of the lamp pooled in the bedroom's dark spaces. For the first time in the history of the house, in the history of the farm, in the history of the Smoky Mountains, in the entire geologic timeline of the earth, the glow of an electric light softened the wilderness of Wild Woman Ridge. It didn't waver and it wasn't unpredictable, like a flame. Steady and safe, it reflected dependably off the soft reds and browns of the chestnut walls and glinted in the stained-glass window across from the bed. The room might be small and sparsely furnished, but the bed looked comfortable and colorful, and the lamp made me happy. Light is a happy thing.

I plugged a CD player into the power strip, and a clock. On the floor I set a small, tolerable electric heater. It had sisters in the living room and kitchen. They gushed warm air across the maple floor as they swiveled back and forth like summer fans. I left one outlet free on my bedroom power strip. "You can put another lamp in here," Delta noted.

I gave a dull chuckle. "No, this outlet's for my vibrator."

She laughed so hard she clamped a hand over the front of her jeans. "I think I wet myself. The curse of middle-age."

"My porta-shitter is through the hall door, across the sleeping porch, out the screened door, down the steps, then past the first oak on the left."

She laughed harder and hurried outdoors.

I stood there alone, gazing at the lamp, the bed and the outlet for my vibrator. *I don't need Thomas to keep me warm and satisfied. I have impersonal electricity instead.*

All right, I admitted it. I missed him.

Chapter 19

Thomas
Chicago

My brother's house was full of electronics. His darkly paneled study included a high-definition flatscreen TV, two computers, a Play Station, CD players, DVD players, several iPods, a Blackberry, TiVo, and a wall full of software and manuals. It was like sitting in the command station for a space shuttle, only with more controls. *The Best of Steely Dan* rocked softly from an iPod speaker berth, and digital fish swam across the computers' screen savers. The study's mantel brimmed with blue Hanukah candles, Christmas garland, and robotic toys. The only non-electronic, organic elements in the room were John, me, and the flames on his gas fireplace logs.

"Dad," Jeremy called over the house's intercom-slash-security system. "Mom says we can go skateboarding at the rink tomorrow if you and Uncle Thomas promise to keep us off the Super Slalom of Death."

"Sure."

"She's standing right here. She says you have to say it out loud so it's a promise."

"No wiggle room for semantics, this time," we heard Monica say in the background.

John laughed. "I solemnly promise that Thomas and I will do our best to prevent all three Mitternich boys from attempting the Super Slalom of Death."

"I hear loopholes," Monica said. "If anyone comes back with broken bones, I'm making all of you play dreidel every night this week, and for matchsticks, not chocolate."

"No broken bones. I promise."

"Then so be it."

The intercom clicked off. I sank further back on the room's deep leather couch, cradling a fine cigar and a cup of coffee. *Ethan should be going to the rink with his cousins.* Lounging beside me with his socked feet on an ornate teak coffee table, John glanced at me, froze, then said quietly, "I'm sorry."

I shook my head. "How do you have the faith to let them out of your sight for even a minute?"

"They have a mother who does all the worrying for me. She imagines every possible disaster and buys a helmet for it."

"Seriously."

John inhaled his cigar, blew out a long stream of smoke, then said, "I'd rather be afraid of losing them than not have them at all."

"I hope you never lose one."

"Brother, I know we were raised Catholic, but when did you turn into a Mel Gibson movie?"

"What?"

"You know, the whole 'torture me some more' and 'suffering is good' thing."

"The day Ethan and Sherryl died."

"You weren't responsible. How many times does everyone have to tell you? You couldn't have saved them. Yes, you were supposed to keep Ethan at home that day, but you had a fight with Sherryl over whose schedule was more important, so she took him with her. That's life."

"Could we drop this subject?"

"No. On a related note, I wish I could figure some way to block every form of communication between you and Ravel. Sherryl's sister is a twisted woman with some kind of secret guilt of her own. That's the only explanation for how she treats you. You did nothing wrong, and the fact that you still refuse to believe that shows just how far she's sunk her tentacles into your brain and short-circuited your common sense. She's lurking in her lair at Trump Tower just waiting to make your life miserable again. How's she going to top herself *this* January?"

"I deal with it when it comes. I don't want to talk about it."

The tone of my voice set him back. We smoked in grim silence for a minute. "What's up with the two little girls?" John asked.

"What do you mean?"

"Girls. Young human females. One approximately seven, the other approximately twelve. You asked Monica to pick out Christmas gifts for them. See, this is how it is with happily married people. They share information. Monica told me you're playing surrogate dad to a couple of little girls."

"I'm nobody's father figure. Just trying to do my part for a couple of needy kids. Cora and Ivy. Good kids. I don't want to talk about them."

"Hmmm. Then tell me all about Cathy Deen. Is *she* a safe subject?"

"There's not much to tell."

"Pardon me, but, uh, you're in a relationship with the woman who's made People Magazine's *Most Beautiful People* issue every year for the past decade. Throw me a bone or two. Some information. Anything."

"It's not a 'relationship.' We're friends. She likes talking to me. She needs me. But she could have any man she wants. Even now. She thinks she's ugly, but she's still got *it*."

"'It'?"

"She—" I searched for words in the hypnotic movements of the fake computer fish. "She could inspire an army just by smiling."

"Helen of Troy? You're falling in love with Helen of Troy?"

"I'm not—dammit, John, don't make me wrestle you to the floor and give you a wedgie."

"How bad are the scars?"

"Remember the drywall foreman who played poker with the old man? The one who'd been burned in a firefight in Vietnam?"

"Oh, my God. The guy we called 'Freddy Krueger' behind his back? Her burns look like his?"

"Yes. As if someone scrambled the skin, raked a fork through it, then tanned it badly with several shades of leather stain. Red, pink, white, brown."

"Damn. She let you see her scars? I mean, the ones that aren't on her face?"

"Not deliberately. But there have been some . . . circumstances."

"Ah hah."

"Not like that."

"Come on, don't be coy. Admit it. She can't resist you."

"Oh, yes, she can."

John nodded sagely. "Cathryn Deen wants to nail my brother."

"Don't make me hold you down and rap your skull with my knuckles."

"This sexy movie star wants to *do* my brother," he continued, grinning. "My brother looks like a big, hairy, survivalist troll—even with a trimmed beard, courtesy of the sexy movie star—and he's practically a self-flagellating martyr, but he's caught the world's most beautiful movie star. Even if she's scarred she's still Cathryn Deen, the 'it' girl. Wow. Can I tell Monica? This ought to earn me some hotness by association."

"I haven't caught her. I've just sneaked up on her and stunned her into friendship."

"Incredible women fall for you, and you don't get *why*. Sherryl could have married royalty, Greek shipping heirs, Fortune 500 trust-funders, or one of the Kennedys, but she fell for you."

"I'm gentlemanly and I have nice teeth. Politeness and good dental hygiene are the key to hotness."

"You were Sherryl's rock," John said gruffly. "She wanted somebody to stand up to her rich family, to tell them all to go take a flying fuck, and you did. You gave her a chance to live her own life, and whether she appreciated that fact later on or not, she loved you for having the balls to marry her without expecting even a penny of her inheritance. And you were *my* rock when we were growing up and the old man treated me like crap for being fat and shy. You stood up to him. You looked out for me. If it hadn't been for you I'd have turned into a screwed-up monster just to show the old man I could be a tough prick." Even as I began shaking my head to dismiss his praise, John clamped a hand on my shoulder and went on, "You're the rock that never cracks. I have no doubt Cathryn Deen sensed that about you from day one."

I swirled my coffee then downed it in a single long swallow. Once, standing in Jeb's gem shop watching him cut and polish a rough, purplish ruby into a rounded cabochon, I heard him telling the biker who had bought the ruby for a big-ass ring, *Even the hardest stone has a fracture line in it.*

Ethan and Sherryl's deaths had created my fracture line. I knew the fissure was still there, that a dangerous crack existed in the rock everyone assumed couldn't be broken. If I believed I could be with my son again, I'd have killed myself long ago. That crack had never healed.

Loving Cathy made me even more aware that I wasn't solid anymore, and might never be again.

Cathy

The slippery clay floor of the barn's milk stalls and calf pen now sported a deep, pristine layer of new pea gravel, and the walk-in feed crib, where gaps in the old gray planks let in cold, damp air, received a brand-new plywood floor and walls. Thinking of Thomas, I dutifully helped nail the old planks over the new plywood, to hide it.

Suffice to say I'd never hammered a nail before in my life, and Alberta knew it. My nails skewed at odd angles or bounced free and took flight. One pinged Alberta on the forearm, and she flicked it off as if I'd spit on her. On the next try, my hammer missed its mark and thumped my own left thumb.

I saw stars and leaned against a wall, sweating inside my head scarf. Not only was I clammy with nerves, I was roasting under a silk scarf. Even high in the Appalachians, a Southern December can turn warm overnight. The daily temp hit sixty-five degrees that week. Balmy. The other two women working in the crib with us were dressed in t-shirts. Alberta wore a light flannel pullover. One of the women patted me on the back.

"You're doin' pretty good for a gal who spent most of the past year in the hospital or at home in bed," she said.

"We read all about you hiding in your mansion," the other put in kindly. "We saw the stories in the check-out line at the Ingles in Turtleville. Sorry. Those gossip magazines are hard to ignore when the store puts 'em right next to the candy bars."

"I understand. Thank you." I only managed to talk between dizzy spells.

Alberta snorted. "If you took off that damned silk burka you're wearing, you'd be more comfortable and you could see what you're nailing." She levered her hammer with ninja-like precision. Sixteen-penny galvanized nails disappeared into the wood after only two or three skillful slams. She pounded another nail into place smugly. "What are you going to do with this barn, anyway?"

"I don't know, yet."

"Turn it into some kind of guest house? I know, maybe turn it into a potting shed where your landscape man can store the lawnmower and all the chemicals you're gonna have him pour onto the wildflowers you'll call 'weeds.'" Alberta chuckled ruefully as she whacked nails into a board only inches from my sweaty face. "Let me guess. This spring you'll have your landscaper plant beds of blooming azaleas around this barn, and camelias, and some nice evergreen arborvitae to give it that *Italiente* touch city people think is so elegant, and some tulips already up and budding."

I wiped my forehead with a shaking hand. "So what's your point?"

She hooted and looked at the others. "Up here in the mountains, what do we call all those plants I just listed?"

They looked uncomfortable. Bullies have a way of making people hate themselves for playing along. "A salad bar for the deer," one answered.

Alberta guffawed. "Salad bar. For the deer."

The other woman hurried to add, "But Ms. Deen, your yard sure would be pretty for a day or two, before they ate it."

Alberta guffawed again.

I went in the house, washed my face with my ice-cold well water, changed the clingy silk headscarf for a lighter cotton one, then headed for Macy's encampment under the front oaks. Macy worked at a laptop on a small folding camp table in the winter sunshine, bundled up except for fingerless yarn gloves, charmingly Victorian except for the modern camp stove where she created giant pots of stew for lunch everyday. When I pulled up a lawn chair she was listening to a CD of Robert Frost poetry. *Two roads diverged in a wood, and I, I took the one less traveled by, And that has made all the difference.*

"Hi," Macy said, and flicked off the CD. "Alberta, again?"

"Excuse me for asking this about your spouse, and I don't mean to pry into her personal life, but . . . is Alberta the Antichrist?"

Macy laughed so hard her braids shook. When she finally caught her breath she folded her hands in the lap of her work skirt and looked at me solemnly. "You need to understand. I came out to my parents when I was fifteen, and they loved me anyway. But Alberta was *thrown* out when her parents learned she was gay. She lived on the streets of New Orleans for several years. She was beaten up, raped, nearly died from overdosing—you name it. Finally, she cleaned herself up and got a job in construction. She really has bootstrapped it to get where she is, and if she comes across as merciless and mean, it's just that she feels that it took tough love to set her on the right path, and so that's what she doles out to other women. So it's nothing personal."

The horrifying details of Alberta's background settled on me like a hair coat. How could I despise her now? "You really know how to take the fun out of my plot to strangle her."

Macy smiled. "Oh, don't feel sorry for her. Give her hell."

"She hates me because I'm pampered, rich, and whiny."

"Don't forget *straight*. She hates you because you're straight, too."

"Great. I've hit a home run on this one."

"She thinks straight women have it easy. Nothing—"

"Personal. Okay, maybe she's right about that. But it's not like I woke up in my baby crib one morning and said, 'Gee, I think I'll choose to grow up white, pretty, rich, Protestant and heterosexual."

"No, but be glad you had it easy."

I pointed to my face. "Does this look easy?" I asked quietly.

Macy gave me a wistful and even sympathetic smile. "No, but it looks no worse than the scars the rest of us carry around."

Okay. I was not going to get much sympathy from Macy, either. I decided to change the subject. I gestured toward her CD player. "I thought you'd be listening to poems by women. Sylvia Plath, I guess."

"Just because I'm a lesbian doesn't mean I like suicidal women poets." But she looked impressed. "You like Sylvia Plath?"

"I was briefly in the running to play her in the movie. Gwynneth Paltrow got the role. This was a phase when my agent thought I might be a serious actress."

"I love your movies."

"You don't have to say that. I was the queen of brainless romantic comedies."

"You brought a wonderful presence to the screen. A wonderful personality. I always wanted to *be* you when I watched your movies. A *gay* you. Don't tell Alberta, all right?"

"You liked me. Really?"

She gave me a quizzical frown. "Of course. What an odd question from someone who enjoyed such fame, wealth and universal adoration."

"I've seen all the mean things that were written and said about me after the accident. All the gloating and the nasty jokes in the media. The critiques of my recklessly happy life. A lot of that came from women, not men. How could women say such mean stuff about a . . . a *sister*?"

Macy wagged a finger at me. "Those are women so eager to please the male power structure that nothing else matters to them. They instinctively distance themselves from females who are no longer valuable to men. They secretly fear that your fate is a warning to them. 'See what happens to women who don't measure up to men's standards anymore? See what happens to women who seek status in the world?'"

Macy sighed. "Generally, I don't frame my beliefs in traditional feminist dogma, but in this case . . . when you lost your beauty in the accident—and, as a result, you lost your career and your status, all because of a superficial asset the male power structure deemed most valuable about you as a person—your fall from grace illustrated just how fragile the female power base is. You see, women who deliberately attract attention to themselves—not only by their beauty, but also by their brains or athletic prowess—women who dare to be something besides demure and submissive servants—are a threat to the male ego and an equal threat to the brainwashed egos of women who haven't got the courage to demand recognition in their own lives."

I stared at her. "That sounds much better than thinking I was just a pampered twit and everybody secretly hated my guts. Thank you."

She patted me on the arm. "Women shiver when something innocent is snatched away by random fate. Your beauty was innocent, you understand. I don't mean in a child-like way, or naïve, I mean pure." Macy brightened. "But, on the other hand, losing it was a good thing. The universe clearly has important plans for you, and you need to progress to a new level. This is just a transition."

"But I was happy being vacuous and pretty."

"Were you?"

"I got the best concert seats, the best men, the best food, the best vacations."

"In a few years you'd have become morbidly obsessed about maintaining your looks. Fighting to stay in the limelight. And your husband was obviously a bad choice for a life mate."

"Now, don't go trying to make me feel *better*."

"I'm sorry. The truth is a necessary pain in the butt."

"Okay, you're right. Since the accident I've thought about all the beautiful people—not just in show business but in boardrooms and offices and warehouses and walks of life everywhere—clinging to something so fragile. Lucky me. I'm done clinging, whether I like it or not. I don't."

Macy chuckled. "Well, at least you've identified your dilemma."

"So . . . you like Robert Frost. Why?"

"I'm a sentimentalist. Emily Dickinson. The Brownings. Frost, Carl Sandburg. Their poetry is music." She leaned closer and confided, "When Alberta and I exchanged rings, she gave me a volume of the Romantics. She said, 'There's no poem in the world that can say how much you've saved my life and made my life *worth* saving.'"

"You love her dearly," I said quietly. "And she loves you. I've watched how you two look at each other. I'm envious of that level of partnership and devotion." I regained my grumpy footing. "It's what keeps me from skewering her with a screwdriver." Macy chuckled. I went on, "Delta told me . . .let's see. You were a history professor before you and Alberta met."

She sat back, nodding. "Was, back in my late twenties. More than ten years ago. A different life."

"You're a PhD?"

She shrugged. "Yale."

Oh, great. Thomas had married a Harvard girl and one of his best friends was a Yale girl. "Okay, I need a thesaurus and an IQ implant before we talk anymore."

"I wasn't brilliant, just good at academics. I got my bachelor's at Duke, here in North Carolina, then my PhD at Yale. Then I came back to Duke to teach. Then my parents died, and I gave it all up."

"Died?"

"Were murdered in a carjacking outside Boston. Where I grew up."

"I'm so sorry."

"Me, too. I miss them every day. I always will."

"You left everything and started on a new life path?"

"I went to work for a church, was transferred to New Orleans, and met Alberta there."

"How could you give up your old life that easily? Tell me how to do that."

"There's something very freeing about losing the anchors that have always defined you. Frightening, sad, but exhilarating in a poignant way, as well. You're free to float to the moon and evaporate or sink to the bottom of the deepest ocean. But you're also free to explore. Some people confuse that with *drifting*, I suppose. I like to think of it as *growing*."

I shook my head. "I don't think I'm growing. I think I'm shrinking."

"Give yourself time."

"Was Alberta 'growing' when you met her? Or just mutating?"

"She was working at a downtown mission, helping the homeless. Go ahead and say it."

"What did she do—*scare* them off the streets?"

Macy laughed. "Sometimes."

"How did the two of you decide to come here?"

227

"I'd visited this area a lot when I was at Duke. These mountains . . . Alberta and I love them. They have the most incredible energy. Don't laugh, but a lot of people believe they're the most powerful spiritual vortexes on the planet."

"I was raised Episcopalian. I'm sorry, but we laugh at *everybody's* beliefs."

"I was raised Methodist, and all I remember is wearing a pink dress with a poofy, pink crinoline skirt to Easter services. I think I was five years old. About 1970. Did you know they still made crinoline skirts in 1970?"

"You're forty years old?"

"Don't say it like it's a curse. Alberta's thirty-five. I'm forty. We've been together for nearly ten years. Tomorrow I'll bring pictures of our two kids to show you. Alberta is their birth mother. I have fibroids. I assume you know that Santa Whittlespoon is their father? Everyone knows; we just pretend it's a secret."

"I'm still trying to apologize for saying you're forty. You look younger."

"Happy people look young. You're really afraid of getting older, aren't you? You should only be afraid of getting less happy."

"I'm afraid of both."

She scooped her hands toward her nose. "Inhale the energy of these ancient mountains, feel the power of these vortexes, and you'll know how young you are by comparison." She patted her thighs. "Your vagina is a vortex, too. Feel its magnetic pull. Rejoice in the siren song it sings. Can't you hear it?"

"I thought I'd just forgotten to turn my radio off."

Macy laughed. "The pseudo-scientific people argue that these mountains have an abundance of quartz rock, which acts as a kind of electro-magnetic generator. The Cherokees designated some of their most sacred sites here. They believed a person can't truly know herself unless she has a strong sense of place. Alberta and I found our place here. We found ourselves."

I loved Granny's mountains, but I wasn't ready to admit I'd found myself and my true calling by getting roasted in a fire and running here to hide. Since I couldn't think of anything profound to say instead, I looked at Macy earnestly and announced, "Krispy Kreme Doughnuts started in North Carolina."

She laughed and nodded. "I see you channel your spiritual discussions through food analogies and tourist trivia."

"When I was struggling to make it through each day back in California, Delta's biscuits came to symbolize every good memory I had of my grandmother and her home here. I was never happier as a child than when I visited her. I knew who I wanted to be, here, and it had nothing to do with my looks. This was the only place in the world where I was allowed to forget what I looked like. Granny gave me biscuits with cream gravy and didn't care if I gained weight. So yes, biscuits represent a lot of things to me. Rebellion and freedom, to name a couple. Biscuits are a state of mind. A North Carolina state of mind, to me."

"All right, good. Let's see, can I think of other famous state foods?" She squinted and looked skyward for a second. Then, "No. But here's some other trivia. "Andy Griffith *and* Ava Gardner are from North Carolina. Edward R. Murrow, O Henry, the Wright Brothers, oh, and Blackbeard the pirate. He wasn't from here, but he spent a lot of time hiding around Ocracoke Island."

"Andy Griffith and Blackbeard. I smell a reality TV show. 'Mayberry, Arrrr. F.D.'"

She laughed. "The state motto is *Esse quam videri*, meaning "To be rather than to seem."

To be, rather than to seem. I sagged a little. "I was happy just seeming to be somebody."

"No, you weren't. Once you accept your reality, you'll be ecstatic at your transformation."

"I'll have a chat with my vortex about that and get back to you."

She sighed. "You're still working through your denial phase. I understand. I see that a lot among the women at our farm. We talk about it in our counseling sessions."

I stared at her. "Are you saying I have the attitudes of a battered woman?"

"The desperate need to win approval from men, the feelings of unworthiness, the lack of self-love. Yes, some of the same issues we see at the farm, sure. It's nothing to be ashamed of."

I groaned. We sat for a moment, at an impasse. Macy picked up a CD. "On a lighter note . . . did you know Carl Sandburg retired to Flat Rock? It's south of Asheville. Beautiful little town. These mountains lure poets and artists and singers. You can feel their heights in your soul." She pressed the CD to her heart and recited, "'Come and show me another city with lifted head singing, so proud to be alive and coarse and strong and cunning.'"

"An ode to Alberta," I said drily.

"That's from Sandburg's 'Chicago.'"

Chicago. Thomas. I had a deep need to be near Thomas in some small, harmless way. Just a quick inhalation of his essence, a toke off the energy of his vortex.

I looked at the hulking orange Kubota tractor sitting in my yard. Slow, sturdy, safe. "Can you teach me how to drive that tractor?" I asked Macy.

"Of course!" She smiled. "See, the power of the machine is the power of the universe, and you instinctively want to connect."

No, I instinctively wanted to see Thomas's cabin. But whatever.

🐾🐾🐾🐾🐾

Two roads diverged in a wood, and I, I took the one less traveled by, And that has made all the difference.

Seated atop a humming diesel mammoth, I looked up and down Ruby Creek Trail. Through the deep winter forest I could just make out the rutted side-trail that led to Thomas's land. Delta had warned me that his road was even rougher than mine, and that the road dipped down into Ruby Creek. I'd have to drive through rushing, foot-deep creek water.

Maybe I should try this trip again tomorrow. Pat myself on the back. Take baby steps.

No, Alberta will smell defeat on me. She'll know I wimped out. She'll eat my liver with homegrown strawberry preserves on it.

"Onward, beast," I said to the tractor, shifting its gearshift and gunning the engine. "Robert Frost and I are fearless. Let's take the road less graveled."

🐾🐾🐾🐾🐾

I stood in Thomas's front yard, admiring a high-mountain pasture with long views in nearly every direction. I walked among the perfectly aligned grape trellises, trailing my fingertips over the wooden posts and steel wires, stopping here and there to gently stroke the woody, gnarled vines already reaching the top wires.

"He'll have a harvest this year, for the first time," Delta had said. "I put in a word with somebody at the Biltmore Estate, and they'll buy the grapes. He could have himself a business, just selling grapes."

I turned in a slow circle, picturing the ridgetop full of luscious trellises filled with fruit. There's something about a man who grows things, who nurtures other living beings, even plants, that's warm and sexual and reassuring. I walked up the hill to his cabin with twinges of guilt on my spine.

"You made yourself at home at *my* house the past few years," I said aloud. "It's only fair that I get to take a look around *your* house."

His cabin was functional and authentic, built of logs with clay chinking. At the corners, the logs had been notched to fit together. Even a girly-girl like me recognized the pioneer craftsmanship. I walked completely around the tiny structure, touching the clay-chinked river rock of the fireplace, the coarse roundness of the logs. I walked over to the outhouse, sniffed delicately—no odor, thanks to a proper design and a strong mountain breeze—studied the half-moon carved into its door, thought about taking a look inside at Thomas's most private sitting spot, then wondered what kind of animals might have moved in while he was away, and walked quickly back to the cabin.

I sat down in a cane-seated wooden stair on a small front porch hooded in rusty, salvaged tin. His shovel and rake and other tools hung neatly from wooden pegs. My eyes kept flitting towards two small windows high on the wall. No curtains.

Don't you dare look in those windows.

But there aren't any curtains.

Don't you dare.

Just a peek.

I stood on tiptoe and looked inside.

Monks' cells had more décor.

The bed was more of a giant cot than a modern bedstead, built of rough logs and covered in piles of quilts and blankets. It occupied about half the available floor space and sat not more than spitting distance from the rock fireplace. Chills went over me. One popped ember and he'd wake up in a burning cocoon.

What I did next has no explanation other than 'I couldn't help myself.' And I mean that seriously. The depth of my fears swallowed calm reason. I couldn't leave that bed close to that fireplace. No matter what the consequences, I had to move it. My hands shook as I tried the cabin's plank door. I was fully prepared to take a sledge hammer from Thomas's tools and break the door off its bolt if I had to.

I didn't have to. It wasn't locked.

I looked at the door suspiciously, pushed it with my fingertips, and it swung open. I stepped inside and looked around, breathing hard. What a claustrophobic space, with a bucket on a ledge instead of a sink, one chair, and an old aluminum TV table. Deep shelves lined one end of the room from floor to ceiling. Stacks of canned food shared the space with rows of vodka bottles and dozens of books—mostly art and architecture texts, but also a Bible and an eclectic mix of novels and nonfiction, Studs Turkel, Hunter S. Thompson. Working-class homages to rebellion.

Then I saw the special shelf. About head high, not jumbled and packed like the others, but a small, sacred clearing among the clutter. It held children's picture books, a fat white candle that had been lit so many times the wick guttered in a smoky cavern, and saddest of all, the blackened, mangled remnant of a metal toy truck. The toy Thomas's son had held when he died. I stood there crying, with my hands spread like birds' wings on my chest. Beside the ruined toy was a framed photo of a smiling, brown-haired toddler. Ethan.

I should never have invaded Thomas's shrine to his son. I turned wildly, staring at the obsessive spectre of the damned bed too close to the fireplace. If I moved it, he'd know I'd trespassed. But if I didn't move it, I'd have nightmares about him burning alive.

"Move it," I ordered aloud. "Move it and let him be furious with you. Maybe you'll keep him safe. That's all that matters."

I grabbed a bed post and began tugging.

An hour later, exhausted, aching and all-too-aware that even the most charming neurotic can't justify trespassing, I staggered out the front door and shut it behind me. Inside, the bed now lived among the shelves, and the chair with the aluminum tray table lived next to the fireplace.

The sun was sinking in a blue-gold cloud. Cold wind whipped around me. I should head back to my house that instant, but I felt the need to leave some soft statement of apology, something that said, "I'm a friend, not a stalker."

I hurried across the pasture and into the woods, found a small pine tree, broke off an armful of its boughs, and carried them back to the cabin. Using a fragment of steel wire from the grape trellises, I tied the boughs together. I got Thomas's hammer, rummaged up a nail from a storage can, and efficiently hammered the nail into the upper-center of his door. "Take that, Alberta," I muttered.

Then I hung my Christmas decoration on the nail. Green pine boughs with a wire belt. It didn't make enough of a statement. I pulled my scarf off my head. It was a dark winter plaid, russet and gold—Old English Christmas colors, one might say. I tied it around the pine spray, knotted it in a bow, and stepped back. Martha Stewart would be proud.

By the time I drove the tractor back into my own yard my mood had sunk. What in hell had I been thinking? Darkness began closing in. Alberta and Macy, with their crew, stood around their trucks. Obviously they were waiting for me to bring their expensive tractor back before they left for the night.

"We were worried," Macy said as I climbed down. "Are you all right? What happened to your scarf?"

I gave up all subtlety and covered the right side of my face with my gloved hand. "Sorry, I took longer than expected. See you in the morning. G'night." As I strode past Alberta, she grunted her usual grunt and said, "Let me guess. You lost your idiotic scarf and you've spent all this time looking for it."

I pivoted and looked her in the eyes. "There are a lot of ways to deal with the nasty little fears of ordinary life. Everyone handles them differently. You act as if you've earned the right to badger and judge other people, but *no* one has that right. I expected someone who's been through what you've been through to have more compassion, or at least more basic decency. You're a disappointment, Alberta, but that's your problem, not mine." I took a deep breath. "To sum it up, if you fuck with me right now, I'll beat you to death with your own hammer. My aim may be amateurish when it comes to nails, but I guarantee I won't miss a single whack on your fat head."

I stomped inside the house.

For once, Alberta was speechless.

I took some solace in that.

Thomas

A few days before Christmas I became the star attraction at a cocktail party John and Monica hosted. Their mini-mansion glowed with synthetic garlands and silk poinsettias. Everything felt beautiful, clean and safe inside that bubble of money and possessions. An electric menorah flickered in the atrium window of the foyer, next to a twenty-foot Christmas tree done by an interior designer with a fetish for white—white lights, white ornaments, white flowers. Bing Crosby even sang *White Christmas* on the intercom music system.

In my rustic honor, I guess, the holiday style du jour among my brother's friends was something I'd call "outdoorsy hiker at the mall." Everyone wore expensively casual tweed-and-chinos, and that was just the women. As for me, I wore the latest Crossroads holiday fashion—running shoes, knee-scuffed brown corduroys, and an ancient Jerry Jeff Walker pullover Santa had traded for a fifth of Smirnoff. The title of Jerry Jeff's classic, *Up Against The Wall Redneck Mother,* was printed on the shirt's chest, but, being a gentleman, Santa had faded 'Mother' to a ghostly hint, using some bleach.

Everyone stole glances at me as if I'd recently come back from a foreign detainment camp or missionary work among the natives. I sipped a soft drink and pretended I didn't want a triple Absolut on the rocks.

"I understand you live in that area of the Appalachians where Eric Rudolph was captured," a banker in a Ralph Lauren sweater opined over his imported beer. "Is it true those mountain people supported his terrorism?"

"No, most of them didn't like having a murderer in their forest." Pike had helped the FBI track Rudolph, and everyone in the Cove was glad to see Rudolph arrested.

"But they're still very gothic and tribal, aren't they?"

"No worse than the average college fraternity." I tossed back another rakish soda—non-diet, caffeinated, the hard stuff. Before I settled in the South I'd have been quick to believe stereotypes, too. A somber black woman took me by one arm. "Have you met any, you know, groups of 'clannish' men in pointed hats?"

I smiled. "Only Shriners. Oh, and the volunteer fire department puts on elf hats during the Christmas parade."

An investment broker in a flowery brocade vest—this was a man, by the way—whispered, "So tell us, have you been to any snake-handling sermons or seen any albino banjo pickers?"

"No, I hang out with pot dealers and lesbian folk singers."

Suddenly, David ran into the crowded party. He stared up at me with a six-year-old's awe. "Santa's on the phone! He wants to talk to *you!*"

My Santa, Joe Whittlespoon, obviously couldn't be David's Santa, aka St. Nick, and it scared me that Joe had a reason to call me in Chicago. David grabbed me by one hand and pointed to a portable phone on a lamp table. "He's right there! Calling from the North Pole!" I strode to the phone. David ran ahead of me, thrust out a remote, and activated the speaker feature. "Santa, here's my uncle!"

"Thomas, that you?" Joe's drawl boomed through the room.

My gut twisted. "What's wrong?"

"I went by your cabin to check on things like I promised you I would and, uh, well, somebody had decorated the door for Christmas, and, uh, when I checked inside . . . your furniture was rearranged."

"Was anything missing?"

"Nope. Pike came by and looked around, and couldn't find anything wrong, just . . . strange, you know."

"Let me get this straight: Nothing was stolen, but the furniture had been moved, and somebody decorated the door."

"Yep. Somebody 'decked your halls' with pine limbs and a scarf tied in a bow." He laughed. "You've been the victim of a drive-by decking."

"Any suspects?"

"Oh, we already got your trespasser red-handed. Delta put the word out to her social circle for tips, and, well, the culprit 'fessed up the second she was confronted."

"Who?"

"Cathryn Deen."

Cathy? *Cathy.* "Cathy rearranged my furniture and decorated my door? Why?"

"She said that's between you and her. She didn't mean any harm, for sure. Looked embarrassed. Maybe she was doing some kind of *feng shui* thing to your décor. All I know is Cathryn Deen wanted your bed moved, so, by God, she moved it. If I was you, I'd be thrilled. This is probably some kind of 'nesting' thing. She wants you. She wants you bad. Here's my take on it: She's hoping you'll walk in, trip over the new arrangement, and fall head over heels. It's like she dug a pit to trap a wild hog."

Cathy had moved my bed. Her hands on my sheets. Sheets I stained in her honor before I left for Chicago. I casually reached down and fluffed the bottom of my untucked Jerry Jeff Walker shirt to hide an erection. Time to end this public conversation. "Cathy's okay?"

"Yeah, just kind of surly and sheepish. It's some woman thing."

"I'll call you back."

"Merry Christmas, Santa!" David shouted. "Am I'm getting the new Robosapien with the laser eyes?"

"You betcha, little dude." To me, "Is he, Thomas?"

"He is *now*."

"Ooops. Bye."

"Bye."

I straightened. The party had gone quiet. Someone had even turned Bing Crosby off. When I turned, dozens of laser-surgeried and eyebrow-lifted eyes—and that was just the men—gazed at me in fascination. John and Monica wore open-mouthed smiles. Everyone else looked as if they'd just heard the bum in the corner owned a Ferrari and had season seats next to Jack Nicholson at Lakers' games.

"Cathryn Deen?" a man asked. "That Cathryn Deen?"

Monica couldn't resist. "Yes," she told everyone loudly. "That Cathryn Deen. She and Thomas are an item!"

"You heard it here, first, folks," John announced, grinning. "Cathryn Deen has a thing for my big brother's bed."

Everyone crowded around me, questions posed on their tongues. I began backing toward a door. The women looked at me as if I was hung like a porn star. The men looked at me as if I knew some secret to attracting world-famous beautiful women that didn't *require* being hung like a porn star. Just as I'd become a kind of morbid VIP after nine-eleven—a touchable, collectible commodity like the other survivors of that day—I was now elevated to celebrity status by winning a movie star's personal attention. Now these people could drop my name into a conversation at the gym or the office. *As Thomas Mitternich said to me the other night—he's one of the heroes of nine-eleven, and he's dating Cathryn Deen—as he confided to me over drinks . . .*

I'd been spotlighted by sly gods who know every person's darkest desire is to be special for something, anything, even by mere association.

I dodged outside into the frigid Chicago night. There, alone in the suburban semi-darkness of my brother's patio, I took a deep breath. The darkness filled my lungs, connecting me across the curve of the earth to the deep mountain darkness at Wild Woman Ridge, to Cathy. I put aside what strangers saw and thought just this: *She was worried about me sleeping too near the fireplace. She was worried about me.*

Cathy

Macy—sweet, deceptively nice Macy—ratted me out. Something about "promoting an honest examination of honest motives," or so she claimed. When Delta asked around at the café's Saturday night quilting bee to see if anyone had any clue who might've re-decorated Thomas's cabin, Macy dropped a dime on my tractor trip. That tip led to my capture.

Now everyone in the Crossroads and greater Jefferson County was gossiping about my mysterious obsession with Thomas's furniture. I was so humiliated I locked my gate and stayed home for the rest of Christmas week. Delta wheedled, cajoled and threatened. "Please come to Christmas Eve dinner at my house. Please. Don't you want to come see Cora and Ivy open your gifts? I'm keeping the girls for the holidays. Laney's gone again. Spending the holidays in jail up in Nashville. Her and her boyfriend got caught forging checks at liquor stores."

I groaned. "I told Ivy to call me for help the next time her aunt disappeared. Thomas gave her his number, too."

"Ivy's never going to ask *anybody* for *any* kind of help, no way. She's scared of the social worker in charge of their case, one 'Mrs. Ganza,' over in Asheville. Mrs. Ganza is on the verge of hauling Ivy and Cora to foster care, again."

"No! We need to keep them here, where they've got a home and a chance to make friends. What I can do to help? If it's about money—"

"Hon, it's about friends and community, and we've got plenty of both here. Dolores and the Judge caught wise to the girls' situation when they noticed for two straight days that Laney's car wasn't parked at the cottage. They let Pike know. He practically had to hog-tie Ivy. Poor little Cora just tagged along, talking to some invisible friend. 'Santa won't forget about us like our aunt did. Thomas and Cathy won't let him.'"

"Oh, God."

"Don't worry about them, I'm tellin' you. They'll have a good holiday. Thomas sent them a bunch of gifts. Add those to the pile of gifts from Neiman Marcus on your nickel—Anthony said his whole UPS truck smelled like some kind of perfume by the time he delivered everything to the Crossroads—and those little girls are going to have the best Christmas of their entire lives so far. Hey, by the way, what did you get *me* out of the Neiman Marcus catalog? I've been shaking the box. Let me guess. It's a gift certificate for a custom Jaguar with my monogram on the vanity plate. Or a solid-gold spatula."

Actually, my Christmas gift to Delta was a diamond pendant in the shape of a biscuit. "I'm staying home for the holidays," I told her again. "I have a Lean Cuisine turkey-and-dressing dinner in my new little freezer. I have a microwave oven. I have the Log Splitters' 'Goddess Holidays' CD. I'm staying put. Tell everyone they can gossip about me freely. My holiday gift to the community."

"Oh, honey, people think what you did was . . . well, okay, they don't understand about you moving the bed, but they think the door decoration was mighty sweet. In fact, you've sparked a new fashion among the trendwatchers. A bunch of Turtleville's social divas have put pine boughs tied with scarves on their front doors."

"I don't want to be a trendsetter. And I don't want reporters to start poking around here."

"Honey, other than somebody from HGTV looking for you to do a show about decorating with scarves, I doubt you've got much to worry about. Come to dinner."

"I'm staying home. Really. I'm happy. I've got heat, a bed, a vibrator."

"Speaking of love machines, Thomas isn't mad at you. He told Santa. Said what you did to his furniture was between him and you, and nobody should bug you about it."

"When's he coming home?"

"He didn't say, but I hope he'll stay at his brother's until New Year's. Get himself off to a fresh start for next year. Anyhow, please come to dinner."

"Delta, just knowing I have an invitation is enough for me. Thanks, but no thanks."

"I'll come pick you up. You don't have to drive. You know, maybe you should buy a tractor. Now we *know* you can drive one of those. Why, you could get you a great big Kubota or a John Deere with a front-loader to scare off on-coming traffic, and drive it all over the county. Pike wouldn't give you a ticket for driving an unauthorized vehicle on a public road. He'd look the other way."

I groaned. Now everyone knew I was afraid to drive a car. My humiliation was complete. "I'll talk to you on Christmas Day. I'll call you. I promise."

"You're a hard cousin to browbeat," she said sadly.

On Christmas Eve, I ate my microwaved dinner in my warm but still unfurnished house, listened to Alberta and Macy sing folk songs about the empowerment of Mrs. Santa Claus, then crawled into bed with my vibrator. It wasn't a dildo-type but one of those giant massage wands. It had a vibrating head like a flying saucer and three speeds. I called them First Kiss, Second Date and Weekend in Las Vegas.

"Merry Christmas, Thomas," I whispered, and flicked the switch to

Vegas.

The next morning, shivering next to my space heater on the living room hearth, I carried a microwaved cup of coffee to the window and pulled back the quilt-drape for a look at Christmas morning weather. Cold and clear and . . .

Christmas tree?

Someone had covered a wild cedar at the edge of the forest in colorful ornaments, garland and tinsel, with a cheerful plastic star on top. I grabbed my shotgun and crept outside. I'd padlocked the new driveway gate. No one could have gotten here by car, only a trespasser on foot. Looking around furtively, I didn't see anyone lurking in the forest. I sidled over to the tree. A note dangled from one branch.

Goldilocks seen in neighborhood. Porridge eaten, beds moved. Three bears call cops. But me? I like her style. Thomas.

Thomas. He was back. He was home.

I gently carried the note inside and set it on the living room shelves among the jars, the old photos I'd found in Granny's attic, Cora's fake ruby and Ivy's drawing of the ruby-mining sluice.

My Christmas keepsakes.

PART FIVE

Taking joy in living is a woman's best cosmetic.
—*Rosalind Russell*

I'm not happy, I'm cheerful. There's a difference. A happy woman has no cares at all. A cheerful woman has cares but has learned how to deal with them.

—*Beverly Sills*

Chapter 20

Thomas
The Dark Side Of Winter

I thought I had a better handle on the January depression now. I told myself Cathy was all the inspiration and motivation I needed to stay in the light. But when the calendar clicked past New Year's Day a black pall settled on me, just like every year since nine-eleven. I couldn't think straight. I returned to drinking with a vengeance to stop the nightmares and the flashbacks.

I should have known it would happen. Many nine-eleven survivors are serious head cases, still fighting off bleak moods and random fears. At least my January mood could be linked to a specific cause. A package always arrived from Ravel in the third week of the month. The contents always flattened me. Dread squeezed me like a vise.

The vodka bottles on my shelves emptied themselves one by one into my bloodstream. I looked and felt like hell, and I didn't want Cathy to see me that way. Snow closed in and everything froze hard for nearly a week. I sat by my fireplace and drank, and waited for the package, and talked to myself.

Just get past that package, and you'll be okay.

Cathy

"Cathy, I want to warn you about something," Delta said as she drove my Hummer along a narrow, winding two-lane perched high along the rocky banks of Upper Ruby Creek in downtown Turtleville. I huddled in the passenger seat, sweating inside sunglasses and a heavy, hooded jacket, clutching a small fire extinguisher in my lap.

"That we're going to die a fiery death in the river gorge if you don't slow down?" I said in a shaky voice.

"I'm only doing thirty."

We flashed by small shops and pretty little houses clinging atop boulders that looked down on the river. Dapples of cold winter light dropped like pearls through bare hardwoods and the feathery limbs of tall evergreens, flickering across the road before disappearing down the ravine into whitewater currents. I hugged the fire extinguisher. "This is a road for trapeze artists with safety nets. Not cars."

"Try to think about something else. Listen to me. I want to warn you. Thomas has dived back into the bottle. That's why you haven't seen him since Christmas."

Instant alert. I craned my head at her and forgot the road. "What's wrong? What's happened to him?"

"Same ol' same old. He always gets worse around certain dates. September eleventh, naturally. And his little boy's birthday. But January is the worst. It's his wedding anniversary."

"Well, of *course* he still grieves for his wife, even if their marriage was shaky."

"No, this isn't about grievin'. It's about that cold-hearted sister-in-law of his, up in New York. She always sends him something that makes him feel like shit. Every year, the day before his anniversary, a package comes. One year she sent him his wife's diary from when she was a little girl."

"Why?"

"The sis-in-law had red-lined all the parts where Thomas's wife fantasized about marrying a prince or a movie star and living to be an old lady with lots of kids and grandkids."

"Oh, my God."

"Another year she mailed him a letter his wife wrote to her family when she and Thomas were dating. The letter said how Thomas was the man of her dreams and how she just knew he'd die to protect her. Had a line in it something like, 'He'd throw himself into a burning building if

I were trapped inside.' Thomas nearly jumped off Devil's Knob after his sis-in-law stabbed him with that poison dart. Jeb and Santa followed him around like guard dogs for weeks."

I groaned. "Why does he humor his sister-in-law's viciousness that way? Why does he even open the packages?"

"Because he can't resist pouring salt into his wounds. The sis-in-law *knows* he can't resist. The mean bitch. She doesn't ever want him to make peace with what happened. In her crazy mind, he didn't try hard enough to rescue his wife and son."

"Maybe she won't send a package this year."

"Oh, she will. After he called her for help back when you were in the hospital? She was smug and furious. That woman's armed for bear, this year."

"Called her? About me? What do you mean?"

"Gawdamighty, I never mentioned what Thomas did to get your phone number in the burn ward?"

"No!"

Looking grim, Delta told me how he'd used his sister-in-law's connections in the hospital industry. How he'd bribed her with an antique pocket watch that had been both his wife's family heirloom and his sentimental keepsake.

I sank back on the seat. "Oh, Thomas."

"Hmmm uh. He might as well have cut his chest open and told his sister-in-law to rip out his heart. She let him live, but she's been biding her time ever since."

We crested a ridge. Suddenly Delta turned the Hummer down a steep road overlooking a vista of mountains. My stomach lurched. "Let's intercept the package," I announced as I reached for a pill bottle in my jacket. "Does it come through the post office? Just set it out where I can happen to notice it, and I'll steal it and throw it away." An Internet headline flitted through my mind. *Cathryn Deen's Bizarre Behavior Continues—Now Feds Charge Her With Mail Tampering.* Complete with a bleary, disheveled mug shot. All right, for Thomas I'd take my chances. "Does it come through Anthony, the UPS man? Then tell him to leave it where I can accidentally find it."

Delta sighed. "You think I haven't considered doing that? If it came by Anthony, well, no problem. Anthony's aunt's husband's brother's wife is a New York City policewoman who's been on anti-depressants ever since nine-eleven, so he's sympathetic, and he'd throw the package in a ditch to save Thomas more grief. But Thomas's sis-in-law is no dummy. She always sends the damn package by special courier, with Thomas's signature required—so the delivery guy comes to the café, calls Thomas from there, and Thomas comes down from the ridge and picks up the package. Just like a sacrificial lamb knowing it's headed for the altar."

"But the courier has to meet him at the Crossroads. So you'll know when the courier gets there. You can let me know."

"And then you'll do *what*?"

"Be there when Thomas comes to get it. I'll talk to him about it. I'll talk him out of looking at it. I have influence. He'll listen to me."

She clucked her tongue. "Cathy, where this thing is concerned, nobody can talk him out of it."

Delta swung the Hummer into the gated entrance of a mountain estates community. *Blue Ridge Vistas, Estate Homes, Private Golf Community, Mountain Views,* said an elegant wooden sign set on a stacked-stone foundation. As we careened to a halt at the guard's office, she turned to me sadly. "Hon, when that package comes the Thomas we know will disappear even deeper inside himself for awhile. And all we'll be able to do is wait and pray that he comes back safe and more-or-less sound, like always."

As she drove into the resort subdivision with a security pass hanging from the Hummer's rearview mirror I frowned and hunched down in my seat. Pre-scars, I'd always been able to wrap men—and their moods—around my little finger. Thomas's depression would have been no match for my geisha-beauty-queen skills. Now I had to rely on reason, personality and tact.

A challenge, but I'd try.

I was still deep in thought when Delta turned into the cobblestoned driveway of a miniature villa. "Okay, here we are," she said cheerfully. "Like I told you, Toots Bailey and her husband used to own an interior decorating business down in Atlanta, and she says this living room furniture she wants to sell you is the bonafide 1920's mission style you're looking for. Solid cherry wood and leather cushions so deep you can lose your butt in 'em."

I barely heard a word. I stared at the vintage Trans Am in the driveway next door. Black-and-gold, late nineteen-seventies model. With the firebird emblem on it. Exactly like the one I'd crashed. Cold shivers went through me, and I threw up some bile in my throat. Delta shoved her door open and began climbing out, not realizing I was frozen in place. "What you waiting for?" she chirped, peering at me. "If you sit still too long around this neighborhood, you'll get hit by a golf ball."

"Delta, I . . . I don't know if I feel all right. Maybe we can come back later—"

"Delta, help!" Our furniture-selling hostess, Toots, burst out of the house yelling and waving a phone as she ran toward the Hummer. By the time she reached Delta she was gesturing wildly up the street. "You remember Frank and Olinda Hunsell? They own car dealerships over in Tennessee. Olinda left Frank this morning! Now Frank's drunk and he's out in their backyard waving a gun and threatening to shoot her poor little dog and its puppies! I've called Pike, but I don't know if he'll get here in time!"

"Damn," Delta said, stabbing a hand into the oversized leather tote on her shoulder. "The one day I left my pistol at home. Come on, Toots, I'll try to talk some sense into him." She tossed her tote in the Hummer. "Cathy, you stay here and hold the fort, okay, hon?" Then she slammed the door and followed Toots across the neighboring lawns at a chubby trot.

"Frank has a gun!" I shouted belatedly. Delta and Toots disappeared around the corner of a two-story shingle-and-stone bungalow several doors down. "I don't believe this," I said weakly, dabbing my forehead with a gloved hand. I looked up the street in the dire hope I'd see Pike's patrol car right away.

A gunshot made me jump so hard I bit my tongue.

I threw my sunglasses on the dash, tugged my jacket hood further over my face, pushed my door open, and clambered out on rubbery legs. Still cradling my fire extinguisher like a baby, I headed for the Hunsell house at a staggery lope, giving the next-door neighbor's Trans Am a wide berth.

The Hunsell back yard was surrounded by a tall, wooden privacy fence, but its gate was open wide enough for me to glimpse Delta, Toots, and another woman from the neighborhood clustered inside. I crept along a line of bushy, red-tipped-photina shrubs, watching. Toots and friend, looking terrified, huddled behind Delta.

Delta tried to reason calmly with Frank Hunsell. "Now, Frank, put that gun down before my husband gets here," she cajoled. "You don't want to make my husband mad by waving that gun at me. You don't want him to turn you into a big, hairy *stain*, do you?" I heard puppies whimpering. "Put the gun down, Frank," Delta repeated. "Don't take out your revenge on the rest of these poor little dogs. It's not their fault your wife ran off."

"This is what all you ugly bitches deserve," Frank yelled. "A bullet in the head. My wife left these bitches behind. I shot their ugly bitch of a mama, and now I'm going to shoot both of her ugly bitch puppies."

I charged through the gate and made a left turn toward Frank's angry voice. Frank was balding, beefy, and had the generally disheveled look of a country-club executive on a bad bender. A delicate, tri-colored Sheltie twitched her last moments of life into a puddle of blood on the brown fescue lawn. Her two half-grown, mixed-breed puppies cowered nearby.

Frank waved his pistol. "Ugly bitches get what they deserve," he said again. Then he pivoted toward the puppies and took aim.

I didn't know what else to do, so I hit him in the head with the fire extinguisher.

His knees buckled and he sprawled on his back, moaning. I shoved the gun away from his quivering hand with the toe of my *Gucci* mule—style is always important when threatening a man—then leaned over him with the calm fury of the queen-mother monster in the *Alien* movies. In case he moved again, I aimed the extinguisher at his head like a short, fat baseball bat.

"Some of us ugly bitches fight back," I said.

🐾🐾🐾🐾🐾

"It was just like something in a movie!" Delta exclaimed, waving her hands and pacing excitedly in the frosty afternoon air outside the Crossroad's general store. Jeb, Bubba, Becka, Cleo and other assorted family members stood there steaming up the air with their rapt breath. Pike looked grim. He'd just returned from arresting Frank Hunsell at the Turtleville Emergency Clinic. Hunsell had a mild concussion and a long list of charges to face. He also had a bruise on one cheek, since Pike slammed him against a wall.

"And then," Delta went on, bending herself into a chubby crouch that made the back of her winter coat stick out like a duck's tail, "here comes Cathy through the gate. Like a football player headed for the end zone, only she's carrying a fire extinguisher instead of a ball. Frank Hunsell puffs out his chest and curls his lip and growls, 'Ugly bitches get what they deserve,' and then he turns—" Delta pivoted with an evil look on her face. "He turns toward those shivering little puppies, and he points his gun at them and then . . . *wham!*"

She mimicked a fire extinguisher being rammed against a head. "Cathy slammed that canister against his skull, and the sound it made echoed for *miles*. He went *down!*" Delta feigned a slump, though she wasn't enough of a method actress to actually fall down on the graveled parking lot. "Like a sack of wet flour!" She straightened, lifted the imaginary fire extinguisher, then leaned over the imaginary Frank Hunsell. "Cathy glared down at him like so. I'm telling you, green fire shot out of her eyes. And she said, 'Sometimes us ugly bitches fight back.'"

Everyone applauded. Delta was a storyteller in the great Southern tradition. Thanks to her, my legend would be told around campfires for generations to come. I sat dully on the store's wooden steps, my hooded head propped on a gloved fist. I couldn't stop worrying about Thomas. I also kept seeing the puppies' dead mother. I looked up at Pike. "Don't you have to file some kind of charges against me? If so, can I turn myself in tomorrow? I've got a lot on my mind today."

"Charge you?" He smiled grimly. "For what? Using a fire extinguisher to put out a *gun*?" Pike shook his head. "Hunsell was waving a loaded pistol at three women, one of them my wife. He'd already committed one act of animal cruelty and was about to commit more. No, you won't be charged for stopping him. Too bad you didn't hit him harder."

"Is there any way to keep this incident off the front page of the *Jefferson County Weekly Messenger*?"

Delta patted my shoulder. "Since the editor is my third cousin once removed on the Aymes side of the McKendall line, I'll have a word. It's a family thing."

I relaxed a little. "The fire extinguisher *did* make a satisfying sound. When I hit Hunsell on the head it was like a sound effect in a cartoon. It went 'conk.' I just wish I'd gotten there before he shot the puppies' mother."

Everyone nodded somberly. Jeb and Becka headed into the store. "We'll get you some supplies for your new babies," Becka said.

"Thank you." I stood slowly, my knees quivering, and made my way over to the Hummer. Banger lurked there, looking up at the rear passenger-side as if jealous. "You can't eat my puppies," I said. He gave me a china-eyed glare.

I opened the back door a few inches and peeked inside. The puppies looked back at me uncertainly, their eyes sad, their shaggy tails set on half-wag. Their mother's small, still body lay in the back of the Hummer, wrapped in a clean garbage bag. I couldn't bear to leave her laying where Frank Hunsell shot her. Her babies needed her nearby, if only in spirit.

"Toots says your father was a miniature Schnauzer," I told the puppies. They were a grayish-brindle color, with white splashes on their chests and faces. Both had floppy little ears that folded over to the front, and both had chin whiskers. "Since your mother was a Sheltie, that makes you two 'Sheltzers.' Okay?"

Their tails wagged half-heartedly. I leaned closer, stroked their heads, and made soothing noises. "I'm sorry about your mother. Will you be *my* babies, now? You're *not* ugly." My throat ached. "The three of us, *we're* not ugly."

As if they understood, their tails went wild. I was a little startled. I knew nothing about dogs because I'd never had any kind of pet as a child. Daddy said we traveled too much to care for animals. By the time I was old enough to make my own choices my career took all my time. Now, suddenly, I got my first lesson in doggy devotion.

Two sets of front paws climbed my shoulders. Two pink tongues attacked my face. They licked the good side, they licked the scars, they licked the hood of my jacket. Puppies don't see "ugly," they see love. I stroked their heads and struggled not to cry.

"Thomas is here," Delta whispered behind me.

I wiped my face hurriedly as I shut the Hummer's door. Here I was, smelling like dog saliva. Not to mention having just auditioned for a *Sopranos* episode in the Hunnell back yard. My nickname as a made mafiosa? *The Fire Extinguisher.*

I'd tell him that. I'd make him smile. I'd find a way to talk to him about his sister-in-law. I'd convince him to throw her toxic anniversary gift in the nearest trash can without opening it. I turned around and froze. He stood a few yards away, frowning as Delta gave him the *CliffsNotes* edition of the afternoon's drama. I didn't expect his haggard face, his bloodshot eyes. His beard was beginning to look ragged again. There was a bone-weary droop to his broad shoulders.

When I ran over to him he registered nothing warmer than a tired nod. I said as lightly as I could, "I have two furry little creatures in the Hummer. I think they're commonly referred to as 'dogs.' Do you speak 'dog' or any related dialect of dog language? I could really use an interpreter. Why don't you come to my house tonight and translate for us until I learn enough words of dog to communicate with them?"

Not a flicker of amusement. "What you did today proves how capable you are. When other people—or animals—need you, you're there for them. All you have to do is recognize your own strength."

"You didn't see me throw up on the hood of a *Trans Am* after I whacked Frank Hunnell." I turned my face just-so, charmingly luring him with the good side. I dipped my chin, smiled and looked up at him from beneath my lashes. My box-office close-up. How many times I'd used it in films. The eyes, the smile. The megawatter. "I really need your help and advice with the puppies. Please come to my house tonight. I'll microwave a protein bar and some crunchy granola for you. Please?"

"I know what you're trying to do, but I have to handle my problem alone."

So much for movie shtick. I stared up at him bluntly. "The hell you do."

"This is a part of who I am." He bent his head close to mine. His voice became a hoarse rasp. "Cathy, this is *my* burn scar. All right? You can't fix it."

I grabbed the front of his coat. "The fact that you drove down here to check on me today means you *don't* want to be alone."

"I drove down here to meet the courier. He called."

I looked up at him in dismay. Delta, eavesdropping nearby, hurried over. "He's delivering your package a week earlier than the other years!"

"Good. I hate long waits."

A van bearing a delivery company's logo pulled into the café's parking lot. Thomas pried my hands off his coat then walked over to meet the driver. I turned to Delta urgently. "I can't let him go back to his cabin like this. Tell Pike to arrest him for his own safety. I'll . . . I'll get my fire extinguisher and hit him on the head. Whatever it takes. I am not going to stand here helplessly and watch him walk into a pit of despair alone!"

Delta clamped a hand on my forearm. "I'll tell you what I told him about *you* before Christmas. *Back off.* He has to find his own way."

"How can you say that?"

"Hon, if he's about to go down in flames, you're not the one who can save him. He's got to make peace with himself. You can't do it for him."

"I can try."

Thomas was now walking to his truck with a slender package tucked under one arm. What had his twisted sister-in-law inserted in that benign-looking envelope this year? How could something so flimsy have the power to tear him apart? I followed him at a trot. My feet crunched on the fine gravel, and he turned slowly as I reached him. "Go home, Cathy. That's not an option. That's an order."

"Why is it that you have the right to meddle in my life when I need help but I don't have the right to meddle in yours?"

"This isn't about keeping score."

"If I had a bottle of pills in my hand you'd stop me from taking them. Just as you did a few months ago."

"That was different. Leave me alone, goddammit."

This bitter, cursing man wasn't the Thomas I knew. "Why don't you open that letter now and read what's inside, and then we can talk about it? I'm a good listener." My voice broke. I flung a hand toward the deformed ear hidden under my hood. "No matter how this looks, I *can* hear with it. Please, Thomas. I can listen. Please."

"Go home. If you need anything, I mean in an emergency, call me. I'll get there."

"Even if you're too drunk to stand up?"

"I'm never too drunk to stand up."

"Will you promise to call me if you feel . . . desperate?"

"Cathy, go home. Leave me alone."

"I'll come to your cabin, day or night. Just call me. I'll get in the Hummer and drive. I swear. Or I'll walk. I'll walk to your cabin if you need me."

He lifted a hand, unfurled it, pointed at me. "*I don't need you.*"

Thomas left me standing there, got into his truck, and drove away.

Chapter 21

Thomas
Sherryl's Letter To Her Sister

Good morning, Sis—
In terms of the legal issues, everything's in place. I'll
file for full custody of Ethan immediately after telling
Thomas I want a divorce, and if Thomas fights the
custody issue (which I'm sure he will, because he's a
devoted father and he loves Ethan) I'll back off and
offer joint custody as a bargaining chip. Thomas has a
deep need to salvage and restore neglected treasures, and
my approach to the custody issue will give him a sense
of satisfaction. In his mind, he will have salvaged joint
custody of our son from the ruins of our marriage.
I know you think I should abort the pregnancy, but I'm
not comfortable with that choice. However, I will follow
your advice and tell Thomas about it only after I file
for divorce and custody of Ethan. I want to be settled in
London before I let him know he's going to be a divorced
father to Ethan and a second child, too.
Call me sentimental or call me a coward, but I don't
want to deal that blow to him in person. Once upon a
time, when we daydreamed about having a little brother

or sister for Ethan, Thomas loved the idea. He'll no doubt
be despondent over my news that our second child will
not be raised by the two of us inside the confines of our
marriage. Of course, there's no reason in the world he
can't visit Ethan and the new baby in London, as long
as we can be civilized in general and on the subject of
Gibson, in general.

Thomas has long suspected Gibson of being more than a
friend to me, so I know that won't come as a shock to him.
But naturally I don't want my relationship with Gibson
to complicate the divorce, so Gibson will have to lay low
for awhile.

Sis, I know you think I'm far too concerned with
Thomas's feelings, and you've always believed he was
secretly after my money and could be bought off should
the need arise, but no, as I've said many times, he really
does believe what he believes, he is a good person, stalwart
and true and idealistic, and I dearly wish I were the
kind of woman who could give up a view of Central
Park to live in crusty old buildings by his side.

There was a time when I thought marrying an idealistic
man without money was the epitome of soulful maturity,
a respectable elective in the School of Life. Unfortunately,
it has turned out that I really do like the freedom
only filthy lucre can offer, and so it's time to move on.
Everyone deserves one "practice marriage," right?

I'll drop you another email after I get home this
afternoon. I'm meeting Gibson for an early lunch
at Windows on the World. Thomas thinks I've got a
morning meeting with a caterer there, to plan your
birthday party. I hate sneaking around in full view of
the daily restaurant crowd at the World Trade Center,
but I'm taking your advice that "visibility is the best
defense." Besides, Gibson loves the view from the North
Tower. Thanks for suggesting it.
Love, Sherryl

❧❧❧❧❧

That's all Ravel sent in the envelope. No note, just the brutally simple print-out of Sherryl's email to her, written by Sherryl around 7 a.m. on nine-eleven, while I was in the shower and Sherryl was at her computer. I remembered her switching to the screensaver as I walked into our bedroom in a robe, toweling my hair. Since we shared very little about ourselves by then, the small, furtive gesture only made me head sooner to the kitchen for my first cup of coffee.

I should have known. I should have *known* she was in love with someone else. We hadn't touched each other in several months. Apparently, our last time in bed had been ripe and careless. But I didn't suspect she was pregnant.

So there it was. I'd lost two children on nine-eleven, not one. And I'd lost my wife to another man, someone I vaguely recalled meeting at parties, someone from her law class at Harvard. Had they been together before we met? After we met? The whole time of our marriage? To me, all that mattered was this: She and he were going to take Ethan and the new baby to London. My son, and my second son or first daughter, would have been raised on the other side of an ocean from me, and Sherryl would have fought me for sole custody, using her family's money and clout, bolstered by her sister's cold-blooded encouragement.

I would have lost the court battle. I would have lost my children. My children would have been raised by another man. Ethan would have slowly forgotten me, not by name or title, but by significance. I would have been the father who visited, not the father who walked him to school or sat on the sidelines at games or taught him to ride a bike. And the baby, the baby wouldn't have known me at all. Not even a hint of a memory of me in the house. I'd have been no more important than a friend of the family's.

I slid through the dark doorway of those thoughts as I drank and read Sherryl's email, and drank and re-read it, a drink, a reading—drink, read and repeat. Dazed, I found myself outside the cabin in the cold blue light just before sunset. A blood-red sliver of cloud clinging to Hog Back as if the mountain were being gutted from the spine down. The thought hiding deep inside the black doorway of my mind rose up like the fetid smoke off a burning corpse.

My children would have forgotten me. I'm glad my children died, instead.

"Jesus Christ," I said softly.

You're a loser. You should have died, not them, the vodka whispered. I staggered inside to pack. I'd leave in the morning, when I was sober. A clean getaway, no trouble, no interventions. By the time Cathy or John, Delta or Pike or Jeb or Santa—the people who thought they knew me, who thought I was worth caring about—came looking for me, I'd be halfway to somewhere. Mexico, maybe. A foreign land. A place with deserts and mesas and spaces too big for meaning. Somewhere vast and empty and hard to search.

I didn't want anyone who cared about me to find my body.

Cathy

Even as I agonized over Thomas's state of mind that evening, I couldn't forget my new responsibilities. I had a dog to bury before dark. I'd never used a shovel before in my entire life, so no, I'd never dug a grave with one, either, or ever had the need to do so. Hurrying before the light failed, sweating in the cold, my scarf down around my shoulders, my coat on the ground, blisters stinging my palms, I finally stepped back and surveyed the deep hole I'd dug, and I felt grimly proud. A real woman can bury the dead with her own two hands, if need be.

"She'll be happy, here," I told the puppies, as if I could make promises for the dead, as if they understood. They wagged their fluffy tails at my voice, I knew that much. I waved a hand at the Nettie tombstones among the deep gloaming. "Lots of people who liked dogs are here. And their dogs along with them. And cats. And a goat. Y'all can visit here anytime you feel like it. That path we walked from the house? Just follow it."

More tail wagging.

I knelt beside the small, sad form of their mother's body, still wrapped in a black trash bag. The puppies huddled on either side of me. I put a hand on each of their delicate little bodies. Tears rose in my eyes, and my throat ached. I was so worried about Thomas. I tried to think of something hopeful from the Episcopal funeral liturgy to comfort me and the puppies, but couldn't. Daddy didn't go to funerals and my aunts preferred cremation or stuffing. For their pets, that is. I shivered at the memory of small vases in one aunt's china cabinet and a stuffed tabby alongside the golf trophies of another. No, I'd have to wing this service.

I stood and cleared my throat. "Little Miss Sheltie was a good mother," I began. "She died trying to protect her babies." I looked down at the puppies. "I'm so sorry y'all won't have her here in the flesh anymore, because it's hard to grow up without a mother, I know, and there'll be so many days when you'll wish you could hear her voice again, just *once*; you'll wish she could tell you what you thinks of how you're doing, if she's proud of you, and those small, important moments, like when you get your period the first time, or your first date, or your first kiss, or your first, your 'first,' you know, and you'll wish you could ask her advice, but you'll have to just hope, just have faith that somehow, some way, she's listening and she's speaking to you in quiet little ways you aren't aware of. Sometimes she may speak through other people, and sometimes she may speak through your dreams, and sometimes, like now—" my voice broke, and the puppies licked my shoes and whined—"sometimes, she may speak to you through someone else's mother, through that mother's sacrifices or victories."

Tears slid down my face. I knelt again, gathering the puppies in my arms. They licked my cheeks. "Parents are not perfect," I whispered. "But the best ones really do have good intentions. My father tried to keep me away from this farm, away from my Granny Nettie, because he thought she was a bad influence. He was wrong about that, but he didn't mean to hurt her, or me. In his own way I suppose he thought he was honoring my mother's memory, doing what she would have wanted. My mother left this farm and made a new life for herself in Atlanta. Maybe she rejected Granny's way of life, maybe she broke Granny's heart without realizing it. I can't say. I don't know, and it breaks *my* heart to not know what she and Granny really went through. All I can say now is, 'I'm here. I'm back, Granny. I'm back, Mother. You and Granny have to work out the past for yourselves. Just help me work out the *future*, all right? Help me take care of these babies, these puppies. And please, please, help me take care of Thomas. He's suffered so much already. Please help me understand how to help him. Please.'"

I nuzzled the puppies. "Sometimes you just have to bury your mother and go on with your life and try to be a good mother yourself." I kissed the puppies on their heads, gently set them aside, and laid the body of their mother into the grave. "Goodbye, sweet little dog," I whispered as I sprinkled the first handful of dirt. "Goodbye from me." Another handful. "Goodbye from my mother and grandmother." A handful. "And most of all, goodbye from your two loving daughters." Two handfuls. I stood again, shivering in the falling temperature of a January night. I shoveled the rest of the dirt into the grave, tamped it with my feet, found some rocks to pile on it, then stepped back. The puppies leaned against my legs.

"I'll get her a marker," I promised them. "But I don't know her name. Toots couldn't say, none of the neighbors knew, and I'm not asking Frank Hunnell. We'll think of a name to put on the gravestone, all right? Something better than 'Little Miss Sheltie.' And I don't know *your* names, either. I'm Cathy. Cathy Deen. And *you* are?"

Of course, they just looked up at me and said nothing.

"If I were Alberta, I'd name you 'Thelma and Louise.'" No response. "If I were Delta, I'd name you 'Biscuit and Gravy.'" No response. "If I were the old me, I'd name you 'Vera Wang and Coco Chanel.'" No response. "But I'm not sure who I am, anymore." I shut my eyes. "Mother? Granny Nettie? Mother of These Puppies? Could the three of you help me name these girls? Tell me who I am, and who *they* are."

No response.

I opened my eyes wearily. "Okay, we'll work on the names later. Maybe we have to figure this out for ourselves, girls." I put the shovel on one shoulder and looked at the grave one more time. The puppies circled the stones, sniffing at them, touching them with curious paws. I clucked at them, and they came to me. "We're on our own tonight. Let's go home." They wagged their tails. A good sign. We were a family.

Watching out for the shadows, picking our way through the woods, we went back to the house. I kept thinking of Thomas, and death.

Thomas

Liquor, like most mind-altering substances, including food and sex, is a multi-layered temptation, a seductive genie corralled in the bottle of our common sense. Let the genie out carefully, persuade it to grant your more benign wishes, and you'll be okay. But turn your back on it, let go of the leash, and the genie will drag you inside the bottle and chain you to its floor. And there, my friend, you'll find a hell of your own making.

I prided myself on controlling the vodka genie. I knew how to set it on 'stun' for hours on end, keeping the effect just below 'stupor' and just above 'pain.' Even that night, after my decision to leave the Crossroads and die, I kept the genie on a leash. I packed my big canvas tote neatly and slowly, pausing to drink and read Sherry's email to Ravel again every hour or so. I built a fire as the cold night settled in, and I turned my bed down, and I ate canned meat with crackers. I was calm, I was deliberate, I was numb. I didn't want to think about the letter—in between reading it—and I didn't want to think about the death wish I'd put on Ethan and his never-born sibling—and I didn't want to think about Cathy.

If I got out of her way now, she'd be able to tell people I was just someone she'd needed in transition, while she was getting her life back together, not someone she regretted ever meeting. And Delta. Delta would never forgive me, but Delta was good at putting sorrows in perspective, and she'd be all right.

My brother. John. He'd never forgive me either, but John had seen this coming a long time. He wouldn't be surprised. I'd leave the email. John would read it and understand. He'd get over my death. He had a loving wife and children to live for. He was a family man. Clearly, I wasn't.

I set the tote on the seat of my truck. I laid my pistol on top of it. An Enfield No. 2 Mk 1, a workhorse of a revolver, .38 caliber, British, their standard sidearm during World War II. I'd bought it from an old Japanese businessman in New York years earlier. He would only say, "It came to me through a family connection who cherished the bravery endowed in it," leaving me to wonder what soldier in his family fought the soldier who died holding it.

This gun had seen too much honorable war to be shocked by my peacetime despair. This gun considered me an afterthought in its legacy. Good. I walked back inside, coatless, not shivering in the below-freezing temp. A white, crisp moon rose over Hog Back, silvering the high pasture, my unfinished vineyard homage to Frank Lloyd Wright, and me.

Cathy
Midnight

I couldn't sleep. The puppies wisely grieved for their mother only in their dreams, so they were curled up, sound asleep, in the jumbled quilts of my bed. I wandered through my house from one waggling-headed electric heater to the next, still dressed in jeans, a heavy sweater, and wrapped in one of my grandmother's quilts. I carried my cell phone with me in case Thomas called. He didn't. The darkness beyond my windows was only leavened by the stark, white moon.

I stood in my empty living room, among the boxes and cot and ad-lib curtains, feeling my thoughts echo off the smooth, empty chestnut boards of the walls. *This house needs furniture. I have puppies now. They need a couch to chew. I'll go back and buy Toots' furniture. I'll get Thomas to go look at it with me. See if he thinks it fits the mood of this place.*

I pulled the quilt tighter around my shoulders. Even with space heaters, the house was cold. Tea. I'd brew a cup of hot Earl Grey in the microwave, with sourwood honey Macy had given me, made by lesbian bees. That would soothe me. In the kitchen, squinting in the shadowy pool of light from a small lamp on the counter, I scuffed my socked feet over the red-clay constellations, fetched a plain ceramic mug from a cabinet, and twisted the handle on the primitive faucet of my sink. Ice-cold water trickled into my mug. I dropped a tea bag into the water and idly bounced it. Lost in thought, I gazed out the uncurtained window over the sink.

I wonder if Ivy and Cora are still enjoying their Christmas gifts? I should call Thomas and ask if he's seen them lately. It's only midnight. I should call him.

Suddenly, I saw him in the window. His reflection, over my own. No, not his face. His hand. Like a close-up in a film. I simply understood it was *his* hand. And his hand was . . . dead. It sprawled in the window pane, palm up, flecked with red.

Flecked with blood. His blood.

I dropped the mug. It hit the hard sky of the constellations and burst into ceramic chunks. Cold, tea-stained water splashed my socks.

I didn't bother changing them. I shoved my feet into loafers and fumbled in my purse for the keys to the Hummer. "Sleep tight, I'll be back," I told the puppies. I, who had not driven a vehicle more demanding than a garden tractor in ten long months, I, who had panic attacks just sitting in my own Hummer's passenger seat, I went outside in the moonlight and climbed up into that big, hulking Fear on Wheels, and I cranked the engine.

And, shaking, I headed for Thomas's cabin.

Praying I wasn't too late.

Thomas

The rumble of an engine woke me from a dazed sleep by my fireplace. I staggered from the chair Cathy had moved by the hearth, knocked over the half-empty bottle by my feet, and shoved the stained letter away from an ember on the hearth's stone ledge. By the time I looked out a window I saw Cathy, carrying a flashlight, walking toward my truck in the moonlight. I'd left the driver's door open. She looked in, leaned in, and I knew what she was seeing: The revolver, my wallet, my keys, and a wad of cash laying atop the duffle bag.

My plan couldn't have been more obvious.

Dull anger crowded the despair in my mind. I'd told her not to come here. I slammed the cabin door open and strode outside in the cold moonlight. She jumped, looked at me wildly, dropped the flashlight, but then turned back inside the truck's cab. When she pivoted to face me, she held the revolver in both hands, held it out from her on her palms as if afraid it might explode. But then she flipped the chamber open with surprising expertise and began methodically shaking the bullets out. I reached her as the last one hit the ground. With one quick swipe I pulled the empty revolver from her hands.

"Give that back," she ordered. "Goddammit, you give that gun back to me."

"I can't do that." We were carved in shadows; I heard her hoarse sound of rage before I saw the flash of her hand. She drew back her scarred right hand in a fist.

And punched me in the mouth.

It barely hurt, though I was dimly aware of tasting blood. I was too numb, too drunk, to care, though she hit me hard enough to make me take a step back. She grabbed for the empty gun, and I lifted it away from her reach, while bracing one hand on her shoulder. I held her at bay. She uttered another sound, deep and feminine and furious. Twisting away from me, she shoved my arm aside and got free.

We faced each other like boxers in a ring. "How could you?" she yelled. "How could you sneak away and blow your brains out? Was that the plan? You care so little about yourself, about me, about all the people who need you, that this is how you do it?" She slung her hands at me and gave a fierce, broken laugh. "You think I couldn't stand to find you laying out here with your brains spattered across your grape trellises? So instead you'd run off to somewhere safe, someplace among strangers? How dare you!" She fell to her knees, searched the ground, then leapt to her feet with something clenched in her fist. "Here, go ahead, let me watch, now that I know what to expect!" A small, sharp weight hit my arm. Bullets. She threw another one. The tip caught my cheekbone. "How could you do this to yourself!"

I hadn't flinched, hadn't moved. "Go home," I said in a low voice. I couldn't think; the liquor and depression controlled me, there were no eloquent words left. I loved her, I didn't want her to know I'd wished my own children dead.

She groaned, a sobbing, feverish sound, and shook her fists at me. "You can either drag me into your truck and drive me home, or you can shoot me. Those are the only ways I'll leave. Give the gun to me."

"You remember what you said to me in the Privy that day? 'I never asked you to care.'"

"I was a fool. We can't decide who cares about us and who doesn't! The only reason I'm alive today is because you and Delta decided to care about me. Now I care about *you* and there's nothing you can do about it. You can't pretend your choices don't hurt other people when you hurt yourself!"

"I live with my choices every day. I know who I've hurt."

"Really? No. You don't know a damn thing about your choices! You're letting liquor and depression and your manipulative psycho-bitch of a sister-in-law make all your choices *for* you! You let *them* control you. How about giving *me* the privilege of controlling your life, instead?"

I let the gun drop to the ground. "I'm taking you home. Stop asking so many questions."

"You're too drunk to catch me, and if you do, you won't get me into the truck without hurting me, and without me hurting you. I know you, Thomas. You're not going to hurt me. You haven't got it in you. And you're sure as hell not going to catch me." She turned and ran a dozen yards or so, stopping atop a knoll, silhouetted in the white moonlight, against the starry sky.

I walked slowly up the knoll towards her. She balled her hands into fists by her sides and braced her legs apart. "I thought I could trust you," she yelled hoarsely. "You weren't a photographer trying to screw me, you weren't Gerald trying to make money off me, you weren't all the men who've loved me only for my looks, you weren't the world. I thought you'd always be here for me. Don't tell me I was wrong!"

I halted, looking up at her. "I can't be what you want me to be. You don't know me."

"You already are what I want you to be. And I know you better than I've ever known any man before in my entire life!" She pummeled the air with her fists. "Why don't you just admit that you don't want me? That the thought of . . . of fucking me really *is* repulsive to you. The kindness and the flirting and friendship has all been some kind of sick game to you, hasn't it? You don't really want to touch me. You don't want to see me naked. Admit it!" She jabbed a hand at me. "You'd rather kill yourself than touch me."

261

"This is insane."

"Is it?" Her voice rose. "Is it?" She shrugged her coat off, slung it aside, grabbed the hem of her sweater and pulled the sweater off over her head. Her furious breath puffed white in the moonlight. She threw the sweater down the knoll at me. "Touch me, then! If you're going to kill yourself soon, you won't have to stand the memory of my naked ugliness very long, so go for it!"

"I'm warning you for the last time, Cathy. Go home."

"Liar. You never *wanted* me. You were just being kind to me. Pitying me. Hoping to wheedle the Nettie farm out of me. Me, the grotesque and pathetic and lonely Cathy Deen. Was that it?"

"You know that's not true."

"All I know is you'd rather die than be with me." She unzipped her jeans, shoved them down, kicked off her shoes, then the jeans, then stood there in her bra and panties. I couldn't see the scars down the right side of her body, I only saw the incredible silhouette of her, against the sky, the moonlight. Nothing could make me want her less. Nothing could stop me from wanting her, always.

"I'm right," she said through gritted teeth. "I'm right. You won't even try to touch me." She shoved her panties down, kicked them aside, unfastened her bra, threw it aside. "It doesn't get anymore humiliating than this, Thomas. And all I'm asking you to do is have the guts to admit I'm ugly. Admit you can't make yourself touch me."

I knew what she was doing to me, I knew she was *playing* me, but there was no way back. I was frozen in place, my life revolving around this single moment in time, everything hinging on who she demanded I be for her, for now, for then, for the rest of my life. She sobbed and turned her back to me. Put her face in her hands. Her shoulders shook. This was no acting job, this was real misery on her part. She was the essence of loneliness, of despair. My mirror. My life.

I ran to her. I ran. I put my arms around her from behind and dragged her up and against me and stroked my hands over her from chin to thigh and back again in rough, urgent exploration. Cathy gasped and held onto my forearms. "Not there, not that side," she said, trying to twist her head. I sank one hand into the thick, dark hair along her temple, held her still, and kissed the ruined flesh along her neck and face. She could play me, but I could play her, too.

She cried out as I dragged her to the cabin. Inside we went down on the hard wooden floor, me on my back, her straddling me, cushioned on top of me with her knees digging into the thick, woven cotton of a country rug Delta had given me. Her hands were as rough as mine as we wrestled my jeans open and down. I groaned as she jammed my cock inside her. She didn't care if she was wet enough, and at that moment, I only cared that I was alive, that she was alive, that we were together. I lunged upward to meet her, my hands on her breasts, her riding me with her head bent over me so the unscarred side of her face was against my hair. I dug my fingers into her hips and came instantly, convulsively, as if I'd never released myself before. *I want to live.*

She held my head with her hands in my hair on both sides, and bent her forehead to mine, and cried with relief.

With my arms tight around her, holding her on top of me against the cold, I cried, too.

Chapter 22

Cathy
Halfway to Dawn

Thomas and I were a mess that night. Too many emotions, too much to say, so we kept it simple. Everything turned on the pulse of sex—sex to forget and forgive, sex to heal, sex to bond. I wanted to know what was in the letter, but that would have to wait.

An antique mantel clock chimed three times. The cabin was pitch black. The fire he'd built before I arrived was long gone, and I, of course, would rather shiver than build another one. We sprawled on the floor by the hearth in a jumbled nest of quilts and pillows, naked, sweaty and exhausted in each other's arms, shivering whenever the cold air hit our bare skin. His hair streamed over his shoulders in brown tangles, his beard was wet with me. He loved all the parts of women, all the nether regions, the caves where only the brave and the noble go. I preferred a term my aging Southern-belle aunts had optioned.

Tunnel.

That woman is decorating her tunnel for traffic.

You'd better put a toll booth on your tunnel, or you'll surely pay the price.

Thomas loved all the tunnels of a woman's body, heart and soul. He and I weren't sure where to tread, what to say, or how to say it, so we shoved and grabbed and licked and bit and slammed into each other until

I felt bruised all over and his bloodied lower lip was swollen and raw. The mood was urgent, not tender. And yet very gentle.

I fumbled for the overturned vodka bottle on the hearth, found just enough liquor to fill my mouth, and, holding that warmed fluid on my tongue, pushed him down, bent my head to his cock, and cleaned it with a quick, efficient suck. He was hard again in an instant. Thomas groaned and curved his hands over my head, lacing his fingers in my hair. But then he pulled me away, guided my head upwards, kissed me. He was on my tongue and lips, his semen, the blood from his lip. He cleaned my lips with his tongue.

"Since we're dealing in moments of truth," he said grimly, "you're going to build a fire."

I went very still. He slid out of the quilts, and his naked heat became a shadow in the blackness. My heart raced at the melodic thud and rustle of split wood being arranged on the iron grate only a few feet away across a narrow apron of flat stone. Bile rose in my throat, and the clammy claustrophobia of terror hummed inside my brain. Hugging a quilt around me, I scrambled backward, stopping only when I backed into the rough wooden posts of his narrow bed.

He closed a hand on my shoulder. "You can do it."

"No." High-pitched, horrified. "Not yet."

"Cathy." His disembodied voice was deep, calm, but unrelenting. "You threw bullets at me and punched me in the mouth. When I carried you in here you cared more about taking care of me than you did about the dying embers on the hearth. You can build a fire."

I crept forward until I felt the coarse hearth stone beneath my knees. He slid his hand down, parted my quilt and outlined one nipple with a forefinger. Then he bent his head to my breast and sucked the nipple gently. The effect was overtly seductive, and very effective. Thomas versus the flames. Thomas won. He sat back, then reached behind him for firewood stacked on the hearth. I watched anxiously as he arranged it with kindling underneath.

When he finished he took my right hand, his fingertips gentle on the sensitive scar tissue. My arm coiled against my body even as my thighs dampened for him. He pried my arm free, extended it. My hand shook. Thomas wedged a smooth, metal obelisk inside my curled fingers. "It belonged to my old man. He lit three packs a day with it. That's why he died of emphysema the year I married Sherryl. I keep it because I forgive him for fucking up his life, but I don't want to be like him. Click it and prove you want me more than you want to be afraid of the fire."

I rolled my thumb on the tiny, coarse wheel. A blue-orange flame popped up. My hand jerked, the flame snapped off, and Thomas caught the lighter as I dropped it. "Try again," he said.

"I can't."

"You can."

He pressed the lighter back into my palm. I clicked it. The terrible little flame shot up, again. I stared at it. Beyond it, in its faint, flickering light, I saw Thomas's strained face, the injured lip, the handsome, tired eyes, needing to put my miseries ahead of his own. "Help," I begged, holding the lighter out stiffly. He guided my hand to a fragile pile of kindling and crumpled newspaper beneath the logs. I touched the deadly little flame to the paper and pulled back all my nerve endings as the edge of the paper flared and blackened. The kindling caught. The fire was started. "There," I said hoarsely, and snapped the lighter shut. "Now make it worth my while."

Thomas pulled me to him and kissed the top of my head. I pressed the good side of my face into the crook of his neck. Shaking, I held onto him and stared as the fire rose to a cheerful, crackling pyramid of aromatic orange and red flames, just an arm's length away. I hated it.

He laid me down and stretched out over me. I wrapped my legs around him and he slipped inside me without a hitch, as if buttered. The deep thrust, the filling sensation radiated outward, comforting muscle and skin and memory. Tragedy and fear seep into our cells like a poison, they aren't just intangible thoughts, they change our DNA. Trust and desire have to be re-learned at the core. I curved my arms around his neck. In the soft, terrifying firelight I looked up at his face, that strong, sad, compelling face, marred by ragged beard and shaggy hair and wounds I had given it.

And all I thought of was him.

Thomas

Cathy came the last time. I wasn't sure about the other times that night, when she was intent on saving my soul or staring worriedly at the fire or both, but the last time, I had no doubt. The deep breath, the electric arch of her back, the incredible stroking contraction around my cock. And then she relaxed under me, turning her face languidly to the burned side. This was how I knew she'd had an orgasm: She forgot to pose.

266

A proud moment for us both.

In the last, deepest hour of full night I built up the fire again and we sat, dazed, in the eddying river of the quilts. She squatted behind me, wrapped only in a blanket that formed a tent around us both, on an old milking stool I'd bought at a flea market. Her knees hugged the sides of my arms; occasionally I felt the hard nub of a nipple caress one shoulder as she bent over my head. My gardening shears weren't meant for cutting hair. She had to concentrate.

Cripz. The sound the thick blades made as she snipped my foot-long hair at the nape of my neck. She methodically pinched each shorn section, handed it to me over my shoulder, and I laid it on the hearth. I threw the first section she handed me into the flames; the odor of burnt hair went up, and her hands shook so badly she dropped the pruning shears on the floor. She didn't say a word, but I realized why the scent gave her flashbacks. From then on, I laid my hair on the stones.

"Done," she said, handing me the final section. She stroked her fingers through the shaggy remnants. I relished the feathery caresses on my scalp, the tops of my ears, my temples. Her touch went straight into my brain, a gentle therapy. She got up, holding the blanket around her as if suddenly shy, moved around in front of me, and sat down cross-legged with her knees against my mine. She studied the new me solemnly. "You're the most handsome man I've ever seen," she said, "with a bad lip, a bruised cheekbone, a ratty beard, and a haircut from hell."

I nodded. "It's a start."

"Is it? Don't you think it's time you told me what was in that letter from New York?"

I offered it to Cathy without a word. She took the letter in both hands and bent her head close to the words in the dim light. I stared over her into the fire.

"Oh, my God," she whispered at first. Then, "I'm sorry you were the last to know." But finally, after reading further, she drew back, staring at the paper with no sympathy at all. "Ravel is one sick, sad woman. Now, I see why."

"Why?" I said wearily.

"Your sister-in-law blames herself for what happened. No wonder she's spent the past four years trying to unload that guilt on you. It must be hell for her to live with it."

I frowned at her. "What are you talking about?"

"She suggested the restaurant at the World Trade Center that day.

Your wife went there to meet a boyfriend because her sister recommended it as a safely public place where they wouldn't be suspected of having a romantic tryst." Cathy tapped the paper with a hard fingertip. "Didn't you read that part?"

"What part?"

"*Thomas*," she said in hoarse rebuke. "You've accepted your blame for so long that now you can't see the truth, *can* you?"

"I saw that my wife intended to take our kids away from me. When I realized what she was saying—that my children would have grown up without me, with another man acting as their father—when that sank in, I thought one thing, and one thing only: *If I couldn't have them, no one should.* Do you understand, Cathy? Do you get what I'm saying? *I was glad my children died.*"

There. The bloody hulk of my real self lay exposed. Poker-faced, Cathy looked up at me. Her eyes shifted slowly, scanning my face, scraping the skin off my skull, boring into the bone, searching inside the folds of my mind. Whatever she was looking for, she found it. She exhaled and relaxed. New breath curled from her lungs to mine. My ribs expanded. I felt my heart slow down. *She looks relieved.*

"I don't mean to sound flippant," she said gently. "But . . . *Thomas*. A thought is only a thought. Not a wish. Not a plan. Not a hope. Just words in the rough draft of a movie script. Not reality. You didn't want your children dead."

"Yes, I did. I wanted revenge, even if it hurt them. I was no better than the men who destroyed the towers. The men who killed three-thousand people that day, including Sheryl, Ethan, and our unborn baby."

"Oh, Thomas, *no*. If you could wish Ethan alive again, if you could hold him and your other child in your arms, would you?"

"Of course."

"There. See? You've nullified the other thought. No thought can be taken seriously in the heat of the moment. Especially when fueled by liquor or drugs or depression. Thomas, if thoughts were destiny, if all thoughts were serious, I'd be in prison now."

"This is no time to joke, not even to make me feel better."

"I'm not joking. I planned to kill Gerald."

"Come on."

"Really. I planned to lure him into visiting me, to hide a kitchen knife in my robe, and when he stepped close, I'd stab him. I made the arrangements. I invited him to my house. He thought I wanted to discuss the details of my promotions contract for *Flawless*. He thought I was eager to forgive and forget, to help him sell his products." She touched the scars on her face. "He thought I'd work for him behind the scenes, of course, where I wouldn't make anybody squeamish."

I studied her eyes the way she'd studied mine. Yes, she had been capable of murder that day. "What stopped you?"

"One of your letters. It doesn't matter which one, what the subject was, it was just a typical letter from you, one of the letters I loved reading, about my grandmother's house. It came with a box of Delta's biscuits." Tears gleamed in her eyes. "I ate biscuits and read your letter about an hour before Gerald was supposed to arrive. I definitely meant to kill him that day. I was drugged on tranquilizers, and I'd downed most of a bottle of wine, but as I lay on my bed reading your letter one clear thought came to me: 'If I go to prison for murder, Thomas might not write to me anymore.'" She gave a shaky chuckle and wiped her eyes. "Whether you know it or not, you saved Gerald's life that day. And you kept me from a life behind bars."

I sat there looking at her, drinking her in, absorbing the strange comfort she offered inside a maze of conflicting ideas. Every time I'd written her, I thought, 'I want to keep her alive.' I had wanted everyone I loved to live. I didn't want my children dead. I didn't mean it. I didn't want Sherryl dead, or even Gibson, her boyfriend.

All this time, the only person I had wanted dead was me. Life sometimes came down to such simple realizations. I bent my head beside Cathy's. "I wish my children had lived," I whispered, absolved. "I wish Sherryl had lived."

Cathy made a soothing sound and put her arms around me. "I know."

I sat back and took the letter. It fluttered from my hand, falling lightly among the long streamers of my hair on the hearth. "There's some symbolism there, but I'm not sure what," I said.

Cathy nodded. "Burn the letter." She looked toward the shelves where Ethan's mangled toy truck lay. "And bury Ethan's toy. Put a part of your heart into the ground with his memory. Then go on and live your life, the way he'd want you to. When you're ready."

"I'm not ready to let him go like that, yet."

"Okay. When you're ready, you'll know."

I picked up the letter. My heart broke, but the fracture was manageable, for once. "I had a second child on the way," I said gruffly. "I lost another son or daughter."

"I know," Cathy soothed again, leaning close, patting my blanketed knee gently. "I know. But it wasn't your fault. It wasn't your fault, Thomas. " Her voice shook. "I'll put that letter in the fire for you, if you want me to. It'll be the first time in ten months I can honestly say I like what a fire can do."

Courage. What she'd do for me. I touched the back of my fingers to her scarred cheek in gratitude. Then I leaned toward the fire, laid the last truth about my marriage, my wife, and my children, into the flames, and watched it turn to clean ashes.

I took her in my arms. She put her head on my shoulder, scarred side up. We lay down, burrowing inside the quilts, holding on tight, then relaxing, breathing easier. The first hint of daylight made ghostly rectangles at the cabin's windows. "I think we can rest now," she murmured.

I pulled her hair to my nose so the scent would fill me and nestled my forehead against her temple. I shut my eyes as close to her face as I could get. We had survived the elements—fire, ice, water, wind, heat, cold. We had climbed mountains, fallen off cliffs, been lost inside black monoliths of memory and forgetting. This was something we'd had to work out of our systems like a poison, to get it to the surface, the air and the light. It had taken all night, and every sensation, and every emotion, until we were exhausted and newly opened, rebirthed.

We had lives, now. Imperfect, newly minted, the skin still fresh and vulnerable and easy to burn, but we wanted to live. She had tested her scars, and mine, by fire.

"Cathy?"

"Hmmm?"

"I'd have written to you in prison."

She tucked her right hand between us and unfurled her fingers along my heart. "Good thing I didn't know that then," she said.

We slept.

Chapter 23

Cathy
Beginnings

The next morning I buried Thomas's revolver in the deep loam of
the forest below his cabin. I also quietly removed all his vodka bottles while
he slept, pouring out their contents on the frosty ground. I was walking
up the hill to the cabin when he stepped quickly outside, dressed only in
jeans. He scraped a hand over his raggedly chopped hair when he saw me.
It was nice to him look relieved. He strode down to meet me. "There's
blood on the quilts. Did I hurt you?"

"Oh, ye of grand ego," I said as lightly as I could. "My period
started."

"You're sure? It was a hard night. I've never roughed up a woman
before."

"You didn't rough one up, now. And if anyone looks abused, it's
you."

"I'm fine. Are you? No condoms, no responsibility. That's not
me."

"Not my *modus operandi*, either. But I think we're okay, this time."
I looked up at him tenderly. "I haven't had a period for months. Stress,
medication, all that. I'm . . . back in the flow of things, now. Good."

"If you're happy." He studied me carefully, making sure.

I looked up at him the same way. "Are you? Will you be? I buried your gun where you can't find it. And I poured out all your liquor. But look at the lovely display the empty bottles made. I'm an expert with bottle arrangements."

He glanced at the creative display of empty vodka bottles on one corner of his porch. "All right. But . . . you can trust me with the gun. I swear to you. I'd like to have it back. It's an antique."

"Good. When archaeologists dig it up a thousand years from now, they'll be impressed."

A stalemate. We looked at each other a long time. "If that makes you happy," he conceded.

I nodded.

He exhaled. "Okay."

With that understanding in the bag, we stood looking at each other a minute more, like teenagers at an awkward prom, trading a thousand unspoken memories from the darkness, sensations, the exposed soft spots, the vulnerable moments, the feverish images that make knees weak and blushes rise even in the freezing air of a winter morning. "It's cold out here," he said gruffly. "Come back inside and I'll heat up some Spam for breakfast."

"I bet I have an old protein bar in the Hummer. We can share it as a side dish to the Spam."

"A feast." He held out a hand. I took it.

We went back to the cabin.

🐾🐾🐾🐾🐾

His cell phone rang three different times in quick succession. Thomas raised his head from my breasts, scrubbed his eyes, wrapped a quilt around his waist, and got to his feet. By the time he found the phone on one of his shelves, I was sitting up with a hand to my head, thinking responsible thoughts.

I have puppies at home, now. They need breakfast. I'd left them so much food and water they couldn't possibly be hungry, but it was the principle of the thing. I was a mother, now.

"Mitternich," Thomas said into the phone, frowning. The morning sun poured through the window, washing his bare arms and broad chest in warm, white-gold tones. I lost my train of thought, gazing up at him. He glanced at me. "No, Delta, don't worry. I know where she is. She's fine." As his expression tightened into a grim mask I gathered my scattered clothes.

"I'll bring her," he said. "We'll be there in a few minutes. Tell Ivy to calm down. Tell her I keep my promises. She'll know what that means."

I was already on my feet getting dressed as he clicked the phone off. "What's wrong with Ivy and Cora?"

He looked at me somberly. "Laney's dead."

🐾🐾🐾🐾🐾

Laney Cranshaw had been beaten to death by a boyfriend outside an Atlanta nightclub. Her battered body lay in Atlanta's big-city morgue 150 miles and one state line south of the Crossroads. Cora and Ivy, at the tender ages of seven and twelve, were now officially alone in the world. When Thomas and I drove into the yard of Laney's cottage, Cora was hiding in a closet along with Princess Arianna the cat and Herman the rooster, and Ivy was guarding the closet door. Delta, Pike, Dolores and Benton sipped coffee in the kitchen and looked grim.

"The social worker from Hades is on the way here," Dolores intoned. "Even Benton doesn't have the judicial authority to hold her back."

"I'm trying to think of an excuse for a restraining order," Benton said.

"She's from Asheville," Delta explained. "Been assigned to our area since our local gal transferred six months ago. We're still waiting for a *human* to take her place."

"Stickler for rules," Pike added grimly.

On an unrelated note, everyone stared at Thomas and me. After all, we'd been found together at the end of Thomas's cell phone and we'd arrived together in my Hummer. We were rumpled, hollow-eyed, smelled vaguely of vodka, woodsmoke and sex, and Thomas appeared to have been beaten up by me.

"Big night?" Delta whispered. I nodded. Her eyes gleamed.

I followed Thomas down the cottage's narrow hallway and into the pink bedroom the girls shared. Ivy was planted in front of a closed closet door. My heart twisted at the stark misery in her freckled, pale-brown face.

"Don't bullshit me," she said fiercely, glaring up. "We're going to some shitty foster care home somewhere, aren't we? No one wants us."

Thomas dropped to his heels in front of her. "You're not going anywhere you don't want to go. You have my word."

"You're a guy. They don't pay attention to guys. You can't be a foster

273

dad. Not for girls. I know the rules."

"But *I* can be," I said. "Be a foster . . . mom."

She stared up at me. So did Thomas, pivoting slowly on his heels and gazing up at me with quiet warning. *Be careful what you promise.*

Did we have a choice? Was I going to let some officious state agent whisk *my* girls out of *my* rental cottage? My spine stiffened. I lifted my chin. "Yes, I can be your and Cora's foster mom. How would you feel about living with me at my house?"

Ivy craned everything—head, neck, black eyebrows—in wary hope. "Why?"

"What do you mean, why?"

"Why do want us to live there?"

"Because I like you."

"You just met us one time, before Christmas, and then you threw up."

"I didn't throw up because of *you.*"

"How's Cora?" Thomas asked gently.

"She's hiding in her cave until the monsters go away. I keep telling her they're *never* going away."

"Let us talk to her, please," I said.

Ivy frowned and chewed her lip, but finally edged aside and opened the closet door. "It's cool," she said to Cora. "Thomas and Cathy are here."

Cora was crouched in the floor, hugging her cat. The rooster perched overhead on the wooden clothes bar. Cora's face was ashen and streaked with tears. Her lower lip trembled. "The social worker lady won't let us take Herman and Princess Arianna to a foster home," she said brokenly. "Herman and Princess Arianna won't have any place to live. What'll happen to *them?*"

I got down on my knees and held out both hands. "You and Ivy come and live with me, and Princess Arianna and Herman can come, too."

Cora brightened. "Forever?"

Ivy said in a quick, stern tone, "There's no such thing as 'forever.'"

I glanced up at her. "Let's just take things one day at a time. Okay?"

Ivy glowered at me. "You just want to try us on for size, like a pair of curtains you ordered. See if you like how we decorate your house. Then you can return us if we don't look good. That's what happened the last time we went to foster care."

Thomas nudged me with an elbow. *Let me talk.* "Cathy's giving you a choice. Maybe you won't like *her*."

"Excuse me?" I said. "I'm very likable."

"We like you just fine," Cora whispered, tears sliding down her face. She clutched the cat harder. "Me and Princess Arianna and . . ." she glanced upward, "Herman." Her face crumpled. "Where did Aunt Laney go?"

"It doesn't matter," Ivy said grimly. "She's not coming back."

"But where'd she *go*? The same place as Mama?"

Ivy pounded a fist on the wall. "I don't know. Forget about her, all right?"

Cora sobbed. "Why doesn't *anyone* stay with us for long?"

"I'll stay," I blurted, tears in my throat. "I'll stay. Forever. I promise. Come and live with me. If you don't like my house, you can leave. But I won't leave *you*."

Thomas's face went from quiet disapproval to resigned tenderness. I was making promises on the spur of the moment, on the wings of angels, on the hope of the night past. He knew it. But he couldn't resist, either. "We'll take care of you," he told Cora and Ivy. "I promise."

Cora bent her head to the cat's. "We'll go live with Thomas and Cathy until they get tired of us. Then we'll find somebody else to love us. I promise." She stoically clambered from the closet and into my arms, cat and all. Ivy retreated behind a sarcastic shrug. "Whatever. We'll go for now, at least."

This was not going to be easy.

🐾🐾🐾🐾🐾

Mrs. Ganza, the Child Protective Services worker from Asheville, was a big, flashy, flinty-eyed woman with an affection for rules. She distrusted Thomas and me at first sight. Understandable, considering how we looked when she met us that first day. We immediately followed her to the courthouse in Turtleville for a quick ruling from a family court judge on our foster-care application. Delta stood with us, scowling at Mrs. Ganza on our behalf. Mrs. Ganza could not recall ever having seen one of my movies and said bluntly she only watched nature shows on the Discovery Channel.

"She likes the shows on crocodiles," Delta whispered. "Reminds her of her family reunions."

Mrs. Ganza regarded Thomas as if she'd stepped over him on a sidewalk. "*What* did you say your relationship to Ms. Deen is?" she demanded, arching a gray brow beneath an inverted bowl of gray hair.

"I'm her architect. She's hired me to renovate her home immediately to make it more suitable for Cora and Ivy. She plans to enlarge and modernize the house."

I stared up at him in surprise. He nodded.

Mrs. Ganza didn't seem impressed. "What is your *personal* relationship to Ms. Deen?"

"She rescued me from a life of sin in Tijuana. I was working as a stripper at a *tapas* bar."

"If you find this interview amusing, Mr. Mitternich, perhaps I should tell the judge you're not serious about your role as a father-figure for Cora and Ivy."

"I'm very serious about that role. But my personal relationship with Ms. Deen is *personal.*"

She tapped a form on a clipboard. "I don't place children in foster homes occupied by unmarried couples."

"I don't live with Ms. Deen."

"See that you keep it that way."

I intervened quickly. "I'd like to have you notarize what Mr. Mitternich just said about enlarging and modernizing my house."

"Are *you* making jokes, Ms. Deen?"

"No, I'm making sure Mr. Mitternich installs an indoor bathroom."

"Add on, not install," he corrected. "We can make exterior, not interior, changes. Maintain the house's internal integrity."

"I want a bathroom *inside* the house," I said tightly.

"It'll be accessible to the original floorplan."

"That sounds as if you want to build a walkway to the porta . . . toilet." I'd almost said 'porta-shitter' in front of Mrs. Ganza. Not a good idea.

Thomas arched a brow. "A Craftsman-style arbor over a walkway to the outside toilet could be nice."

"Oh, you have *got* to be kidding—"

"Perhaps," Mrs. Gaze interjected loudly, "I need to make a *personal* assessment of your extremely rustic-sounding domicile, Ms. Deen. You and Mr. Mitternich can continue your argument at your leisure. In the meantime, Cora and Ivy can stay with a dependable married couple. In Asheville."

"No! Please. We're only debating details, not the important issues."

Thomas added quietly, "I apologize, Mrs. Ganza. Believe me when I tell you that Ms. Deen and I will find every way possible to cooperate."

She snorted. "With each other? Really?"

"You have my word. Cathy?"

"My word, too," I said, nodding. I darted a look at Thomas. *Inside bathroom.*

He gazed back without retreat. *Walkway.*

Mrs. Ganza didn't notice the silent battle because she was too busy giving me more slit-eyed scrutiny. "Ms. Deen, I'm very familiar with Cora and Ivy's situation. I've been assigned to their case in the past. Personally, I believe they'd be best off with people of their own racial and ethnic mix. White-black-Hispanic."

"Oh, come on," Delta interjected. "Those little girls don't care about skin color or country of national origin. They care about being loved. They need to stay *here*. With people they've come to know and trust."

"Ethnic and racial diversity aren't trival concerns."

Delta slapped her thighs and hooted. "Diversity? Well, shoot, Cathy's grandma was part Cherokee Indian, so that makes Cathy part-Cherokee. And Thomas, here, why, he's part-Yankee. He used to be all-Yankee, but I've fed him so much Southern soul food he's gotten diluted."

"Very, very funny." Mrs.Ganza resumed glaring at *me*. "Ms. Deen, do you have *any* idea what it takes to be a parent? Do you have any idea what these two little girls need? A few years ago, after Ivy was sexually abused, she went through a self-mutilation stage. Have you seen the scars on her stomach? Did you even know that?"

"I . . . no. I didn't." I slumped a little. When I glanced up at Thomas, his eyes had gone dark. He said slowly, "We don't know everything about the girls, but we know what's important. If you take Ivy and Cora away from here they'll lose their chance at being part of a family and a community. Ivy may never trust anyone again."

Mrs. Ganza sighed. "She may already be a hopeless case. Cora, on the other hand, is very willing to bond with a loving couple. Perhaps it would be best to separate the girls. Given a structured environment, without Ivy's negative influence, Cora would progress well and—"

"If you break up those sisters, you'll burn in hell," Delta said grimly. "And I'll light the bonfire."

Mrs. Ganza gaped at Delta. "Are you threatening me?"

"If the shoe fits, wear it. By the way, what size shoes *do* you wear on those cloven hooves of yours?"

"Stop!" I ordered. "Mrs. Ganza, I promise you I'll take good care of Cora and Ivy. If they need outside help, I can afford it. I'm extremely wealthy."

"And extremely *odd*, if my sources are correct. From what I hear about your anxiety attacks and reclusive behavior, well, to put it politely, you're not fit to take responsibility for a pet hamster, much less children."

"I am perfectly capable of—"

"Assaulting a man with a fire extinguisher. Refusing to drive a car. Trying to hire somebody to dig a moat around your house."

"That was a joke!"

"And *you*." She pointed at Thomas. "An alcoholic with suicidal tendencies."

Thomas said quietly, "I've never harmed myself or anyone else. I'm sober and I plan to stay that way."

"So you admit you've had a problem."

"I admit that my problem is behind me. I'm healthy and responsibile."

"Are you sure? Cora and Ivy need a normal home, with foster parents who aren't distracted by personal problems." She pointed at me. "I don't care how rich you are. Do you *know* how to make a home for children? Can you cook, can you listen to their woes, can you help with homework, can you offer kindness tempered with discipline?"

"Yes! I'll shower Cora and Ivy with wonderful toys and clothes, and I swear to you, I swear, I won't inflict my issues on them. I can hire plenty of people to help me. I'll fly help in from Asheville, if I have to. Trained nannies. By helicopter. Every day."

"These girls need stability, not a rich, crazy woman who intends to foist them off on paid help choppered in from Asheville like a special forces patrol."

"I didn't mean it that way. I'm only trying to tell you I'll do *whatever* you want."

"I'm afraid I can't accept your reassurances. When I speak with the judge I'll have to recommend—"

"I'll not only vouch for Thomas and Cathy," Delta put in grimly, "I'll sign whatever papers you want me to sign to share responsibility for the girls."

"It doesn't work that way, and, considering your belligerent and threatening nature, you're hardly an acceptable surrogate."

"Look, I catered your boss's family picnic way over in Raleigh last year. Don't *make* me call your boss. He *loves* me and my food. He eats at the café every time he's in this part of the state. His staff orders my ham biscuits by the dozens. I ship biscuits to your boss and his people at least once a month."

"*He?* My 'boss,' if by that you mean the head of my department, is a woman. She has no family here. She's from Michigan."

Delta craned her head like an angry cat. "I'm talking about the *governor.*"

Silence. We watched Mrs. Ganza slowly deflate. When she reached the size of a shriveled birthday balloon she hissed in my direction. "These are the conditions, Ms. Deen. You have to get your quirks under control. I don't want to hear any more rumors about weird behavior."

"Agreed!"

She jabbed a finger at Thomas. "No drinking. No cohabitating without marriage. And get a haircut. You look like you were attacked with a chainsaw."

"Agreed."

"Then I'll recommend a three-month trial period." She walked away.

Delta pressed her hands to her heart and gazed at us joyfully. "I'm so proud. You're a pair, now, a couple. Right when God needed you to step up to the table and make a meal for two children who need you, you're ready to cook! The Lard cooks in mysterious ways."

Thomas and I traded a quiet look. *We can do this. Yes, we have to try.*

"As long as the Lard doesn't mind cold food," I said. "And He lets me have an inside bathroom."

🐦🐦🐦🐦🐦

We buried Laney Cranshaw's ashes in the cemetery of Crossroads Methodist Church. The minister and church board presented her plot to me in honor of the huge donation Delta had channeled from me to the church some months back. My square space of winter grass on the edge of the graveyard was a short stroll from the plot that contained my grandmother's body.

"I'm going to move Granny to the farm," I whispered to Delta during the chilly graveside service. "Where she should have been all along."

Delta leaned close to me while the minister praised Laney's good intentions and Cora, crying, held Thomas's hand. Ivy stood like a grim soldier beside them. Delta bent her ruddy face to my black wool hood and whispered back, "You don't have to move your grandma. She's already under your front stepping stones."

Later, when I recovered from swallowing my tongue, Delta confessed that she and other relatives of Granny's had quietly ignored my father's directives and buried my grandmother at the entrance of her beloved home on the ridge.

"According to Delta, Granny Nettie's right about here," I told Thomas that evening, as we stared down at several large gray stepping stones between the remnants of the front yard's gate posts. I pointed to a post. "Right beside the spot where I shot your cell phone. I blasted a cell phone to pieces right over her grave. Granny, I apologize."

"I doubt she was disturbed," Thomas said gently. "Unless her long-distance roaming charges kicked in."

I sat down on the cold earth, laid the palms of my hands on the stepping stones, shut my eyes and bent my head. *Please help us make this house a home.*

PART SIX

People are like stained glass windows: they sparkle and shine when the sun is out, but when the darkness sets in their true beauty is revealed only if there is a light within.

—*Elizabeth Kubler-Ross*

The really happy person is one who can enjoy the scenery when on a detour.

—*Unknown*

If one is lucky, a solitary fantasy can totally transform a million realities.

—*Maya Angelou*

Chapter 24

Cathy
February

Three months, the family court judge decreed.

Thomas and I had three months to prove we could be parents. Three months to decide if we were able to deal with the realities of everyday living. Three months to find out if we could earn the trust of two little girls who wanted desperately to believe we would always be there for them in a world where no one had ever stayed.

Renovating Granny's house became the challenge that defined us.

Thomas set up a bachelor campsite inside my barn. At night we made love there; during the day we argued passionately. We agreed the house needed wiring, central heat and air, indoor plumbing, more closets, and bigger rooms. But that was like agreeing the universe needed stars and planets. Okay, how many, and where? We struggled for compromises.

The least hint of disagreement—even our most placid debates—sent Cora and Ivy into a quiet froth of anxiety. They feared we'd abandon them and each other at any moment. Nothing we said could reassure them. We knew we were soulmates. They didn't.

Cora talked out loud to her imaginary friends, asking them, 'Thomas and Cathy would never, ever get mad at each other and go away, would they?' and Ivy secluded herself in the bedroom she and Cora shared, hiding behind books and a small laptop computer that would access her favorite chat rooms on the Internet the moment our phone line was installed.

Even our pets sometimes seemed fearful and insecure. The puppies chased the cat, the cat terrorized the puppies, and the rooster sequestered himself in the screened sleeping porch, peering out at us with one-eyed alarm from a light-bulb-enhanced nest Thomas nailed high on the wall. He crowed loudly every morning at dawn, as if calling for help.

❦❦❦❦❦

"We've named these *dogs*, but only because you told us to," Ivy said. Thomas and I turned from hanging curtains in the living room to find her and Cora standing in the hallway entrance, each holding a puppie. Since we'd noticed both of them avidly petting the puppies when we weren't looking, it seemed a good bet they secretly loved their new pets. But Ivy wouldn't even admit she *wanted* a puppy, and Cora seemed afraid to love another small, needy soul.

Thomas stepped down from a ladder, carefully avoiding a tangle of extension cords and cardboard packing boxes on the floor. The room was a jumble of new lamps, accessories and furniture. "Well, let's hear the decision. Their names?"

"I named mine Marion," Ivy said.

"Marion?" I asked, perched on a stepping stool with yards of drapery fabric in my hands.

"After Marion Mahony Griffin. She worked for Frank Lloyd Wright. She was an architect. Thomas told me about her." Ivy shrugged. "I've decided I want to be an architect. Like Thomas and Marion. So . . . I named my puppy Marion."

"A good name," Thomas said gruffly.

Cora hugged her puppy to her chest. It licked her chin happily. "I named mine Half-Pint. From the book Cathy started reading to us last night. *Little House on the Prairie*. If me and Ivy have to move to a new home one day, can we get one on a prarie?"

"You won't have to move," I said, with tears in my throat.

"Well, just in case we *do*, I want a prarie with covered wagons and buffaloes and dragons, but only the tame kind." Cora nodded firmly. Ivy frowned. Carrying the puppies tightly, they went back to the bedroom they shared.

The month before, I'd asked the spirits of my mother and grandmother to help me name two orphaned puppies. Now, they had. I turned and looked up at Thomas, whose face was a miasma of emotion. "Do you believe God gave us those puppies because Cora and Ivy needed them as much as the puppies need Cora and Ivy?"

"I've seen no evidence that God cares about children or puppies," he said grimly. "But if He gives us half a chance, *we* can save them. We just have to figure out how."

❦❦❦❦❦

Thomas drew up a sketch for a new front gate directly over Granny's grave. It would be made from remnants of chestnut lumber torn out when we began expanding the house's tiny bedrooms and kitchen. *If* we ever agreed to do that. The gate was about the *only* mutual victory in the debate. He and I had very different definitions of the word *expand*.

We stood outside with his impressively detailed gate sketch in hand, looking from it to the worn stepping stones over Granny's resting place. "At least it's a start," I said tartly. "Today a front gate, tomorrow, indoor plumbing. Hmmm?"

Thomas chuckled darkly. "Stick to the details." He tapped his drawing with a fingertip. "All right, we agree on the design and the materials of the gate. Since it's going to double as Mary Eve's gravemarker, I suggest we put a brass plaque on the top crosspiece."

"Yes! That's a great idea! It can read, 'Mary Eve Nettie. She Smiles Down On Our Flush Commode.'"

He arched a brow. "Or how about, 'Here lies Mary Eve Nettie. An original design, with solid integrity. She didn't believe in turning closets into bathrooms. She also didn't believe in sliding glass doors, track lighting, or white baseboards on antique maple floors.'"

"She would have *liked* white baseboards," I said between gritted teeth. "They're *cheerful*."

❦❦❦❦❦

In the midst of the madness, I decided to take up baking. If I could make biscuits, surely I could make a family.

"Pile up the flour to look like a little volcano," Ivy relayed from Delta one cold February afternoon. Ivy sat on the kitchen counter, a cell phone to her ear, listening to Delta at the café.

"Done," I said, doodling a lava crater into a mound of white flour in a mixing bowl.

"Now add the baking soda and the salt."

I poured the ingredients into the crater. "Done."

"Now add the lard, she says."

I scooped creamy white lard from a gooey brick and raked it off my fingers into the volcano of flour. "Done."

"Now scrunch it all together until it's, like, 'crumbly.'" I scrunched. "Now, add some milk to make it doughy."

I added the milk. "Houston, we have lift-off of the biscuit dough."

"Now roll it out on the floured board, she says. About an inch thick."

"I can roll," Cora offered anxiously, standing beside me on a stool.

I plopped the dough on the board and handed Cora the rolling pin. Chewing her lower lip and huffing a little with the effort, she rolled out an apron of dough.

"Tell Delta we have achieved a flat doughy thing on the board," I intoned.

Ivy told her, listened, then relayed, "Now cut out the biscuits with your clean tomato cans."

I handed Cora one can, and I took a second one. We pressed neat round circles all over the dough. Thomas, watching from behind us, said loudly so Delta could hear, "The biscuit prototypes are relatively symmetrical and consistent. Looking good."

Ivy waggled the phone. "Delta says put them in the greased baking pan." We arranged the biscuits. "Now, just pop it in the oven for about twenty minutes, or until the biscuits look golden brown."

Here's the terrifying part. My hands shook as I looked at the hulking, stainless-steel, propane oven we'd installed. I nearly dropped the pan. Thomas rescued me. "I'll do the honor," he said. He slid the pan into the oven and shut the oven door.

"Biscuits!" I proclaimed weakly, applauding. "For the first time in twenty years, this house has Granny Nettie's biscuit recipe cooking in the oven!"

Ivy clicked the phone off. "Delta says don't be upset if you don't get it right at first. She says there's magic in biscuits and they won't be right until you get the magic in your hands."

"How hard could it be?"

Twenty minutes later, Thomas took the perfect-looking biscuits from the oven. As the cook and heir to the Nettie biscuit throne, I got the first bite.

My mouth filled with flaky crust followed by a center of hot, gooey, raw dough. I spit the biscuit out. "Damn. I'm no good at this. I'm scared of the oven, I don't know how to cook, and I'm never going to make this work!"

That one thoughtless remark made Cora burst into tears. Ivy hopped down from the counter. "It's our fault, isn't it?" she hurled at me. "You don't know how to be a mom, and somehow *we'll* get blamed for it."

I held out my hands. "No, no. I promise you, I'm just upset about *me*, not you. I didn't mean—"

"Yeah. Sure. Right." Ivy grabbed Cora's hand, and they retreated to their bedroom.

"Let me talk to them," Thomas said. He headed after the stricken girls. I grabbed the phone and called Delta. "I can't do anything right. Just now I said the wrong thing and the girls are having a nervous breakdown because of it. I can't even make biscuits. *My biscuits suck.* It's all symbolic."

She snorted. "Well, what did you expect? An overnight miracle? Families take time to build. And so do biscuits. If your heart's not peaceful, they won't turn out right. When you really come to believe in yourself, the biscuits will know it. And so will those girls."

Obviously, I had a long way to go.

Thomas

I was now the man of a ragged little family. That family consisted of two subdued, uncertain little girls who'd never learned to trust a father-figure, a chaotic menagerie of rescued animals, and the obsessively determined ex-movie star I loved more than my own life, despite the fact that she agonized over every element of our house renovation, our relationship, the girls' happiness, and her inability to perform the simple yet profound act of baking edible biscuits.

Cathy and I collided in the barn every night despite the deep cold of a mountain winter. After the children and the pets were asleep we rolled each other in a makeshift bed of sleeping bags and quilts. She urged me to move into the house; there were, after all, three bedrooms—one for her, one for the girls, and one for a guest. But I didn't want to test Mrs. Ganza's patience.

"You'll freeze out here in this barn one night," Cathy protested.

"No, I'll build a campfire with all that firewood I bought for the house. If you're never going to use the living room fireplace, I might as well burn the wood myself."

Her face went pale. "I'm not ready for a fire in my own living room."

I pulled her deeper into my arms. "Try it. Just once. I'll be there right beside you. Nothing bad will happen. I swear to you." An empty promise. No man can protect his loved ones from every quirk of fate. I still hadn't made peace with that fact. I hadn't been able to save Sherryl and Ethan, so what made me think I could make bold promises to Cathy and the girls? I said the words and I wanted to believe them. I had to try.

She pressed her face into the crook of my neck and shivered. "All right. A fire. Agreed."

As snow covered the ridge in white, I carried an armload of firewood into the cottage's living room. It was now a comfortable, if chilly, enclave of leather couches, thick Turkish rugs, fat oak side tables, russet drapes and big lamps waiting for electrical outlets. I began stacking logs in the berth of the newly unboarded fireplace. Soon I sensed eyes boring into my back, and when I glanced over my shoulder I saw Cathy standing there staring in nervous dread, with an anxious Cora and stern Ivy flanking her. Cathy, dressed in baggy faded overalls, a striped sweater and one of Delta's *The Lard Cooks In Mysterious Ways* aprons, held a fire extinguisher in her hands. The puppies and the cat sat by her feet. Ivy and Cora wore baggy overalls and striped sweaters, too. My matching tribe of worried girls. If Cathy was afraid of something, the girls picked up her signals. Cathy tried to hide her phobias for their sakes, but Cora and Ivy had sharp instincts.

"You're sure the chimney is in good shape?" Cathy asked.

"Absolutely. Clean, solid and it draws air upwards like a wind tunnel. Perfect."

Cora looked up at her plaintively. "A fire in the fireplace would be fun." She looked down at her puppy. "Half-Pint says, 'Let's sit by a fire just like Laura Ingalls did.'"

Ivy grunted. "Anything to get warm. Marion's got frostbite on her paws." She scowled at the living room's gyrating space heaters.

I met Cathy's worried gaze. "It'a no-brainer. We have to make a fire *pronto*. Marion has frosted paws."

She feigned a cheerful smile. "Okay. Then what are we waiting for?"

I piled kindling under the logs, pulled my old man's lighter from my jeans' pocket, and started the fire. Orange flames crept up the wood. The good scent of oak wafted into the room. Cora and Ivy looked up at Cathy, whose face went stark white, emphasizing the red spiderweb of scars on one side. "Come on," Ivy said to her quietly. "It's okay to be scared."

Slowly they tugged her to the hearth. I held out a hand. She gave me the fire extinguisher, and I set it by a pair of iron tongs I'd found in the barn. Cora and Ivy settled on the hearth beside me. The puppies snuggled by their feet. Cathy sank onto a fat leather couch that faced the blaze. In the soft, flickering light, her anxious, beautiful, scarred face reminded me of that emotional night at my cabin, and I shifted to hide my erection.

Outside, night began to cover the snow, a small herd of deer nibbled corn we'd thrown out, and the raccoon rummaged around his plate on the porch, eating leftover cat and dog food. The cat stretched out on the couch beside Cathy, purring. Cats don't worry about existential danger. They simply seek the heat.

"I made a pot of vegetable-beef stew," Cathy said, nodding stiffly toward the shadowy hall, toward the tiny kitchen with its evil gas stove. "It tastes like salty tomato *goo*, but when you mix my burnt biscuits into it, the effect is a kind of, well, heartily semi-edible." She kept trying to bake biscuits and the biscuits kept giving her the finger.

"The stew's not so bad," Ivy lied sincerely.

"Half-Pint and Marion like your biscuits," Cora said. "Better than chew bones."

"I'll eat a few spoonfuls of stew without making a face," I promised.

Her mouth quirked. Still staring fixedly at the fire, our first family fire in the fireplace, she had to admit the house wasn't going to burn down. Settling back on the couch warily, she nodded. "A fire in the fireplace of Granny's house. Okay. It's a good fireplace. Nothing to worry about."

The girls smiled. So did I.

Sometimes just *pretending* to feel safe will get you through the night.

❦ ❦ ❦ ❦ ❦

Attaching arms to the Venus de Milo. Straightening the Leaning Tower of *Pisa*. Painting both ears on Van Gogh. Adding rooms to the Nettie house.

Tampering with classics seemed so wrong to me, no matter how much I agreed in principle. But the old cottage needed more space. We had to decide on a blueprint soon and get construction underway by spring. I could hear my old man's voice. *If you haven't got the guts to do the job right, you don't deserve to do it at all.*

I secluded myself in the cottage's empty third bedroom for hours every day. With only a space heater to fight the room's chill and a clamp-on utility light for illumination, I hunched over a crude drafting board I'd made from plywood on two-by-four legs. On large sheets of paper I sketched and discarded dozens of designs. The crumpled paper littered one corner of the room. Occasionally the cat and the puppies snuck in and pounced on the pile for fun. At the end of each session I gathered the wadded balls and burned them in the fireplace so Cathy and the girls couldn't sneak a peek.

They watched me with anxious silence. Cathy couldn't quite figure out what to say to Ivy, who didn't care for girly things, and she coddled Cora too much, like a damaged doll. One morning, as I donned a coat to drive the girls down to the schoolbus stop at the Trace, Cathy held out a trembling hand for the keys. "What kind of mother can't even drive her kids to the schoolbus?"

I put the keys on her palm then cupped my hands around hers. "Are you sure you're ready to brave the Hummer?"

"No, but I'm going to try. I never rode a bus. I went to private schools, and the servants drove me. But I always *wished* I rode a bus, and that I had a mother to take me to the bus stop. So . . . I'm driving the girls to the bus."

She stared at the Hummer as if it were a bull she had to wrestle, but from then on she drove Cora and Ivy down to the Trace to catch the school bus. If she rolled so much as one tire of the Hummer past that point, she broke out in a sweat and had to take a pill. Cora and Ivy watched her worriedly, as always.

"How will Cathy know when it's okay to believe in happy things?" Cora asked me. "Is there a magic word we can say?"

I didn't have an answer for that.

Every afternoon she went back and picked the girls up. When she realized the bus driver and kids were craning their heads to get a look at her, she began shielding her face with hoods, scarves, and sunglasses. At our Saturday night poker game Pike drew me aside. "You think Cathy'll ever get over the hood thing in public?"

"I don't know," I admitted.

"The kids on the bus are talkin'. Word's gettin' around. We don't want Mrs. Ganza to get wind of it. Those kids see Cathy sitting there in the Hummer every day with a scarf draped over her head, looking like a terrorist or the Grim Reaper or something. I mean, there's nothing strange about wearing a head scarf in the wintertime, but the way she does it, with the sunglasses and the scarf pulled low over her eyes, it just looks weird. Folks in Turtleville are starting to joke about Michael Jackson living here."

I tried to talk to Cathy about the cover-ups, but she cut me off every time. Just as I cut her off when she tried to soothe my dilemma about the house design. She hid from the world, and I drew imaginary houses.

One afternoon while Cathy picked up the girls I slaved over yet-another unsatisfying idea. When Cathy returned I heard two sets of frantic footsteps in the hall. I suddenly realized the puppies were barking outside. Ivy flung my door open. "Cathy needs your help!"

Beside her, Cora wrung her small hands. "Hurry, before he eats the seats! He already took my pencil!"

He? I ran outside. Cathy stood beside one of the Hummer's open passenger doors, scowling. The puppies circled the big vehicle feverishly, barking and wagging their tails. When Cathy saw me she jabbed a finger toward someone or something in the Hummer's back seat. "Get him out. Use your cell phone as bait if you have to!"

I strode to the open door and looked.

Banger, standing on the seat with goatish arrogance, stared back at me. "Bah," he said.

I stifled a laugh. "There's no law that says you have to give a goat a ride home from school."

"The little monster was lurking on the side of the road by the bus stop, and when Cora and Ivy opened the back door, he jumped in. And *nothing* we said or did could get him out."

"I petted him," Cora announced. "And he tried to eat my hair."

"Smells like a moldy old rug," Ivy grunted.

I took Banger by the collar. "Hop down, you four-footed stowaway."

He leapt to the ground, white tail twitching. Gazing around the yard with what appeared to be contentment, he nuzzled his horned head against my thigh. Cathy snorted. "I guess he's missed you lately."

I rubbed Banger's head and looked into his china-blue eyes. "So you missed sleeping in the truck bed with me? Admit it." He nibbled the sleeve of my Giants sweatshirt. I nodded. "He can live in the barn. I'm sure Delta and Pike don't care if we keep him. I'll put down some hay.

We'll be roommates."

"If he chases me the way he did at the café that time, he'll be your *only* roommate," Cathy said meaningfully, arching a dark brow.

"I'll lock him in the calf stall at night. He'll be warm, he'll be placid, he'll be behind bars."

Banger wandered around the yard, taste-testing twigs, rocks and dirt. It was as if he knew the farm had been home to a goat herd in the historic past, headed by his spiritual ancestor in the Nettie cemetery, Bah Ba Loo. The puppies followed him curiously, but he ignored them. On the back screened porch, the rooster crowed. We glanced over our shoulders at the cat, which was watching Banger from the veranda. The audience was complete.

Ivy gave us a dark half-smile. "Maybe we should just build *sheds* on both sides of the house. So Banger can live on one side and Herman can live on the other. Banger could be an indoor house-goat and Herman could be an indoor house-chicken."

"Not a bad idea," Cathy deadpanned. "With Banger in the house we wouldn't need a garbage disposal."

"I could feed Herman at the kitchen table!" Cora said excitedly. "He has good manners! He always lets you know when he's about to poop. He fluffs his feathers. I bet he'd used the kitty litter box if we asked him to."

I stared at the house. Sheds. On the sides. I dropped to my heels beside Ivy. "Take that thought to the next level. The sheds. Be creative with it."

Her dark eyes widened. "Me?"

"Tell me how you'd add rooms to this house."

Ivy gaped at me then, slowly, faced the cottage. "Well, like, if the whole point is to keep people noticing the old part, the original part, without noticing the new parts too much, then . . . " She spread her arms. "We could build . . . wings. So the house will be the middle of these new wings, you know, like . . . it would have matching wings, like in a computer game when you look down an alley and the alley makes you look right there, right in the middle. So wings on the house would make everybody look right in the middle at the old part. You know, like . . . an illusion." She dropped her arms, shifted uneasily, then shrugged. "Aw, that's all just stupid, I know."

"No. No, it's perfect!" Her stunned eyes went wider. I nodded over her head to Cathy, who was watching us with a quiet smile. "It's so simple. I was making it too complex. All we have to do is extend the sides of the house equally. Open up the existing rooms by expanding outward. That way, we'd leave the central interior virtually unchanged. Everything new will be in the extensions."

"Including bathrooms?" Cathy asked.

"Including bathrooms." She and the girls applauded. "The original house is covered in shingles, so we'll cover the new wings in stone facades. That contrast will lead the eye to the center, to the original cottage." I stood excitedly, framing the house with my hands, gesturing. "Add some evergreens, the right curve to the landscaping in the front, here and there, and over there, and the house will maintain its original integrity. The illusion will honor the concept, inside and out."

Cathy whooped. "'Pretty is as pretty does.' I like it when that happens."

I looked at Ivy. "Want to help me draw the blueprints?"

"Really?"

"Really. It's your design, so you have to supervise. We'll move the drafting board into the living room. The light's better and there's room to pull up a second chair."

"Okay!"

Cora looked a little forgotten. "Hey," Cathy said to her gently. "Ivy can help Thomas with the blueprints, but once the new rooms are built I'll need your help decorating. So we'll need to start looking through house magazines for ideas, okay?"

Cora beamed. "I like picking out colors!"

"Good. That's settled, then." Cathy saluted me. "*Team Nettie Homeplace* is ready to build, Sir."

I saluted back, then waved the troops toward the house. "Homework and dinner, first. Then we'll sketch some house plans."

The girls raced indoors.

Cathy took my hand and looked up at me in a way guaranteed to get her laid in the barn that night, even with a goat watching. "The girls needed to feel that this house is theirs, not just ours. You've made that possible. Thank you. Maybe we'll get this parenting thing figured out after all."

I kissed her. "Maybe we need more goatly inspiration. Imagine what might happen if we bought a whole *herd* to keep Banger company. What do you say?"

She thought a minute. "Not just 'No,'" she answered sweetly. "But '*Hell*, no.'"

Chapter 25

Cathy
Clearing The Way

Soon we had a blueprint. One Thomas and I both liked, and to which the girls had contributed lots of ideas. We were ready to begin building.

On a chilly March morning I woke to the weight of two girls, two puppies and a cat sharing my queen bed, all of them having been too excited to sleep the night before, until they fell asleep with me. They needed me, all of them, and I had hugged them to me, each of them, all night, for comfort. My night had been nearly sleepless and tainted by bad dreams. My hands shook; I was an emotional mess, I needed to forget who I was and what I looked like. But the girls slept soundly. For once I'd managed to hide my emotions from them. They had no clue what the date meant to me.

I inhaled the aroma of coffee, slipped out of bed, dressed, and padded to the kitchen wearily. Thomas often woke me up by slipping into the house and making coffee. That morning I cherished the scent of him and his ground roast even more than usual.

It was the first anniversary of my accident.

Thomas stood with his back to me at the kitchen sink. I paused in the doorway, aching at the sight of him. Lots of flannel and corduroy, a good barber-shop haircut, big shoulders, nice ass, no vodka since January, plenty of hope. *Don't think about this day last year.* I wanted my morning cup of Thomas, the feel of his arms around me, the slow kiss.

"Good morning," he said. He gave a little flourish with his hands as he finished pouring two cups of Starbucks from the big vintage percolator he'd bought at the Turtleville flea market. He pivoted slowly.

And presented his shaved face to me.

"In honor of fresh starts," he explained simply, watching my reaction carefully. "It's a day to celebrate new looks."

His brown beard was entirely gone, along with its mustache. For the first time since I'd known him I saw his angular jaw, his strong chin, the irresistible dimple next to the right corner of his mouth. He pointed at the dimple. "I just wanted you to see the Mitternich birthmark."

"It's a winner," I said, smiling and crying. He wanted to please me. To say that change was good, even *my* changes, my scars, though I'd never accept that claim. I wished I could believe he truly found me beautiful the way I was now.

I never would.

🐾🐾🐾🐾🐾

That evening, as the sunset turned Hog Back to chilly gold, Thomas, the girls and I stood beside the gray-white expanse of the house's newly poured foundations. "See those, girls?" Thomas said, pointing to white pipes rising from the cement. "Plumbing. That's a bathroom, and that's a bathroom, and that's for the new kitchen. I've made my peace with the modernization of this house. Or at least the modernization of the new wings. But let's always remember how it looked before this day."

"Last night Half-Pint drank out of the portable potty in our room," Cora said earnestly. "I think she'll like drinking out of a real commode better."

Leave it to Cora to put things in perspective. I arched a brow at Thomas. He sighed and looked at the concrete in silence.

The house would fit this gray footprint some day soon, would spread its wood and stone wings, its heart, over these two broad, flat arms. The room additions would more than triple Granny Nettie's wonderful cottage in size, would turn the old bedrooms into sitting rooms for the new bedrooms, turn the original kitchen into an entrance and pantry for the new one, turn the small dining room into a buffet nook for the new dining room, add two fireplaces, three full baths, several big closets, two side halls, and lots of big, sunshine-filled windows guaranteed to make any traditional Craftsman-style lover cringe from the light like an architectural vampire. But the heart of the house, the big living room with the fireplace and the built-in cabinets, would remain exactly as it was.

Welcome to the home I made for you, my grandmother whispered from the front walkway, from the arched veranda, from the front door with its mountain-scape in stained glass, from the living room, from the space where the new rooms of her house would rise. *You survived, see? It doesn't matter who you were, anymore. It's all about who you are, now. You'll be all right.*

Granny, I wish I had your faith.

Thomas put an arm around me. "We need to commemorate this building site. Get some sticks, girls. We'll sign our names in the concrete before it finishes drying."

When we were all armed with sticks, we knelt by the cool gray apron. *Cathryn, Thomas, Iverem and Cora,* the scrawled etchings said. I drew the month and day, Thomas drew the year. We sat back on our heels and gazed at the evidence that we were here, that we were all alive on this date in history together. I wanted so badly to feel joy and satisfaction for surviving, to make some peace with what had happened to me, but I wasn't ready yet, any more than Thomas was able to bury Ethan's toy truck. He now kept it on a shelf in the barn.

"Baaaah," Banger chortled suddenly, appearing from the shadows at a gallop. The puppies enjoyed chasing him and he enjoyed pretending to run. He bounded onto the concrete with all four cloven hooves, with the puppies behind him. We stared as he and they left a jagged trail across the fresh tablet of concrete. Thomas nearly exploded. "That section will have to be re-poured, dammit." Suddenly the cat raced across, too, chasing the others. Little kitty prints now paraded after the hoofprints and puppy paws. The animals' carefree absurdity colored the moment with a patina of faith. Life doesn't take itself seriously for long. Joy leaves an imprint in even the hardest sorrow.

Cora began to giggle. Then Ivy, helplessly unleashed from her tough self, chortled. Thomas put a hand to his stomach and bent double, laughing.

And I couldn't help smiling.

We all made our marks, that day.

Thomas

"Her," Cathy said, pointing furiously. "Not her. Not her, again."

Cathy didn't sound happy, to say the least. We stood in the yard that chilly spring morning, welcoming Jeb and his crew to Day One of house construction. Stacks of lumber and insulation filled the yard. Pick-ups rumbled on the driveway. Bert and Roland, my chain-gang mates, who were good carpenters and dry-wallers, waved at me. "I brought you a Baptist stone monkey for the roof," Roland yelled out his truck window, and held up a plastic owl he'd bought at a Wal Mart.

But the truck Cathy jabbed her finger at was Alberta's. Rainbow Goddess Farms. It carried Alberta and her womanly carpenters. Cathy pulled a colorful spring scarf closer around her face and adjusted cheerful pastel sunglasses. "Her," she muttered again.

"Sorry, but Alberta's women do some of the best house-framing in the county. Be glad we got them. They're in demand. Another month and they'll be too busy at their farm to do construction work."

"Okay, but don't let me have a hammer around Alberta. I can't be held responsible for what part of her I might thump *accidentally*."

Alberta, small and brawny in an *Indigo Girls* sweatshirt, cargo shorts, and hiking boots, strode up to us. She ignored Cathy and thrust out a hand to me. "I like your blueprint. Helluva plan. Thanks for hiring us." We shook.

Cathy held out her left hand, palm down, for a squeeze. She never shook with the scarred hand, and Alberta knew that, but Alberta gave the proffered left hand a sniffy glance. That glance rose to Cathy's pastel scarf and sunglasses. "What are you pretending to be this time? The Easter Bunny's crazy secret helper?"

"Fuck you," Cathy said flatly, and went inside.

I frowned at Alberta. "A little more compassion on your part would go a long way."

"Thomas, don't baby her, she's not your kid, she's your *woman*. Let her fight her own fights. If you don't push her harder, she's gonna be a needy little whack-job the rest of her life."

"I don't baby her. Besides, I *like* whack-jobs. I'm one, myself."

"You coddle her more than you realize. Women turn into resentful children when men take care of them too much. And men turn into daddy-figures or bullies. Don't risk it."

Before I could say anything else in Cathy's defense, she burst out of the house with her purse hanging from one shoulder and the Hummer keys in her hand. "The school called. Ivy's been in a fight. They're suspending her. I have to go."

I immediately reached for the keys. Cathy pulled them away. Breathing hard, her hands shaking, she glared at Alberta. "I can handle this alone."

Drive on pavement? All the way to Turtleville? That would be interesting. I desperately wanted to talk her out of it. But maybe Alberta was right. I did try too hard to protect her at times. "Okay," I said. "Call me on the cell phone if you need anything."

Cathy nodded shakily and climbed into the Hummer with great dignity. But as she rolled out of the yard she lowered her window, held out her rejected left hand, and flipped Alberta a bird. After the Hummer disappeared down the driveway Alberta slapped me on the back. "See? Cathy'd rather eat nails than look weak and helpless in front of *me*. Good. No extra charge for the therapy session."

Whistling, she went to unload her tools.

She had some big ones.

Cathy

I was a nervous wreck, and everyone at Jefferson County Elementary School knew it. At least in my imagination they did. And it wasn't my imagination that heads popped out of classrooms as I hurried down a hall to the principal's office. It wasn't my imagination that teachers gasped as they glimpsed the scars peeking from beneath my scarf. Not my imagination that they whispered fervently to each other as I went by.

The principal confirmed my suspicions.

"I'm so sorry for everyone's reaction," she said, hustling me into her office and shutting the door. I noticed that her own face was stark white and she avoided looking directly at me. "The entire faculty attended a disabilities sensitivity seminar over in Asheville, not six months ago." She smiled awkwardly. "Oh, Lord, I didn't mean to imply you're *disabled*. I'm *sorry*. Forgive me. I just didn't know what to expect about your appearance. How bad it . . . oh, Lord, I'm sorry, again."

"Relax, no problem," I lied cheerfully, while I shriveled inside. "If there *were* a sensitivity seminar about my situation it would be called *Burned-Up Celebrities*, and the sub-title would be, *Why It's Impolite To Stare At Bob Crane's Crispy Corpse*."

She darted looks at me as she ushered me to a chair facing her desk. "Excuse me? Bob Crane? Who?"

"He starred in *Hogan's Heroes* during the sixties. His personal life got a little out of control after the TV series ended. He burned to death in a motel room out west. Some lurid and mysterious sex scandal involving . .

. " My eyes fell on a big cartoon bunny who smiled from a poster on the wall behind the principal's desk.

Think Happy Thoughts, the slogan said.

"Nevermind." I sat down wearily. "Sorry for the disruption. Let's talk about Ivy, instead."

The principal took a deep breath and sat down facing me. "Ms. Deen, regarding your foster daughter—"

"Call me 'Cathy,' please. Did I mention I intend to join the PTA?"

"We call it the PTSA, now. Parent-Teacher-Student Association."

"Oh. That's good. I think I knew that. I just . . . forgot."

The principal smiled patiently and still avoided looking at my face. She cleared her throat. "Now, about Ivy. This is the third time since fall that Ivy's physically injured a fellow seventh grader. The first two times, of course, I called her aunt, who couldn't have cared less and refused to meet with me. Now, unfortunately, the problem is yours."

"Look, she's going through a hard time."

"I understand, believe me. Ivy has lots of potential."

"Yes! She's been an honors student despite the way her aunt moved her and her sister around. I suspect she's bored. She needs to be in accelerated classes. When she goes to middle school next year I intend to talk to her teachers about that." *Just as soon as I get over my phobia about being stared at by strangers in public.*

"Yes, fine, but . . . we've got to address the *current* problem. She's defensive, belligerent, foul-mouthed and violent."

"Well, so am I, on occasion."

"Excuse me?"

"Come on, she's a walking target for the other kids. Do you have *any* other mixed-race children in this school? I mean black-white, like Ivy."

"Contrary to what you may think, people around here are not mouth-breathing Ku Klux Klanners, all right? We've got students with Native American backgrounds, East Indian backgrounds, Asian backgrounds and Hispanic backgrounds. Ivy's problems aren't racial, they're personal."

"Can't we agree that her touchiness is understandable?"

"Punching other children in the mouth is not 'touchiness.' It's anti-social behavior."

"You don't have to mention this incident to her caseworker, Mrs. Ganza, do you?"

"Yes, I do. I'm sorry."

I glanced around the office. My eyes lit on a fund-raising poster.

"What if I make a large donation to the school?"

"Don't try to bribe me, Cathy."

"Oh, I'm not, I promise you. I'll make the donation anyway, all right?"

"Thank you."

This was not going well. I'd never had to bargain with people in the old days. Getting what you want is easy when you're rich, famous and beautiful; good-looking celebrities get away with a lot. I sagged a little. "Exactly what did the other child say to her?"

"I'll call her in and let her tell you herself."

A few seconds later Ivy slunk into the office. Her black, goth-style backpack hung from one shoulder. Her hands were shoved into the pockets of oversized camo pants, her shoulders made a miserable hunch inside a faded pink Hawaiian shirt over a blue sweater. A half-dozen woven bracelets lined each pale-brown arm, and her reddish-brown hair sprang from my white-girl attempt at frontal corn rows like a wild, high hedge. I'd wanted so often to offer fashion and makeup advice, but her streetwise-goth-tomboy attitude made it clear she didn't want any part of my girly nonsense.

When she saw me she halted and stared. "How'd you get here alone?"

"I drove."

Her eyes widened with fear. "Is something wrong with Thomas?"

"No. He's supervising the construction work at home."

"So you . . . drove here by yourself? You must *really* be pissed at me."

"No, I was *worried* about you. Tell me what happened."

She frowned. "I'm not apologizing."

"I didn't ask you to. Just tell me the truth about what happened."

"Some douche-bag called me names. I punched him in the braces."

"What did he call you?"

She shifted uneasily. "Who cares? Let them suspend me. I don't give a—"

"You've used up your quota of indelicate language in front of me and your principal."

Ivy grimaced, chewed her lower lip then shrugged. "Let them suspend me. I've got nothing to say."

The principal sighed. "The victim of Ivy's attack called her a 'fat, ugly, nappy-haired nerd.' He'll be disciplined for that."

Ivy stared at me unhappily. "'Nappy-haired' is redneck for 'nigger.'"

The principal scowled. "It most certainly is not."

"I know when somebody's calling me that name. I've heard it plenty of times."

"But not this time. You're letting your imagination get away with you."

My motherly instincts raised their hackles. "This boy who Ivy hit. Has he been suspended for taunting her?"

"Yes."

"For two full days, like Ivy?"

"Nooo."

"Why not?"

"Because the hitter always gets more punishment than the hittee. It's a rule."

"Generally speaking, that sounds fair. But not when the hittee provoked the hitter with hate speech."

"Hate speech? No. Look, if she'll apologize for striking him, and promise not to hit any other of her fellow students, I'll reduce her suspension to one day, just like his."

"I'd like a mutual apology. Her for hitting him, him for calling her derogatory names."

"I'm sorry, but this negotiation is over. My best offer is on the table."

I stood. "All right. Ivy did the crime, and she can do the time. Even if it's not fair. Come on, Ivy, we're going home. If the kid calls you a racist name again, you have my permission to clobber him again. I'll pay for his new braces."

"Wow," Ivy said, staring at me.

The principal stood quickly. "I hope this doesn't sour you on the school. We could use a donation. We desperately need a computer lab. We have a lot of disadvantaged students who need every chance they can get if they're going to survive in a world full of technology."

"I'll pay for the whole lab."

She gaped at me. "Even though you're unhappy with my decision regarding Ivy?"

"I'm not going to punish the school because I disagree with your judgement. I was raised better than that."

"Thank you!"

"I'll pay for the lab on two conditions: Put a plaque by the door naming the lab in my grandmother's honor—Mary Eve Nettie—and hang a quote about fairness and tolerance on one wall. Something by Dr. Martin Luther King, Jr. And Ivy gets to pick the quote."

"It's a deal!"

We shook. "Ivy will be back in class two days from now. Good afternoon."

I took Ivy by the hand. She was speechless. As we headed down the hallway, teachers popped out again. I glimpsed several rising hands with camera phones in them. Ivy glared at them. "Hey, mind your own business! I'll feed those phones to my goat! Quit staring at Cathy!"

"Ssssh." I tugged my scarf further over my face, jerked Ivy's hand, and we ran. Not exactly a dignified mother-daughter day at school, but we proved we might be good together in a two-legged sack race.

In the Hummer, driving back to the Cove at a heady thirty miles per hour with my hands shaking, I felt Ivy's dark eyes boring into me from the passenger seat. "You defended me. How come?"

"I'll always defend your right to be treated fairly."

"I didn't mean to cause trouble. I don't want Mrs. Ganza finding out. What if she—"

"Don't worry about Mrs. Ganza. But let's come up with some ways for you to handle future incidents without smashing some little redneck's dental work."

She sank back in the seat. "It's not that easy. Nobody's ever called *you* names."

"Oh, really?" I told her about the incident with the protestors at the Four Seasons. "And a movie reviewer called me 'whitebread with big teeth.' Another one said I was 'eye candy with more charm than talent.' I've also been called 'gorgeously inoffensive.' Which made me feel like off-white carpet."

Ivy said quietly, "But you're not fat and ugly, and I *am*."

"You're not fat and ugly."

"And I do have nappy hair. And I am a nerd."

"There's nothing wrong with any of that. Besides, isn't 'nappy hair' a cool thing to have, now?"

"I want to look like Halle Berry. Like you. You look like a white Halle Berry. I mean, you know, pretty in the same way."

"You don't have to look like Halle or me or anybody else to be pretty. Be yourself."

"You don't really believe that."

"Excuse me? I do mean it. Girls cannot let people intimidate them about their self-image. They have to be unique. Be confident."

"If you really think looks don't matter, then how come you still won't show your face to strangers?"

I clenched the steering wheel. "Being famous means I'm at the mercy of photographers who want to exploit—"

"You just don't want people to call you 'ugly.' You're always scared of being called ugly. Nothing Thomas says makes you feel any better. He loves you but you don't really see how he sees you. No matter how much Cora and I try to show you that we don't care about how you look, you don't listen." Her voice rose. Tears gleamed in her eyes. "What if you freak out and decide you can't ever go out in public anymore? Mrs. Ganza might decide you really *are* crazy and take us away from you!"

I pulled onto the side of the road, turned to her and grabbed her hands. "Ivy, honey, I promise you, I'm not going to let my problems get in the way of—"

"I'm ugly and I'll never be good enough for anybody to love! I know it! I know it! Just like you! I'll never think I'm good enough for people to love, and neither will you, and some day you'll freak out for good, and then Cora and I won't have a home anymore!"

She turned away, sobbing.

🐾🐾🐾🐾🐾

"You tried your best," Thomas said that night. We sat in the kitchen. "Ivy gets emotional. Don't blame yourself."

I hunched over a cup of tepid tea. "But she's right. I have no self-confidence, so how can I lecture her on the subject?"

"I have a suggestion. Maybe you and the girls need some time together. See how you get along on your own. Just a couple of days without me here."

I looked up at him quickly. "Where are you going?"

"New York. I have unfinished business with Ravel."

"Do you really want to open that can of worms, again?"

"It'll be all right. Just something I've been meaning to do. Can you handle staying here alone with the girls? Jeb and Alberta will be here working, so--"

"Maybe you should wait a week or two until Ivy is speaking to me, again."

He pushed my lukewarm tea aside and took my hand. His somber eyes bored into mine. "I want to protect you against everything that frightens you. There's a part of me that would do that for you without question, forever. But I'm trying very hard to get past my need to guard my loved ones with all-consuming obsession. You've got to help me. Kick me out of the nest every once in a while. Prove you'll be just fine without me."

After a moment, I nodded. He had such a good way of making it sound as if *he* had issues to resolve, not me. "I recognize 'tough love' when I see it. We'll be fine while you're in New York. Absolutely. I want you to go."

He drew my scarred hand to his lips and kissed it. I managed a smile, but inside I curdled. *I won't be just fine. I depend on him more every day.*

Thomas

Leaving Cathy and the girls for even two days was hard to do. Tough love? Hell, it was tough on *me*. I flew into New York, took a cab into Manhattan, and left a handwritten note for my sister-in-law with a concierge at Trump Tower, handing it over in the empty grandeur of the famous atrium with its pink-veined marble.

> *Ravel—*
> *Whatever you and I wish we'd done differently on nine-eleven no longer matters. Neither of us wanted our loved ones to die; neither of us deliberately caused the deaths of Sherryl, Ethan, and the baby Sherryl carried. If I could have traded my life for theirs that day, I would have. I'm sure you feel the same way. I'm moving on with my life. I hope you can move on with yours. Good-bye.*
> *Thomas*

Even if she only told me once more to fuck off or die, it would be closure for both of us. When no response came, that was all right, too. Sometimes making a statement is more important than receiving an answer.

Cathy

Just as I feared, Ivy didn't say a word to me after Thomas left for New York. But when Cora and I went out to the cow pond the next morning Ivy couldn't resist wandering along behind us. Cora and I held hands as we studied the water. "This spring we'll add some pretty rocks, a fountain, some waterlilies, some reeds, and some fish," I told her. "*Voila.* We'll have a goldfish pond. It'll attract frogs and turtles and dragonflies and butterflies and thirsty deer and turkeys and songbirds."

"And fairies!" Cora added.

"You bet. Hey, I've got an idea. We'll name the fish. What would be some good names for goldfish?"

Cora's eyes gleamed. "Nemo and Dorie and Simba and—"

"Simba is a cartoon lion," Ivy grunted. "Stick to cartoon *fish.*"

Slowly, holding my breath, I turned to look at her. "But isn't there something called a 'lion fish?'"

She shrugged. "Yeah, maybe. Sure."

Cora stared at her with great patience. "Lions are gold, and goldfish are gold, so there *can* be a goldfish named after a lion."

"Whatever."

I feigned deep thought. "What else is gold? Or yellow? Sunflowers. Butter. Okay, I'm naming my goldfish 'Sunflower' and 'Butter.' Oh, and orange juice. I'm naming one of my goldfish, 'Orange Juice.'"

Ivy stepped up to the pond's edge. "I'll name my goldfish, 'Pus.' Pus is yellow."

"Don't forget 'snot,'" I offered. "That's sort of yellow, too."

Her mouth quirked. She couldn't resist me. "'Pus' and 'Snot.' Cool. Pus and Snot the goldfish. Yeah!"

"Y'all are gross!" Cora squealed, giggling.

"And *PeePee*," I intoned. "We need a goldfish named *PeePee*, too."

Cora thought that was the funniest thing she'd ever heard. Just naughty enough to be hysterical. She went into giggly overload. Even Ivy smiled. When I nudged her with an elbow—sort of the girly version of a backslap—she nudged me back. We were friends again, at least for now.

"A fish named PeePee," Cora repeated, and giggled harder. Ivy and I traded a smile and rolled our eyes. In the midst of that reassuring moment Granny whispered to me the way she often did, disguised in my own thoughts. *You'll never look at this plain old cow pond the same way again. You'll remember laughing over goldfish. You'll remember, and so will these girls. The memory of laughing and feeling loved with be here from now on, in this water.*

Suddenly I had had the urge to call Thomas and let him know he was loved, too.

Thomas

Marcus Johnson and I stood at Ground Zero, looking over a railing at the raw footprint where the towers had been. A cold wind chapped our faces. Marcus, a New York fireman who'd been on duty during nine-eleven and in the months afterward, had become a good friend among the blood and dust of the ruins. He'd lost fellow firemen there, and he was determined not to lose *me*. Marcus was the one who handed me a respirator mask on my first day as a volunteer and said, "Wear this all the time, Mitternich, or your lungs will turn into raw meat. There's environmental shit in this air that could screw us all."

Thanks to Marcus I wasn't among the thousands of Ground Zero workers with lung problems. Neither was he. "What fuckin' happened here?" Marcus asked wearily, as we leaned on the rail. He opened his big, dark palm and let a few blood-red rose petals lift into the cold wind. "Man, will we ever know the truth about who knew what, and when they knew it, and whether this could have been stopped?"

I took a rose from him, crushed it in my hand, and let the petals float away. "People we cared about died. That's all we'll ever be certain of."

"The suits are fightin' over what to do with this property."

"I know. I was asked to comment on the design of the memorial. I told them I didn't care *what* they built here. I don't need a memorial to remember what happened, and no matter what architectural marvel they put in place of the towers, those towers are all I'll see when I look at this site."

Marcus nodded. "The suits will be fightin' for control of this place for years to come. Greedy bastards."

"It's just another restoration project now. For everyone but the people who were here that day, and the people who lost loved ones here, it's a historical site where tourists can snap a picture and buy a postcard."

"Maybe that's good, Thomas. To put it in perspective that way."

"I don't know. I wish I believed in easy answers."

Marcus's cell phone played the opening bars of Ray Charles' *What'd I Say?* He flipped the phone open and clamped it to his ear. "Yeah?" Silence;

him, listening. Then, "You're jerking my chain, lady. Yeah, right, and *I'm* Denzel Washington." Marcus pressed the phone to his jacket and stared at me. "You know any women who sound like Scarlett O' Hara? This one says she's Cathryn Deen. The actress. The one that got roasted in a car accident last year."

"She is."

Marcus gaped at me. "You're shittin' me."

"I'll tell you about her and me over a cup of coffee. It's a long story."

"She says she just wants to know if you're coming home tonight or in the morning. 'The girls are making him a cake,' she says. 'Tell him I bought him a new cell phone,' she says. 'The vet says Banger passed the other one with no problem.' Who's Banger?"

"Tell her I'll be home tonight. Late. I'll call her from Asheville. Tell her I love her. Tell her to tell the girls I love them, too."

"You're shittin' me. Cathryn Deen. The real Cathryn Deen."

"The real one."

He put the phone to his ear. "Babe. He'll be home tonight. He loves ya. He loves the kids. He'll call from Asheville. Yeah. Kisses. *Smooch.* My wife's a big fan of yours, by the way. Always with the Cathryn Deen movies. Got the DVD's, too. Love you, too. Bye-bye."

Marcus stuck the phone in his pocket, staring at me open-mouthed. We looked out over Ground Zero again. "*Man,*" he said. "Cathryn Deen must be psychic. What timing. Cause now I'll look at this place and think about her calling. And so will you."

I nodded. My heart lifted a little. Cathy had effectively cast her own aura over the memories here. Something good to add to the mix. It would never be entirely dark here, again.

Cathy

Apparently my timing had been excellent. Thomas was standing at Ground Zero. As the girls continued to hurl bawdy goldfish names at each other I walked to the house, squatted by the front steps and spoke to Granny.

"Thank you," I whispered. "I got the message. And so did Thomas."

Chapter 26

Thomas
April

I picked up my mail one April afternoon at the Crossroads post office during a lull in construction at the cottage. As I flipped through catalogs and other junk I came across a letter from a stranger. Some doctor in Florida.

> *Dear Mr. Mitternich,*
>   *I'm contacting you on the advice of your brother,*
> *John, who handles some investments for me. I understand*
> *that you may be able to put me in touch with Cathyrn*
> *Deen . . .*

What the hell was John thinking? He knew better than to tell his clients about Cathy. But my surprise and anger faded as I read on. By the time I finished the letter, I understood why John had encouraged the stranger to write me. And I knew what I had to do next.

I just hoped Cathy understood, too.

Cathy

I sat morosely in the café's kitchen. Delta patted my arm each time she hustled past with a platter in hand. A busy lunchtime on a Saturday was

307

no place for brooding. I'd come to watch Delta make biscuits. Mine still refused to cooperate. But she was too busy cooking to humor me.

"Ms. Deen?" I looked up warily from beneath a floppy felt hat over a silk scarf tied low around my forehead like a biker's do-rag. A slender, graying man in a windbreaker and corduroys stepped through the doorway. "Thomas Mitternich told me I'd find you here. I've spoken to him several times by phone and we met here in person yesterday. He's checked out all my credentials and he'll vouch for me if you want to call him right now. I just need a minute of your time."

I stood quickly. Thomas didn't send strangers to meet me, especially not without warning. The man probably had a miniature camera hidden in his jacket. I backed gracefully toward the kitchen door. "Just let me check on something outside for a moment, then I'll be right back—"

"Ms. Deen, please, don't panic."

"Oh, I'm not. I have to check on a delivery of . . . tomatoes. You see, I'm in charge of . . . tomatoes."

He held up his left hand. It was grotesquely disfigured, missing two fingers. "I'm a burn survivor, like you."

I studied him for a long minute, finally gesturing for him to follow. We walked outside in the cool sunshine. He nodded his thanks. "I'm Dr. Richard Bartholomew. I'm from Jacksonville, Florida." He indicated his ruined hand with a nod. "Backyard grilling accident. About five years ago. I used to be a surgeon."

"You can't perform operations anymore?"

He nodded. "But I can teach, I can consult, and I serve on the board of directors for SEBSA."

"SEBSA?"

"The Southeastern Burn Survivors Association. We have about two thousand members, from all over the region."

"I had no idea there was a . . . a club for people like us."

"Indeed. We offer advice, fellowship, sharing. We direct burn survivors and their families to local support groups. We have a newsletter about new treatments, new therapies, et cetera. And . . . we have an annual conference. It'll be held in Asheville this year. In the fall." He looked at me kindly but intensely. "Would you consider being one of our speakers?"

I inhaled sharply. Thomas intended to push me farther out of my comfort zone than I'd ever fallen before. "I'm really not able, I mean . . . not in front of the public, no. I'm sorry if Thomas gave you the impression I'd be able to do that."

"Oh, he was very frank about your concerns, and he made it clear you worry about being exploited." Dr. Bartholomew paused. "He made it abundantly clear my motives had best be pure."

"So he didn't scare you off."

"No. Please, just think about speaking at our conference this fall. Take your time." He handed me a business card. "Whatever you could share with others would be appreciated. Burn survivors need all the inspiration they can get. You could draw attention to the needs of victims, make the public more aware of safety issues, and motivate survivors to believe in themselves, again."

I stifled a grim laugh. Me? A poster girl for self-confidence? "I'm nobody's role model. Trust me. But I'll be happy to donate money to the organization."

"I'm not asking for money, Ms. Deen. I'm asking for something more important. You."

"I don't think I have as positive a message to share as you assume."

"Please, just keep the conference in mind."

He nodded his good-bye and left. My chest constricted and a prickly flood of new panic slid through my skin.

Speak? In public?

No way. Never.

🌑🌑🌑🌑🌑

"You *can* give that speech. You can do it." Thomas said quietly. "Just tell Bartholomew you'll try. It's that simple. You've got months to get ready. Look, I'm sorry I blindsided you, but I knew I'd never get you to talk to him any other way." We sat on the veranda, watching the sunset over Hog Back. I was furious with Thomas. We'd sent Ivy and Cora to visit Delta's grandkids at the café so we could argue all we wanted without them hearing.

I shook my head. "Your ambush wasn't fair."

"Would you have met with him willingly?"

"No. Why should I? I don't know what to say to an audience of burn victims."

"You're kidding me. How are they different from you?"

"They weren't known as Vanity Fair magazine's 'Sexiest Superstar of the Silver Screen' before they were scarred for life, I'm guessing."

"So?"

"They've made peace with their scars. I haven't. What can I tell them?

309

'Get over it?' Just like I have? That's pretty much what a burned person has to do, isn't it? Just get over it. To coin Ivy's favorite word: Bullshit."

"Alberta warned me not long ago that if I need to push you harder. I didn't believe her at the time, but now I do. You've *got* to get out in public. This speech would be the perfect start. I'm telling you, you have to do it."

I stared at him. "You're taking advice from *Alberta* about me? You're telling me what to do? You're ordering me? Nobody orders *me* around. I'm not some little nobody of a girlfriend you can lord it over. I'm . . ." My voice trailed off. Oh, God. I suddenly realized how arrogant I sounded. This was Thomas I was talking to. Thomas.

His jaw tightened. "Yeah, I get it. You're Cathryn Deen. You're special. So the rest of the world can go fuck itself while you do exactly as you please? While you continue to build a life as the recluse of Wild Woman Ridge? Even if you hurt and disappoint everyone who loves you? Me, included?"

He got up and went inside, slamming the door so hard my grandmother's stained-glass mountains rattled. I put my head in my hands.

I could *not* give a speech in public, even if he never forgave me.

Thomas

I was pushing Cathy too hard. I knew it. We made up, made love; we claimed we didn't mean what we'd said. By late April we were able to pretend we'd never argued over the SEBSA invitation, but I found Dr. Bartholomew's business card in the trash beside my drafting board, where Cathy had thrown it conspicuously. She wanted to make sure I understood the subject was closed. Okay, I'd play along. I chewed my tongue and kept quiet—a bad habit from my marriage to Sherryl. The tension remained, and festered.

Hog Back and the Ten Sisters shimmered with a dozen shades of green. Rows of baby vegetable plants filled the big gardens Delta cultivated near the café. The spring shrubs were all in bloom. The season's first bees buzzed lecherously around all the pollen-dusted stamens. The café bustled with warm-weather visitors, and on Saturday nights Alberta, Macy, and other local musicians held jam sessions in the blossom-scented darkness of the front porch. Campers and locals brought chairs and coolers to the small concert. Late one Saturday, after all the visitors had gone for the night,

Cathy, the girls and I lounged in the shadows of the yard beside Delta, Pike, Dolores and the Judge. Cathy climbed onto the porch, borrowed Macy's electric violin, and played a haunting bluegrass rendition of *Blue Moon Of Kentucky.*

We listened in surprise. "Why, girl, you're a fiddler!" Pike said when she finished. Alberta looked flabbergasted. Macy smiled and applauded. So did the rest of us. Cathy gave a sardonic little bow then walked back to her lawn chair and sat down. "As a child I took a few lessons in the stringed instruments," she said, giving me a dark look. "See? I'm happy to perform in public, as long as I'm with people I know and trust."

I kept my mouth shut and merely nodded.

I stayed busy with construction issues at the house and its growing collection of farm buildings. I drew plans for a heated, air-conditioned, Craftsman-style chicken house and upgraded the barn to make a comfortable palace of goat-loving proportions for Banger and his future harem. Sometimes Cathy and I made love there, sometimes we simply fucked. It's amazing how two people can love each other so much, be so good for each other, yet build a wall between themselves so quickly.

I recognized the raw wound inside me that needed to control situations, to build protective walls around the people I loved. Even if Cathy and I still had problems to work out, wasn't it time to make a decision about Cora and Ivy's future? There was no doubt the girls wanted to stay with us, although Ivy was often morose and Cora still assured imaginary friends that we weren't going to desert them.

Sure, they still had trust issues, but Cathy and I could overcome all that just as we settled the burn-speech issue—by ignoring the problem. I was ready to accept formal, signed-on-the-dotted-line responsibility for Cathy and the girls; to prove I'd never let terrorists get near them, never let a skyscraper collapse beneath them, that I'd guarantee them utter and total security. What better way to do that, in my mind, than asking Cathy to marry me?

The day seemed perfect for a proposal.

Cathy
The Proposal

I should have known Thomas was going to ask me to marry him that day. Delta looked far too innocent when she invited Cora and Ivy to go for a *Dairy Queen* dinner and a *Disney* double feature at the one-screen

Turtleville Cinema with her and her grandkids. But I just thought she was giving Thomas and I a chance to christen the first officially finished part of the house addition. Granny Nettie's little kitchen, with its wonderful constellation floor and handmade tile counters, was now the grand entrance to the new kitchen and its dining nook. The constellation floor led to a wider floor of polished slate, and light fixtures of copper and geometric stained glass—a classic Craftsman style—filled the kitchen with warm glows at night. Granny's big, deep metal sink had a place of honor beneath a modern faucet on a new wall with a broad window and a wide sill for potted herbs over the backsplash.

I loved Granny's aged sink. If spirits live on in the wood and stone and metal of a home, Granny's flowed in that deep basin. I honored it like a shrine. Electrical lines had been run. A hot water heater had been installed. Thomas, the girls and I held a ceremony to turn on the kitchen faucet the first time, and we all solemnly put our hands under the warming water.

In contrast, I'd secluded the big, scary stove in a stone nook with cherry-and-glass cabinets around it, next to a huge refrigerator and freezer. *Cold trumps hot*, I thought. Nearby was a long, antique-primitive table of oak slabs from trees so old each board measured nearly two-feet across. We'd surrounded the long table with handsome dining chairs of cherry with upholstered seats. The kitchen was sumptuous, an architectural meal, the comforting yet elegant equivalent of a biscuit covered in rich honey.

As I waited for Thomas to arrive for our first private dinner there, I opened the stove's oven door, pulled my latest pan of biscuits out and stared at their crusty, blackened tops. Damn.

I still don't have the magic touch. This kitchen knows I'm not worthy. It knows I'm scared of the stove, scared of the future, scared of the outside world. Just like Thomas knows.

I grimly threw the biscuits away, sipped a glass of wine, stirred a pot of gooey potato-leek soup, fluffed a bowl of salad, straightened the new silverware on the new placemats on the old table, then looked out a broad panorama of big windows that faced Hog Back. Even Thomas admitted the house was better for that lovely scene and all the sunshine that came with it.

I heard the rumble of Thomas's truck. The puppies wagged their tales and ran for the front door. I hurriedly smoothed my hair and patted everything else—breasts, stomach, butt—draped in a slender, long-sleeved white sweater and flowing white-on-white lace peasant skirt. My pulse increased, my pelvis softened, my body anticipated him. No matter what our problems, I couldn't imagine my life without him.

I heard the front door open and shut, then his footsteps on the hall and the scampering of the puppies as they circled his legs. I posed artfully by the table, as if I'd just happened to pause there in a decorous way. "I'm back here cooking for you," I sang out.

"I smell the wonderful aroma of your biscuits," he called.

"Only because I forgot to turn on the new ceiling fan and spray air freshener to hide the charcoal scent."

He rounded the corner and stopped in the doorway. He carried a huge bouquet of spring flowers in one hand and one of Granny's two-gallon milk jars in the other. He was dressed in faded jeans, a good belt, and a white dress shirt, open at the collar. He looked me up and down, slowly, and didn't stop looking at me as he walked to the counter. He put the flowers in the milk jar, filled the jar with water at the sink, then set the arrangement on the table between our place settings. All that time, looking at me. And me looking at him, with my hands by my side and my chin up, my body angled just-so, my heart racing.

He stepped close to me, parallel to me, fitting his body to mine yet not touching me, leaving a very fluid, very intense space between us. I raised my face, turning the scarred side away, trying to forget it, as always. I took his hand. "We're going to make love in a real bedroom. In my real bed."

His fingers closed snugly around mine. "That," he said as he pulled me to him, "would be wicked."

🐾🐾🐾🐾🐾

Good sex always makes life seem so simple. That's the danger of it. We lay together, naked, in my rumpled bed. Thomas was one of those rare men who liked to talk after sex. I loved that about him in general, but not lately. Too risky. Distractions were safer. I reached under the bed, fetched my vibrator, and trailed its bulbous plastic tip over Thomas's bare stomach. "I want to show you," I said, clicking the switch, "the miracle uses of modern electricity."

He put a hand over mine and stopped me. "Let's get dressed and go down to Ruby Creek. I want to show *you* something."

"It had better be as exciting as this," I intoned, waving the vibrator at him with a coy wink while dread formed in my stomach.

"Even more so," he said grimly.

❦❦❦❦❦

We knelt by the creek in the soft shadows of the spring evening, holding the shallow tin mining pans Thomas had brought. "Slide your pan into that sandy spot right there," he directed. "Scoop up the sand along with a little water, swirl it around, let it drain out one side of the pan. Do it gently, and the sand will wash off, leaving the good stuff behind."

"You're sure we can find rubies or sapphires in this spot? Why here?"

"The physics are perfect. I've calculated the curve of the currents, the percentage of water volume, the force of fluid transporting sand into these sub-surface inclusions right here, the hydraulic lift versus the metric tonnage."

"Even I know technical b.s. when I hear it."

"Trust me, just scoop, all right?"

I scooped some sand, swished, dumped it, prodded a few gray pebbles in the pan, tossed them, sighed, and scooped again. Something substantial weighted my pan. "Hey! I found a boulder or something." I swished. The sand washed away from a small black box. A jeweler's box. I stared at it. "Thomas, what have you—"

"Open it," he said gruffly.

My hands shaking, I set the pan down, held the box on my palm—the unscarred left one, of course—and opened the lid. Inside, there gleamed a gold and white-platinum ring in a pattern of exquisitely delicate, interlocking rectangles, topped with several small rubies around one large diamond. It was beautiful, it was unique, and he had, no doubt, designed it himself.

Thomas knew I wouldn't accept it the moment I looked at him. He blew out a long breath. The expression in his eyes broke my heart. "I'll wait as long as it takes," he said. "Just tell me what the hell is happening to us."

I slumped. "What happens when you finish 'restoring' me? And then you realize—" I pointed to my face—"that, no matter what you do, this won't ever look like the original?" I looked away from him, fighting for control.

He bent his head close to mine. "Do you really think I sit around wishing your face weren't scarred? You really think that's what defines how I see you? How I see our future?"

I looked up at him tearfully. "It's not just my face. It's me. Inside and out. You want me to be a strong, confident woman who can stand up in front of people without flinching. I can't do it, Thomas. Maybe I'm always going to be a recluse. Maybe I'm going to turn into the crazy recluse of Wild Woman Ridge."

"You're not. I refuse to give up—"

"*You* refuse to give up. Exactly. But what if I give up? What happens if I can't change, and you can't change me, and one day you begin to feel even more disappointed in me than you do, now, and you decide my limitations are stifling your choices, your life, your dreams? Thomas, I don't want to be a disappointment to you, or to Cora and Ivy."

"I love you. You're making our simple problems into a big deal."

"Going out in public again is not simple to me. I love being with you, and the girls, and the animals, secluded up here on the ridge. Isn't that enough, for now?"

"You don't 'love' being a recluse. You've accepted it. There's a difference. And I've made it easier for you by being here all the time. Well, no more. I refuse to live in the barn any longer. I'm going back to my cabin next week."

I groaned. "How can you do that to me? How can you upset Ivy and Cora that way?"

"What do you think goes through their heads now? They worry all the time that you and I aren't going to stay together. *I live in the barn, Cathy.* They know that's not good. I hate the pretense of it. Either we're together, we're a family, we get married, or we stop pretending. No half-measures, all right? At some point, loving someone is always about taking a chance. I've learned that lesson the hard way. You need to learn it, too."

"I agree with you. I know I need to be stronger, braver, better. But it's not about taking a chance on you. It's about taking a chance on me."

"Just tell me you'll give that speech in the fall. Just try. That's all I ask."

"I can't. I can't. I'm sorry." I got up quickly and he leapt up, too. I was crying harder, now. He had tears in his eyes, too. I gripped his arm ferociously. "Don't tell the girls you're moving. They won't understand why. Don't tell them, yet. Give me a few days to think about this. About what to say to them."

He nodded. "A few days."

Miserable, we went back to the house, walking side by side, not touching.

Chapter 27

Cathy
At The Crossroads

"You and Thomas really like to keep things complicated, don't you?" Delta said helpfully, as I dusted her round cheekbones with blush. "You look like you lost your best friend. And Thomas looks the same way. He won't talk to me about it. He's a man and I can't crack him. But I can crack *you*. Talk."

I tossed the brush into my makeup kit then slumped beside her in one of the café's slat-bottomed dining chairs. It was a Monday afternoon, and the café was quiet and empty, always closed on Mondays. Delta had borrowed a video camera from one of her grandchildren; I'd offered to be her director and camera-person for a practice video. I'd talked her into auditioning for the Food Network.

"You're still not talking," she complained as I stared out a café' window.

"It's going to storm. Look at those clouds. A bad thunderstorm."

Delta grabbed an eyebrow pencil from my kit and held it like a skewer. "Don't make me use this."

I sank deeper into the chair. "I love him. I want to marry him. I just don't want him to push me so hard to be 'normal' again."

"Aw, come on. If people waited to get married until they were normal, nobody'd ever walk down the aisle."

"His expectations for me are too high. When you marry somebody you make a promise to be the person your spouse wants you to be. I can't take that oath in good faith right now. I'd be lying. When I married Gerald I didn't really believe the vows I took. I thought I did, but they were just words. I don't want them to be just words this time."

Delta rolled her eyes. "Married people say lots of things they don't mean and can't live up to, but at least they try. Sure, they'll disappoint each other from time to time. So what? What would be the fun in it if married folks didn't fight and sulk and worry and come back for more? The only way to stay happily married is to keep changing, to keep adjusting how you see each other. As long as the core of love is there, as long as that person is right for you, down deep where nothing changes, then the rest is just butter on the biscuit." She waved the eyebrow pencil at me righteously. "Is anything else wrong? Don't tell me you're not over Gerald, yet, that mule pecker."

"Oh, please. I wasn't really married to Gerald. Not here." I tapped a finger to my heart. "Gerald has nothing to do with this."

"Okay, then have you've got some deep, dark secret Thomas doesn't know? Do you turn into a werewolf when the moon is full?"

"If I did, I'd have chased Banger down and shredded him by now. Did I tell you he ate a pair of my walking shoes last week? He even ate the laces."

"Don't change the subject. You're waiting for lightning to strike? Magic moments of happiness to anoint you with the shivers? Your scars to miraculously disappear?"

I looked at her for a long, tense moment, then gave up and nodded. "That last one. That's it."

"Oh, cousin. You know that's never gonna happen. What you have to do is, you gotta change how you see yourself. You've got to stop being the Wicked Witch and be Dorothy instead."

"Excuse me?"

"Dorothy. From *The Wizard of Oz*. Click your ruby slippers together and say—"

Thunder boomed over Ten Sisters. I nodded toward them with a grim smile. "Don't disrespect the Wicked Witch of the West." I shut my eyes and curled my hands under my chin. "Okay, I'll be Dorothy. 'There's no place like home, there's no place like—'"

"That's not what you need to say. Here's what you need to say, if you want to get back home." Delta put her hands together, shut her eyes, and chanted, "There's no face like mine. There's no face like mine. There's no face like—"

I looked at her askance. "That doesn't even make sense."

She cupped her chubby, work-reddened hands around my face. "Take pride in the face you have, not the face you had. Look at this beautiful face, scars and all. When you see that face in a mirror, you'll be home."

I bowed my head. "I'll never see myself that way. Every time Thomas looks at me—every time for the rest of our lives—I'll have the urge to turn away a little, to hide. And he knows it. He knows I cringe a little, Delta. He tries to pretend he doesn't mind, but some day he'll run out of patience. He'll get tired of my quirks. I can't marry him until I can look at him and let him look straight at me, until I can look at him and think only how much I love him, not how ugly I am." I took her hands from my face, squeezed them, then stood up. Lightning flickered. "I better go see where the girls are with those flowers."

Delta sighed.

Cora and Ivy ran into the dining room with their arms full of cuttings from the last of the café's pink azaleas. "It's scary out there!" Cora said worriedly.

Ivy looked concerned, too. "The clouds are moving fast, and some of them are the color of bruises. On the Discovery Channel they said most tornadoes occur between three p.m. and nine p.m. and from March to May. It's three-forty-five and it's the first week of May."

Delta dismissed statistics and the force of nature with a wave of her hands. "It's just a thunderstorm, sweeties. These old mountains rumble like a bear, sometimes. Come on. Let's get those azaleas in some vases." She smoothed a preening hand over her turquoise outfit. "We'll arrange them on the 'set' of my show, so my kitchen looks pinkish and blossom-ish."

She steered the girls toward the kitchen, where I'd already set up the camera on a tripod. I'd also clamped several utility lights here and there to fill in the shadows and brighten the ambience. I'd never realized how much I knew about basic stage craft before. Martin Scorsese had nothing to worry about for Oscar competition, but I could definitely produce and direct Delta's audition tape for a cooking show.

As I followed Delta and the girls a blinding flash of lightning made me jump. Its immediate thunderclap shook the entire restaurant. Cora shrieked. I peered out the windows and halted. Storms didn't usually scare me—even I couldn't imagine being toasted by lightning—but the churning brew of clouds over Ten Sisters made a knot in my stomach. The parking lot had gone so dark the automatic light on the café's sign suddenly switched on. Huge gusts of wind rocked the trees.

My cell phone buzzed. Thomas. He was building new pasture fences at the house with a crew that included Santa. "I'm coming down there," he announced. "Pike says a tornado's been sighted west of Turtleville. Heading your way."

"Relax. Delta tells me the Cove almost never gets tornadoes. Ten Sisters and Hog Back form a natural obstacle course. The funnel clouds break up trying to cross the mountains."

"Tell that to a tornado while it's sneaking up the hollow along Ruby Creek. I'll be there soon. In the meantime, convince Delta to take you and the girls on a tour of the root cellar."

"Only if you stay up on the ridge and take our construction team on a tour of Granny's root cellar. Don't you dare start this way in that tin can of an old truck."

"Don't *dis* my truck. Go downstairs," he ordered. "Now."

Click. I frowned at the cell phone, stuck it in the pocket of my jeans, then jumped again as lightning struck so close the air snapped. *Boom.* The café's windows rattled. An enamelware coffee cup made a loud clatter as it fell off a display shelf. Cora squealed and came running my way. I swung her up into my arms and hugged her tightly. "It's okay, *Corazon*, sssh." Delta, with Ivy on wide-eyed alert beside her, appeared in the kitchen door waving a flashlight. "Who wants to see where my grandpa hid his liquor still?" she asked cheerfully.

We quickly followed her down a back hall toward the cellar door. Halfway there, the café suddenly began to shiver. The ceiling lights went out. Framed antique calendars and folk-art paintings of farm scenes danced on the walls. And a roar—yes, like the train people always describe—filled our ears.

"Into the toilet!" Delta yelled.

We darted into the café's indoor restroom, a small one-seater where an old white sink and avocado-green commode vied for attention among framed photos of Delta's celebrity fans. I found myself face-to-face with an autographed picture of Garth Brooks. "Get down!" Delta shouted. The four of us huddled on the floor. I pushed Cora and Ivy under the sink.

"We'll be fine!" I promised them, touching their faces.

"Hang on!" Delta shouted above the noise. Everything was shaking. Everything was dark. Suddenly I was back in the Trans Am, speeding out of control. Panic blurred my brain.

The restroom door slammed shut behind me. The café shrieked and groaned. I heard Delta cry out in shared misery. Her beloved café, *our* beloved café, was suffering. Timbers crashed, wires ripped free, windows shattered. Suddenly the hallway collapsed against the restroom door, making it bulged inward on its sturdy old hinges. The restroom's ceiling began to dribble plaster on us, then bits of wood. I threw my arms over the girls and burrowed under the sink with them as the restroom's big ceiling fixture hit the sink. Chunks of glass sprayed in all directions, and the fixture's heavy metal base bounced off my shoulder.

I heard Delta groan. Chills went through me. I flung out a hand and gripped the front of her turquoise suit.

She didn't move.

And then it was quiet.

The train moved on, lifted back into the clouds, caught the fast track to oblivion. I began to hear Cora's soft whimpers and Ivy's rattled breaths. It was dark, it was hot, and the café—or what was left of it—creaked and shifted around us. A draft of damp air curled down from the attic through a foot-wide hole where the light-fixture had hung.

"It's all right, it's over," I heard myself telling the girls, while I fervently patted their heads and faces, instinctively checking for warmth, life, praying for no slick texture like blood. When I fumbled one hand over Delta's head I wasn't so lucky. I drew back my hand at the wetness. "Delta!"

She moved a little and mumbled. "Guess I . . . was wrong. About tornadoes."

I scrambled around and located her flashlight. With a click of my thumb, we had light. A quick survey showed Cora and Ivy were terrified but unhurt. When I trained the beam on Delta she was slumped against the restroom wall, squinting in pain. A wide stream of blood trickled down the right side of her face. I aimed the light at her scalp, probed gently with one shaking forefinger, and found a small gash in the center of a swelling lump.

"I'm not doing your makeup anymore if you insist on bleeding," I teased hoarsely. She managed a smile. I turned to the girls. "Ivy, squeeze in here beside Delta." I pulled a wad of toilet paper from a roll. "Hold this on her cut. She's going to be just fine. And so are we."

Ivy wedged herself next to Delta and pressed the toilet paper on the wound. "How are we going to get out of here?"

"I don't like this cave," Cora mewled.

"Come here, sweetie." I pulled her into my lap. "We're just fine, and all we have to do is wait for Thomas to come. Okay?"

"Okay."

"You hold the flashlight for me. Good girl." I pulled out my cell phone, blessed the day it was invented, and started to punch the speed dial number for Thomas. But he beat me to it. The phone buzzed.

"Tell me you're all right," he said into my ear. I heard the deep rumble of the truck's engine, speeding. His voice was deceptively calm. He had flat-lined his fears, his memories, his horror. *Not again*, he must be thinking.

"I'm just fine, really." Casual. Relaxed. And the critics said I couldn't really act. Hah.

"The girls? Delta?"

"Fine, too. But the café is a wreck."

"I'm only five minutes away. I've got Santa with me. Jeb's on the way, and Pike, and everyone Pike can marshal."

"Delta's got a scratch on her head, but it doesn't appear to be serious. The only problem is, we're stuck in the bathroom. The door's blocked." I guided Cora's wobbly hand, holding the flashlight, and we looked up through the hole in the ceiling. "The light fixture fell, and I can see all the way through to the attic. Well . . . what's left of the attic. Delta, your bathroom has a skylight, now. With a nice breeze." As I aimed the flashlight through the hole, something caught my eye. A wisp of gray moving through the air. Just the faintest whirl of dust? Sure. Or just my imagination. Of course. Of course.

My skin went ice-cold. My blood retreated to my bones. Terror seeped from invisible burns submerged by scars. My body would never forget those wounds, would never forget the effect of fire.

"I smell smoke," Ivy said in a low voice.

So did I.

Thomas

My heart stopped in my chest. Not fire. Not again. Not for Cathy, not for Ivy and Cora, not for Delta. Not for Ethan, or Sherryl, or the child that had lived inside her. Not for me. No. Not this time. Never, again.

"Call the fire department," I told Santa, throwing the phone to him as I drove. "Get the forestry service. Get anyone with a hose and a bucket and a shovel full of sand. *Get them.*"

"Oh, shit," Joe groaned, and began punching numbers.

I drove. My ancient truck roared dutifully along the creek trail. I steered around downed trees. The tornado had ripped massive hardwoods and firs from the creek banks. I swerved onto the pavement of the Trace and the truck skidded. Two wheels left the concrete. But the squat, strong old workhorse didn't roll; it hugged the road like a friend. It knew it was still respected, still needed, it had a job to do.

I stomped the gas pedal. We careened up the road.

When the café came into view I saw a thin plume of smoke already rising from the wreckage. Bile rose in my throat. I spit it out the truck's open window. The wind brought back the faint sound of sirens heading from Turtleville. Pike was racing from the opposite end of the county. Jeb and the crew from the house weren't far behind me and Santa.

I stared at the smoke. *Cathy, I won't let anything happen to you, or the girls, or Delta. I swear to you. I swear. I swear to you, Sherryl, and Ethan. Not again.*

It looked as if the café had been sideswiped by an enormous hand. The entire right side of the house had collapsed inward, and that end of the roof was scattered in pieces through the pasture beyond the oaks. I slid the truck to a stop inches from the wreckage of the side porch. The Privy was now just a two-foot-high pile of debris. Flattened. "I've got to get into the attic," I yelled to Santa. "I can get them out of the bathroom through the ceiling."

"You can't climb into that wreckage; you can't get up there! Hold up, wait for the boys from the fire department with the ladder truck!"

I gunned the truck's engine, threw it into low gear, and aimed for a wall of the Privy that had tilted on the debris. I'd use it as a ramp. Santa whooped as the truck climbed the pile the way a beetle lurches up a pile of twigs. By the time the axle finally jammed on a timber the truck halted, nose up, front wheels spinning in thin air, but with its front grill snuggly set against the jagged edges of the attic floor.

"Brother," Joe said breathlessly, "You just turned this piece-of-shit old truck into a mountain goat."

I pulled my tire iron from beneath the seat, climbed out, vaulted onto the truck's hood, and crawled under what was left of the attic roof.

Smoke wafted around me gently, closing like a lethal blanket over my lungs. I smelled the dust of the World Trade Center's North Tower, I felt the impact of air weighted by doom. *Welcome back to your nightmares*, it whispered. *Will you and Cathy beat me this time?*

Cathy

I heard noises outside, but I was too panicked to analyze them. Hot. It was hot in the tiny bathroom, and the air already seemed to thicken, ready to smother, to suffocate us. "Hold these over your noses," I told Delta and the girls, handing out paper towels I soaked in the sink. I splashed water on the front of my t-shirt and wiped my face. The acrid smoke couldn't be ignored, now. Sweat dripped from my skin as I climbed onto the commode, furiously jabbing the wooden handle of a commode brush at the rim of the hole left by the fallen light fixture. Flecks of wood and torn ceiling tile rained down on me, Delta, and the girls.

The foot-wide hole slowly widened a little. The commode brush handle splintered and snapped. A thin shard stabbed my palm. I barely noticed. "There, done!" I called to the girls. "Cora, climb up. Ivy, you give her a boost. Then I'm going to lift you up, Cora, and you're going to climb through the hole in the ceiling. It's big enough for you. Once you're out, I'll work on it some more, and then Ivy can crawl through. Come on, now."

"I'm scared of the dragon's breath," Cora said, crying. Smoke slithered through the cracks in the ceiling.

"He's just snoring," Delta said, holding a hand to her bloody head. "He won't hurt you. Go on, Cora. You can do it."

Ivy grabbed her around the legs and lifted her. "Go, Cora. I'll come up right after you, okay?"

"I'm scared!"

I hoisted her and, straining, lifted her as high as I could. "Stick your arms up through the hole, Cora!"

She squealed, shut her eyes, and thrust her hands into the attic. "It's hot! The dragon's breathing hot air up there!" She jerked her hands down and sobbed.

"Cora!" I lowered her enough to wedge one arm under her butt and brush the sweaty hair back from her face so I could see her eyes. "Look at me!" When she did, I smiled. "Even in fairytales, princesses get scared of dragons. It's okay to be scared, all right? But don't stop trying to *fight* the dragon! Okay?"

She cried harder but nodded. I held her up to the ceiling again. She stuck her arms and head through the hole. "I'm looking," she said, "But I don't see the dragon. We better hurry, though."

"Just climb up on my shoulders, okay?"

"It's smoky, I'm scared!"

"Fight the dragon, Cora!"

She wiggled a little higher. "I'm stuck!"

Oh, God. I pushed. She screamed. More sweat poured off me. My scars began to throb with the heat. My skin knew what was coming. That we were trapped. "Don't give up, Cora!" I begged.

"Thomas! Thomas is here!"

I heard heavy footsteps above us. Suddenly, as if by magic, Cora was whisked upwards. "I've got her," Thomas yelled. "I'll hand her to Santa and be right back." I heard his quick steps leading away. Below me, Ivy and Delta began to cough. I thrust down a hand to Ivy. "Come on, you're next. Climb up."

"The hole's too small for me. You know it is."

"We're going to try it, anyway! Get up here!"

She climbed atop the commode, then onto the sink. I grabbed her by one hand. Delta braced her by the legs. We all looked up at the hole. Ivy squeezed my hand and shook her head. "I won't fit," she moaned. She was right. God, we were running out of time.

"Cover your heads," Thomas shouted. He was back, standing over the hole, smoke billowing in his face. "Watch out, I'm going to work on this ceiling with a tire iron."

We all ducked as he attacked the wood above us. Chunks of wood pelted us. Boards split, nails squealed. The hole widened by slow degrees. "It's big enough for Ivy now!" I yelled. He dropped the iron and, coughing, thrust his hands down. "Let's go, Ivy. I'll pull you up. I promised you I wouldn't let anybody hurt you, and I meant it."

She held up her hands. He grabbed her around the wrists. "I'm too fat—" she began, but the protest ended in a gasp as Thomas pulled her into the attic. "Carry her out," he yelled to someone. Then, to me and Delta, "Jeb's here."

"Hang in there, Mama," Jeb yelled. "Daddy's just pulled up in the yard. He's here."

"Don't you let your daddy climb up here," she shouted. "He'll throw out his back again."

Smoke billowed into the bathroom from an air conditioning vent high on one wall. I covered my nose with the tail of my soaked t-shirt. A tiny orange flame curled through the metal vent. Like the obscene tongue of some smiling monster—a dragon, yes—it licked the air in my direction.

This time you won't get away.

"Cover your head, Cathy!" Thomas yelled. Jeb handed him a chain saw. He jerked the starter cord. The motor buzzed, the long blade spun.

"Hunker down!" Delta yelled, and tugged at my arm. I dropped to my heels atop the commode. She and I burrowed our heads together, coughing, as Thomas sliced a large opening in the ceiling with the powerful saw. When he finished he dropped to his stomach and thrust the entire length of his arms toward me. "Cathy, grab on."

Every cell in my body wanted to flee that bathroom, even if it meant deserting Delta. To go first. All my life, I'd been the golden girl who always went first. But I couldn't do it this time. I wasn't that person, anymore. I had kin to think of. Delta coughed violently beside me. I stumbled to my feet. "Delta goes first! She's not breathing well, and she's hurt!"

"Cathy, let me get you out. Then—"

"Not this time!" I clambered off the toilet seat and shoved Delta toward it. "Go, go, go. Climb up. You can do it!"

Coughing so hard she couldn't argue, she hoisted her plump self atop the commode seat. I pushed like a tugboat until she was standing safely on the porcelain rim. She raised her arms. Thomas grabbed her by the wrists. He pulled, I pushed. Delta yelled and swung her feet. By the time Thomas got her head and arms through the hole Pike bounded into the attic beside him, grabbing Delta beneath the arms. "You'll hurt your back!" she cried.

"Yell at me later," he yelled in return. He threw his arms around her but she struggled and turned to look back at me. "Cathy!"

"Go!" I yelled. "I love you, cousin!"

"I love you, too, cousin!"

Pike practically had to drag her out of the attic. Thomas flung himself back to the floor. Soot smeared his face. The smoke was so bad at times I couldn't see him. He thrust down his arms again. "Cathy! Here! Here! Come on!"

But I flattened myself in one corner of the bathroom as the tongue of flame in the vent sprouted new tendrils. They crept out of the metal grate in all directions, turning it into a horrifying blossom of fire. One eager tendril headed for the hole in the ceiling, that delicious conduit for the outside air. The flame gave a low, hissing *poof*, like a magician's sound effect.

Suddenly, fire circled the opening. Thomas was wearing one of his Giants jerseys. The left sleeve smoked then burst into flame. The sight of him on fire made me scream when nothing else had. He beat the flame with his hand, jerked the jersey off over his head, then threw it down to me. "Soak it and throw it back!"

I shoved the wadded jersey into the commode bowl, withdrew it with blue, sanitized water streaming everywhere, and tossed the sopping bundle up to Thomas. He drowned the flames on one side of the ceiling hole, threw himself down atop the soaked material, and reached for me. "Now!"

I leapt onto the toilet seat within inches of the vent fire. Nothing could keep me from staring into that terrifying maw of flame. It drew me, it taunted me. My arms refused to rise toward Thomas. In order to escape I'd have to get close, risk having that flame touch me. I couldn't do it.

"Get out of here, Thomas. I don't want you to die with me. Leave. Now."

"Stop looking at it! Look at me, instead! Goddammit, Cathy, *look at me.*"

Slowly I dragged my gaze up to his. Through the smoke, the fear, the growing despair, I saw his face clearly for just a second. He looked straight at me, at my scars, at me, not them, with unwavering devotion. *He'll literally walk through fire for me. He'll never turn away.*

Thomas thrust down a hand. "We leave here together or we die here together! You decide! I'll burn to death with you if that's your choice!"

He meant it. He'd die here with me. I faced the fire again. *I've given you all I'm going to give. You won't get the best of me anymore. I won't let you have Thomas.* I raised my arms. The heat licked the air close to my right arm, and the scars prickled with pain. I shut my eyes and prayed. Thomas closed his hands around my wrists. He struggled to his knees, lifting me. I rose along with him. The lurid tendril of flame sent a tiny, curious tongue my way. As I rose past it I opened my eyes defiantly. *I'm going to live.*

With one strong heave of his body Thomas birthed me onto the hot, smoking attic floor. I threw an arm around his waist, and we staggered from the attic.

We were grabbed by the helping hands of Jeb, Santa, the Judge and others. I never let go of Thomas, and he never let go of me. We climbed down the hood of his poor truck, now a sacrificial lamb atop a pyre of smoking wood. As we stumbled onto safe earth we both looked around wildly for the girls—there they were, over by the road, wanting to run our way but held back by Becka and Cleo and Dolores. And there was Delta, yes, safely sitting on the roadside with Pike beside her. A paramedic from the volunteer fire department tried to dab the wound on her head. She shooed him away. Who wants help for a flesh wound when your heart is being ripped out? When she saw us she shut her eyes in gratitude, then opened them, looked at the dying, burning remnants of her beloved café, and sobbed.

We ran to her and the girls, hugging them and them hugging us. Holding their hands, we turned and, with Delta, looked at the lovely old house, the heart of the Cove, the touchstone that had brought us all together there.

As we watched, The Crossroads Café burned to the ground.

Thomas

Cathy and I made out on the couch at home that night like lovers reunited after a thousand years in exile. We were dirty, sooty, smoky, blistered, exhausted, and sad about the café, but we couldn't keep our hands off each other. Ivy and Cora—scrubbed, soothed, fed and hugged—slept soundly in their beds with their pets and their newly assured trust. Their doubts had vanished. Cathy and I would never abandon them. They would never worry about us again.

I turned Cathy's hand and forearm. Gauze covered the underside from elbow to wrist. The skin had been lightly blistered. Does it still hurt?" I asked gently.

She nodded. Her eyes met mine with wonder. "But it'll heal. I know that, now. It *will* heal."

I pulled her onto my lap. She stroked my face. "I love you," she said.

"I love you, too," I answered softly. "I always have."

Cathy slid off my legs and knelt before me, taking my hands in hers. For the first time since I'd known her she looked up at me without angling her face to the good side. No more posing. No more hiding. "Today I finally understood the real meaning of *trust*," she whispered. "I trust you with my life, my love, and my future, and I want you to trust me with yours. I promise to go to Asheville and speak at the burn conference in the fall. I promise to stop hiding from the world. As long as you look at me the way you're looking at me right now, I can face anything the world throws my way. Thomas Mitternich, will you marry me?"

I reached inside my shirt and pulled out a necklace with the ruby and diamond band dangling from it. I took the ring from the chain and slid it onto Cathy's left hand. "Have I told you lately," I said gruffly, "that you're the most beautiful girl in the world?"

That night we went to bed peacefully in Mary Eve's magical house, sharing a bed that faced the plastic-draped opening where a wall had been removed. Soon the small, intimate bedroom would expand to welcome a new legacy, our legacy. We made love in the light of a spring moon shimmering outside a stained-glass window Cathy's grandmother had set into the wood with her own wise hands.

When we slept, I dreamed Cathy and I ate biscuits at the café. It looked the same as always. A good dream.

Like us, the café could be restored.

Cathy

Her face swollen from crying, Delta stood in front of the café's charred ruins. Thomas and I craned our heads from the back of a crowd that included the Whittlespoon clan and most of the café's neighbors in the Cove. Pike stood to one side, his expression dark and his arms crossed over his chest. Delta cleared her throat. "I called you all here today to say something that's hard to say." Her voice trembled. She looked to Pike for support but he only scowled harder. Rebuffed, she sucked in a deep breath, steadied herself, and stared at everyone grimly. "This sweet old place will never be the same. My heart's just flat broken. How could the *Lard* do this to me? I'm not rebuilding the café. Don't even talk to me about it."

As we gasped and traded stunned looks she walked to her car, got in, and drove up the lane to her house. She went inside, and that was the last we saw of her for days.

Delta had lost her faith in biscuits.

🐾🐾🐾🐾🐾

People all over the region flooded Delta with sympathy and encouragement, to no avail. The governor called, and various mayors, and a senator. Artists showed up to cry and carry off sentimental shards of the Privy, promising to adorn a new one when she re-built the café. But Delta remained inside her home, resolute and inconsolable.

The girls held my hands as we looked at the ruins. "Cathy, were you scared we were gonna die?" Cora asked in a small voice.

I shook my head. "Nope. I knew Thomas would come and get us."

Ivy nudged Cora's shoulder. "Thomas keeps his promises. We don't have to worry about anything anymore. Because we've got Thomas." She looked up at me with gleaming eyes. "And we've got you."

My throat closed with emotion. I loved these girls, these little people who needed Thomas and me as much as we needed them. We were a family. Even Mrs. Ganza recognized that. She'd emailed us after the fire.

> *Dear Ms. Deen and Mr. Mitternich,*
> *I was wrong. You do know how to be good parents.*
> *When you file for adoption I'll give my full approval.*
> *In return, when the café reopens I expect you to send me biscuits.*

I had no intention of telling her that the café's future might be in doubt.

Thomas walked over to us. He'd been scrutinizing his scorched truck, which now had been towed from the debris. He smoothed a hand over the girls' heads and they grinned up at him. "The good news," he announced, "is that my truck doesn't look much worse now than it did before. I can fix it. In fact, in honor of its heroism I'm going to restore it to its full glory. Mint condition."

I smiled wistfully at him. "We're *all* going to be okay. Mint condition. But what are we going to do about Delta?"

Thomas put an arm around me. "We're going to do what she did for us: We'll refuse to give up on her."

❦❦❦❦❦

Pike ushered us into the Whittlespoon house that warm spring night. He looked worn and tired. "She's in the sunroom. Whatever y'all have to say, I hope it's powerful. Because like I told you on the phone, now she says she's going to *sell* the café so everyone will quit hovering around it waiting for her to change her mind. She says she'll sell everything that can be salvaged, and then she'll sell the ground it sits on. And the rights to the name. The menu. Her recipes. Even her biscuit pans, at least the ones that didn't get ruined in the fire. Everything a person can sell."

Thomas shook his head. "She can't be serious."

"She is. She really is heartbroken. She's convinced the place will never be a sanctuary again. Never have the same spirit. She's always felt safe in the café. After our kids drowned it became a sacred place to her, where nothing bad could happen to her or anybody else she loves. Now God's put the *kabosh* on that notion, and she's so mad at Him she wants to spit. He burned her restaurant down. Why did He let that happen? Cleo keeps quoting the Bible to her, trying to calm her down. 'We aren't meant to understand the Lord's ways. He really does cook in mysterious ways,' and on-and-on. But Delta isn't listening. She's mad at God, so she's not going to minister to people with her cooking anymore." Pike frowned. "*No more soul food.*"

"I'll talk some sense into her," I announced boldly. I headed for the sunroom, waving at Pike and Thomas to stay back while I worked my Southern-belle-geisha-movie-star charm.

Delta lay in the dark on one of the wicker lounges, dressed in an old chenille robe with a pair of pink coffee cups embroidered on the front. She stared grimly into space. I sat down on the lounge next to hers. "Hi, cousin. Get up off your butt and bake me some biscuits. I'm in biscuit-withdrawal."

"You can't talk me out of selling the café."

"Yes, I can. You're not a quitter."

Her shoulders slumped. "I was raised in that house. I was taught to cook in that house. My first two babies were born in that house. After they died I turned to that house as a comfort and for a living. When I cooked in that house, when I served food to people in that house, I nourished all my memories. Sure, I can build another café, but I can never rebuild *that* house. I just don't have the heart to try."

"So you're saying that leftovers aren't worth saving? You're saying there's no point in salvaging what's no longer perfect? That it can't be wonderful in a new way?" I pointed to my face. "Are you saying that everything you told me to believe about myself was wrong?"

Delta's eyes snapped. "You know that's not what I mean."

"Then tell me what you *do* mean."

"All I've done is feed people and meddle in their lives. I don't see any evidence that I've changed *anybody's* life. People change on their own. You didn't need me to tell you how to live. Neither did Thomas. I fed you, that's all. And now I can't even do that."

"So . . . you just took an interest in me for fun? You were just being pleasant to your movie-star cousin? You really didn't think my life was worth saving or rebuilding? You really didn't care if Thomas killed himself? To you, we were just two more paying customers?"

"Quit trying to poke me a long stick until I give in! I'm done caring about that café, I tell you! Looking at it the burned-up ruins of it makes me sick to my stomach! It's like a dead person. I can't resurrect the dead! Leave me alone!"

I leaned closer. "You taught me to never give up. You gave me my life back, even when I didn't think I wanted it. Now a fire has stripped away your self-image just as a fire stripped away mine. My face was how I connected to the world. The café was your connection to the world. Thomas says you once told him I was trapped in a dark place and he had to be my light. Now I'm going to be *your* light. Even if you don't want me to."

"I'm selling the place. Don't argue with me anymore. Get out!"

"All right, if you insist, *I'll* buy the café from you. Name your price." I reached for the purse I'd dropped on the tile floor, pulled a checkbook and pen from it, and signed my name. "Here. You fill in the numbers." I laid the check on her pink-teacupped chest. "I'm buying the property, the name, the right to all your recipes, and the wreckage. Thomas is already drawing up a blueprint for a completely restored building—with a modern kitchen and a few other new touches—but we want to use as much of the original materials as we can salvage."

"There's no way y'all can make the place feel right, again." Delta snorted. "You can't even make biscuits."

"I don't have to cook. I'll hire Becka and Cleo to do the cooking and run the place. Even if their biscuits aren't as good as yours, it'll be all right. You know, running a restaurant is just about marketing an image. People don't have to know you're not in the kitchen anymore. They'll just be happy that The Crossroads Café is up and running again."

She stared at me. "I want to see y'all pull this off. Go ahead. It's a deal."

My heart sank. So much for my charm. I pinned a casual smile to my face and thrust out my hand, the scarred one. "Good. Shake on it."

We shook. I grabbed my purse and walked out.

Pike paced on the front porch. Thomas leaned against a post, staying out of his way. Both of them looked at me hopefully. "Did you talk some sense into her?" Pike asked.

"No, but I bought the café."

"You what?"

"I should have known I couldn't bluff her. So now we move to Plan

B. We rebuild, we go forward, and we hope Delta changes her mind. Thomas is already working on the blueprints."

Pike pivoted toward Thomas. "Can you do it, Tommy-Son? Bring the place back to life, just like it was?"

Thomas shook his head. "No. I can only create the illusion. Delta has to do the rest."

"What if she doesn't bite?"

I gave Pike a hug. "She never gave up on me. She never gave up on Thomas. We're never going to give up on her, either. She'll bite."

I looked at Thomas. He nodded firmly for Pike's benefit but looked less certain when he stole a glance my way.

The sacred biscuit of hope was in our hands, now.

PART SEVEN

The future belongs to those who believe in the beauty of their dreams.

—*Eleanor Roosevelt*

It's wonderful to watch a pretty woman with character grow beautiful.

—*Mignon McLaughlin*

It matters more what's in a woman's face than what's on it.

—*Claudette Colbert*

Chapter 28

Cathy
Restoration

Everyone in the county had something to contribute to the new café; everyone wanted Delta's faith in biscuits to be restored. Alberta and Macy showed up from the start, with their hammering women. "We're here to work, even if you don't like it," Alberta grumbled, obviously pissed that I owned the place. "You don't even have to pay us."

"Good. I enjoy being verbally abused for free."

"You're not really serious about managing the restaurant yourself when it's finished, are you? That's a joke, right?"

"Oh how I adore your sunny confidence in my abilities."

"You can't just give the restaurant a makeover and think Delta will buy into your fantasy."

"Watch me. A good makeover can change a woman's life."

Alberta glared at me. "Is that kind of superficial shit still all you think about? The world can't be fixed by a new hairdo and the right shade of eye shadow. Looks aren't everything. Haven't you learned anything since you got roasted in that Trans Am?"

I stepped towards her so fast she blinked and took a step back. "Self-image is not a frivolous thing, and makeup is not the enemy," I hissed. "Some women feel empowered by their brains, some by their brawn, but other women feel empowered by their mascara. You could use a good green eyeliner and a beige foundation that takes the red out of your complexion. A makeover wouldn't undermine your image as a burly butch goddess."

Alberta sputtered. "You can kiss my un-madeup ass."

"No doubt that could use some makeup, too. And probably some cellulite cream and a good waxing."

I thought Alberta was going to hit me. I balled up my fist to hit her back. Then a miracle happened. A chuckle bubbled up in her mouth like indigestion. It bulged her lips, and she fought it, but it finally escaped. *Bwahahaha.* "Correction. That's 'burly *bitch* goddess.'"

Macy, watching from the sidelines, looked relieved. I thrust out my scarred hand to Alberta. "I accept your apology."

Her chuckle evaporated. "For what?"

"Oh, don't make me go through the whole long list."

She stared at my hand. No more demure, girly, left-handed squeezes. A womanly shake. Macy nudged her. Alberta sighed. "All right. You're tougher than I thought. For a beauty queen and a third-rate heterosexual actress. But you're no Angelina Jolie."

"Don't make me come after you with a pair of sharp tweezers."

We shook. Sort of arm-wrestled, but it was a start.

Thomas

I knew I could rebuild the café in a way that saved all its quirky charms. That never worried me for a second. But people see what they want to see in buildings, and yes, old buildings have a feel about them that not even the most meticulous attention to detail can't salvage.

"Okay, here's what we're going to do," I told the crowd, fronted by Cathy and the girls. Armed with old knives and forks, we gathered around stacks of pristine new lumber in the café's parking lot. "Poke these planks, scrape them, do whatever you want. When we're done, we want every plank to look as if it's a hundred years old."

The sound of cutlery hitting lumber filled the warm air. As Cathy prodded a board with a steak knife she looked at me askance. "Are you sure these boards will end up with a fashionably 'distressed' look, or will they just look *mad*?"

"After some creative paint work they'll look like the café's original lumber, I promise." I dragged a tarnished, gnarled salad fork over the wood. "The problem with a restoration is that the new edition of an old building turns out too pristine, too clean. The scars are erased. The character is gone. Without imperfections the appeal is only superficial."

I continued forking the board, and she said nothing else. Her silence worried me, and I looked over. She was gazing at me in a way that instantly made me hard. "I know I've asked you already," she said softly, "but will you marry me?"

Women. I'd never understand how their minds worked. Offer them a little architectural philosophy and they get hot.

Not that I was complaining.

"Sure," I told her.

Like most men, I didn't fantasize about weddings. Couldn't tell you what the rituals were for, why the tiny flower girl had to zigzag down the aisle like a fluffy pinball, why the ringbearer had to be barely old enough to wear a tiny tux over his Huggies, much less carry the ring pillow right side up, or why women spent so much time agonizing over the exact flowers for the bouquets and the exact configuration of the tables at the reception.

All I knew was this: I wanted to marry Cathy, to have a wedding with her, but I had to rebuild the café first to do it.

"We're agreed then," we said. "We want to hold our wedding at the café, when it re-opens in the fall."

Sentimental, the perfect place, a meaningful setting, yes.

Agreed. Dammit. To wait until fall.

In the meantime, we divided our days between the renovation at the farm and construction in the Cove. The girls threw themselves into the busy schedule, and we enjoyed a lot of happy days, family days. We cooked big meals in the new kitchen and listened to the Grand Ol' Opry via streaming audio on the living room computer on Saturday nights. We walked the woods and panned for gems in the creek and visited a goat breeder and bought Banger a harem of beautiful Cashmere does, then went to a chicken house and bought Herman a flock of robust Rhode Island Red hens. They towered over him in the new yard of the fancy new chicken house like big red *hausfraus* to his one-eyed, scrawny Barney Fife. He was thrilled. We hired a lawyer in Turtleville to start the adoption process for the girls, and we sat down with Cora and Ivy one night in the living room to make sure they understood.

"This is permanent," Cathy told them. "Okay? We're going to be a family in all the ways we can be one. You'll live with us permanently, and you'll tell everyone you're our daughters. You can tell everyone we're your mom and dad, if you like."

I added, "We'll hold onto you both so tightly that, sometimes, you'll wish we'd let go."

"Promise, Mommy?" Cora asked.

"That's cool, Mom and Dad," Ivy said.

Pretty simple. The most profound decisions often are.

That night, after the girls were asleep, Cathy drank a good red wine and I sipped from her glass. The toxic vodka demon was gone. I had a harmless taste for the vintages of grapes. "To our daughters, and to our vineyard," Cathy said, holding up the wine glass.

"We're going to have a vineyard as well as daughters? You've decided?"

She nodded. "You like the idea?"

I thought about it. Grapes, wine, wine-tastings, cheese, crackers, friends, family, fertility. To be a vintner. To have vinted. "Yes," I said emphatically.

She smiled. "I've got an idea for a name. A name for our label. 'Tree of Life .' What do you think? 'Tree of Life Wines.' A salute to your idol, Frank Lloyd Wright. And we can put an aerial picture of your 'Tree of Life' trellis design into the vineyard brochure. And use the abstract tree logo on t-shirts and coffee mugs. Think of the merchandising!"

I stroked her cheek with the backs of my fingers. "Why don't we call the wine label 'Wild Woman Ridge,' instead? Good alliteration. 'Wild Woman Ridge Wines.'"

She looked pleased. "But what would the logo be?"

"How about a crazed woman with her hair on fire, chasing a goat who's eating a cell phone?"

She stared at me wide-eyed, processing the image from a slightly lubed perspective. For a second I was afraid the fire joke had been too much. Then that famous smile, the little-seen-in-recent-times megawatter, lit her face. "Okay. We'll work on it."

A few days later, Cathy bought me an early wedding present. It arrived right after we finished the new master bedroom. Bert and Roland picked it up in Asheville for her and delivered it on Bert's aging, open flatbed. The sight of it in several big boxes marked BED must have entertained most of Jefferson County by the time it reached our ridge.

"It's a Stickly," Cathy said, looking up at me anxiously for any hint of displeasure or rejection. A man can go a long way on an adoring look like that from the woman he loves. "A reproduction, because Gustav Stickly didn't make king-sized bedsteads originally. But it's the Stickly company,

Delta traveled a lot that summer. She never came to the construction site, and when forced to drive by it, she looked the other way. She and Pike even took the grandkids on a Caribbean cruise, though Jeb confided to us that his mother still had bad memories of children in the thrall of water.

Alberta and Macy held an impromptu Log Splitter concert that night at the quilting bee. "We like to think we're developing a Dixie Chicks sound," Alberta announced over the microphone. "Only edgier, and with no love songs about men."

I chewed my tongue and wisely made no comment.

Becka launched the quilt project with this announcement. "We could be traditional and do a pattern—'Crazy Patch,' or 'Sampler,' but I think this calls for something different. So. Everybody. Just stitch your little squares together in whatever form you want, and we'll piece it all into one big crazy-patch quilt top later. It'll represent all of us, and it will be unique, if nothing else."

I watched Dolores parcel out yellow and green fabric. "What are you making?" I asked.

"Abstract yellow roses."

Toots organized her fabric squares in splotches of green and pink. "What are you making?" I asked.

She smiled. "A golf course. The fifteenth hole at the Masters, to be precise. The pink section is the azaleas."

Ivy immediately arranged her fabric squares into stacks sorted by print pattern, and began outlining a large architectural shape. "Are you making the Vatican?" I asked.

"The Biltmore mansion," she explained patiently.

Thomas had taken the girls to see the fabulous estate in Asheville. Ivy and Thomas spent their visit discussing the architecture. Ivy gazed at my jumble of squares. "What are you making?"

"I call it . . . 'Oscar Night.' This tiny little red-rose print represents the red carpet. These blue and gold fleur-de-lis squares are the bleachers where the fans sit." I pointed at a garish purple square. "And there's Joan Rivers."

"Do you miss it?" she asked. "Being on the red carpet and all that stuff?"

I could lie, but I didn't. "Yes," I said.

Later, as I hunched over my creation, Thomas came over, gently placed his hands on my shoulders, and studied my work. "No photographers on your red carpet?" he asked.

"Never."

He pressed his fingertips into my muscles, massaging, trying to take the memory of the cruel lens at the crash away.

I shivered. Photographers. Cameras. I'd have to face them again soon. The speech in Asheville was never far from my mind.

Chapter 29

Cathy
The Speech

The café was finished. Closed and empty, but done.

Thomas and I scheduled our wedding ceremony for October. It would be a small, loving event with the girls as bridesmaids, Delta as the matron of honor and Thomas's brother, John, as the best man. John and Monica would be bringing their boys. They'd meet their new cousins, Cora and Ivy, for the first time.

"Maybe we can lure Delta inside the new café by threatening to hire a caterer," I told everyone. "Surely she wouldn't let a stranger take over her kitchen."

"Looks like the old café, only cleaner," Pike proclaimed. "A good job." The Crossroads Quilters—of which Ivy and I were now regular members—hung our weird quilt on a wall in the new dining room. Ivy's Biltmore Estate design impressed everyone. My homage to Oscar night looked more like a strange garden with a red walkway. But people were polite in their praise.

Thomas handed Delta the key to the café's new front door. She sat at her sunroom's wicker table, pretending to read a newspaper. "I installed the old lockset in a new front door," Thomas pointed out. "So that's your original key. And it opens the door just the way it always did."

She continued to read the newspaper, or pretend to. "It's y'all's restaurant, now. Y'all keep the key."

I pushed the key under her newspaper. "No, you keep it. Think about the possibilities."

She pushed the key away. "I don't have to think about the possibilities. I'm retired."

I pushed the key back. "You're only fifty."

She pushed the key away. "Becka's pregnant again. Now I'll have time to play with a new grandbaby, not just plop it on a prep counter while I salt a squash casserole."

I snapped. "All this time you lectured Thomas and me about how to live our lives. About never giving up. About keeping the faith, the hope. And we believed you. We rebuilt the café because we were sure you'd come back to your senses. If you really believe you can stop caring about other people—that you can stop nurturing and nourishing other people—then hide here in this sunroom for the rest of your life. But if you want to see how much your inspiration has changed my life, then take this."

I slid a folded card toward her. "This is an invitation to my speech at the burn association's meeting in Asheville. If you don't come to see me, I'll know you never really cared."

I walked out.

🐾🐾🐾🐾🐾

Terror. It soaked my bones, slithered through my veins, layered ice onto my skin. As Thomas pulled the Hummer into the parking deck of the Asheville Civic Center that crisp autumn afternoon I sat stiffly, frozen in the front passenger seat, silently rehearsing my speech again. It was neatly printed in large, bold type on a sheaf of papers. I had memorized it, recited it a thousand times, performed it in front of the girls, Thomas, the cat, the puppies, the chickens, the goats, and all the wildlife on the ridge.

But I had not performed it in front of strangers. Strangers in public. Strangers in public who had cameras. All these months, every step I'd taken outside the sanctuary of the Cove had been carefully orchestrated, my face covered by hoods, scarves and then artful hair, my audience a trustworthy one of friends and neighbors, people who didn't take pictures, people who didn't talk to reporters, people who didn't judge.

"Can we go to dinner after you talk, Mommy?" Cora asked from the back seat. "I want pizza. Daddy says we can go out and eat like regular people after you get over tonight."

Ivy shushed her. "Mom's concentrating. There's lot of statistics in her speech. She's gotta get 'em right. Chill out."

"What are statistics?"

"Numbers, sweetie," Thomas said, glancing in the rearview mirror as he shoehorned the Hummer into a parking space. "Your mom likes numbers more than personal anecdotes."

Mouthing the last page of my speech, I ignored his snide implication. I wasn't interested in confessing intimate details of my experience to a room full of gawkers. I planned a formal performance, an impersonal act. As I lipped the words I tilted my head, angled my shoulders, lifted and lowered my chin—every move a practiced nuance. I'd crafted every inflection, every facial expression, every body pose, for the entire thirty-minute speech. My topic? *The Beauty Culture—An Insiders' Perspective On Self-Image.* Thomas and Ivy had helped me research all sorts of serious psychological and sociological studies. My speech was filled with factoids and summaries of scientific opinion. It sounded important, solemn, academic. *Look, the Southern-belle geisha knows big words and percentages.* Yes, and the actress knew how to sell a boring speech that revealed nothing about her personal pain.

"Showtime," Thomas said gently, breaking my anxious reverie. The Hummer was still and silent. We had parked. He and the girls watched me worriedly. I folded my speech, tucked it in my purse, and checked my face in the visor mirror. Shield of hair over the scarred side, check. Snug turtle-neck sweater to hide my scarred neck, check. Tailored jacket and pants to hide the scarred arm and leg, check. Pleasant, unrevealing expression on my face, check.

"Showtime," I echoed in an octave high enough for a piccolo.

As we walked into the civic center the girls trotted close beside Thomas and me. Cora held our hands and swung them merrily. Ivy tucked an arm through mine and patted the sleeve of my jacket. "Mom," she said quietly, as we entered through a service door, "Even if you throw up, it'll be cool, okay?"

I hugged her. "I just hope no one photographs me hurling chunks. I don't want to be the star of a sixty-second spew-video on the Internet."

Dr. Bartholomew smiled sheepishly as he greeted us in a back hall. "I'm sure you're accustomed to drawing a crowd, but we're stunned at what's happening."

"I'm trying not to think about it."

He had scheduled me for an ordinary workshop room, as he'd

promised back in the summer. Thirty, forty people in the audience. But a couple of days later the burn association blurbed my appearance in its online newsletter, and afterwards the programming chair was flooded by media inquiries—*USA Today* and the *Los Angeles Times*, to name a few, and all the big entertainment magazines, like *People* and *Star*, and *Entertainment Tonight*—plus a stampede of members asking that the association move me to a bigger room. So Dr. Bartholomew had switched my speech to the civic center's ballroom, which seated a few hundred. But then so many reporters asked for press passes, and so many members asked for a bigger venue, that Dr. Bartholomew had asked my permission to super-size my audience one more time. I'd agreed fearfully.

"Exactly where am I giving my little speech now?" I asked in a small voice.

His smile became a hopeful wince. "The Thomas Wolfe Auditorium."

"That sounds big."

"It's where the Asheville symphony performs." He paused, wincing harder. "It seats 2,500." Another pause, and now his face was a prune of apology. "It's packed."

My knees went weak. Thomas grabbed me by the elbow. "She needs a minute to adjust to this idea. Some place private."

"Absolutely. Follow me. I'll take you backstage."

I numbly let Thomas tow me to the auditorium complex. The girls hurried along behind, their mouths open in awe. "Wait right here with Dr. Bartholomew," Thomas told them, then led me into a dressing room and shut the door.

He took me by the shoulders. "You've performed in front of tough audiences all your life. These people are burn victims and medical professionals who treat burn victims. They're on your side. You can do this, Cathy. You can do it."

I pulled away from him and paced, hunching a little, clutching my stomach with shaking hands. "National media. Dozens of photographers. All wanting the first pictures of me and my scars."

Thomas blocked my way, pried my hands away from my navel, and held them to his chest. "You," he said in a graveled voice, "are the woman who didn't scream when nurses scraped your raw skin. You are the woman who crossed the mountains in a snowstorm to find your grandmother's house and then camp out there without heat, without electricity, without running water, alone. You are the woman who saved the lives of two helpless puppies. You are the woman who made a home for two unwanted little girls. You are the woman who put everyone else's safety ahead of your own during the fire at the café. You are the woman who refuses to give up on Delta." He lifted my hands to his mouth, kissed them, then finished, "You are the woman who saved my life, and who makes my life worth living. *You can give this speech.*"

I gazed up at him, sagged a little, and nodded. "I'll get through it. I will. Somehow."

He kissed me on the forehead so as not to smudge my makeup. "The girls and I will be in the front row, rooting for you. Just look at us and forget everyone else."

I exhaled long and slow, then straightened. "Okay. Okay." *Settle. Breathe. Focus.* "Okay." My mantra. Okay.

"I love you."

"I love you, too." Thomas headed for the door. Just before he walked out I said, "Thomas? All the things you listed? I couldn't have done them without you."

He looked back at me with a quiet smile. "And we'll get through this speech together, too."

The door shut quietly behind him.

I faced the dressing room's brightly lit makeup mirrors. For the first time since that day at the *Four Seasons*, nearly eighteen months earlier, I was stepping in front of the world. That time, I saw biscuits and tragedy in the glass.

This time, I only saw my fear.

Thomas

"Will Mommy be okay?" Cora asked as we found our seats on the front row, center. She stared up at the crowded balcony, then the packed main floor. "All these people came to see Mommy? But Mommy doesn't want to see *them*."

I nodded. "But she'll be fine."

Ivy nudged me. "Dad, look at all those guys with cameras right in front of the stage. There must be, like, a hundred of 'em. She's gonna freak."

"No, she won't. She's a star. You'll see."

I wish I felt as confident as I sounded. We sat down. I looked at Delta's empty seat next to mine, and crossed my fingers.

346

🌣🌣🌣🌣🌣

"Ladies and Gentlemen, SEBSA is pleased to welcome Cathryn Deen."

Applause. The deep, rolling clatter of it, an orgasmic wave of sound. In the old days I'd love that swell of appreciation, the whistles, the sound of my name being yelled among the clapping.

Now I had to force one foot in front of the other, had to make myself smile as I walked onto the elegantly lit stage before all those people, all those cameras. Blinding, terrifying. *Trapped. I'm trapped out here, now. All I can do is throw up, run off the stage, or collapse. A pathetic sight, just like last year at the accident, captured for the curious and the mean and the greedy to enjoy, preserved in the uncaring ether of a computer's mind, to be shared in seconds with people all over the planet.*

I shook Dr. Bartholomew's hand. He waved me toward a spotlight. I tried to breathe normally. The portable mike on my turtleneck would pick up even the smallest groan of hyperventilating horror. I walked numbly to a handsome podium and laid my speech there, then stood, staring at the cameras, the glaring lights, the audience. Applause. It went on, rising and falling. My hands shook by my sides. I couldn't inhale. If I didn't get myself under control my voice would fracture, I'd squeak when I talked, and these people, the whole world, would realize how weak I really was. I'd never cracked on stage, before. My heart pounded so hard the mike might pick up the staccato drumbeat.

Finally, the audience grew quiet. I still just stood there, afraid to speak. Slowly I began to study the faces looking back at me. So many of them were scarred, deformed by fire. Much worse than mine. What could I say to people who had suffered worse that I had? What kind of statistic or mealy-mouthed formality could sum up what they'd been through, what they lived with, and what they now understood about life without the veneer of physical perfection?

I darted a frantic gaze over the front row, squinting past the wall of cameras. Thomas and the girls. If I could just find them. There. There they were. Looking up at me with all their love. Thomas sat on the edge of his seat, trying to appear calm, supportive, casual, no-big-deal-if-you-go-catatonic-honey. But failing. He looked worried.

He wanted so badly for me to do well. I managed to gear my frozen eyes down to the text of my speech. The words were big and bold and dull and waiting. *I want to thank the Southeastern Burn Survivors Association for inviting me here today. I'm here to talk to you all about the meaning of personal appearance in American culture . . .*

I opened my mouth. Nothing came out. I swallowed hard, reached for the glass of water on the podium, sipped some, watched water splash from the glass because my hand was shaking so hard.

I can't do this. I can't. Thomas, I'm sorry. I can't.

People shifted a little in their seats, glancing at one another, holding their breaths. I sensed the worst thing a performer can feel in a theater—the dreaded vibe of the awkward silence. *Ignore it. Look at Thomas and the girls, look just at them, and try to ignore everyone else and . . . say something, say anything!* Frantically I peered at the front row again. I locked my gaze on Thomas, but he nodded to his left. My eyes responded automatically. Left. Look to his left.

Delta.

Delta sat there, looking up at me with tears in her eyes and one hand on her heart. She knew I was sinking fast. She grabbed a big, plasticware serving plate off her lap, flipped the lid off it, and held the platter up.

Biscuits, she mouthed.

Biscuits. She was baking again! Our symbol for everything good, everything hopeful, everything worth believing in, everything worth fighting for. She had brought biscuits as an apology for her temporary loss of faith and to remind me who I was, and who I always would be. I was Mary Eve Nettie's granddaughter and Delta Whittlespoon's cousin. The heir to the sacred dough.

I looked down at my speech. *It's now or never. People will see you the way you want them to, but you have to tell them who you are, not who they think you are. Tell them. Tell them. Tell them.*

I picked up my speech. I held it high, turned it sideways, put one hand on either end. I tore the papers in half. Then I tore the halves in half, and the half-halves into fourths. Then I tossed the pieces into the air like confetti. Cameras flashed.

The entire auditorium went even more silent. People gaped at me. At least I had everyone's rapt attention. I left the podium and, still not saying a word, walked to the edge of the stage. I looked down into the bank of cameras, then out at the audience. I shrugged my jacket off. The turtleneck was sleeveless. I tossed the jacket behind me onto the podium, then gracefully raised my scarred right arm so everyone could see it. Like a game-show hostess outlining a prize washing machine, I swept my left hand along the length of the right. *Here's the new Cathryn Deen arm, from shoulder to fingertips, see the deep pink scar tissue of the arm and the gnarled flesh of the hand. This fine appendage is yours to photograph, to look at, to stare at in open pity or even disgust. Free!*

Cameras flashed.

Next, still not speaking, I angled my right foot forward, the knee flexed slightly, the toe pointed. I swept my hands down it. *Abracadabra. And now for the new Cathryn Deen leg.* I hitched up the flared pants leg until it clotted above my knee and I could pull it no higher. The scars swirled down the outside of my knee and calf, ending at a grotesque tendril that curved over the top of my foot.

Cameras flashed.

I let my pants leg drop back into place. Next, I raised my hands, palms up, then palms down, fingers fanning toward my face. *And now, for the grand finale.* Sinking my hands into my carefully coiffed shield of hair, I fluffed wildly, destroying the hair-welding alchemy of mousse and gel and spray. Then I swept my freed hair back from my face. I turned my head so everyone could get a good look at the scars, the ruined hairline, the ugly ear. Some people gasped.

Cameras flashed endlessly.

I posed. I gave them what they wanted—no, this time, I gave them what *I* wanted. My timing was impeccable. I still had what it took to mesmerize a crowd. Let the photographers get their fill, let the entire auditorium full of reporters, photographers, fellow burn survivors, doctors and nurses and therapists see the reality, let them all get a good, long look.

The only people whose opinions I cared about were seated in the front row, and when I looked calmly down at them, they were all smiling. The girls grinned up at me. Delta laughed and cried with her arms circling the platter of biscuits; Thomas had tears on his face but he nodded his fervent approval. *Yes, this is who you are, and I love you for it.*

I strolled back to the podium, folded my jacket, and rested my hands on either side of the lectern. I cleared my throat. "Just like everyone else with a less-than-perfect body in this auditorium tonight, I'm not a burn victim. I'm a burn *survivor*. A year ago, every time I looked at myself, I wanted to die." My voice was clear and strong and confident. "But today I can honestly tell you that if I could turn back time and prevent the accident that scarred me—but that would mean giving up the people who've become part of my life because of that accident, the people I have come to love in this new life of mine, in this new body of mine, the people who love me regardless of these scars—if I could choose to be beautiful again, but lose those people—*I'd choose to be scarred.*"

The audience went wild. People leapt to their feet, clapping with scarred hands, crying with scarred faces. I would stand there for the next hour-and-a-half, telling them the story of the past eighteen months in honest detail, about the pain, the fears, the failures, but also about the love, the lessons, and the victories. They would applaud again and again, and the standing ovation I would receive when I finished would go on for ten minutes.

But for the moment I basked in the simple pleasure of my own courage, amazed that I could stand there comfortably, looking out at my people—I had people, again!— and then I sought Thomas's loving eyes, and I gave him my biggest smile, the movie-star one. And he nodded and laughed.

The night was all good, from then on.

Thomas

Cathy did it. She reclaimed herself, got her mojo back, told the world to look at her on her terms or go take a flying leap. An incredible night, heady, laughing, joyful. Delta being there, that was the key. The gravy on the biscuit, yes. Afterward, Pike, who couldn't get a seat at the packed event, met us in the civic center's ballroom, where the SEBSA organizers quickly set up a reception for her adoring audience. Cathy stayed for an hour, signing autographs, posing for pictures with other burn survivors and medical people. She offered to participate in fundraisers for burn research, making Dr. Bartholomew and the other board members ecstatic.

What she wouldn't do was talk to the press. I'd never seen reporters sweat that hard to push burn patients out of their way without success. It wasn't pretty.

"They got what they wanted when they took all those photos of me tonight," she explained with a shrug. "They couldn't care less what I have to say. They got the pictures." She wasn't bitter, just practical.

And then we left. "We have kids to feed, and we're going to dinner," she said. Priorities. We took the girls, Delta, and Pike to a pizza restaurant, and we sat in a corner and laughed and ate and relived the extraordinary speech while people stared and some came over to ask for Cathy's autograph, and some of those took pictures of her, for which she smiled and waved.

Then Delta reached into her purse and got our two torn halves of Cathy's check for the café, and laid them on the table in front of Cathy.

"I reject your offer," she said. "It just took me a few months to say so."

She and Cathy got teary and hugged and we toasted with a round of beer, and then we ate a second pizza. Cathy and I drove back to the Cove with the girls happily asleep in the Hummer's back seat. At home, with the girls in bed and a new moon peeking over the red-and-gold autumn forest, we changed into jeans and Giants jerseys then sat on the veranda steps with one of Mary Eve's quilts around us.

Cathy reached into a pocket of her robe and held out a small, torn package. "This came two days ago from New York. Anthony delivered it. Delta waylaid it. And I, I admit shamelessly, I opened it to see what it was. Because it's from your sister-in-law."

I took the open bubble mailer from her with a sense of fatality. "I should have known Ravel would go for the jugular one more time. But don't worry. I've made my peace with her, whether it's mutual or not."

"Take a look at what she sent you."

I pulled wads of bubble wrap from the package, unfolded it down to a clump that fit in my palm, then slowly reached inside.

The watch. The heirloom silver pocket watch Sherryl had given me on Ethan's last birthday. I turned it in my hand tenderly. "Was there a note?"

"No. I think the watch says it all."

I nodded. I tucked the watch into my jeans. Enough said, yes. I had my keepsakes, all of them. "A new moon," I said to Cathy. We huddled together and watched it rise.

Thomas

I carried a shovel and the small package, wrapped in one of my Giants jerseys, to the Nettie cemetery behind the house. It was a beautiful morning, a little before nine on September eleventh.

The first plane hadn't struck the towers, yet.

I dug a deep, narrow grave among the heirloom tombstones of Cathy's people, my people now. Then I knelt beside it and unfolded my jersey for a last look inside. I ran my fingers over Ethan's toy truck. I rested my hand on the keepsake, one last time.

I buried my grief for my son, not my memories, but my grief. I cried. Then I stood and wiped my face, and put the shovel on my shoulder, and walked back up the path through the woods.

Cathy and the girls were waiting for me at the edge of the back yard. When they saw me walk out of the woods, Cathy patted the girls on their shoulders. *Now. Go see him, now.*

Cora and Ivy ran up to me and held out their hands. They looked up at me with worried, gentle eyes. "Are you okay, Dad?" Ivy said.

"Are you okay, Daddy?" Cora whispered.

I took their hands, curled them inside mine, met Cathy's smiling tears, stalled until my voice would work, then said to our daughters, "Yes, I'm fine. I really am."

And we walked back inside together, the four of us, on that morning.

Cathy

"Mom, you're on CNN!" Ivy called. She and Cora, followed by the galloping cat and barking puppies, ran into the kitchen, where I was stoically waiting for another batch of inedible biscuits to come out of the oven. Thomas, sitting at the kitchen table checking the news via a laptop computer, nodded. "Your mom's everywhere. They're showing clips from the speech all over the Internet. Calling her 'a remarkable story of courage and inspiration.'" He grinned at me. "Don't get big-headed about it."

"I've got biscuits to mangle. People can call me whatever they like. Talk won't brown a biscuit, that's all I care about."

"Mommy, you *are* a star!" Cora exclaimed, hugging me by one leg. "Does this mean we're stars, too?"

"Absolutely." I stroked her hair absent-mindedly as I peered through the oven's glass door. Damn biscuits. They didn't seem to be rising at all, this morning. I'd never get them right. I sighed and sat down across from Thomas. The girls flopped into chairs beside us. Ivy laid my cell phone on the table. "Shouldn't we turn this back on and see if anybody's called since last night?"

"I guess. Sure."

I'd turned the phone off on the way home from Asheville. I knew there'd be calls from reporters. The usual fluff. Ivy switched my phone on and hunched over it, studying the screen. "Whoa," she said softly. "Dad, look."

Thomas glanced at the phone and did a double-take. "I'd say you have a few messages here. In fact, so many you're getting a notice that your message capacity has maxed out."

I *harrumphed* and got up. "Big deal. I've got Rhode Island Red eggs to scramble while I wait for the biscuits to finish doing whatever awful thing they're going to do this morning."

"Mom!" the girls wheedled.

"All right. Ivy, play a few messages back on the speaker function, where we can all enjoy the sillier questions. I bet you a nickel the first ten calls are from tabloids wanting to know if I'm going to start my own line of miracle scar-reducing cream or if I'm having an alien-hybrid baby with George Clooney."

Thomas arched a brow. "I didn't suffer through that alien probe so you could get jiggy with *him*, instead."

I grinned as I cracked big brown, homegrown eggs into one of Granny's ceramic mixing bowls. Ivy fiddled with the phone. "Okay. All set. Here goes."

Beep. "Cathryn, hi! This is Brad Harris with ProtoToon. I'd love to talk to you about some doing voice work in our proposed Robin Williams animated feature. Great speech last night. I totally see you as a lioness."

Beep. "Cathryn, babe! Marcia Steen Conklin here. Casting director. You'd make a perfect mother for Superman. The next sequel. Flashback to his Smallville years. Young Mrs. Kent. We can work your new look into the script. I am so serious. Call me, okay?"

Beep. "Cathryn. This is you-know-who. Don't make me beg. Call me, all right?"

Everyone looked at me. "Who was that lady?" Ivy asked. "Her voice sounded really familiar."

"Oprah," I said.

It went on like that for dozens of calls. Offers, solid ones, and 'call me's' from all the major players, including studio heads. My agent had left a dozen messages. The first one said, "Hey, I told you to find some great guy and get married and have some babies, but I didn't think you'd get a fiancé, two daughters, a farm, a café, a vineyard, pets and a goat within a year. Listen, what I said before about your options? Forget it. It's a whole new world after that speech. You're not just an actress anymore, not just a movie star. You're a symbol. You're a role model. And good role models can get good roles."

And then, finally, there was the call that brought me to a halt with my hand on the oven door.

"Gerald, here," the deep, pompous voice said. "Cathryn. Come on. Be a team player. Let's put you back out in public. New campaign. The face of Flawless doesn't have to be Flawless. You looked fabulous last night. With the right lighting, hey, the sky's the limit. I never gave up on you, you know. We can still do business together."

Click.

Thomas and I looked at each other. He looked at the phone. His jaw tightened. So did mine. A small vein throbbed in his cheek. A larger one throbbed in mine. I walked over, picked up the phone, and said quietly, "Allow me."

I went out the new kitchen door, through the side yard, and out to the fresh new fences of the goat pastures and the palatial goat barn. Thomas and the girls followed me. Banger and his ladies looked up from a delicious pile of hay. I held the cell phone through the fence to him. "A special treat. This one's loaded with high-calorie sweet-talk. Want it?"

"Bah," he said happily, and crunched the phone between his teeth.

I pivoted to find Thomas's grim look fading to a smile. The girls looked up at us, frowning.

"Mom, you're not going to take any of those offers?" Ivy said. "Not even Superman's mother?"

"We're not moving the Hollywood are we?" Cora asked. "I don't think the chickens'd be happy there."

"We're not moving," I promised, holding Thomas gaze. "But I might accept a good offer from time to time. Can't hurt to make a little extra money here and there. And get some publicity for Wild Woman Ridge Winery. Hmmm?"

Thomas chuckled and nodded. "I totally see you as a lioness."

So did I.

Ivy turned toward the farm road, listening. "Somebody's coming."

Pike's patrol car rumbled into the yard. We hurried over. "Delta's cooking," he yelled. "Come on down to the café. She's back in the kitchen!"

"Grab your coats," Thomas told the girls. "I'll feed the puppies and the cat, and—"

"My biscuits are still in the oven," I moaned, running for the house. This would be the worst batch ever. I rushed into the kitchen, flung the oven door open, and peered inside as I swiped a pair of oven mitts off the counter.

I halted, staring.

"The Lard cooks in mysterious ways," I whispered.

❦❦❦❦❦

Word spread like the aroma of good food. The Crossroads Café reopened that morning without any pre-opening publicity, yet the parking lot was full by the time we arrived. Thomas and I headed into the new kitchen via the new back door.

"Fry that ham a little harder," Delta commanded cheerfully. "Get that new griddle up to temperature! And somebody, please, somebody stir another stick of butter into those grits."

Becka, Cleo, Jeb, Bubba, Alberta, Macy, Dolores and the Judge hurried in all directions. Thomas and I ducked into a safe corner. Delta pivoted and saw us. "Make yourselves useful!"

I came towards her like a peasant bringing a gift to a queen. I held out a shallow bread basket draped in one of my grandmother's embroidered dish clothes. "I did it," I whispered.

Thomas ceremoniously pulled the cloth from atop the basket. A small mountain of golden-brown biscuits waited underneath. Delta laughed and applauded. "I told you it was all about having the right heart. They look perfect!"

"More important, they taste perfect."

She plucked one from the top, studied it the way a wine connoisseur studies a great cabernet, then broke the biscuit apart with her hands. "Flaky, buttery-smelling, just right," she crooned. Slowly she put a piece in her mouth, shut her eyes, chewed and swallowed. She gave a laugh, looked at me with glowing eyes, and held out her arms. "You're a biscuit-maker now, cousin!"

We hugged. "How would you like to meet Oprah?" I asked.

"Oh, sure. Any ol' day. And the Queen of England, and Dolly Parton." She thought I was joking. I let it go, for now. Plenty of time to discuss my plans for her cooking show. Forget the Food Network. We'd produce and sell our own videos. 'Cooking at the Crossroads with Delta,' or something catchy like that.

Delta took my biscuits and set them on a steam table. "Serve those up," she told the gang. "Biscuits aren't meant just to be admired; they're meant to nourish the wounded soul and feed the aching heart."

My biscuits were whisked into the new dining rooms. On that morning I began to feed the soulfully needy, to share my wisdom of the golden crust. Thomas kissed me. "Flaky," he said, "but just right."

I laughed. "What can we do to help around here?" I asked Delta.

Delta pointed to a crate of apples. "Peel and slice. I feel some apple cobbler comin' on!"

Thomas and I carried the apples outside. We sat down under the oaks with a wash tub and paring knives, in the sunshine of the fall morning. Everything in life leads us where we're supposed to go. It's not always easy to see our destination in the middle of the journey. Thomas lost his son but found me and the girls. I lost my beauty, at least the easy version of it, but I found him, and the girls, and Delta and the café.

I wouldn't trade any of them for a perfect face. Never.

I looked at the breathtaking autumn panorama of the mountains. I listened to Cora and Ivy's laughter as they played with friends in the café's backyard. I thought of our animals at home, well-fed and safe. I inhaled the aroma of the café's kitchen. I thought of the warmth and friendship of the coming years. I looked at Thomas, contentedly working beside me. We'd have lots of happy decades to come. Years full of biscuits. Homemade and satisfying, filled with love. I put a hand to my heart.

This is how it feels to be beautiful.

Delta's Biscuit History and Recipes

"*Biscoctus.*"

That's Latin for *biscuit*, and it translates as "twice cooked."

According to food historian Lynne Olver, editor and researcher at foodtimeline.org, the traditional Southern biscuit—a soft, leavened bread instead of a hard cracker—was mentioned in travelers' journals as early as 1818 and appeared in Webster's Dictionary by 1828. Nineteenth-century recipe books—especially those in the South—included instructions for "soda biscuits" or "baking-soda biscuits," and by the 1850's cookbooks also noted a curious cousin, the "beaten biscuit."

Though often called the "Maryland Beaten Biscuit," the beaten biscuit was a staple of Deep-South and Mountain-South kitchens, often served up with thick slices of ham. Cooks literally beat the biscuit dough for at least thirty minutes to tenderize it, usually employing a wooden mallet or rolling pin, but a hammer or ax handle would suffice, too. While it's hard to pinpoint the exact ethnic origins of Southern biscuit-beating, we know for sure that English cooks were pummeling biscuit dough as early as the 1500's.

Beaten or not, the historic Southern biscuit consists of these basics: flour, salt, baking powder, water or milk, and lard—evil, wonderful, saturated-fat, high-cholesterol lard. Rendered pig fat. A Southern delight. Lard is white, gooey, delicious and a fabulous cooking ingredient due to its high smoking point. (People used it not only for baking, but as a topping, like butter.) It produces incredibly light, flaky biscuits (and also great pie crusts.) Many traditional cooks feel lard's charms outweigh its health risks. Just enjoy all foods in moderation, and never forget, as Delta says, "The Lard cooks in mysterious ways."

Purists *still* make their biscuits with lard, particularly the premium "leaf lard" rendered from high-quality fat around the pigs' kidneys. But in 1911 Proctor & Gamble introduced *Crisco*, a hydrogenated vegetable oil that was tasty, easy to store, and cheaper than either lard or butter. To teach housewives about the new product, Proctor & Gamble provided a cookbook full of *Crisco* recipes and hired home economists to demonstrate those recipes all over the country. (Read the history of *Crisco* at www.crisco.com.)

Of course, we now know that both lard and hydrogenated vegetable oil have nutritional drawbacks, but what's the thrill of Southern soul food without a little hellfire! Why, taking the flaky, fatty goodness out of a great biscuit would be like taking the moonlight out of the magnolias. Sacrilege!

Some Good Biscuit Recipes

A little trivia: Here are a few of the sacred names you'll see on the pantry shelves in a Southern kitchen: *White Lily* or *Gold Medal* (flour,) *Crisco* (vegetable shortening,) *Calumet* or *Clabber Girl* (baking powder.) A baking tip: Use a deep biscuit pan, not a cookie sheet. And make sure your baking pan is *shiny*. A dark pan will cause your biscuits to brown too much on the bottom.

Chuckwagon Biscuits

This one's only for a serious outdoors cook. You need a bed of coals and a black-iron Dutch oven. The feet of the oven let air circulate underneath as it sits in the coals, and the rimmed lid lets you pile coals on top to brown the biscuits.

Ingredients:

3 cups flour (not the self-rising kind)

6 teaspoons baking powder

3 tablespoon lard

1 cup of milk

1 teaspoon salt

1 tablespoon sugar

Grease your Dutch oven and let it start heating up in the coals. Set the lid in the coals—you want the lid warm, too.

Sift the dry items together then mold the lard into them by hand until the dough's texture is flaky. Add the milk to moisten the dough. Roll or pat the dough out on a floured board (the dough should be about an inch thick when you're finished,) then cut into biscuits. A clean tin can makes a good cutter!

Place biscuits in the oven—touching is okay, but don't crowd them together. Put your pre-warmed lid on the oven; fill it with coals. Now set the covered oven on glowing coals. The average baking time is about 20 minutes. Lift the lid and check to see if your biscuits are brown on top and bottom.

Old-Fashioned Soda Biscuits

2 cups flour (not self-rising)
1/2 teaspoon baking soda
1/2 teaspoon salt
1 teaspoon cream of tartar
2 tablespoons lard
1 cup milk

Sift the dry items together, add the lard, then add the milk while you slowly stir (a fork is good for stirring dough.) Roll the dough out on a floured board to about 1/2" thick, cut into biscuits. Bake at 425 degrees for about 15 minutes.

Old-Fashioned Beaten Biscuits

4 cups all-purpose flour (as always, this means not self-rising)
1 teaspoon baking powder
1/2 teaspoon salt
1 teaspoon sugar
1/2 cup lard
1/3 cup milk mixed with 1/3 cup water

Mix the flour, baking powder, salt and sugar. Add the lard and knead until you have a coarse, mealy consistency. Add just enough milk/water to make a stiff dough. Knead the dough then place it on a floured board.

Beat the dough for about 30 minutes. Turn it several times. The end result should be dough that "pops," and feels both smooth and elastic.

Pull off small chunks and shape into smooth balls by hand. Place on a cookie sheet; then be sure to prick each biscuit with a fork, making 3 rows of holes. Bake in a preheated oven at 400 degrees for about 20 minutes. The biscuits should be a light, golden brown.

THE CROSSROADS CAFÉ
READING GUIDE

1. If you could be any beautiful woman in the world, who would you be? Why?

2. Do you feel that your looks—good, bad or ordinary—have played a major part in shaping your life? How?

3. Our obsession with physical beauty is a focus of the book. Do you feel that society places unfair expectations on women in regard to their personal appearance?

4. Even in today's supposedly enlightened world, are women still judged primarily on their youthfulness and looks?

5. Does it concern you when notable women in business, academics and politics are critiqued for their appearance? Do you feel that men receive similar critiques in public?

6. Is it still true that "Men get character lines, but women get wrinkles?"

7. Do you feel that beautiful celebrities, like the book's Cathryn Deen, represent unrealistic and even destructive ideals for physical appearance?

8. Studies indicate that men enjoy looking at pretty young women more than women enjoy looking at pretty young men. In other words, that men rank physical appearance higher than women do. Do you agree?

9. Food—and all it represents in terms of family, comfort, and heritage—plays a thematic role in The Crossroads Café. What part does food play in your own family memories and reunions?

10. Thomas Mitternich is consumed with grief for his wife and son even four years after their deaths. At what point do you think grief becomes self-destructive?

11. Thomas's ability to see past Cathryn's scars is one of his most endearing traits. Despite Hollywood images of beauty and perfection, many people in "real life" lead happy, fulfilling love lives regardless of severe physical imperfections. Discuss true anecdotes from your own circle of family and friends.

12. Have you ever made—or seen others make—negative assumptions about strangers who are physically unattractive? Studies show that pretty people are assumed to be smarter, more successful and more likable.

Dedication

The inspiration for this story, the first ingredient of the recipe that later became this novel, started with a trip in search of flowers and food. Three women on a hunt for roses and lunch.

On a spring day many years ago, my mother and I, and our pal, Ceil, piled into a car at our Asheville hotel and headed north into the high Blue Ridge peaks of western North Carolina. Our mission was to find a rare-plant nursery we'd read about in a tourist brochure. And, as always, to eat a good meal. Women don't just shop. They shop and eat. It's a given.

An hour later, dizzy from weaving along a narrow two-lane road that zigzagged over the mountains like a snake wrapped around a rock, we wondered if we'd lose our lunch, not find it. One more double-back turn with nothing but perpendicular mountain rock on one side and thin air on the other, and food would be the last thing we wanted.

Finally, the roller-coaster road deposited us on the other side of the world in a high cove tucked between even higher ridges beneath a dome of Delft-blue sky. Sighing with relief, we cruised past wonderful little farms, chicken houses, fields full of cattle, and the greening squares of spring gardens. This was a place where most civilized roads competed with rocky creek beds for their route; there was always a creek to our left or right, hooded with big evergreens, its banks filling with lacy ferns. Elves. Elves must live in those North Carolina mountains. And unicorns and tiny dragons. The creek bottoms harbor magic.

Without really knowing how we got there, and with no idea what to expect, we found a quiet intersection in the woods. Our companion creek meandered nearby, passing beneath a narrow bridge before disappearing toward Tennessee. A crossroad headed to parts unknown. A few aged highway signs hinted that a mapmaker might be able to pinpoint this crossroads, but it would take a magnifying glass.

In one corner was a beautiful little farmhouse surrounded by gorgeous flower beds. On the opposite corner was the modern equivalent of a stagecoach stop: a mom-and-pop store, a couple of sun-faded gas pumps, a graveled parking lot, and, glory be, a small diner. We hurried inside and flopped down at a booth beside a huge picture window that overlooked the creek. A sturdy, smiling woman brought us handwritten menus listing the day's offerings. We gawked at a list that included every staple of a heavenly Southern meal: fried chicken, cream gravy, biscuits, casseroles, turnip greens, stewed peas, cornbread, creamed corn, homemade pickles, chow-chow, banana pudding, apple pie, and on and on and on.

We fanned ourselves with excitement. Nothing gives heart palpitations quicker to Southern women of a certain size than the prospect of a plate piled with all the major food groups cooked in a pound of lard. And don't forget the fatback. And the butter.

After we settled on our side dishes we chose fried trout that had been caught fresh from a local pond that morning. When the platters (not plates, platters) arrived, sidling up to tall, sweaty glasses of iced tea so sweet it made the teaspoons stand at attention, my mother bowed her head over the repast and prayed, "The Lard cooks in mysterious ways. Amen." Not bad for a lapsed Methodist-turned-Universalist keeping company with a Catholic and a tree-hugger.

And we ate. And ate. And ate, all while gazing happily out the big picture window at the creek, the farm, the woods, and the mountains. That day we enjoyed the most secluded five-star dining experience on the planet, with the best, world-class view. And what made it even more special was that it came to us as a hidden treasure, a surprise we hadn't dreamed we'd find. Food always tastes best when you've cooked it, farmed it, or hunted it yourself. In our case, when you've discovered it after you thought you were merely lost in a high mountain valley.

We staggered back to the car, drowsy and satiated. Our energy for exploring restored, we found the rare-plant nursery nearby. We bought heritage rose bushes and homemade rose-petal potpourri, and we drove back to our hotel in Asheville inhaling the scent of our grandmothers' gardens and reminiscing about our grandmothers' cooking. Food and flowers, you see, bring back the spirits of our ancestors. I make meals from my grandmother's recipes. I grow my grandmothers' heirloom tea roses and irises and tiger lilies and daffodils in my yard. My grandmothers live in the flour and the flower and the heart and the hearth.

I never forgot that day in the mountains above Asheville, that meal, that fellowship at the crossroads.

And so this book is dedicated to all the mountain grandmothers of the Appalachian South who welcome strangers to their tables, who love the food and the wilderness and the roses and the creek roads and the high ridges only the hungry and the brave will dare to travel for a glimpse and a taste of heaven.

Thanks to y'all, the Lard really does cook in mysterious, and wonderfully soulful, ways.

Also, many heartfelt thanks to everyone whose help, encouragement and inspiration made this book possible. My undying gratitude to my good friend Linda Wolfowitz, not just for serving as my consultant on all matters Yiddish, but also for her praise, patience and enduring pen-pal support. To all the readers, booksellers, and librarians who contacted me as I shared the opening chapters of this book via email, many thanks for your enthusiasm and input. I fixed the typos and learned to spell "extrapolate."

To everyone at Google: Without you, I'd still be prowling a library for the geologic history of the Appalachians, the breed history of Guernsey cows, the exact route of California's Ventura Highway, the treatment protocols for burn wounds, a street map of lower Manhattan, and a hundred other details that would not otherwise, I guarantee you, be in this novel. You're doing God's work in a world of harried writers.

To my husband, Hank, thank you, as always, for loving and supporting and waiting and hoping and helping and never, ever losing faith. I love you. To my brother and sister and theirs: Thank you for showing me what a family is, and what a family isn't. You have transformed my understanding of true family spirit, and, trust me, I will never forget the lesson. To my mother: Thanks for being here now and being there then, the day we made that trip outside Asheville.

To all the gals who took such good care of the home front in recent years: Sue, Marie, Judy, Sandra and Bobbie. You performed more than a job, and your compassion was much appreciated.

To my grandmother, Agnes Nettie Qualls Power, who made the best biscuits in the world without ever measuring so much as a pinch of flour or a dollop of lard, thank you for that memory. Grandma baked by instinct and love, and her food nourished more than the body. I was just a child when she died, but my heart still knows the comfort of her meals.

To my tribe, aka my BelleBooks partners, aka my longtime friends, aka my sisters of the heart—Debra Dixon, Sandra Chastain, Martha Shields and Nancy Knight—this book wouldn't exist without you. Its foundation and its process would be meaningless. Any success it enjoys would be without merit. In short, I hope we all make a lot of money off it. We'll buy that BelleBooks beach house, yet.

But most of all, this book is for Gin Ellis. Gin, we hope you know how much we miss you. Your flowers are blooming, your pottery and art and books and photographs and words of wisdom are spread among us for safekeeping. Not long ago we stood in your empty home and cried and smiled and thought about you. We will never forget.

We'll see you later, okay?

About Deborah Smith

With more than 2.5 million copies in print worldwide, Deborah Smith is one of the best-known and most beloved authors of romantic, stylish, contemporary Southern fiction. Her novels have been compared to those of Anne Rivers Siddon, Pat Conroy, and other prestigious Southern writers. Among other awards, her work has been nominated for the *Townsend Prize for Literature* and she has received a *Lifetime Achievement Award* from *Romantic Times* magazine, which also named her 1996 *New York Times* bestselling novel, *A Place To Call Home*, one of the top 200 romantic novels published in the twentieth century. In 2002 *Disney* optioned her novel, *Sweet Hush*, for film in a major six-figure deal.

As partner, co-founder and editor of *BelleBooks*, a small Southern press owned by her and four other nationally-known women authors, Deborah edits the acclaimed *Mossy Creek Hometown Series*. She lives in the mountains of north Georgia with her husband, Hank.

www.bellebooks.com

www.deborah-smith.com

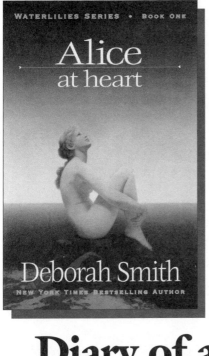
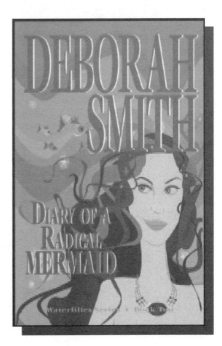

Non-Fiction

BRA TALK

by Susan Nethero

You'll learn:
- tips on selecting bras
- wear-and-care instructions
- how to overcome any figure problem
- what to expect from a professional fitting consultant
- where to find bra shops in your city
- and much more!

As seen on the Oprah Winfrey show

No matter what your size, no matter what your problem, you can look great and feel great in the right bra.

BRA TALK gives you the facts.

There is no one perfect bra for all women. Your body shape and size isn't to blame for a poorly fitting bra. The most comfortable bra isn't the one that fits the loosest. If you're big breasted, "minimizer" bras aren't the solution. If you're small breasted, the right bra can add a full cup size.

Also available from BelleBooks

ALL GOD'S CREATURES

by Carolyn McSparren

Say hello to Maggie McLain, an unlikely Southern debutante in 1960s Memphis. Gawky, restless, smart and opinionated, young Maggie isn't cut out to fill the patent leather

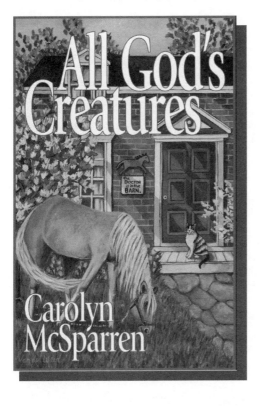

pumps of a Southern belle. When she ditches a Cotton Carnival ball to save a drowning pup, Maggie realizes her destiny.

Is the land of mint juleps and Elvis ready for a woman veterinarian? Maybe not, but Dr. Maggie McLain sets out to prove otherwise.

Over the years, Maggie earns the devotion and respect of crusty farmers, snobby horse breeders and doubtful pet owners throughout western Tennessee. She's an inspiration to up-and-coming women vets, a loving wife to her proud husband, a patient mother to her demanding kids, and above all, a champion to sick and injured animals.

When loss and grief knock Maggie off her pedestal, she falls hard. It may take a miracle for her to understand that sometimes even the best doctor must struggle to heal her own heart.

THE MOSSY CREEK

MOSSY CREEK

Book One

The first book in the series introduces a mayor who sees

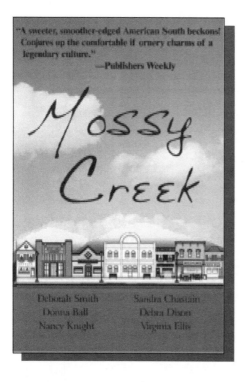

"A sweeter, smoother-edged American South beckons! Conjures up the comfortable if ornery charms of a legendary culture."
—Publishers Weekly

Mossy Creek

Deborah Smith   Sandra Chastain
Donna Ball   Debra Dixon
Nancy Knight   Virginia Ellis

breaking the law as her civic duty and a by-the-books police chief trying to live up to his father's legend. We've got a bittersweet feud at the coffee shop and heartwarming battles on the softball field. We've got a world-weary Santa with a poignant dream and a flying Chihuahua with a streak of bad luck. You'll meet Millicent, who believes in stealing joy, and the outrageous patrons of O'Day's Pub, who believe there's no such thing as an honest game of darts. You'll want to tune your radio to the Bereavement Report and prop your feet up at Mama's All You Can Eat Café. While you're there, say hello to our local gossip columnist, Katie Bell. She'll make you feel like one of the family.

"MOSSY CREEK is as much fun as a cousin reunion; like sipping ice cold lemonade on a hot summer's afternoon. Hire me a moving van, it's the kind of town where everyone wishes they could live."

— *Debbie Macomber, NYT bestselling author*

HOMETOWN SERIES

REUNION AT MOSSY CREEK

Book Two

This time they've got the added drama of the big town reunion commemorating the twenty-year-old mystery of the late, great Mossy Creek High School, which burned to the ground amid quirky rumors and dark secrets. In the meantime, sassy 100-year-old Eula Mae Whit is convinced Williard Scott has put a death curse on her, and Mossy Creek Police Chief Amos Royden is still fighting his reputation as the town's most eligible bachelor. There's the new bad girl in town, Jasmine, and more adventures from the old bad girl in town, Mayor Ida Hamilton. And last but not least, Bob the flying Chihuahua finds himself stalked by an amorous lady poodle.

Deborah Smith Sandra Chastain Debra Dixon
Virginia Ellis Martha Shields Nancy Knight
Carolyn McSparren Sharon Sala Dee Sterling
Carmen Greene

"Mitford meets Mayberry in the first book of this innovative and warmhearted new series from BelleBooks."

— *Cleveland Daily Banner, Cleveland, Tennessee*

THE MOSSY CREEK

SUMMER IN MOSSY CREEK

Book Three

It's a typical summer in the good-hearted mountain town of Mossy Creek, Georgia, where love, laughter and friendship make nostalgia a way of life. Creekites are always ready for a sultry romance, a funny feud or a sincere celebration, and this summer is no different. Get ready for a comical battle over pickled beets and a spy mission to recover hijacked chow-chow peppers. Meet an unforgettable parakeet named Tweedle Dee and a lovable dog named Dog. Watch Amos and Ida sidestep the usual rumors and follow Katie Bell's usual snooping. In the meantime, old-timer Opal Suggs and her long-dead sisters share a lesson on living, and apple farmer Hope Bailey faces poignant choices when an old flame returns to claim her.

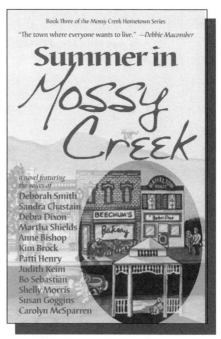

"In the best tradition of women's fiction, MOSSY CREEK points to a genuine spirit of love and community that is our best hope for the future."

— *Betina Krahn, NYT bestselling author of* The Last Bachelor

HOMETOWN SERIES

BLESSINGS OF MOSSY CREEK

Book Four

The good-hearted citizens of Mossy Creek, Georgia are in a mood to count their blessings. Maybe it's the influence of the new minister in town, who keeps his sense of humor while battling a stern church treasurer. Maybe it's the afterglow of Josie McClure's incredibly romantic wedding to the local "Bigfoot." Or maybe it's the new baby in Hank and Casey Blackshear's home. As autumn gilds the mountains, town gossip columnist, Katie Bell, has persuaded Creekites to confess their joys, troubles, and gratitudes. As always, that includes a heapin' helping of laughter, wisdom, and good old-fashioned scandal.

"A fast, funny, and folksy read. Enjoy!"

— *Lois Battle, acclaimed author of* Storyville, Bed & Breakfast, *and* The Florabama Ladies' Auxiliary & Sewing Circle

THE MOSSY CREEK HOMETOWN SERIES

A DAY IN MOSSY CREEK

Book Five

Maybe it's the post-New Year's boredom. Maybe it's the cold, frisky air. Whatever the cause, the citizens of Mossy Creek seem determined to get into trouble on a clear winter day in mid-January. Police Chief Amos Royden and his loyal officers, Mutt and Sandy, can barely keep up with the calls. Hank and Casey Blackshear's great aunt Irene, 93, leads a protests march of angry seniors -- on their electric scooters. Louise and Charlie Sawyer battle renovation pitfalls (literally) in their cranky house. Pearl Quinlan fights her sister, Spiva, over a plate of brownies. Patty Campbell performs a makeover on Orville Gene

Simpson's front yard, against Orville's will. All that and more! Last but not least, Amos and Ida finally stop fighting their secret attraction, but then the trouble really begins!

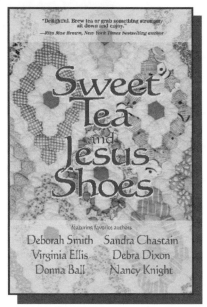

CREOLA'S MOONBEAM

by Milam McGraw Propst

Author of
A Flower Blooms on Charlotte Street
the book that inspired the acclaimed
feature film

"Don't miss this delightful, heartwarming journey into friendship."

—*Haywood Smith, NY Times best selling author of the Red Hat Club series*

My decision was firm.
Sliding out of bed, I jumped into my warm-up suit and running shoes. I grabbed my manuscript from the bedside table, tiptoed down the hall, and hurried out the kitchen door. Lifting the garbage can lid, I hurled the papers into a smelly stew of last night's meat loaf, coffee grounds, egg shells, rice, and butter beans.
"Good riddance to you!"

Honey Newberry, a successful Atlanta writer, has been hit by a double whammy: Writer's block and the middle-age crazies. She heads for the Gulf beaches of Florida, determined to spend the summer getting her groove back. There she finds unexpected inspiration from a joyful neighbor—the mysterious and flamboyant Beatrice—whose zest for life reminds Honey of another wise woman—Creola Moon, the wise and amazing nanny who encouraged Honey's childhood dreams.

As Beatrice lures Honey into a series of adventures, Honey shares her funny, poignant stories about marriage, children, sisterhood, and the fabulous Creola. Together in spirit, Beatrice and Creola teach Honey what it truly means to enjoy life.

Also available from BelleBooks

Available in all fine bookstores and direct from BelleBooks

Mossy Creek Hometown Series

Mossy Creek
Reunion at Mossy Creek
Summer in Mossy Creek
Blessings of Mossy Creek
A Day in Mossy Creek

Sweet Tea Series

Sweet Tea & Jesus Shoes
More Sweet Tea
Sweeter Tea

WaterLilies Series

Alice at Heart
Diary of a Radical Mermaid

Everyone's Special Children's Series

KaseyBelle: *The Tiniest Fairy in the Kingdom*
Astronaut Noodle

Other Fiction

Creola's Moonbeam
All God's Creatures

NonFiction

BraTalk